THE PRINCESS

⅃ℲℲ Ⅎ⅄ℿℲℾℳℴℴℴ

Ariel MacArran

The Princess
By Ariel MacArran

©2016 Ariel MacArran

Cover Design: Steven James Catizone

Published by Here Be Dragons
ISBN-13: 9780-692-72435-4
ISBN-10: 0-692-72435-4

Also available in eBook publication

PRINTED IN THE UNITED STATES OF AMERICA

The Princess
By Ariel MacArran

©2016 Ariel MacArran

Cover Design: Steven James Catizone

Published by Here Be Dragons
ISBN-13: 9780-692-72435-4
ISBN-10: 0-692-72435-4

Also available in eBook publication

PRINTED IN THE UNITED STATES OF AMERICA

1

Storm

"My mother will see you skinned for this!"

Imperial Daughter Saria, Heiress of the Az-kye Empire, bared her teeth even as she was forced further back into a corner of her once sumptuous quarters.

"And I am sure you will understand"—Uthar kept his blaster aimed at her heart—"why I have no intention of allowing the empress that pleasure, Your Highness."

The warship—a sleek cruiser of the newest design, the finest vessel of her mother's fleet—bucked under Saria's feet. Energy cyclones of the Badlands tore at the ship's hull, forcing Saria to brace herself just to remain upright. Her quarters, newly redone to convey her on this diplomatic mission—and her very first time off the homeworld—now lay in ruins from Uthar's assault, the stench of smoking flesh and blood choking her. The plasma storm, its terrifying scarlet fury hammering the high, arched viewports, was rapidly draining the ship's power, causing the lights to flicker nightmarishly over the broken bodies of her attendants.

The women's fine gowns were bloodstained and surely these maids had shown more courage than any warrior ever had. When Uthar and his men stormed her quarters the women had surrounded her, rallying to their princess's defense armed with only desperate pleas and soft hands.

The door of her quarters gaped open, the lock disabled at the moment of attack. The hallway beyond was littered with the bodies; those of Uthar's men and her own guards too, honorable warriors who had fought with swords against treasonous attackers armed with Tellaran blasters.

Naret of the Az'larna, so gentle and respectful, honored to the point of reverence to be her first lover, was among them.

Handsome as if his form had been carved by the goddess Lashima herself, Naret's chiseled face was turned away now and Saria was grateful for that small kindness. The black leather of his warrior's clothes was split open across the chest, his long dark hair pulled free of its tie.

The last of her protectors to fall . . .

Saria glared at the commander of her flagship. "It does not matter if you escape Imperial justice—Ren'thar Himself shall avenge this betrayal!" She indicated the windows, the swirling crimson beyond. "He will destroy you—along with your ship!"

As if to underscore her words the vessel shuddered around them, the tarasteel girders groaning under the energy storm's onslaught, the god of war's fury.

Uthar sent a wistful glance at the ceiling. "She was a fine thing, was she not? Gliding among the stars like a jaha floating on a warm breeze." He shook his head, his long gray hair tied smartly back. "To order her here to be destroyed . . ."

"Then the storm—We were not caught by an eddy? You set course into the Badlands?" She shook her head. "You have gone mad, Uthar. What of your men? Your ship!"

"Sacrifices well worth the reward. Well worth all I have done. What I *will* do."

"All to clear way for another to take the throne." Her throat was tight. "Who?"

He was the image of an Az-kye warrior now—powerful, stoic, expressionless.

"Will you not tell me to whom you have sworn yourself to in my stead, Uthar? To whom you would betray me—betray even sacred honor itself?" She searched his face, seeking any hint that the man who had safeguarded her since babyhood remained. "What great reward has she offered you? What can she guarantee you, this one who may—or may not—win the throne in the end? Mine are not empty words, whispered promises!" Saria drew herself up. "My inheritance has the weight of law; I am already the acknowledged Heiress. Think you of what *I* can offer you! Calculate the riches my mother will bestow to—"

"My reward for returning you to the homeworld would be execution," he interrupted sharply. "And the obliteration of my clan. Think you—after all my time at the empress's side—that I do not understand her mind? Or *yours*? From the day you took your first step, the throne called to you." His dark gaze narrowed. "And I am not the only one who saw the ambition that burned in your heart. How being Second, consigned to live out your life as a princess with no hope of power, chafed at your soul."

She was stunned into silence, her cheeks burning at having been so transparent.

"Why could you not find contentment as Second?" he cried suddenly, throwing his arm wide. "You would have been left in peace! Lived in ease, with no more asked of you than to bow to another as empress!"

"I have long struggled against my own aspirations." Her eyes stung. "Yet I can be no other than as the gods made me."

"Nor I, but I would it had never come to this. In my heart," he said hoarsely, "you have always been far more niece than princess."

"And you far more uncle than guard." She spread her hands, reaching toward him. "There is time yet to reclaim your honor. Be my protector again and *hold* that place when I come to the throne. Return me to my mother and—"

"Quick and clever as always," Uthar broke in. "With words sweet as a kytala bird's song. Think you I believe you would keep *this*"—he indicated the ruin around them—"secret? That once you were safely within the palace walls you would not stand at your mother's side to watch the skin flayed from my body?"

Of all the names she had the right to call him now, "fool" was not among them.

"I have made my bargain." A shadow crossed his face. "My path now one I cannot turn from. And you cannot imagine the wrath that would await me—and my family—if I tried."

"Who has plotted against me?" At his silence she sent a meaningful look at the blaster he held. "Surely, if my fate is set, you can tell me that much."

He shook his head. "I am sworn never to breathe her name, even to the dead."

"You say you know me well." Saria's voice was rough. "In my heart that burns with ambition—do you not also see the love I have for the Az-kye; the devotion I have for our people?"

"Yes, Princess," Uthar said gravely. "I do."

"Then tell me the name of she who would rule in my stead! Let me be assured that she is capable of not just seizing the throne but of holding it." Her vision blurred.

"Let me enter the City of the Gods with my heart at peace, knowing that I leave our people to be ruled well by her."

His expression softened at that. "I can offer you this much, Princess—she is one with more right to the Az-kye throne, and one far better trained to it, than you."

"*More* right? There *is* no one better trained, with more ri—"

But there is.

Saria's hands went to her ribs, her voice cracking. "Alari?"

Uthar's lips pressed together at mention of her elder sister's name.

Saria suddenly recalled huddling beneath the covers with Alari when they were children, hidden from their attendants' view, to giggle and whisper secrets to one another. She remembered, too, each of them holding their father's hand under his watchful, indulgent eye as they crossed the courtyard of the Imperial Palace together, both too young to know not to skip . . .

"No!" Saria shook her head sharply. "No, my sister loves me! She would never—!"

Would she?

Her sister's whole life had been spent preparing to rule an empire so vast it spread from the Badlands separating the Az-kye Empire from Tellaran territory to the uninhabited Nelari expanse. Alari had been First Daughter, the eldest girl, born to be the Imperial Heiress, her inheritance assured until . . .

Until she chose Kyndan Maere—a *Tellaran*—as her mate. The empress humiliated Alari before the entire court, disinherited her and raised up Saria, the younger sister, in her stead. In the space of a few hours Alari had lost all. Saria had become First, Heiress to their mother's crown.

Alari now had to walk a pace behind Saria in state processions, as Saria had once had to walk behind her. Alari was an Imperial Daughter but not even Second, no longer in line for the throne at all.

Their mother had borne only two children and her sister had once been a much beloved First Daughter. Without a proclaimed Heiress, their mother risked a civil war; the strongest of the clan leaders would rise up, each seeking the crown for herself. If she were dead, the empress would have no choice except to—

Saria shut her eyes. But was it so difficult to imagine Alari wanted her rightful position back? That Alari's gentle, kind face concealed the cunning to plot her sister's murder?

Certainly theirs was a heritage stained dark with royal blood. Saria would be but one of many Imperial Daughters who fell victim to a sister's hunger for power—tenderness and love be damned . . .

But the same blood that ran in Alari's veins—the vital power of a thousand generations of women who had risen to claim the throne for themselves—also sang in Saria's own.

And love be damned!

"I will see you destroyed—you and that bitch!" Saria clenched her fists, nails digging into her palms. "I *will* take the throne that is lawfully mine!"

"You, Princess," he said evenly, "will not see the start of the next hour."

But her fear suddenly evaporated, her mind clear as Lashima's sacred pool.

I cannot die here. To have revenge, I must return to Az-kye. I must survive.

Saria was a tall woman but Uthar was taller by a head, even at his age a powerful warrior. She was no match for him physically.

But an Az-kye woman's strength lies in her wits.

"And what of you, *false* warrior?" she demanded, satisfied by the tiny flinch her taunt drew. Az-kye honor ran deep. "With me dead, you will have failed beyond redemption. No one—no matter how high born—could risk aligning herself with a disgraced warrior. Return to the homeworld, *coward*," she mocked. "I may enter the City of the Gods today but you will end your days a slave!"

"I am spared that disgrace at least." He sighed, as a schoolmaster might when burdened with a particularly dull student. "I, like you, am fated to die here."

"Die *here*? You will not even attempt escape?"

"No." His mouth quirked upward a bit, touched with bitterness. "I have only one task left now: to assure you die here with me."

"But . . ." Saria scrambled. "Your family—your reward—"

"Ah," he said with a nod. In that moment, her hope surged. From the hallway she saw a slow, pained stirring. A familiar and beloved form, struggling to rise.

Naret!

She forced herself to keep her attention on Uthar, her expression unchanged.

"The reward will be my clan's, not mine." His gravelly voice softened with longing. "I will not live to see it but they will be raised up, a great family, with wealth and influence—"

"And with those of your blood as honorless as you are," Saria interrupted tartly, "they should rise high indeed, in the court of this *new* empress."

His grip on the blaster tightened till his knuckles whitened yet he did not fire.

But why?

He should have killed me already! Taken the first opportunity when they breached the door! Why hold me here, talking?

Alari, pious enough now to spend hours praying in Lashima's sanctuary, might fear offending the gods by the murder of her sister. Saria's maids, her guards, the crew of the ship, were another matter. They might suffer the cut of a sword, the singe of blaster fire, but Saria herself—

The ship rocked hard, as if something had struck the vessel. Somehow Saria held her balance.

She wants the storm to kill me!

Naret heaved himself up, her beautiful lover, swaying on his feet for a moment. His face was tight, the stuttering illumination highlighting the blood from his head wound, the bright metal of the sword in his hand—

Her heart hammering, Saria curled her lip. "Kill me then—*coward*!"

Even now—when he had betrayed all their culture revered—that taunt had the power to flush Uthar's cheeks.

"Go on! Or do even I—a woman, alone and unarmed—make you tremble in fear?" She threw her arms wide, startling him a bit. "Do it, coward—cast away the last shred of your honor! You have already disgraced yourself— the clan Ar'tyn's very *name*—beyond redemption!"

"Be you silent!" Uthar flared. "Or I will silence you!"

"I am your princess—whom you swore to the god of war himself to defend!" Saria raised her voice to a shout as the ship rattled. "Do you hear His fury? Ren'thar Himself will greet me at the Gate! And there I will demand every ancestor of the Ar'tyn be summoned before me! Let *them* answer for the son who cut me down with a *Tellaran's* weapon!"

When his face went almost purple Saria saw she had played her part only too well—

Then Naret was on him, seizing Uthar's wrist so hard Saria heard bones snap. Naret was wounded, weakened, but strong enough to run the man through. Uthar cried out in agony, his fingers moving reflexively. A flash of blue light shot from his blaster and hit the wide skirt of Saria's court gown.

Saria screamed as the dress burst into flames around her. Wild with terror, she instinctively tried to flee, only to find herself trapped against the corner of the room.

A large strong hand caught her by the back of the neck. In the next instant she was flung forward, hitting the deck hard, a heavy weight smothering her. Blinded, clawing in an effort to get away, Saria could only whimper as the weight lifted and fell on her again and again—

Suddenly she was free, gulping to draw air into her lungs.

He had used the tapestry that had once hung on the wall beside her bed to smother the flames. A hand-woven work, precious and ancient, commissioned thousands of years ago to capture the splendor of Empress Liri's coronation day, its threads were scorched, the fragile image destroyed.

Her mouth parted at the ruin of such a rich cultural treasure. Naret seized Saria's shoulders with strong hands to lift her and turn her. Naret's face was soot-smudged and sharp with fear.

"How badly are you hurt?" he asked, tearing the remnants of her gown away to see for himself before she could answer.

"I d-do not know."

She was an Imperial Daughter: she knew court etiquette and devoured Az-kye history, could use a jaha feather fan with fetching skill. But physical pain? Of that, she had little experience.

Stinging ran up her leg as he probed; her knees and elbows throbbed. Saria's hand went to her face and she winced when her fingers touched the bruised spot where her cheekbone hit the floor.

"The fault is mine," he said roughly at her flinch. "I should have left the door to the guards, been at your side—"

"He would only have shot you."

Naret's sword protruded from Uthar's chest, the elder warrior's fixed eyes wide with dread as he beheld Ren'thar at last, clutching a Tellaran's weapon in his hand.

"I admired him, even as a boy, strove to emulate him!" Naret's voice was tight. An Imperial Commander—Uthar, the great and honored warrior!"

"And Alari's creature."

"Alari?" Naret exclaimed, in his disbelief forgetting to refer to her sister by her title.

"My sister is not the sweet soul she appears," Saria muttered. "And no one was better played like a hitiwood pipe than I."

"But surely that cannot—"

A shudder ran through the deck beneath them and Naret's arms tightened around her. "I must get you off this ship!"

Saria stared as he yanked the blaster from Uthar's hand. "What are you doing?"

"An Az-kye sword is no match for a Tellaran weapon and you are far more precious than my honor. We cannot know which warriors on this ship are loyal to you, my

Princess, and which have thrown their lot with your sister." His hand tightened on the blaster. "We must trust no one."

Naret stood, drawing her up with him. Her legs were shaky, her garments in burned tatters around her, the elaborate twists of her hair hanging down in places, the jeweled combs askew, but it was he who groaned when they took a step toward the door.

She rested her hand on his chest, searching his face worriedly. "Naret?"

"Come," he said, gritting his teeth. His face was tight as he led her over the bodies in the hall. Past the carnage outside her door the hall was clear and they moved quicker. "Gods grant us a way clear to the shuttle bay."

"But if we made for the bridge—"

He shook his head. "Either this ship cannot break free or those on the bridge are your sister's warriors and have been ordered to keep it here even unto deaths. Even armed with a blaster, I cannot overcome such men and hope to pilot the *Ty'har* out of the Badlands before she breaks apart."

They came upon the bodies of three warriors and, lying nearby one of the men, a young woman dressed in the white smock of a slave.

"Will a shuttle withstand this storm?"

"It had better," he panted. "Or it will answer to m—"

"Naret!" She caught at him, scarcely able to keep him upright.

He leaned against the wall, his arm over his chest pressing hard, his face white. "A moment—"

Her hair hung in her face and with one hand Saria yanked the last of the jeweled combs that held her now ruined coils. She tossed the bauble away, and her dark hair, set free now, spilled over her shoulders and down her back.

Naret stared at her for a moment then looked at the bodies nearby.

She followed his glance. "What is it?"

The warriors had been shot, but it was clear from the way her head lay at an unnatural angle that the woman's neck had been broken.

"Quickly, take her smock." Naret indicated the slave. "Put it on."

Instantly Saria recoiled at the idea. "I will not!"

"Your gown is a ruin," he pointed out. "That one is no worse."

"The white of the clanless?" Saria drew herself up. "It is by thousands worse!"

"Your sister's men control this ship. But how many would know the Imperial Heiress without her fine clothes, her maids and jewels?" His jaw hardened then, not in anger but in determination, and a frisson of fear ran through her belly at how his face had blanched. "They are hunting an Imperial Daughter," he said as if forcing the words out. "Not a slave."

She was filthy, her hair a tangled mess, but—

"I would rather die in a princess's rags than live wearing slave's white!"

"You—" His legs suddenly gave out from under him and he slid down the wall, collapsing in a heap on the floor.

"Naret!" Saria threw herself down to kneel beside him and his head lolled her way.

She had been schooled in ceremony and court life; she had no knowledge at all of how to care for the sick or injured. "I will find a healer—"

He caught her hand before she could rise, his grip terrifyingly weak, and he looked as if he were having trouble focusing on her. "There is . . . no time . . ."

"You need only rest a moment, Naret, then we will continue on." Her grip tightened on his hand. "Together."

"I have been honored to serve you. I am honored . . . to die for you."

"You cannot! I—I do not give you leave to go!"

A smile lit his face for an instant then a spasm of pain contorted his features.

"There must be something I can do!" she cried. "Tell me what to do!"

Blood appeared at the corner of his mouth. "Saria—" He looked toward the slave, at her smock. "Please . . ."

She crawled over to where the woman lay as Ren'thar's fury battered at the ship. With shaking hands Saria maneuvered the smock off the poor wretch. The girl was not much older than she, her staring, dark eyes the same shade as Saria's own. Swallowing hard, Saria spared an instant to lay the sad tatters of her gown over the girl's body.

She gripped the dingy white smock in her hands for a moment. Then, with stiff movements, she yanked the slave dress over her head.

"You see?" Naret asked, when she knelt beside him again. His hand, cold now, reached up to touch her cheek. "Even a slave's garb could never sully you, my Princess."

"Do not leave me, Naret," she pleaded, resting her hand over his, her vision blurring. "Please."

His lids were closing. "My love . . ."

"No. Please—"

She caught his hand tightly in hers, her tears overflowing. But his face was peaceful, the fingers that had stroked her to gentle pleasure slack.

Alari will answer for this as well.

The rapid approach of heavy boots brought her head up.

He was a tall man, strongly built, with the dark eyes of an Az-kye, but he was bearded, his hair cropped short as no warrior would wear it. His clothes too—gray trousers tucked into boots, topped with white shirt and black jacket—showed him no son of the empire.

As did the blaster he instantly trained on her.

A Tellaran? Onboard the Imperial flagship?

"Well, Arrena's tits—" His teeth flashed in a quick grin, startlingly white against that closely trimmed beard, his Tellaran words unpleasantly sharp to her ear. "Looks like I'm not the only one alive on this piece of junk after all."

2

ꓘꓤꓥ ꓝꓥꓫꓘꓒꓥ

The Pirate

Jehan's glance darted about, taking in the gruesome scene, the echoing silence of the corridors beyond.

"You alone?"

There were dead Az-kye all over the ship; he'd found passage after passage of them as he'd made his way inward from the shuttle bay. A storm like this could be the cause of *some* of the casualties, but the warriors on this ship looked like they'd killed not only each other but the slaves and the free women too. Only this one slave girl seemed to have survived the carnage.

What the hells happened here?

Az-kye were a lot of godsdamned things but they weren't fucking *insane*.

Well, usually, anyway.

"You!" he snapped off, sharper than he'd intended, badly startling her. "You speak Tellaran?"

Her velvety dark glance darted fearfully to the blaster he held and Jehan raised the weapon, holding it at the "ready" position.

"I do," she said reluctantly.

"Well, that brightens things up for me a little," he muttered. "You alone?"

"Yes." Those long-lashed dark eyes were haunted. "I am alone."

She seemed to understand him okay but Az-kye could be pretty festering literal.

"Is there anyone else alive on this ship?" he asked deliberately.

"I do not know." Her voice was soft, honeyed by the hum her Az-kye accent lent the Tellaran words.

"Get up." She hesitated and he blew out his breath. "I'm not going to hurt you, okay? Just get up."

She rose with a dancer's grace. The warrior she'd been kneeling beside had been half hidden by her body but when she stood the man—and his wound—was uncovered.

"Wait. That warrior"—Jehan's frown deepened—"he was shot?"

Her dark gaze went to her master. He'd been a young guy, almost too pretty to be a warrior—except he was built like a sular on growth stims.

"Yes," she said huskily, wiping at her tears with the back of her hand.

"But—" He shook his head, taking in the other warriors lying here, the dead woman, her ragged clothes flung atop her body . . .

Never one for superstition and certainly no temple-lover, Jehan found himself suppressing a shiver.

It's like they all went crazy.

"An *Az-kye* shot him?" he demanded. "When did Az-kye start using blasters?"

She stared at him, her trembling hands twisting in the skirt of her slave dress.

"Never mind," he muttered. Keeping one eye out, his blaster at the ready, he shrugged out of his jacket and shoved it at her. "Here. Put it on."

"I do not—"

"It's freezing in here. Put it on."

She shoved her arms into the jacket. It was comically big on her and she clutched it closed. She didn't have any shoes but there wasn't much he could do about that right now.

"Come on." He reached out to take her by the arm. "Let's go."

She scrambled back, out of his grasp. "With you?"

Jehan indicated the dead warriors around them. "You got a better offer?"

She didn't budge, stubbornly rooted beside her dead master.

"Have it your way," he said shortly. "Clear skies, sweetheart."

Jehan left her behind and continued on, moving deeper into the ship, picking his way past the grisly corridor. Life support was starting to fail, the warship's heat rapidly leeching into space, and he cursed himself for giving away his jacket like that.

Mig's right. I am an idiot.

"Wait!"

He halted at her cry and she stopped short when she saw him, as if afraid to get too close to him.

Damn, but that bothered him.

"You want to come with me, you do what I say, when I say." He held her with the same narrow look he used to keep his crew in line. "Or I leave you behind. Got it?"

Apparently his harsh tone worked. She nodded, watching him with big, scared eyes.

"And I'm not going to waste any time looking for you if you wander off, so don't," he warned. "I've scanned this ship from stem to stern and that hallway back there—where *you* were—was the only life sign I detected. But just in case the storm's mucked up the readings and we come across any

Az-kye your only job is to hit the deck—*fast*—and let me handle them." He lifted his blaster meaningfully. "Understand?"

Jehan could feel the storm hammering at the hull through the deck plating. The warship wouldn't be able to stand up to this punishment much longer.

She must have figured that out too because she gave another mute nod.

"Glad we're getting along so well," he said, turning to lead the way. "Come on. I don't want to be on this flying tomb any longer than I have to."

"How are you here, Tellaran, on one of our ships?" she asked. "Have others of your people boarded?"

"No, I'm the only one crazy enough"—*or stupid enough, depending on how this goes*—"to bust through the shields of an Imperial warship. And maybe you could call me Jehan instead of 'Tellaran'?"

"Jehan?"

"Captain Jehan Dekra." He took a cautious glance around the corner and found it empty. *Maybe the scanner was right after all.* "At your service."

"But—and your eyes! You are Az-kye!"

He rounded on her. "I am *not* a fucking *Az-kye*! Don't call me that again!"

She didn't retreat but her slender hands gripped the jacket tightly as if it would somehow shield her from his fury.

Jehan's cheeks heated in the wake of his outburst. Her own people had already treated her brutally; she didn't need harshness from him too. The side of her face was swollen and bruised, her tunic stained, her knees raw—all testament to how ill she'd been used.

And, really, it shouldn't bother him. Not anymore. Not after all this time.

"Come on," he muttered.

The Az-kye in these chilly corridors were long past worrying about trespassers wandering their ship. Some lay with closed lids, some stared into nothingness with eyes the onyx shade of their people. He was relieved not to have to take on any of the warriors, but finding deck after deck of them—clearly dead at each other's hands—had the hair on the back of his neck standing up.

As if the Badlands needed another ghost story.

"I know who you are." Jehan glanced back at the woman, who trailed obediently after him. "What you are."

Her face blanched. "You do?"

"A slave. One of those they call 'clanless.'"

"Yes," she croaked. "Yes, I am."

"What's your name?" At her frightened silence he gave a short, bitter laugh. "Right. They took that too, didn't they? Fuckers. What *was* your name?"

"I—" She wet her lips. "Liri. I am Liri."

He raised an eyebrow. "Kind of an unlucky name, isn't it?"

"It is a strong name. The Empress Liri survived betrayal, terrible wounds. She rose to become a power to be reckoned with—"

"She was a bloodthirsty lunatic. Didn't she skin her own sisters—*and* half the court—to make her coronation canopy?"

"*That* is only what—" she began stridently then broke off. "I think . . ." she continued, her tone softer, far more deferential, "that tale may be far more legend than fact."

"Well, they named you right, anyway. You've been to the darkest level of the nine hells and come back."

"I do not understand."

"You're Liri again," he said roughly. "This is the Badlands, outside the empire's borders. You're not a slave anymore, you're free."

"As you are?"

He snorted. "I'm workin' on it."

"If you are . . . Tellaran," she ventured finally, "do you know—have your people allied with Uthar then?"

"Uthar?"

"Uthar of the Ar'tyn, Commander of this ship. He—" Her voice tightened. "He is dead now."

Liri's master had died from a blaster shot to the belly. If this Uthar was the one handing out Tellaran weapons it wasn't hard to guess which side her owner had been on.

He didn't have to wonder where Az-kye could have gotten hold of those weapons. He knew exactly where. The question was why they'd *want* to.

No warrior he'd ever known would fight with anything but a sword. To do so would dishonor him. And honor was everything to a warrior.

And he's nothing without it.

"I don't know who Uthar's friends were or weren't but don't worry," he assured. "I'm not allied with anyone but myself."

They made it down another deck but at the next turn she balked.

"That is the wrong way." She pointed to the corridor on the left. "There is the turn for the shuttle bay."

"We'll go to the shuttle bay." His breath was visible now, reminder enough not to slow his stride. "After a quick detour through engineering."

"Engineering!" Her face was openly hopeful when she caught up. "Think you then you can bring this ship safely out of the storm?"

"Oh, hells, no.," he scoffed. "This thing'll never leave the Badlands again."

"Then why go to engineering?" She frowned. "To what purpose?"

"Because there's a fortune in crystals sitting in the belly of this monster and I'm sure as fuck not leaving without them."

"You—you are a thief!"

She'd stopped, glaring at him.

"*That* is why you boarded?" she demanded, shivering in this dim corridor. "To steal?"

"I sure didn't come aboard for the ambience. And who am I stealing from exactly?" he asked, annoyed by how much her scowl bothered him. "The crew's dead. The ship's adrift in Tellaran space. This is a salvage vessel now."

"You boarded with no thought of those in need of your assistance!"

"I took a side trip *your* way, didn't I?" he shot back. "Look at all the accolades that's gotten me."

"This is an Imperial vessel! It is Empress Azara's *personal*—"

"I tell you what, Liri," he interrupted. "If her Imperial Majesty-ness shows up before this bucket gets crushed, she can have the crystals. If she doesn't, they're mine. That's fair, isn't it? I mean, who knows? Maybe she's already onboard but just too lazy to haul her sacred ass all the way to engineering."

Liri's cheeks flushed despite the icy air but she didn't argue. Jehan was actually feeling pretty good about his chances of getting off this beast alive with a handful of astuk gems.

Until she pulled a blaster from the pocket of the jacket—*his* jacket—and pointed it square between his eyes.

3

ᚲᚾ ᚾᚲᚢ

Jewels

"I will not be party to this dishonorable act!"

"Wait, so—" Jehan glanced at the weapon in her hand. "Taking crystals from a shipwreck is 'bad' but blowing my head off is okay?"

The blaster was gripped so tightly in her hand her knuckles were white. "You will take me to your shuttle immediately."

"Sorry, I don't take orders—from anybody." He shrugged. "Guess you'll have to shoot me."

"I shall!"

A shudder ran through the deck under their feet and her face paled.

"Do me a favor, sweetheart, put the blaster bolt through my head now. It's a nice clean death. I'd much rather that than the depressurization when this thing cracks open."

She wet her lips.

"Here, your hand's shaking." Jehan leaned his forehead down to press it against the barrel. "And I'd hate for you to miss."

That shimmer came to her eyes again.

"After I'm dead, of course, you'll have to get off the ship somehow," he continued conversationally, keeping eye contact around the blaster's barrel. "When I docked I saw two other shuttles that should fly. You could make it out of the storm by yourself, if you're a good enough pilot and damn lucky. Or"—he shifted his weight back and she didn't resist when he put his index finger on the blaster's barrel to turn it aside—"you can come with me."

"*You* are a thief!"

"Well, I won't argue the semantics right now but once I've got those crystals, I'll haul ass to the shuttle bay and blast out of here. If you choose to come with me, you have my word—I won't leave without you."

She lowered the blaster to her side but shook her head. "How can I hope to trust a thief?"

"You expect me to trust a slave, one who just threatened to kill me. Speaking of which—"

His left hand shot out and he had the blaster plucked out of her grip holstered at his hip so quickly she gasped.

Her frightened glance met his and he softened his voice.

"I'm really not sure how much time this ship has left, Liri. But I do know, if I'm going to get us both out of here alive I can't fight you at the same time. If you want to go it alone, head for the shuttle bay, I won't stop you. But you need to decide right now." He took a step closer. "Are you with me or not?"

The hall went dark then, plunging them into utter blackness for a long, heart-stopping moment.

He was pulling the lumina from his gun belt when when the lights came back on.

Her lips were white. "I . . . have your word? You will safeguard me?"

"With my life's blood," he said, surprised, even as he spoke, how easily the words came.

She nodded quickly. "Then I am with you, Jehan."

"Good, 'cause"—he clasped her upper arm to urge her on—"I think we've reached the point where we might want to run."

Saria was gasping, her bare feet hurting from their race to the engineering section. She'd lost her slippers when Naret had thrown her down to beat out the fire and she had not even thought to look for another pair.

She had intended to tell him tonight. Tell Naret she would take him as consort, as bound mate . . .

As soon as Jehan hit the control to open the door they both staggered back, overcome by the shrill alarms blaring from the compartment. She cried out, instinctively covering her ears against the painful sound, but he plunged into the room.

"Jehan!" she cried, but the klaxons drowned out her voice so that she could not even hear herself. "Jehan!"

Certainly he did not hear her calls as he moved from console to console. The noise was unbearable but Saria went in after him, preparing to gain his attention with a kick, when the alarms suddenly went silent.

Her ears rang and her hands fell away from the sides of her face, her mouth parting as she took in the scene.

She had been given a tour of the *Ty'har* when she had first arrived on board, Naret at her side, her maids trailing behind. Three days ago every warrior had stood in stoic, respectful silence for their princess, every rail polished to a high shine, every control panel spotless, the deck gleaming.

That same floor was stone cold under her bare feet, stained with the blood of warriors, workers, slaves, all killed by blaster fire.

These men had been loyal to her, loyal to the empress. *And Alari has murdered them all.*

"It's okay," Jehan assured, reaching out to her. "They can't hurt you anymore."

His fingers wrapped around hers, and she spied a few thin scars—now faded to white—that crossed the back of his hand. His grip was strong, enveloping hers in warmth, and she let him draw her along with him, suddenly longing to wrap herself around that warmth.

Saria shook herself a little, her cheeks burning at having for a moment forgotten Naret, dead for her sake, two decks up.

Thankfully Jehan seemed unaware of her confusion. He frowned, studying the control panel to the chamber lock that stood between him and the ship's crystals.

"I'm going to release the safety locks and flood the exchange chamber to cool down the crystals." He let go of her hand to operate the controls. "That way they don't burn right through my fingers, and the deck and the hull—"

The lights dimmed.

"The ship is shifting to emergency power," he said in response to her frightened look, sending a glance at the engineering staff. "These guys must have done a fuck of a lot to keep the primary systems up when the ship was pulled in." He shook his head. "Too bad."

She frowned. "Too bad they were able to maintain the ship's power?"

"That the Az-kye don't reward brains or creativity. Just dumb brute force."

"Such is not so! The empire values its people—"

"*Values?*" He indicated one of the slaves who lay nearby. "For all you know that guy kept this whole fucking ship together—until someone blasted him. If he'd lived long enough to get back to the empire, what would his reward be?" he demanded. "Tell me, Liri—what would a clanless *slave* get on Az-kye if he made it back to the homeworld? Reward? Renown? *Freedom?*"

Hot words bubbled to Saria's lips. Not as devout as her sister, even *she* had never doubted the wisdom of Lashima—how the goddess had interceded, staying Ren'thar's sword when Her infuriated mate sought vengeance against those who desecrated his great temple at Parnat. The goddess met their crimes with mercy, turning their garments white with Her radiance as it wiped away their names.

Saria had never even seen one of the clanless up close until she had come onboard the *Ty'har*. She had stolen glances at them, fully expecting their meanness of spirit to show upon their faces.

But what she had seen instead were souls in unending suffering.

That man, the woman whose robe she now wore, had labored without end, without hope. They died side by side with warriors but no one of their family would ever know of their deeds or dare mourn them publicly. And no act of courage, of strength, of devotion could return a slave his or her name.

Suddenly Lashima's act did not seem like mercy at all . . .

"Damn it." Jehan passed his hand over his face. "I'm sorry, Liri. I don't have to tell *you* what it's like."

Saria shivered, drawing the jacket tighter. "It is growing colder."

"The storm's draining the last of reserve power." Jehan peered at the readings as they scrolled on the control panel. He tapped a few keys. "I'm shunting power away from the bridge and shutting down everything but the shields, the shuttle bay, and engineering."

"What of life support?" she asked quickly, her breath visible.

He kept his focus on the panel. "We've got under ten minutes of life support left, either way. I can't use power to seal off the corridors between here and the shuttle bay because that will shorten it to *five* minutes. But on the bright side," he offered wryly, "we'll freeze before we suffocate."

She caught his hand, trying to urge him toward the door. "We must hurry!"

He resisted her pull, focused on the control panel. "Not yet."

She glanced at the containment chamber but if there had been any change she could not see it. "We will die for your greed!"

"Don't be ridiculous." The chamber door released; the crystals' illumination filled the room, their glow lighting Jehan's face—and his wide grin. "I'm too rich to die."

He reached for the gems but hesitated—worried their heat had not been entirely drained off perhaps—then his fingers closed around the first. Plucking all five gems from their places, he held the last rainbow-hued jewel up between his thumb and forefinger.

Jehan was not smiling now. His face was grave, his dark eyes pensive.

Then his jaw hardened. He shoved the crystals into his pocket, his grin back in place as he caught her hand in his.

"Let's go, Liri!" He urged her to a jog as they plunged into the corridor. "We've got a ride to catch!"

"It is too far! We will never make it in time!"

"Well, don't blame me," he huffed. "You're the one who didn't want to leave the party."

"You are a madman!"

"Hope it doesn't disappoint you but"—he kept hold of her, swinging her along as they reached the corner—"you're not the first to say it."

The floor was like ice under her feet and even at a full run she was shivering uncontrollably. Since girlhood she had been trained in the practice of traditional dance to keep limber and strong, but as an Imperial Daughter she could never set herself against another in an athletic contest. She had not even raced against Alari when they were children; for the Second Daughter to best the First would be unseemly.

"Slow a little—" she begged, her vision turning black at the edges. "I cannot—keep up."

"Life support's—failing—"

The doors of the shuttle bay were open, the weakened shields all that stood between them and the red rage of the storm. A battered, ungainly Tellaran shuttle sat squeezed between her warship's finely crafted Az-kye vessels, a bumbling peasant among aristocrats.

Her vision swam. Her legs leaden now.

"Come on, Liri!" He gripped her arm hard, yanking her upright, pulling her, stumbling, along with him. "That shuttle's—*freedom*!"

The shield holding the vacuum of space at bay shimmered as it began to collapse and Saria's world went black.

4

ᲘᲠᲚᲮᲘᲜᲘ Უ ᲘᲮᲘᲛᲜ

Selini's Song

Saria groaned as she came to, her body at an odd, uncomfortable slump. She was being shaken with a force strong enough to rattle her teeth. Aching all over, she tried to move, to stand, only to discover she could not. Red mist and hazy lights in jewel colors swam before her. She blinked rapidly, trying to clear her vision. Her hands, unfettered, flailed at her sides.

"Where—where—?"

Strong fingers cupped her chin, turning her face to the side, and Saria found herself looking into Jehan's dark eyes.

"You'll be okay," he muttered and dropped his hand. "Once we get out of here, that is."

The blurred colors coalesced into shuttle controls and flashing bright matter that shot across the viewport, the remnants of the energy storm's discharges. Saria looked down to find herself in the copilot's seat, still clad in a slave's smock and Jehan's jacket. Safety straps crossed her body, holding her in place.

"We—" she croaked, trying to speak past the rawness in her throat. "We made it to the shuttle."

"*I* made it. You passed out."

Fighting against the shaking as the storm battered the vessel, Saria pushed herself into a more upright position in the chair.

The shuttle had clearly seen better days; the fabric was patched, and the panel that curved along the front of the cabin was dented and scratched in places. One of the overhead plates was missing and the resulting gap gave alarming insight into the age of the components within.

But then her attention was yanked spaceward, to the once-majestic vessel. "The *Ty'har* . . ."

"One less Az-kye warship skulking around." His fingers flew on the panel. "But trying her damnedest to take us to the nine hells with her."

He changed their heading and she gripped the armrests.

"What are you doing?" she cried as he hurled them toward the warship. "You have set us on a collision course!"

"That demon's between us and the storm's edge." His fingers flew on the control panel. "That's the way out, so that's where we're going, sweetheart!"

The warship suddenly swung upward like a beast in its death throes, as if it did indeed seek to trap them here with it. Saria made a strangled sound as Jehan dove left, passing them so close to the *Ty'har*'s hull she could make out the bolts on the ship's plating.

The lights of her flagship, the pride of the Imperial fleet, went dark. Drained of the last of its power, the lifeless black metal of the *Ty'har* twisted and crumpled in the storm. Ice crystals sparkled as the atmosphere burst free and the warship cracked in two, broken beyond all mending.

Like the Imperial family itself . . .

Suddenly the last angry red tendrils cleared from the viewport to reveal the cool, velvety blackness of open space, the brilliant lights of thousands upon thousands of stars.

"You are to be commended, Jehan," she murmured as the shuttle glided toward that brightness.

"Wow," he muttered, not even glancing up from the control panel. "Is that anything like 'thank you'?"

His tone—combined with her pounding head and sore muscles—made her nostrils flare.

She was an Imperial Daughter, he but a lowborn thief. On the homeworld just daring to speak to her would have earned him a sound beating. A sharp rebuke pursed her lips—

Then her fingers brushed the rough cloth of her slave gown.

Jehan was a criminal and a Tellaran—by choice if not by birth—a man so motivated by avarice he would risk his life to steal from a doomed ship.

What would he do with the Imperial Heiress in his grasp?

Her hands tightened, the white fabric bunching in her grip. No doubt he would demand an outrageous reward for her safe return. It might drain the Imperial coffers but she could resign herself to that—if it were not for the fact he could also just as easily sell her to Alari instead, on the promise of even greater riches when her sister took the throne.

As Second, she had been allowed far more freedom than her sister, but she had not often been let beyond the walls of the Imperial Palace. Even trips to the temple district were tightly controlled. In her life Saria had known little contact with the lower castes and almost none with the clanless.

Jehan's strong-jawed face was in profile. Warriors shaved their facial hair and his black beard, contrasting with the fine cloth of his white Tellaran shirt, only added to his rakish appearance.

He believes me to be Liri; I must pretend it so well he never suspects me other than a slave . . .

Saria wet her lips. "Thank you."

He glanced at her then turned his attention back to the controls. "You look like a scared sercat cub."

"I—I do not know that animal."

"Right," he murmured, his fingers pausing on the controls for a moment. He shrugged. "Well, you'll sure see enough of them. Maybe I'll get you one as pet."

"I thought this a short-range vessel." She took in the rough cabin again worriedly. "Think you it is capable of bringing us safely to a planetary system?"

"It might but it won't have to."

He nodded ahead. The Tellaran vessel was far smaller than her flagship, perhaps a third the size. It was a graceless thing, squat and fierce-looking and it reminded her a bit of a kro'pu. To be certain, that marsupial's yellow eyes, flattened furred body, and crooked yellow fangs looked about as welcoming as that ship did. While not well versed in Tellaran technology, even she could see that its weapons were far beyond what one of its type and class should be carrying.

"*That* is a Tellaran Fleet ship?"

He laughed. "No. But I can name a few Fleet ships that have opened fire on the *Seleni's Song*."

The freighter's shield shimmered, allowing them passage through to land. He set down with such smooth, practiced movements and skill she hardly felt them touch down on the deck.

He powered the shuttle down and released his safety straps.

"Come on, Liri," he said, standing. "Let's see how much trouble they've gotten themselves into while I've been gone."

"Jehan!"

At her cry he stopped in the cabin doorway and turned back, frowning. "What?"

"I . . ." Helplessly she indicated the safety straps that held her in place. "I require your assistance."

His eyebrows rose.

Saria wet her lips. "Please."

"Well," he said slowly as if considering the matter carefully. "I guess I could lend a hand. I mean, since you said '*please*' . . ."

Jehan bent over her, his big body so close she could feel his breath where her neck and shoulder met.

"What is the difficulty?" For someone who could disarm her so masterfully it certainly was taking him a long time to free her. "Are the controls malfunctioning?"

"Hey, give me a minute." He had a warm scent to him—foreign, *Tellaran*, but masculine and clean. "You've got yourself all tangled up here."

"It was you who placed me in this seat!" His beard brushed against her cheek as he shifted to reach around her. She found herself looking down the open neckline of his shirt, the muscled chest beneath. "*You* fastened these restraints."

"You know—" His dark eyes were innocent. "I think you're right."

He leaned in, his mouth close to hers. . .

With a flick of his finger the strap released with a *snap*.

"Lucky for you"—he gave her a slow grin—"I'm good with my hands."

Her cheeks warmed as, chuckling, he stood and once again headed aft toward the cabin door.

"Come on, Liri," he said over his shoulder, laughter in his voice.

Fearing he might think it a fine jest to leave her searching through a strange ship for him, Saria hurried after him.

"Of all the star-blasted, hot-shot, *lunatic* things I've seen you do—" A woman in her mid-thirties, clad in gray coveralls, her red hair a shade only a Tellaran could have, stood with arms akimbo, glaring up at Jehan from the bottom of the ramp. "That was, without a doubt, *the* most *dumb*-ass—"

The woman broke off, staring, as soon as Saria came into view.

"Mig!" Jehan enthused as he headed down the ramp. "Yeah, I'm glad I made it back safely too."

Saria followed Jehan down into the shuttle bay, the deck cold and dirty under her bare feet.

"Hold on a godsdamned minute!" Mig fell in step at his side and threw her hand out toward Saria. "Who the hells is she?"

Jehan snapped his fingers. "My manners! I *knew* I left something behind on that wreck. Right, so Mig, this is Liri. Liri—" He waved at the redhead. "This is the *Selini's Song's* engineer—and my self-appointed conscience— Mig."

"And you just decided to nip her off an Imperial warship?" the woman demanded. "What if the Az-kye come looking for her?"

"They won't," Jehan said shortly, heading for the doors again. "Since I did make it back with my skin intact—and thanks to all for your faith in me—anything I need to know about?"

"Hells, yeah! They've—"

The opening bay doors cut her off and both Jehan and Mig stopped short, Saria behind them. Three men, clad in black hooded ankle-length coats, waited there. One stepped forward to lead and the other two fell into step on either side, a pace behind, coming at them like a shadowy bird of prey.

Mig's freckled cheeks blanched. Jehan's smile did not touch his eyes.

"Kel," Jehan called amiably. "Good of you to come all the way down here to welcome me back."

The lead man pushed his hood back. Intricate black tattoos covered his bald head, snaking around to his upper cheeks and forehead. His attention fixed on Saria and instinctively she pulled Jehan's jacket tighter around herself.

"I see your trip over wasn't a waste after all, Captain Dekra." Kel pursed his lips as he looked Saria over. "Isn't that a fine one?"

Jehan shrugged. "She might clean up okay."

"Body's good," one of the other men said, pulling off his own hood to show himself bald-headed like the first man, but with far less elaborate tattooing across his face. "She'll sell, even with her face messed up like that."

Sell?

Jehan's weight shifted, now partly shielding her from the men's view.

"Take her to The Open Flower," the second man continued. "Bandy'll buy her for sure."

"Van's right. But too bad The Wild Ride isn't buying." Kel smiled, showing yellow teeth sharpened into points.

The third man's brow furrowed. "That girl's going to be like a busy barber's chair: no sooner is one out than another one will be in."

"'Course"—Jehan indicated the man's bare head—"You three don't have much use for a barber these days, do you?"

The leader ran his palm over his scalp fondly. "The Brethren taketh and the Brethren giveth."

"Weighing a little heavier on the taking side, of course," Jehan said.

Kel's smile turned cold. "Which returns us to the matter of this little nibble—and Helock's cut. Tasty to be sure . . ." The man raised his dark eyebrows. "But I do hope she's not the only goodie you got from that ship?"

Jehan spread his hands. "'Fraid so."

"Now that is a pity." The man tsked. "I'm afraid Helock will find it *most* disappointing."

"And who could blame him?" Jehan asked. "That warship was just *ripe* for the picking." He shook his head. "You should have seen it, Mig! Weapons, artwork—that ship was a godsdamned treasure trove! And we could have taken it *all*. If you'd"—he indicated the three men—"gone over there with me when I ordered it, well, Helock would've had *a fortune*. Now he'll get a few creds from the sale of one Az-kye woman to a pleasure house." Jehan folded his arms. "But I'm sure once *you* explain to Helock how he lost his share, Kel, he'll understand."

In the tense silence Mig's hand twitched toward the blaster at her hip.

"Well," Kel said abruptly. "It hardly matters now." He spread his meaty hands. "After all, who's to say what an Az-kye ship—one now lost to the storms—might or might not have had onboard?"

"I can," Jehan said, ignoring Mig's sharp warning glance.

Kel's blue eyes narrowed.

"'Course seeing as I'm captain . . ." Jehan shrugged, "I don't really have much reason to complain to Helock, do I?"

"'Sides, Kel, these days the brothels are full to bursting—likely aren't enough cocks on Halea to fill the ones already there." This Brethren was perhaps twenty or so. His rounded face and long dark lashes made him appear far too gentle to be bearing the black tattoos on his cheekbones and scalp. "Not when so many homesteaders have sent a girl or two to pay their debts."

"You'd know, wouldn't you, Etaran?" Van sneered.

The young man's face flushed, his lips thinning.

"He's probably right though." Jehan eased his weight a bit so his hand fell naturally near the blaster at his hip. "More trouble than it's worth anyway."

"Well, who am I to interfere with tradition?" Kel took a step back. "I think we're best focused on seeing this run completed on time."

"*I* sure wouldn't want to be the man who disappoints Helock," Jehan agreed.

The other men sent dark looks at Jehan but they followed their leader to the exit.

Kel paused just at the threshold of the shuttle bay's open doors. "Enjoy this"—he sent a glance at Saria— "indulgence, Jehan."

Then the doors slid shut behind the tattooed men.

Mig's fist sounded a dull smack as it made contact with Jehan's arm. "Dumb ass!"

"*Ow!*" he complained, scowling as his hand went to the spot. "Godsdamn it, Mig, that hurt!"

"They could have killed you, you idiot!"

"Sorry, I must've forgot you're first in line," he grumbled.

"Don't tempt me!" Mig's face was reddened and she stabbed a finger at the closed bay doors. "You're fucking lucky, you know that?"

"I'm not lucky," Jehan muttered, rubbing his arm. "I'm charming."

"Who are those men?" Saria demanded sharply. "Who is *Helock*? Why would—"

Jehan held up a hand to silence her. "Please hold all questions till the end of the tour." He leveled his gaze at Mig. "And you, kill me later, okay? Right now I need you to get us back on schedule. And for fuck's sake, make *sure* those three are tracked—"

"I know! I know!" Mig said, stomping toward the shuttle doors.

"This is no way to treat your captain!" he shouted after her.

Mig threw back a scowl just as the doors closed behind her.

Saria fixed Jehan with a glare the moment they were alone. "Captain Dekra, I *will* have answers of you! Who are those men? And what did that—*Kel*—mean by he did not want to get 'in the way of tradition'? What tradition?"

"Right," Jehan mumbled, rubbing at his arm again. "Kel was recognizing my claim as captain to the, uh . . . spoils."

"The spo—?" Her eyes widened. "Do you speak of *me*?"

Jehan's tanned cheeks flushed a little.

"Are you . . ." The very thought was utterly absurd, that she, an Imperial Daughter—"Are you saying that as captain of this vessel you somehow now *own* me?"

"*Own* might be a little strong—Oh, hells." Jehan cleared his throat. "That's what it works out to."

Her fingers clenched at the skirt of her borrowed smock. "This is not possible. Tellarans do not keep slaves."

"No, they don't, but"—Jehan shifted his weight—"this isn't exactly Tellaran territory, Liri."

"Not—?" Saria shook her head. "We have passed through Ren'thar's Sword. We are no longer in Imperial space. We must be in Tellaran territory!"

"Okay, yeah." He passed his hand over his face. "*Technically*, this is Tellaran space but the Badlands . . . have laws all their own."

"The kind of laws that have made me your property?" she flared.

"If I hadn't staked a claim to you—" Jehan indicated the closed shuttle doors. "Would you rather belong to Bandy? Or *Helock*? Because if you want my input, of the two, Bandy's pleasure house is the one you want to shoot for!"

"Think you to have won my gratitude by this?" she cried. "That doing such has somehow ennobled you to me?"

His mouth tightened. "In case you didn't recognize that particular fashion choice, Liri, those men are members of the Brethren."

"I do not care what fool name they call themselves!"

"You're in the Badlands now." He took a quick step closer, his tone sharp. "You'd *better* fucking care about the Brethren."

He stood a head taller than she but even his great height would not cow an Imperial Daughter.

"I do not fear them. They are nothing but revolting little snakes!"

"Revolting little snakes who work for a revolting *big* snake named Helock. And," he gritted out, "since I have just crossed the most powerful crime lord in the Badlands for your sake, yeah, you might consider showing the tiniest bit of gratitude."

Her hands balled into fists. "I am *not* your property!"

"Even as my woman you're still freer than you were in the empire!" he snapped, striding toward the doors.

"Captain!" Her voice rang through the shuttle bay imperiously. "I *insist* you—"

Jehan rounded on her. "Let me clear things up for you a bit, Liri. Helock is the Brethren's leader and he wants this ship—*my* ship. Kel's job is to get Helock whatever he wants. If he succeeds, Kel moves up within the Brethren and gets a nifty new stripe on his face to show it off. I may have gotten him to back off a minute ago but I guarantee you, he's out there right now scheming up a way to get hold of this ship—and you." A muscle in his jaw twitched. "Kel wants us *both* on our backs—me with a blaster hole through my chest and you at The Open Flower. So in case you missed it I just saved your"—her face heated as he glanced down at the dark triangle of hair, visible through the thin material of her slave's smock—"*neck,*" he finished. "And if you ever want to make it out of the Badlands, to one of the civilized Tellaran worlds—to *real* freedom—you'll accept my protection, Liri."

He had never been so grim; not even when he was piloting through the storm, not even when the *Ty'har* was on the verge of breaking apart around them.

Gods, they will think me dead! Everyone—my mother, the court. Alari will believe victory already hers.

"Make up your mind," he said shortly. "I've got a few things to drop off in my quarters and a ship to run."

Even if she convinced Jehan of her true identity—and standing here, barefoot and filthy in a slave's smock, she was not at all sure she *could*—revealing her secret now would only put her in far greater peril with these Brethren on board.

"What—" Saria wet her lips. "What do you wish me to do?"

"Just be a good slave." He took her by the upper arm, his grip gentle as he urged her toward the bay door. "You know how to do *that*, right?"

5

ᚴᚠᚹᚠᚠᚴᚾᚴᚴᛃᚹᛝᚠ

Remembrance

Saria garnered curious looks from the Tellarans as she and Jehan made their way through the ship. The crew—male and female both—greeted their captain with respectful nods as they hurried about their business. And it was clear from the crew's attire—ranging from old coveralls, like Mig wore, to tacky, gold-braided finery—this was no military ship.

Nor was it a new vessel, and little effort had been made to enhance the interior's aesthetics. The ceilings were curved and the passageways well-lit, but the carpet worn and discolored in places. Junctures were located at various points throughout the ship where emergency doors could shut in the event of a hull breach; those safety hatches were scrupulously maintained, but along the corridors a number of the wall panels did not match, the patches seemingly made of whatever materials were at hand without thought to appearance or uniformity.

"If this ship is yours—"

His grip tightened on her arm. "Quiet."

Annoyance burned her chest at his hiss but she pressed her lips together and he pulled her into a lift that already held two of his people.

Jehan acknowledged both crewmembers but his hand always hovered near the blaster at his side, as if he trusted his own people scarcely more than he did the Brethren.

Once off the lift, his stride quickened, the tension in his big body so great her glance darted about the empty corridor, seeking signs of imminent attack or ambush.

"Here," he murmured, stopping before a door at the end of the hall. Jehan sent a quick look both ways, his hand now resting on his blaster, but the hallway remained deserted. He triggered the security mechanism and a retinal scan of his eye released the door lock.

Jehan urged her inside, locking the door the instant it shut.

"That went better than I expected," he muttered, letting her go. "Want a drink?" He was already crossing to the other side of the cabin. "I sure as hells do."

It did not take him long to traverse the space either; this room would not take up even one eighth of the Heiress's apartments at the Imperial Palace. The furniture could only be called serviceable, and the walls were a faded beige color. There were no pictures or mementos scattered on the tables or bright carpets beneath her feet. The bed coverings were an equally bland shade of tan.

Little was evident to show that anyone, let alone the ship's captain, occupied these quarters. If she were to be forced to sojourn with the Tellarans for the time being, she sorely hoped not all their interiors would be as dreary and colorless as this. Only the three windows showcasing the turbulent pink and red swirls of nearby energy eddies—beautiful when one was not caught within them—lent some appeal to the space.

"Niman brandy," Jehan announced, holding up a bottle of rose-gold liquid. "Bright as an Apovian moon and smooth as shimmersilk. Now—" He looked around. "Just need a glass . . ."

Spying some on a shelf over the desk, he scooped them up, managing to hold both in one hand and pour at the same time as he made his way back to her.

"Here you go." He pushed the cup into her hand. "Best stuff in the Realm."

She gave the contents a cautious sniff as he downed the contents of his glass. The scent at least was pleasing, and she took a tiny sip.

It was as lovely as he promised: smooth, with a light fruity taste that had her taking another, deeper drink.

He refilled his cup and hers then tapped them together, the crystal making a bright sound.

Jehan held his cup up in response to her puzzled look. "Tellaran tradition. It's called a toast."

Sighing, she obediently clinked her glass to his so she could drink more but at his laugh she stopped short, frowning, the cup at her lips.

"No," he said, the corners of his mouth twitching. "You're supposed to touch the glasses together, choose something to salute, *then* drink." He touched his glass to hers and held up his cup, looking at her expectantly. "So what should we drink to first?"

"It is for me to choose?"

"Sure. Pick whatever you want."

She wet her lips, licking the sweetness from them. "How many things may I salute?"

He eyed the brandy bottle. "Hmm, after the day I've had I'd like to say as long as the bottle holds out but with the Brethren on board . . . let's say, two."

"Then," she said hoarsely, remembering Naret's courage, his rare smiles given just to her in private as befitting the stoicism of a warrior, and touched her glass to

Jehan's. "We will salute the warriors of the *Ty'har* who fell, swords in hand, in service to the empire."

For a moment she did not think he would drink to any Az-kye, no matter how courageous.

"May Ren'thar welcome them to his hall," Jehan replied, surprising her, his deep voice solemn as he lifted his cup, "and honor them as his true sons."

Her throat tightened at the traditional words and she drank deeply of the Tellaran spirits.

"Okay, you got one more." He poured a small amount of the brandy into her glass, just enough for a swallow or two. "Make it count."

The liquor warmed her throat but Saria's heart suddenly felt like a block of ice.

"May Ren'thar's sword sing"—she touched her glass to his—"and avenge the honor of those wronged."

For an instant bitterness tightened his features then he raised his glass. "To Ren'thar."

When her glass was empty he took it from her, placed both on the dining table.

"Enough for now. That Niman brandy hits you hard if you aren't careful." He rubbed the spot where Mig had punched him. "Like their women."

"Your engineer is from Nima?"

"Yeah. Probably haven't seen hair that color before, have you?"

"Only once." Alari's Tellaran mate had a sister whose hair was of a similarly bright shade.

"You saw a redhead?" His eyebrows rose. "In the empire?"

"There were once a number of Tellaran slaves in the Imperial City." Saria looked to the windows, to the stars beyond. "Before the agreement was made to return them home."

That was true enough, although she had never spoken to any of those slaves. Pains were taken to clear the clanless from the princess's sight whenever possible.

"You lived in the Imperial City." His dark eyes were unreadable now. "Were you owned by a prominent family there . . . or cast out of one?"

"I—I was—"

But she had not had time to invent a history for "Liri" and the Tellaran spirits had her thoughts tumbling and crashing over one another. It was as if all the events of the past weeks—Alari's disgrace, the weight of the Heiress's crown being placed on her own head by the High Priestess of Lashima, the wheeze of Naret's last breath—rushed in at once.

"You have nothing to fear from me, Liri," Jehan promised, frowning at her. "I'm not going to hurt you."

"I am not—not—" She was trembling now, so hard her teeth were chattering.

"Shock," he said grimly.

In the next instant he had pulled the coverlet from the bed and wrapped her in it. Then, as if she weighed nothing at all, he swept her into his strong arms and settled onto the couch, cradling her against him.

"It's all right," he murmured, his gentle fingers smoothing her hair away from her face. "It's all right."

"I-I am not a ch-child," she sobbed. "I do not n-need you to h-hold me—"

"Yeah, well—" He settled her closer, tucking her head against his shoulder, his bearded cheek against her forehead. "Maybe I'm the one who needs this."

He rocked her for a long while, until her shaking stopped and her tears slowed.

"I am all right now," Saria said quietly, but she made no move to leave his embrace.

He tilted her face up to look at her, lightly traced the swelling along her cheek with his fingertips. "They do this to you?"

"My—other—dress caught fire. Nar—my owner threw me down and covered me with a tapestry to put out the flames. I did not catch myself in time to prevent the injury."

"That was him—your owner—in the hallway where I found you, wasn't it? One of the ones who died from a blaster wound."

"He . . . deserved better."

He brushed the hair away from forehead with gentle fingers. "Did you—"

The door chime cut him off, his big body tense now.

"Who is it?" she whispered as he shifted her beside him, although even a Tellaran vessel must have adequate enough soundproofing to make it unnecessary. "Is it the Brethren?"

Jehan stood, his blaster already in hand. "I sure as hells hope not."

6

Captain's Perogative

Saria threw off the quilt as the door chime sounded again and forced herself up, standing on wobbly legs.

"Return the other blaster to me," she urged. "I will fight with you."

He stopped to look round at her, his eyebrows raised. "You ever fired a blaster before?"

Among the Az-kye there were no female warriors; her protection was the responsibility of the Imperial guards, of the mate she would someday take. Saria had been raised as a proper Imperial Daughter, taught to wield a fan, not a sword.

But three against one did not bode well for her chances of ever setting foot into the palace again—

"What difference does that make when there is an enemy at the door?"

"Accuracy makes a fuck of a lot of difference to the one who's standing between you and that enemy," he grumbled but his glance at the door's security sensor eased the tension in his shoulders—a bit. "It's Mig."

Jehan activated the door control and the red-haired woman, her freckled face tight with tension and her arms full, pushed past him into the room.

"I'm alone," Mig assured, setting her burden on the dining room table. "Kel's on the bridge and the other Breths are in their quarters."

Jehan followed and indicated the pile. "What's all this?"

"Thought you could use something to eat, maybe some medical supplies." Mig glanced Saria's way. "And clothes."

He grinned. "Mig, what would I do without you?"

She rubbed her hands on the sides of her coveralls. "Let's not find out."

"What's the news?" he asked.

"Kel's skulking about on the bridge, watching everybody like a firehawk hunting snouses. Jul thinks you might want to put in an appearance."

"In the morning," he said, rummaging through the packs she'd brought.

The Tellaran woman glanced toward Saria. "Cap, I think—"

"Go relieve Jul," he interrupted. "I'll take over from you for the day shift."

"Jul's not going to like giving up command when the Breths are aboard. Not to me, anyways."

"If she balks, remind her that she follows my orders or I find a new First Officer."

Mig shifted her weight. "What about engineering? Don't you want me down there?"

"It's on lockout, isn't it?"

"As per your orders," she agreed.

"Trackers on the Brethren?"

She snorted. "Always."

"Then, until we're planetside and the Brethren are off this ship, one of us three is going to have our ass in that command chair. But I need sharp minds up there. Jul's been on duty for over fourteen hours and I'm going on twenty. That leaves you."

"I'm not a command officer," she reminded. "I'm a grease snoth."

"You're a *loyal* grease snoth. Right now that means a fuck of a lot more."

Mig offered a reluctant nod. "Okay, I'll take command."

"Well, as long as you don't mind," Jehan said dryly. "Anything else?"

"A little good news. Ship's systems are all operating in normal parameters and there's no sign Fleet's in this sector. Looks like we've got a clear shot back to Halea, at least."

"The sooner the better," he agreed. "Go tell Jul to get some bunk time. You're in command till *I* relieve you and not before, understood?"

The woman nodded. "Got it."

"Mig!" he called, stopping her at the door. "This order is for your ears and Jul's only—if the Brethren move to take over the ship they get a blaster bolt through the head. We'll worry about kissing and making up with Helock later."

Mig's face lit up. "Yes, sir!"

"*Only* if they move against us," he warned.

She saluted. "Of course, sir!"

"Don't spoil me," he said, waving off her salute. "Dismissed."

Saria pulled the blanket tighter around her shoulders when the door was locked again behind Mig. "If you believe the Brethren intend to seize your ship should you not then be on the bridge, as your officer suggested?"

"What, and let everyone think I'm worried? You probably won't believe this, but I do know what I'm doing." He searched through one of the cases Mig had brought. "At least I'm sure we all hope I do." At her tense silence, his expression softened. "You're safe here, Liri. I vowed to protect you, remember?"

She shifted her weight.

He sighed. "You know you're looking at me with all the confidence of the town wives watching their menfolk descend into the astuk mines after a quake." He lifted a cylindrical instrument. "Let's get you taken care of."

"What is that?" she asked, cringing as he came toward her with it.

"It's just a medscanner—a Tellaran medical instrument." His voice was soothing, patient as he held it up for her to see. "We don't have a bio-bed onboard, worse luck, but even this small scanner can determine the extent of your injuries. It also has settings I can use to treat you. It won't hurt."

She let him guide her to a sitting position. Then, holding the scanner a few inches above her skin, he moved it slowly over her temple then upwards over her scalp and down to the back of her head.

"No concussion or bone fractures," he murmured. "That's good."

He adjusted the controls and passed it over again, this time concentrating on the areas around her right temple and cheek.

"It feels warm." Saria flinched away from the orange light, disconcerted by the strange sensation. "My face is tingling."

"That's exactly what it's supposed to feel like," he assured, gently tilting her face with her his fingers. "It'll speed healing."

He used the scanner over her body, stopping here and there to treat a scrape or contusion.

"Your shins have second-degree burns." Jehan knelt and lifted her feet in turn to examine her soles. "Your feet are cut up real bad too." He scowled up at her. "You should have told me."

"When should I have done so?" she countered, annoyed. "When we were running to the *Ty'har*'s shuttle bay before the oxygen ran out? When the Brethren demanded you hand me over to be sold to a Tellaran pleasure house? When you bid me be silent on the way here?"

He blew his breath out and bent over his work. "Next time just speak up, okay?"

He tended to her other injuries, taking time and care with each, his touch gentle as he removed the jacket he'd lent her, adjusting the slave smock to treat the abrasions at her shoulder.

He met her gaze. "I should check everywhere."

Saria clutched at the smock as if he would tear it from her body. "Such is not necessary."

"Your thighs were burned, I can see blisters above your knees," he pointed out. "You probably have more."

"If I do, they do not pain me," she lied.

He raised his eyebrows. "As I recall, Az-kye aren't usually bothered by nudity."

Her cheeks warmed. She had been bathed, dressed, and undressed by maids her whole life. Surely the love-play with Naret had long since cured her of any shyness about being unclothed in front of a man.

"I am not." But Saria suddenly found it hard to look at him. "It is simply I do not—"

"Trust me?" he finished. "You trusted me to get you off the warship."

"I had no choice but to trust you," Saria said sharply. "I do not know how to pilot a shuttle."

"And here I thought my charm had finally gotten to you." He stood. "Come on, I promise you aren't the first woman I've seen naked." His mouth quirked upward. "And, Arrena willing, not the last either."

"Such is not necessary." She folded her hands, adopting a dignified stance. "I do not require further examination."

"The hells you don't! Look—" Jehan rubbed the bridge of his nose. "We bunked a doctor for this voyage but he— Never mind. The point is, right now I'm the only one on board who's medtech certified. This ship won't make planetfall for another two days and by then any wounds you have might become infected. Whether you trust me or not— whether you're modest or not—you are going to be examined. And treated, if need be. Right now."

Saria remained stubbornly silent and he folded his arms.

"Sorry," he said with a mock-frown. "Did I forget to mention that's an order? The captain gets to do that, you know."

She glanced away, shifting her weight.

"I've never abused a woman, Liri." His expression tightened as if the unspoken accusation wounded him. "I sure as hells wouldn't rape one."

In truth, the skin of her back and buttocks felt as though sand were scraping away at the tender flesh with every movement. She might not trust this man but—

I can hardly return home to demand justice if I die of infected wounds in Tellaran space.

"Very well." She speared him with a look. "But *only* because you have made it an order as commander of this vessel."

"Damn, you're a lousy patient," he muttered, making adjustments to the medical scanner. "You know it's not like I *enjoy* the sight of blisters."

Saria eased herself from under the blanket and winced, her feet tender even after his treatments. She reached for the smock's hem but at the last moment she turned her back to him to pull the slave's garment over her head.

He was silent for a moment and her face warmed.

"You have burns on the back of your legs," he murmured. "Gods, they must hurt like—" His fingers rested lightly on her shoulder as the warm tingle of the scanner treated the skin over her spine. "No more Az-kye stoicism crap, Liri. If you're hurt or in pain, you tell me."

"Another order?"

"If that's what it takes."

He was gentle in treating her burns and, as the pain of them eased, Saria closed her eyes in blessed relief.

"All right," he said finally. "Turn around."

She steeled herself as she turned to face him, expecting some coarse comment at the sight of her bare front.

But Jehan's expression remained focused, clinical. "I only see one burn on your left hip but I'm going to double check with the scanner anyway."

He applied the healing light to her hip and paused over a few other scrapes and bruises.

Finally he finished, and in a smooth movement he lifted the quilt and draped it around her. Instantly she pulled the blanket closed.

"Any other hurts you haven't told me about?" he asked. "Any headache? Or dizziness?"

She shook her head.

"I know the Az-kye don't often bother giving slaves medical care," he said, his voice rough now. "Any . . . old wounds?"

Saria busied herself with the quilt's frayed edge to avoid his searching look. "No."

He hesitated, as if weighing whether or not to press her.

"The areas I treated might be a bit sore for a day or two," he said at last. "Let me know if anything gets worse." He turned, already returning the medscanner to its case. "You hungry?"

"I am but now I will—" She caught herself. "I mean, may I bathe?"

"Sure." He busied himself sorting through the packs, holding one up to examine it then tossing it aside for another. "Fresher's right through there."

Clutching the quilt around her and walking gingerly on sore feet, Saria went toward the door he indicated.

The illumination rose in the small bathroom as soon as she entered. It was utilitarian at best, with a walk-in shower and minimal comforts. The door slid shut behind her and after a moment's hesitation she engaged the lock.

Not that it would keep him out if he wanted to enter. As captain he would certainly have the override codes that would enable him to go anywhere on his ship he pleased.

Her skin prickled as she caught movement in the corner of her eye. She was not alone in here—

7

From the Skin Out

"Gods!"

Wide-eyed with horror at her own reflection, Saria raised her hand to her bruised and swollen face as she shuffled toward the mirror on aching feet. Her waist-length dark strands, only that morning dressed into bejeweled coils by the quick, skilled fingers of her maids, were now the wild hair of madwoman—hanging snarled and dull with soot down her back. Tears had made streaks in the dirt on her face and there were deep shadows marring the skin beneath her eyes. Her hands were reddened and dirty too, a few of the nails broken off short.

No one would know her now for an Imperial Daughter.

No one at all . . .

She was in enemy territory with only a thief's promise to safeguard her. Any plea for help she sent home, provided she could find a means to do so without alerting the Tellarans, could be intercepted by Alari and that would accomplish nothing but inform her sister's assassins of her exact location . . .

Looking into her own reflection, seeing the fear and timidity there, Saria hardened her jaw.

Empress Liri was thrown from the falls and survived to claim vengeance and her throne. What my ancestor did, so shall I. I will find a way to outwit Alari. I will reclaim my place as Heiress.

But before she could hope to return home in triumph, she had to survive here, among these foreign criminals. She must play the role of Liri the slave girl, and make it utterly convincing.

The question was *how*.

Waited on hand and foot since babyhood, Saria did not know how to do the simplest of tasks for herself; she had never even combed her own hair. But no slave would have known such pampering; as one of the clanless, she would have performed any labor required of her, from scrubbing floors to tending livestock.

Saria chewed the inside of her cheek. Jehan already deduced she had been part of a prominent family; her accent, her mannerisms, had already marked her as once one of the privileged caste, but he could have no idea just how high her true rank was.

He—no one—must know.

She would claim to be the younger daughter of a clan leader, a spoiled child, cast out for her willful disobedience, or perhaps the unfortunate victim of a clan war, one who had fallen with the rest of her house into nameless ruin.

Her maids had been drawn from among the greatest families in the Empire. As younger daughters and nieces, they would not inherit their clan's leadership but their bloodlines were impeccable. A number of them had once been Alari's attendants and had clamored to be chosen as companions to the new Heiress when her sister's star had fallen. Eager to rise among her fellows, to make friends with she who would be the next Empress, each sought to engage her in conversation whenever possible.

And from their acquaintance Saria knew even the most pampered daughter among them was capable of fastening her own clothes. Whatever she did not know she would have to learn quickly and without drawing dangerous attention to her ignorance.

Saria squared her shoulders. She may not have done the task herself but she had watched her hair being brushed every day. It looked simple enough.

But the vanity surface was bare with no comb or brush to be seen.

In the apartments of the First Daughter the vanity that held her cosmetics and hair ornaments had been crafted millennia ago from a single tashi tree. The polished drawers had pulls decorated with semiprecious stones and rolled open silently at her maids' gentlest tugs.

There were no such ancient carved drawer-pulls on this battered Tellaran vessel to be sure, but even a room this small should have storage. Saria felt along the front of the vanity. Through trial and error, she discovered that a press to the corner of the drawer front released the latch, allowing each drawer to glide open.

Nothing within appeared to be of any great worth or sentimental value. All Jehan's grooming supplies— what few there were—seemed common enough, as if he could walk out of these quarters at any time, never return, and miss none of it.

But there was a comb at least. She took it in hand, lifted it to her crown, pushed the teeth into the vole's nest that was her hair, and yanked.

She bit her lip as the roots of her hair screamed in protest. Saria sought to pull the comb out, intending on trying it on the other side of her head and found she could not.

It was stuck.

Saria turned her head, hoping to find a quick solution, only to discover that angle just offered a better view of the comb sticking ludicrously from the side of her head.

A sob choked her as she pulled harder, in an attempt to wrench it from her hair.

She who would be Empress!

In the next instant the comb was free, taking an alarming number of her dark strands with it.

Tears blurred her vision and Saria gripped the comb with shaking fingers. Her maids could glide a brush through her hair with such ease it was soothing. How could she hope to survive here alone when she could not even free her own hair of tangles?

Then she recalled one morning when Naret had first begun visiting her bed. Before her maids had come in to tend her, he had playfully taken up a jeweled comb and smoothed her hair himself, gently coaxing out the knots, taking his time with the task to press kisses to her neck.

Saria frowned, trying to recall how he had done it. She took hold of a small section of her hair a few inches up from the ends. Holding it firmly, she brushed just from her fingers downward and managed to smooth it without tearing any more hair from her head.

Emboldened by that success, Saria clasped higher up eventually freeing that small section entirely of tangles. Saria worked her way through her hair, section by section, until her hair was finally smooth and her arms ached from the effort.

Worn out already but desperate to feel clean, she shrugged off the blanket. The baths she had known had been carved, deep tubs of steaming water made fragrant with flowers from the Imperial gardens, but at the moment this was her only option. She stepped around the curved wall to study the controls in the center of the five nozzles there.

An experimental press of one sent Saria, gasping, in hasty retreat from the blast of icy water. She hovered just out of the water's reach, shielding herself with her arm against the chilly spray, then darted closer and managed to shut it off. Shivering, she flung back her hair—so hard won from its tangles and now half soaked—and gritted her teeth. Surely even Tellarans would bathe with hot water. There must be *some* way to coax it from these strange controls.

Her next attempt scalded her fingers, but with grim determination she finally managed to adjust the temperature to a pleasing level, the warmth of the water soothing her sore muscles. Cleanser was available and Saria poured some into her cupped hand. Hoping it was suitable for the washing of hair as well as body she ran it through the strands, scrubbing at her scalp. Her face was tender so she kept her touch there light. Her body scrubbed, she turned her back to the spray and stood for a long moment, willing the water to wash her clean too of the heartbreak and terror of the day.

She found a fresh towel in another drawer to dry herself. Although she could not be certain she was using it correctly a vent affixed to the wall proved an ideal way to dry her hair. She had nothing but the blanket to wear out and she took stock of her appearance as she wrapped it around her shoulders.

Her hair hung free, the strands shiny and smooth. But the swelling and bruising on her face—

A knock on the door made her jump and she clutched the quilt tighter.

She wet her lips as the sharp rapping came again. But surely if the Brethren had broken in to drag her away, they would not take the trouble to knock now. Saria released the lock and the door slid open to reveal Jehan there, a bundle in his hands.

His glance went over her. "You okay?"

"Yes." Had she tripped some sort of panic alarm? "Why would I not be?"

"I was beginning to wonder if you had a concussion after all and passed out or something." Jehan searched her face. "You sure you're okay?"

"I—" Life at court had taught her that lies were best concealed beneath a layer of truth. "I am not familiar with Tellaran technology."

The concern that knitted his brow eased and he gave her a chagrined look. "Damn it, I'm sorry. Of course you wouldn't be. I should have shown you how to use everything."

He seemed genuinely distressed, another unexpected flash of kindness.

"I managed well enough, I think," she said, wincing inwardly at the remembered image of herself with the comb sticking out from the side of her head.

"No, I didn't mean—" His face flushed at bit and he shoved the bundle at her. "Clothes," he said by way of explanation. "Mig brought you coveralls, underthings, boots too."

Keeping the quilt closed with one hand, Saria took them from him. After a moment she remembered to say: "Thank you."

Behind him the table was now cleared and a meal waited there.

"Dinner," he said. "If you're hungry."

"Quite hungry." She glanced at the bundle in her hand. "I have never worn Tellaran clothing before."

"It's pretty simple. Underwear, halter, coveralls, boots, and you're done. You'll figure it out."

If it were indeed that simple, she would not need a maid to help her. "What of my hair? How do Tellaran women dress their hair?"

"Not sure how much help I can be on that subject," he admitted. "You can ask Mig or Jul tomorrow. A lot of women wear it loose. Yours is pretty long so you might want to braid it or tie it back during the day, to keep it out of the way."

"Tie it back?" Her eyebrows rose. "As a warrior does?"

"Tellaran women don't use leather strips like a warrior would," he said, amused. "But the idea is the same. A lot of the women just want it out of the way when they're working. Some cut it short like Jul."

She glanced at Jehan's closely cropped hair.

"Not as short as mine, usually," he said with a laugh. He took a step back. "Get dressed. I'm starving."

8

ᴣ∆ᴧ⌐ᴪ∂ᴧᴣ ⌐ᴧᴧ ᴧᴦ⌐ ᴦ

Monarch and Slave

The coveralls were a bit trickier to get into than she had hoped and Saria was very glad he had left her alone so that no one would witness her fumbling.

It took her some time to close the fastenings up the front of the body. Saria copied Mig, tucking the trouser legs into the flat-heeled black boots and rolling up the too-long sleeves. An attached belt could be pulled tighter to better fit the wearer but the coveralls were clearly a mass-produced item. Intended to fit a variety of body types and shapes, it would fit none of them very well.

Accustomed as she was to the headdresses and wide skirts of an Imperial Princess, these simple clothes gave her an odd, exhilarating freedom of movement. The coveralls' fabric was soft but dull as a cloudy day, with no lace, jewels, or beading to enliven it. Scrunching her nose as she took in her reflection, she found the clothing appallingly unattractive. After all the effort of smoothing her hair, washing, and dressing, the result was more than a little disappointing.

"Ever had Tellaran food before?" Jehan asked when she joined him in the other room.

"No." Leaving the nightdress on a nearby chair, she joined him at the table and tried not to let her dismay show. Lacking the sparkling crystal and elegant finery, the proud touches of the scores of palace chefs laboring to create dishes for her delight, this was as humble a meal as she had ever seen.

There was a single plate at each setting, accompanied by dull metal utensils. Accustomed to dinners that numbered twenty or more courses, Saria examined the three bowls, their unfamiliar contents steaming hot, and a plate of what looked like misshapen disks.

Jehan seated himself. He lifted a bottle and glanced up mid-pour. "Something wrong?"

"No," she said, flushing, and took her own seat.

Of course he would not wait for her to sit first, to beg the indulgence of being allowed to sit in her presence.

I am Liri now!

"Thank you," she said, taking the cup he offered her, pleased to have remembered the courtesy this time. At the Imperial Place it was the servants' task to make themselves as invisible as possible in the performance of their work and hers to offer silent appreciation for their efforts.

Jehan took a swallow of the wine then paused to raise an eyebrow at her. "Liri? What is it?"

She held up her glass hesitantly. "Is the toast tradition not done with wine then?"

"Oh." He straightened. "Yes . . . sometimes."

"But not now."

"Usually it's—" He shook his head a little. "You know what? No, not now." He waved to indicate she should raise her cup. "Go ahead and drink."

She tasted the wine as he served her from each of the dishes and found it unusual but very pleasant.

"The wine is Zartani but the food is assembled from ration packs," he explained. "This is sular stew. That's fried hoss, a vegetable dish." He offered her one of the flat bread disks. "I know it's very different than Az-kye cuisine. Just eat what you like, okay?"

She took a hesitant bite of the sular stew and found it bland, the meat tough.

Some of her reaction must have shown on her face because he gave an understanding smile.

"Ration packs are intended to last years without spoiling. Flavor is kind of an afterthought. But good Tellaran food is *really* good," he said, digging in. "Even Tir-Halea has a couple restaurants worth trying."

Her head came up. "Halea? It cannot be an Az-kye colony? I have never heard of it."

"They tried to establish a colony about forty years ago but it never came to much." The half-smile he gave was touched with bitterness. "There are some old-timers crazy enough to hang on like Anzu but most of the Az-kye left when the Tellarans moved in. There's a Tellaran governor there now, appointed, not elected. Governor Chol hands out permits to, uh . . . *private* spacing companies"—Jehan took another swallow of wine—"in return for a fee—and a percentage of the cargo's sale."

"The Tellaran Fleet is a party to all this?" she asked sharply. "They sanction it?"

"I wouldn't say that. But as long as our good governor collects enough uh . . . *duties* the sector admiral keeps the Fleet out of our way. And to make sure those duties get met he provides special operating licenses."

"To men like you?"

His smile stayed in place but his eyes tightened at the corners. "Yeah, men like me."

"You have chosen a dangerous life, Jehan Dekra. To make such a place your home."

"Tir-Halea's just a base of operations. And 'home' is something for people who don't have to sleep with a blaster under their pillow."

"You do that?"

"Always."

"You do not fear you will accidently shoot yourself?"

Jehan gave a surprised laugh. "I keep the safety on." He refilled her glass. "You're easy to talk to. Has anyone ever told you that?"

"I am surprised that you wish to talk to me at all." She took a sip. "You may recall you ordered my silence."

"Sorry about that." He put the bottle down. "But your value at the brothels goes way up if you already speak Tellaran. You're too tempting to the Brethren already."

"That woman—Mig—knows I speak your language."

"Mig's the last person who'd sell me out to them. They'd like nothing better than to help themselves to my ship and, believe me, she's not eager to be under the Brethren's 'protection.'"

"Why tolerate their presence on your ship at all? There are but three of them," Saria pointed out. "Kill them and be done with it."

"Spoken like a true Az-kye." He took a swallow of wine. "You think if it were as simple as throwing them out an airlock I wouldn't have done it already? If his men don't come back alive I'll have to answer to Helock. He—the Brethren—have a good chunk of this sector under their control and they take offense very easily."

"That is what Mig meant when she said you were lucky? That for defying them, for refusing to hand me over when they demanded it, they might have killed you?"

Jehan shrugged. "I was pretty sure they weren't going to."

"But if they want your ship why would they not—" His glance gave her the answer. "They want you. But . . . if they are so powerful, why not join them then?"

"Me? Not one to take orders, remember? Besides, that kind of power demands a steep price. Your soul, really."

Saria's hand clenched in her lap. "I suppose, to some, great power is worth the cost."

"To some," he agreed. "But not me."

"Many would consider the wielding of such power a matter of honor."

His lip curled. "Honor's never been much use to me either."

"What of the rest of your crew? Have they any sense of honor?" She tilted her head. "I think you do not trust them not to turn against you."

"I hope I can trust them enough to protect their own skins."

"What do you mean?"

His expression hardened. "Back when he was starting out, Helock made a run from the Badlands to Sertar with two ships—a larger freighter, the *Jandar's Fire,* and a smaller vessel, the *Shade*. Just on the other side of the Badlands, they ran into a Fleet ship on patrol. The larger ship, the *Jandar's Fire*, took a wicked beating but Helock had two ships to the Fleet's one. He blew the Fleet ship to bits." Jehan held up his glass to the light, studying the red wine within it for a moment. "He transferred his most loyal crewmembers to the *Shade*—along with the cargo, of course—then sent the rest onto the *Jandar's Fire*. She was badly damaged, adrift really, but Helock stood before them all, put his hand over his heart, and swore before the gods as their captain he would come back for them."

Saria's stomach tightened. "But he did not."

"Oh fuck no," Jehan said easily. "A smaller crew means a bigger share for each. And that smaller crew—the men and women who left their shipmates adrift to die of cold and suffocation on the *Jandar's Fire*—became the first of the Brethren."

"Why are they . . . marked so?"

"Well, it's a great uniform, don't you think? If you want your employees looking scarier than all hells, anyway. But the main thing is, looking like that, none of them can leave. There's nowhere to go, no way to hide. All they've got is their brotherhood—and Helock. No one leaves the Brethren, ever."

"So, like the clanless, they are slaves."

"But these are slaves who don't even realize what they are. Even the smart ones don't figure it out until it's too late."

"Faced with such fanaticism the Tellaran governor must fear the Brethren will take over the sector and deprive him his profits." Saria took a sip of her wine. "That can only mean he is powerful enough to hold the Brethren at bay but too weak to risk open confrontation."

Jehan's gaze warmed. "You are quick, aren't you? Yes, the governor and the Brethren dance around one another like two xekodiles with their barbs out."

"And you dance between them."

His teeth flashed in a grin. "I learned young."

"You took a great risk today, to hide the *Ty'har*'s crystals from the Brethren. To come aboard and swear to them you left with empty hands."

"I didn't leave empty-handed. I brought you back, remember?"

"I was a distraction, then, so the Brethren would not suspect you had anything else of value." Why should that hurt? Did she not have proof enough of his character? "That is why you rescued me."

"Yeah." Jehan drained his glass. "Why else?"

"I suppose your ruse was my good fortune." Saria folded her hands in her lap. "Although to conceal the crystals from them was a very dangerous game to play."

"It's not as if they were going to search me. Not even Helock has balls enough to try that."

"I could have told them."

He shrugged "Consider it a test."

"To see if you could trust me?"

"Something like that."

"What if I were simply a fool?" she wondered. "A dullard who blurted your secret to them?"

"You seemed pretty sharp back on the warship. You must have a good sense of self-preservation to survive as a slave. Oh," he said snapping his fingers as if the idea had just occurred to him, "and *now* you know I have something that I'm hiding from my crew." He raised his eyebrows in mock realization. "Maybe it's even secret you could use later—if you needed some leverage against me."

A lifetime at the Imperial court allowed Saria to keep her expression unchanged but her cheeks heated at his laugh.

"Don't worry. You're pretty good at hiding what you're thinking, Liri; at least"—that grin flashed again—"from most people." Jehan leaned back in the chair. "And now I know I can trust you to think on your feet, to protect me if it's in your best interest. Don't be offended. It's more than I trust most people."

"I trust only myself." She had not meant to speak so plainly and she shifted under his searching intensity. "Why do you stare so?"

"You meet my eye, you argue." His glance took in the plate before her, the carefully laid utensils. "You dine like the daughter of a clan leader."

"How do you know how the daughter of a clan leader dines? Did you spend much time in a clanhouse?"

Jehan's mouth curved into a faint smile. "I know you can't have been a slave for long."

She still had not concocted a full history for the woman she pretended to be and he was unnervingly good at reading her.

"I was not. My family was *gisel* to—" She glanced up. "That is a—"

"I remember what a vassal clan is," he said a little sharply. "So what happened? Was it a clan war?"

Saria busied herself with her napkin. "Our lands are on Az-kanzar, near the river Ut. There was a dispute about territory. I am not even sure what was involved. I was on Az-kye when—"

"What were you doing on the homeworld?"

"I was—" Sent to the Imperial City to finish her education? Visiting a friend? "Our clan leader arranged a post for me at the palace and I—"

"At the *palace*?"

"It was nothing," she demurred quickly. "I was second assistant to the mistress of the wardrobe."

His focus was so intent she shifted uneasily, wondering if he had already sensed the lie.

But when he spoke his tone was gentle. "Doesn't sound like nothing to me."

"It was an honor to serve in the empress's household," she murmured. "I would I were there now."

"Why aren't you?"

"I do not know," she admitted thickly. "Everything happened so quickly. One moment I was safe, assured of a bright future. The next—it was all torn away. I cannot understand what I have done that the gods would visit such a fate upon me." She blinked away her tears. "Forgive me. Self-pity is unseemly."

"From Imperial City to slave," he said quietly. "That would be devastating to anyone."

She had loved Alari, had always believed her sister loved her equally. Now all those precious moments of closeness, those whispered girlhood secrets, were tainted beyond repair.

"I have lost . . . very much." Saria looked down at her clasped hands. "I fear I will never feel whole—or safe—again."

"I wasn't trying to shame you," he said hoarsely. "I just wanted . . ." His fingers went under her chin, gently tilting her face up. "But that whole clanless thing—it doesn't matter, okay? Not here, not anymore. What happened to you was terrible, it was *wrong*." His fingers light, gentle on her cheek, his eyes stripped of mockery and humor, their dark depths filled with remembered pain. "Someday, you'll feel safe again. . ."

Then his expression was wiped clean, as if a wall slammed down between them.

Jehan dropped his hand. "At least you're out of the empire. That's a start." He stood. "And I don't know about you but I could use some sleep."

9

Negotiation

"You do not mean—" Saria quickly pushed herself to standing. "Together?"

"I meant what I said earlier, Liri. I won't take a woman who doesn't want to join with me." At her silence he waved at the couch. "You're welcome to the sofa," he offered, heading toward the bed, "if you don't trust me."

"Trust you? You are a pirate, a smuggler—"

"And a thief," he reminded, sitting on the edge of the bed, already tugging his boots off. "Don't forget about 'thief.'"

He stood to pull off his shirt and tossed it on the back of a nearby chair. Saria shifted her weight as his trousers followed, leaving him bare but for undershorts.

He might not be a warrior but he was as beautifully muscled as any she had ever seen.

"Do you want me to hold up my blade and pledge like an Az-kye warrior? Oh, right." His brow puckered. "It's my raised sword you're worried about. . ."

She caught herself glancing downward. Her face flushed at his grin.

Saria clasped her hands in front of her primly. "You are incorrigible."

Jehan burst out laughing. Her face grew hotter, wondering if she had mispronounced the Tellaran word and made herself look even more the fool.

"You know," he managed, chuckling as he climbed into bed, "of all the things I've been called over the years, Liri, that's going to be the most memorable."

"It was not a compliment!"

"No." He held up his hand. "It was an absolutely stinging insult. See?" he asked, stretching out. "You've felled me with it."

Her eyes narrowed. "You have a Tellaran's sense of humor."

"By that you mean I *have* a sense of humor."

She lifted her chin. "I am not sharing a bed with you."

"Suit yourself," he said, reaching out to dim the room's illumination.

He shifted a bit, adjusting the pillows. Then the tension seemed to run right out of him. Saria pursed her mouth to form a retort when she heard a soft snore.

She stared in disbelief. He had fallen asleep almost instantly.

Saria looked at the couch in dismay. She had never spent the night on anything but a wide bed stacked high with jaha down pillows. Her insistence they not share was only made with the expectation he would gallantly offer the bed to her comfort and choose either the sofa or floor for himself.

For a princess, perhaps. But who would give their bed to a slave?

The sofa was short, too short for her to stretch out comfortably, but, unlike the carpeted floor, at least it was padded. The blanket he'd wrapped her in earlier draped across the back.

Throwing a narrow look at the sleeping Jehan, Saria sat down on the couch.

Before tonight Saria had scarcely done more than kick off her jeweled slippers. Getting her boots off unassisted soon proved far harder than getting them on had. She was forced to tug with both her hands and wiggle her foot to work herself free but in the end she got them off.

Not quite threadbare, the couch's fabric had a disconcerting smoothness to it that made Saria wonder when last it had been cleaned. She pulled the quilt around her and turned, seeking a comfortable position on the sofa. The seat's supports, while tolerable for sitting, sent a sharp pain through her hip as she tried to settle herself. Tucking her arm under her head in place of a pillow, Saria was forced to lie on her side with her knees drawn up to fit on the couch at all.

She tried switching her direction, putting her head on the other end to see if lying that way were any more comfortable, only to find it even worse.

No one could find rest here!

He had not even offered her a pillow for her own and he had four, two he was not using at all. Saria threw off the blanket and stood; surely even he should have the courtesy to spare *one*—

His hand shot out just as she leaned over, seizing her wrist before her hand could reach the pillow, his eyes focused on her with lethal intensity.

Shaken, she pulled against his hold. "Release me!"

"Liri?" The deadly cold look was replaced with a puzzled frown. He let her go and sat up. "What the hells are you doing?"

"I have done nothing!" She held her wrist protectively. "I sought only a pillow for my comfort!"

"You should have told me you were taking one."

"I thought you asleep!"

"I'm a light sleeper. It's a gift. Or a curse," he muttered, freeing himself of the quilts to stand. "Did I hurt you?"

He took her hand in his, his thumbs lightly tracing her skin, probing the bones of her wrist.

"You startled me."

"Sorry. Next time just wake me up. It's not like I won't be able to fall right back to sleep."

He still held her wrist and, awkward now, she pulled her hand away. "I imagine that must be useful for a pirate."

"If you enjoy being a not-*dead* pirate, yeah." He glanced to the other side of the room. "Regretting that you picked the sofa instead of my bed?"

"I require only a pillow of you. Something soft." She was acutely aware of him, of his bare skin over taut muscles. "I will not disturb you further."

"Enough. You aren't going to get any sleep on that thing and we both know it. Get in bed, Liri."

"I am perfectly fine on the—"

"That's an order."

Her gaze narrowed. "As commander of this vessel or as my owner?"

"As whatever will let me get some damn sleep," he grumbled, already getting under the covers. "I've got to be on duty in a few hours."

When she made no move toward the bed, Jehan sighed and sat up, placing his hand over his heart.

"I vow by Lashima you will be absolutely safe from my odious and unwelcome sexual advances."

Saria shifted her weight. "Strange that you make your vow by an Az-kye goddess."

"Fine." Jehan passed his hand over his face. "Certainly wouldn't want to forget my lowly place and offend

Ren'thar's mate by calling on Her. I vow by Arrena then. The Tellaran goddess of love is a lot more egalitarian. Now get in bed."

In truth the bed looked a great deal more comfortable and warmer than that miserable sofa, and sleeping on the floor did not bear thinking about. She lifted the covers on her side, already climbing in, when his exasperated look stopped her.

"Lose the coveralls, Liri."

"But—"

"You'll have underwear and the halter on," he pointed out. "Light sleeper, remember? I sure don't need you tossing and turning because your coveralls are all twisted up around you."

He was right and doubtless it would be more comfortable than sleeping in baggy Tellaran clothing. Her lids were heavy with weariness, her movement slowed by exhaustion as she turned her back to undo the fastenings.

"Everything okay?" he asked.

She wiped at her wet face with the back of her hand. "Yes."

The bedclothes rustled and she turned to find Jehan standing behind her.

"I simply—" She gestured helplessly at the coverall's front. "I cannot seem to—"

"It's okay," he said quietly. "Come here."

With quick nimble fingers he undid the fastenings she could not manage. Accustomed to her maids' assistance, she stood unmoving while he pushed the coveralls off her shoulders and took the hand he offered to help her step out of them.

"Thank you," she murmured, finally remembering the courtesy.

"Come on," he said simply, pulling her into bed. He settled the quilt over her, offering a faint smile as he made a show of tucking the blankets around her. "Everything looks worse to tired eyes."

"I had a governess once who said such," she said with a quick surprised smile.

His grin flashed in the darkness. "I did too. And she was always right." He settled next to her, not touching, but near enough that she could feel the warmth radiating of his body. "Good night, Liri."

"Good night, Jehan."

"You know," he said sleepily. "I like how that sounds."

His breathing grew deep and even, and with a rush of longing she wished he had drawn her into his arms, held her close as he had earlier, murmuring again how everything would be all right . . .

Quietly as she could, Saria shifted closer.

10

ᑫᐧ᠀ᒐᐧᐳᕵᑕᐁᐧ

Entangled

Jehan's eyes snapped open. Already fully awake and alert, he shot his hand out to deactivate the alarm before it sounded.

Waking like that was a skill he'd never lost, not in all these years.

At least some *of Father's training wasn't a waste.*

There was an unfamiliar softness, a gentle warmth curled beside him. Silken hair spilled over his shoulder, her head resting on his chest. His arm was around her, his palm resting on the curve of her back. At some point during the night he'd drawn her close to him.

Liri.

He activated the bedside table, keeping the illumination at quarter power, not bright enough to wake her, and tried to disentangle himself without disturbing her. The shift of his body allowed the lamp's glow to light her face and Jehan's mouth went dry.

Sweet Arrena . . .

A field medscanner had limited power; it sped healing but its full effects took time. Even the ordeal she'd been through yesterday hadn't been enough to hide the lush curves of her body, but with the dirt and bruises and abrasions gone now, her full beauty shone.

Her skin was as smooth as cream, her cheeks softly rounded, her full mouth pink and parted in sleep, her long dark hair glossy like shimmersilk around her oval face. An exquisite creature, curled against him in complete trust.

Trust I'm hardly worthy of.

The temptation to wake her, to explore that softness and feel her arch beneath him in pleasure, was making his cock throb.

But from her reluctance to share the bed with him last night he knew it might not be a joining completely of her own choosing. She might submit simply in fear that he would hand her over to the Brethren if she refused.

Not good enough by half.

The shadows beneath her eyes stood mute testament her exhaustion. Gods only knew how long she'd endured the Az-kye excuse for "justice."

Anybody could see she's walked through the nine hells already.

Jehan carefully eased himself away from her tempting warmth.

What had he been thinking yesterday? Endangering himself, his crew, challenging Kel when he should have been handing her over, vowing to safeguard her like a godsdamn Az-kye pledging his sword to his Lady's protection.

He was no warrior, no matter what his bloodline.

He paused at the bathroom door. She slept bonelessly in his bed, like it was exactly where she belonged.

The empire built no prisons—their whole society was prison enough. With every action judged against the weight of ten thousand years of caste and tradition there was little tolerance for even simple human error. Commit the most minor of infractions, be on the losing side of a clan war, defy the clan leader by choosing the "wrong" mate, and they would tear everything away, even your name.

There was no appeal, no hope, even for the innocent. And it was once you donned the white of the clanless that the real suffering began.

It wasn't hard to guess that Liri's young owner probably made very intimate use of his lovely slave and the idea of it had Jehan rubbing at his face so roughly as he washed, he left the skin reddened.

She wouldn't have had any choice in *that* either.

He dressed quickly, intending to walk right past her, but something about the sight of her there, in his bed, drew him back. He adjusted the quilt over her shoulder and brushed a silky strand away from her face, her skin petal-soft under his fingers. She didn't even stir, looking so fragile in sleep that it wrung his heart. . .

Jehan set his jaw and in the next moment he was in the corridor, the door to his quarters locked behind him.

It's lust. It'll pass.

He'd shared enough women's beds that he knew no matter how much heat one held, another would hold just as much or more. Liri was smart, a quick-witted survivor. Beautiful, no doubt about it, but in her gaze he saw the same stupid insufferable Az-kye pride that set his teeth on edge.

The hallway outside his quarters was brightly lit, indicating the day shift, but thankfully deserted. He was sure as hells in no mood to talk to anyone.

Jehan entered the empty lift and keyed in the code to take him to the bridge.

The Badlands taught him young what it cost to care about someone other than yourself. As soon as they made planetfall he'd wish Liri "clear skies," put some money in her pocket, and send her on her way.

Just as he settled on that sensible plan, a chill, otherworldly whisper raised the hairs on the back of his neck.

Jehan tensed but didn't glance back. Even at fourteen, orphaned, and forced into the back alleys of Tir-Halea, scraping to survive, he knew there'd be nothing to see.

Just as he knew exactly who was there.

Leave it to me to jettison everything Az-kye but a godsdamn shade.

It wasn't often these days, thank the gods, that Jehan felt his father's presence, standing straight and proud at his shoulder. In his mind's eye he could see his sire's stoic expression, his sharp, intelligent dark gaze, the ever-present sword strapped to his back that could be in his hand in an instant. A true son of the empire, a warrior whose honor shone as brightly as the blade of the god of war himself—

Jehan shut his eyes in annoyance.

Shouldn't you be off getting drunk in Ren'thar's Hall or something?

The atmosphere in the lift grew heavy with his father's scowl, offended by his son's disrespect for the gods, the honor of his family, the sanctity of his own spoken vow . . .

For fuck's sake, just go away!

Jehan tapped his fingers on the lift wall, willing the lift to move faster, determined to ignore that prodding at long buried—and laughably useless—instincts.

Even if the Brethren let her be, she'd be an Az-kye woman alone on a world where there was no protection a blaster didn't buy you, no law or justice you didn't grease palms to get. Unfamiliar with even the most basic of Tellaran technology. With nothing to trade on but her beauty, she didn't have a chance of finding work except the kind offered by The Open Flower . . .

Jehan squared his shoulders, fixing his attention on the lift readout.

Not my problem.

She was stunning but clever too; if she was lucky she'd quickly find a protector who'd buy her way out of the pleasure house, maybe even marry her. And if she *weren't*—

He shifted his weight.

She'd wind up like Tesi, dead at the hands of some unknown brute. Or worse, like Onara.

I don't care what I said!

The very air he breathed grew dark with disapproval.

If so worthless is your word, my son, you would have served her better had you left her to die among her own people . . .

"Stupid," Jehan muttered, scrubbing his face with his hands. "Godsdamned, *stupid* Az-kye—"

"Sir?"

Mig frowned at him through the open lift doors. The rest of the bridge crew too sent curious looks his way.

"Morning." His face was hot as he stepped onto the bridge. "You're relieved, Mig. Go grab yourself some bunk time."

"Aye, sir." Her brow knitted. "You okay?"

"Never better," Jehan growled, settling into the command chair.

11

Hole-and-Corner

Klaxons jolted Saria from sleep.

She scrambled back against the bed's headboard, her hands flying to her ears to block the blare of the alarms, her terrified glance darting about the strange room.

Where—?

Light flooded in as the door opened and a bright-haired woman rushed in to babble at her; unfamiliar people hurried by in the corridor beyond.

The woman's nonsensical jumble suddenly crystalized into the Tellaran language and the events of the past day— Uthar's betrayal, Naret's sacrifice, Jehan—came rushing back.

"Cap wants you on the bridge right now!" Mig yanked the quilts off her. "Come on, godsdamn it!"

"What is happening?" Saria grabbed her coveralls from the back of a nearby chair, shakily pulling them on, closing the unfamiliar fastenings with trembling fingers.

"Let's *go!*"

Mig tossed the boots at her but Saria, unaccustomed to catching anything, missed both. The heel of one hit her forearm, the other boot bounced under the bed and she fell to her knees to reach for it.

"What has happened?" Pulling the boots on, Saria raised her voice to a shout to be heard over the alarms. "Where is Jehan?"

Mig grabbed her by the back of her coveralls, hauling her upright. "Move it!"

The redhead pushed her into the chaos of the corridor. A rumpled-haired man fastening his own coveralls shoved past, banging his elbow painfully into her arm as he went.

"No, *this* way!"

Mig pulled her into a waiting lift, hitting the controls as soon as they were inside.

"Come on," the Tellaran muttered as the doors slid closed with agonizing slowness. "Come on already!"

The closed lift doors shut out the blare of alarms, leaving Saria's ears ringing from it.

"What is happening?" Saria pushed her hair out of her face, tucking the strands behind her ears with shaking fingers. "Are we under attack?"

"Oh, believe me, if they open fire," Mig muttered, "we'll know right away."

"If *who* opens fire? Have they identified themselves?"

"We don't need a formal introduction. It's the *Nightfall.*" Mig glared at the readout as if she could speed the lift's progress by will alone. "Come on, damn it."

"A Tellaran ship then."

"Not just any ship," Mig said shortly. "A Fleet ship, battlecruiser class."

"But will they—"

The doors opened and Mig grabbed her upper arm to yank her onto the bridge. Emergency power was engaged but here the alarms had been silenced. On the viewscreen, partly obscured by the scarlet energy clouds, lurked a shadowy image so immense it could only be a Tellaran battle cruiser.

"Jul, just keep backing us up," Jehan ordered, his fingers flying over the readouts beside the command chair.

The bridge crew hunched over their controls, their faces tense with concentration. Kel, forbidding in his black, hooded coat, stood at the bridge's outer curve. His thin lips were tight and the other Brethren, Van, looked equally pale.

"Here she is—as ordered, *sir*!" Mig pushed her toward Jehan. "Can I get you two a cocktail? Maybe light some candles while I'm at it?"

Jehan threw a cursory glance over Saria then turned his attention back to his readouts. "Mig, get your ass down to engineering!"

"Have the engineer *in* engineering during a crisis?" she mocked as she headed for the lift. "What a great idea! Next time send someone else to fetch your bunkmate."

Jehan threw her a black glare. "Now!"

"Aye, Captain!" Mig snapped just before the doors shut.

Just as Saria came to Jehan's side the readouts he was so intent upon flashed red.

He addressed the woman at the helm. "Slow down, Jul."

Jul shook her head, her spiky, short hair a startling platinum. "Any slower and we won't make it to cover before the next scan, Cap."

"We'll make it," Jehan assured. "That last plasma surge is playing havoc with their sensors."

Suddenly the *Nightfall* came about, her nose pointed directly at the *Selini's Song*

"Have they detected us?" Kel demanded, a sheen of perspiration visible on his upper lip, his fellow Brethren looking no less pale.

"No or they'd already have blown us to hells." Jehan eyed the Tellaran ship. "Unless they're operating on 'search and capture' protocols."

"If you're thinking of trading *us* to save your own skin—"

"Now there's a thought," Jehan muttered.

Kel bared his sharpened teeth. "If you do, you—and your crew—will wind up lifers on the Pansh penal colony."

"You don't give yourself enough credit. We're blips on TelSec's screen compared to you three Brethren." Jehan smirked. "You're personally marked for termination on capture, aren't you, Kel? Turning just you in might buy me a pardon *and* a reward."

Despite their dire situation, Saria could not help but smile inwardly at the look of panic on Kel's face.

Then the Brethren drew himself up. "Betray me and you will answer to Helock for it."

"Helock won't give a fuck as long as he gets his cargo," Jehan said coldly. "And it's *you* that's going to answer to him. You're the one who disobeyed my orders and broke comm silence. You're the reason the Fleet sniffed us out in the first place."

"Your orders!" Kel spat, his dark coat billowing as his arms spread. "You don't give orders to the Brethren!"

A blaster bolt slammed into Kel's chest. He swayed for a moment, surprise in his blue eyes, then fell face forward, dead.

The bridge crew turned astonished looks his way but Jehan's focus—and blaster—was now fixed on the other Brethren.

"*My* ship," he said, his voice low and dangerous. "*My* orders."

Etaran nodded quickly. "Yes, Captain."

"Hold position here, Jul." Jehan holstered his blaster. "Any further and we'll get pulled into one of the eddies."

"Are we deep enough in?" Jul asked, her voice tight.

Jehan glanced at the Fleet ship. "We'll find out pretty fucking soon."

Long moments ticked by. Only the instruments' hum and the sound of breathing filled the air.

Abruptly the Fleet ship turned, gone in a flash of engine power.

"It worked," Jul breathed.

"Damn good piloting," Jehan said approvingly.

His First Officer looked back at him. "That was damn good *luck*."

"Well, in that case—" Jehan flashed a quick grin. "I won't give you an extra share of this run after all."

Jul shook her head, half-amused, half-exasperated.

The bridge crew was smiling, offering him words of congratulations, and Jehan waved it away.

"We'll celebrate when we make planetfall." He stood. "That might not be the last patrol we have to slip past."

"We'll make it." Jul came to his side, her amber eyes narrowing at the remaining Brethren. "Long as no one *else* does anything stupid."

"Oh, Etaran isn't stupid," Jehan put in. "He wants this mission to succeed as much as we do."

"I have no argument with you, Captain, or your crew," Etaran said evenly.

"Especially since, with Kel dead, Van moves up and so do you. In fact, once we reach Halea you should be getting a new mark to show it." Jehan gave the man's bald head a meaningful look. "Won't you?"

"I expect so," the young man said guardedly. "As long as we *do* finish the run on time."

"My crew is the best, we want to protect our reputation." Jehan folded his arms. "But more importantly, we want our payment."

"You have no worries on that score—you do your job and I'll see to it you get paid."

"Hey, careful there, Etaran." Jehan raised his eyebrows. "Don't want to start being too decent for the company you keep."

The young man winced and glanced down at the fallen Brethren. "What about Kel?"

"Your problem," Jehan said. "Not mine."

The Brethren sighed. "I'll get Van up here to help me." Etaran raised his eyebrows. "If you'll allow us the use of a sealing storage container to transport the body?"

"Of course." Jehan inclined his head. "I'll add it to your bill."

"Thanks," Etaran grumbled.

"More than he would have done for me," Jehan said shortly, urging Saria along with him. "Jul, you have the bridge—" He indicated Kel's lifeless form. "Such as it is."

"Oh, no danger." The First Officer fixed Van with a glare as Jehan and Saria entered the lift. "It'll be cleared up in five, Cap."

As soon as the lift doors shut and they were alone, Jehan passed his hand over his face.

Saria wet her lips. "You killed him."

"Yeah." Jehan raised his eyebrows. "Oh, sorry. Did you like him?"

She shuddered. "No."

"Good. Neither did I." He sighed, all humor gone now. "I didn't have a choice, Liri. He had a snub blaster already in his hand."

The way Kel's coat billowed out, the odd sharp movement of his arm, the way his hand clenched—

"So you killed him before he could kill you."

"He'd have had to take Jul out next, of course. She's First Officer; the crew respects her. They just might've rallied around her so Kel wouldn't risk leaving her alive. If I hadn't killed him, he'd be in command now."

"Surely your crew would not have followed *him*!"

"Oh, I don't think they'd prefer Kel over me but they'd do whatever it took to save their own skins—just like I would."

"So your life—your *skin*—means more to you than anything?"

"If you're gearing up for a lecture on honor, Liri," he began roughly, striding out as soon as the lift doors opened to the crew quarters level, "don't waste your time."

"So honor means nothing to you?" she demanded, following him into his quarters.

"The question is why it means anything to *you*," he snapped. "You have no claim to honor anymore. You're clanless, without a family, without even a name. Cast out from the Children of Heaven for all time."

"Like you are, you mean? You are a slave too, are you not?"

His dark eyes flashed. "I was *never* a slave."

"Then why not return to the empire? Why not live among your own people?"

"I do live among my own people. I'm Tellaran now, like you are."

She pulled up short. "Tellaran?"

"Well, you're not Az-kye anymore. Tellaran's all that's left."

"I *am* Az-kye." Saria drew herself upright. "And no one will take my birthright from me!"

"I don't think you'd find a lot of agreement about that on the homeworld."

"I do not care what others think! I know what I am!"

"Strange attitude for a slave."

"I am—" She shook her head. "I mean it is for the gods to choose our fates."

He folded his arms. "You think the *gods* are responsible for your exile? So jealousy or pettiness or politics couldn't be the cause of your fall? That—maybe—other innocents have had their name torn away just like you did?"

Their mother decreed Alari, an Imperial Daughter, be cast out for disobedience. If Kyndan Maere had not come to claim her that day, Alari—princess though she was—would have been stripped of title, of clan and name, dressed in a slave's smock and thrown barefoot into the streets of the Imperial City.

Would the gods inflict such cruelty upon a young woman for longing to be free of a loveless match? Or was it merely another weapon the empress could wield, using it to sacrifice one daughter in favor of the younger, more obedient one?

What if it had been she, not Alari, who had refused her mother's choice of consort? If she had been cast from the clan and stripped of her name, would nothing of honor or decency exist in her heart because of the clothes she wore? Or would she know herself to be Saria—even if no other addressed her that way again her whole life long?

Where, then, does honor lie? By the esteem and approval of others?

Or in the heart and mind?

"Is that what happened to you, Jehan?" she asked quietly. "Were you an innocent, punished for another's guilt?"

"You'll find the Badlands burn away a lot of the past, Liri." His jaw was taut, his eyes black ice. "And I'm no innocent. Just ask Kel."

"You acted for the good of your ship, in defense of your crew—"

"Don't try to make it sound so lofty. I did it to save my own ass, to protect—" He glanced away. "I'm not sorry, anyway. And don't put garlands on the crew's heads either, they'd eat a weak captain alive."

"But—are they not sworn to follow your commands? I thought even Tellarans took such vows."

"This isn't a Fleet ship, Liri, it's my personal property. The crew is paid a share according to their rank and I need to be damn sure there *is* a take. The greatest danger to any captain on a ship like this is an unhappy crew."

"You mean a mutiny?"

"Happened on your ship, didn't it?"

"Yes," she said faintly. "Yes, it did."

"And those were Az-kye warriors. Don't worry. My charm buys me cooperation most of the time."

"And when it does not," she pointed, "there is the blaster at your side."

"Always," he agreed.

"What you said to Kel—were you truly thinking to trade him to the Tellarans?"

"Now there I was bluffing. Either Helock is already lining that particular commander's pocket to let the Brethren go—while the rest of us were held on charges—or he was a blaster-bolt straight Fleet man and would have arrested the lot of us."

"Me as well?"

He shrugged but there was an uneasiness to it. "You're onboard a ship known for smuggling but you aren't part of the crew roster. TelSec *might* have believed we rescued you, but you would have been held for questioning at the very least."

"Jehan, why send for me?" she asked. "Why send your engineer to bring me to you?"

"We were on battle alert. I wasn't sure you'd make it safely to the bridge on your own if I called you and I trust Mig—well, as much as I trust anybody. If things had gone badly . . ." Something flashed in his gaze, then he shrugged. "But they didn't."

"Except for Kel."

"Would you have done it?" His dark eyes—Az-kye eyes like her own—focused on her. "Would you kill someone if it meant your life? Or to protect . . . others?"

She was First Daughter, Heiress of the Empire, usurped by her own sister for the throne. Honor demanded vengeance, demanded blood.

Alari's blood.

"Yes."

"You looked away," he observed.

Her face heated, railing at her own weakness. "I will do what hon—*whatever* I am called upon to do."

"Good," he said unexpectedly and indicated the window, where a planet was just coming into sight. "Make sure you hold onto that determination, Liri. You'll need it on Halea."

12

Planetfall

"Well?" Jehan asked, indicating the city of Tir-Halea around them. "What do you think?"

Apparently whoever administered this bustling spaceport favored Jehan—or perhaps Helock. The *Selini's Song* was swiftly routed through to a landing bay and the security officers simply verified the vessel's call numbers and took Jehan's retinal scan, waiving all inspection of the ship or its cargo.

Van delivered the message that Helock had requested a meeting with him and Jehan greeted the news with a careless shrug.

"The run's done on time and the creds are in my accounts." he said. "There's nothing to talk about."

Once the cargo was unloaded, the Brethren departed with it. Jehan excused his crew; he was last off the ship, remaining after the others left to secure the freighter, then threw Saria a smile and urged her toward the landing bay's exit. The spaceport was a curious mix—shiny and new cobbled together with technology of questionable age. The buildings themselves were pre-fab; the newer ones were pristinely white in the late afternoon sun, the older ones cracked and dulled to beige and light gray by Halea's suns. And all lacked the bright colors and intricate carvings that beautified even the humblest structure on Az-kye.

But what the city lacked in beauty and grace it more than made up for in decadence. Every third or fourth structure was a tavern or brothel with names like Golden Tankard and The Petals holo-projected in garish colors over the streets. Laughter, shouts, and music filled the air and a number of the pedestrians—the worse for drink and chemicals—weaved through the streets with unsteady revelry.

On their rare trips beyond the palace walls, she and Alari would peek between the curtains of their litter, occasionally spying one of the splendidly dressed courtesans of the Imperial City. Called "Companions," they were men and women whose accomplishments included engaging conversation and often musical talent in addition to their sexual skills. They were refined creatures, traveling in litters as ornate as any clan leader's daughter and within Az-kye society held a measure of respectability.

It seemed the majority of the men and women who populated the brothels in Tir-Halea could only be called whores.

"It is . . ." Saria spread her hands, "lively."

"Well *that* was diplomatic," he said with a laugh.

"Jehan, isn't that—?"

He followed her glance across the street, to the door of the brothel there and the scantily clad blonde chatting up a young man. "Jul. Yeah, she's very industrious."

"It is fortunate this planet is so temperate." Gone were his First Officer's coveralls and bare face. Her cosmetics sparkled in the afternoon sun and her clothing—what there was of it—showed small sculpted muscles and a lot of smooth tanned skin.

He threw her an amused look. "Do I hear disapproval?"

"She is your First Officer. She should not also be—be—"

"An Ornament? Actually she was an Ornament first, long before she signed on with me. And Jul's got her mind set on buying her own ship. She's smart as hells too. Saves most of her take from her runs with me and works as an Ornament between. She's probably nearly got it all together by now so she'll be quitting soon. It's too bad. She's damn good at her work."

"You mean as a First Officer?"

Jehan raised an eyebrow. "That actually sounded a little jealous."

"Do not be absurd," she said, scowling.

He shrugged. "Just as well, anyhow."

She glanced at Jehan sidelong, his strong profile, how his big body moved with a careless, comfortable gait. Even as he looked perfectly at ease in this unruly crowd, she was certain the blaster at his hip could be in his hand in an instant.

"Why is that?" she asked after a moment.

"Just that Jul and I have kept things strictly business. I guess I should say strictly *ship's* business. Feeling jealous of her would just be a waste of time." His mouth twitched. "So it's a good thing you aren't."

Saria wrinkled her nose a bit at the pungent smell of intoxicant smoke drifting from one of the taverns. "Why do you allow such? Should she purchase a ship, she will be your competitor."

"Jul's going to be my competitor someday anyway, she might as well be a friendly one. In fact she—"

Jehan's words faded away as the late afternoon crowd parted a bit, Saria's attention riveted on three men now visible at the end of the street. Her heart hammering, she slowed her steps, poised between running toward them and running away.

"Liri?"

Jehan's light touch on her arm startled her.

"You okay?" He frowned. "I said your name a couple times. It was like you couldn't hear me at all."

"I—I have been become unused to hearing it." The men were nearly to the end of the street now. "Those are Az-kye warriors."

"Yeah."

"Walking here, openly?' she wondered. "On a Tellaran world?"

"You lived in the Imperial City. Who'd you think was bringing all those Apovian jewels and Niman spices and Sertarian shimmersilks into the empire? Tir-Halea is the nexus for smuggled goods between the Realm and Imperial space." He raised his eyebrows at her shocked look. "You didn't really think I was the only smuggler here, did you?"

"Of what house are they?" She craning her neck. "I cannot see their crest!"

"They don't wear their clan crest here. They're hardly going to advertise that they're breaking Imperial law, are they?"

The Tellarans gave the warriors a wide berth, intimidated by their size, their black warrior clothes, the swords strapped to their backs.

She did not know them.

But they would be returning to Imperial space.

If they are of a lesser clan, a family from one of the outlying colonies, one that has no connection to the Imperial City or the palace . . .

"What's the matter? Are you worried about them seeing you?" He intertwined his fingers with hers, his frown deepening. "Your hand's like ice."

"But—you have had no dealings with them? You do not know who they are?"

"Don't worry, the warriors never stay long. They usually head spaceside as soon as their cargo is loaded. Those three probably won't stay till morning." His hand cradled hers. "Liri, you're safe here. No one's going to take you back to the empire; there's nothing in it for them. You know that, right?"

"Yes," she murmured as the warriors were lost to the crowd. "I do."

Jehan knew he should get her indoors, and his house wasn't far from here. Her beauty was attracting too much attention. It was just inviting trouble to be walking around in this crowd.

But he just couldn't cut it short.

It was a pleasure to watch her take in everything with her wide, dark eyes. In Halea's late afternoon sunlight her hair shone like a dark ribbon down her back, her movements as graceful as the festival dancers of his boyhood.

And it was crazy, but being with her, even on this crowded tawdry street, made him feel somehow like he'd finally come home.

"Are the other Tellaran worlds like this?" she asked, her hand in his.

"I've never been to any of them," Jehan admitted. "I want to, though. I've learned about every world in the Realm's borders but I haven't visited any."

She looked his way, perplexed. "Why not?"

"Tellaran law allows for the free travel between worlds—provided you have an ID."

"But do you not? The men at the spaceport—"

"They're not TelSec: those were Governor Chol's men. The scan they ran on me isn't the same thing. Our good governor keeps track of who lands and departs so he knows how much his take on each run will be."

"Then . . . you cannot leave this sector?"

"All it takes is enough creds to buy a new ID. Luckily for me, some of the best forgers in the Realm happen to have set up shop here."

"I suppose that is no surprise," she said dryly. "So why have you not done so? Purchased this *ID* and left?"

"Well an ID perfect enough so I never need to worry about TelSec is pricy and if there's one thing you don't want to go cheap on . . ." He shrugged. "Besides, no good heading out with my shiny new identity without the means to travel in style—and set myself up well once I get there. I've starved for the last time, thank you very much."

"And now you have all you need."

The crystals from the Az-kye ship were safely tucked into the inside pocket of his jacket. A fortune in purified astuk crystals, enough to buy a whole new life . . .

He should probably get those safely back to the house too.

"Almost," he said, moving protectively between her and a couple of spacers that looked worse for intoxicants. "I have a few loose ends to tie up here first."

"And when everything is tied—" she began and Jehan was proud he managed to hide his smile at that. "Where will you go?"

"Don't know yet," he said honestly, still holding her hand. Her skin was petal soft, her fingers long and delicate. "I might just visit all of them before I pick a world."

Her dark eyes met his.

"I'll take you with me," he blurted, the words tumbling out before he could stop them. "I won't go without you."

She looked away but she didn't take her hand from his. "Why do you vow this?"

"Just makes sense to take you along." He forced a shrug. "Besides, you wouldn't survive long here without me."

Her shoulders tensed. "Think you I need a protector?"

"On Halea? Absolutely. On the other Tellaran worlds?" He ventured a smile. "I hope so."

"Will you not go to Tellar?" she asked after a moment. "And live at the Tellaran center of power and culture?"

"I'm surprised to hear *you* say that."

She sent him a quizzical look. "Why?"

"I thought you'd prefer something more rural. Didn't you grow up in the colony on **Az-kanzar**?"

"Yes, of course. But—once I saw the Imperial City—"

"I guess after the Imperial City anywhere would seem pretty dull in comparison."

Her quick smile fairly took his breath away.

"I am much spoilt in that way," she agreed.

"I lived there," he said quietly. "I was born on Az-kye. In the Imperial City."

"You were? Of what clanhouse were—"

"Never mind," he interrupted. "I don't even know why I brought it up." He urged her along. "This section of Tir-

Halea can get really rowdy at night. Come on. My house is just a few streets over."

They walked in silence for a bit, hand in hand, and he suddenly realized that for all the lovers he'd had he'd never done this before—taking the long way simply so he could go on holding someone's hand.

The neighborhood grew quieter—for Tir-Halea anyway—the farther they got from the spaceport, the brothels and eating establishments here being of the more respectable variety.

"This is your home?" she asked, when they arrived at one of the large prefab white structures.

The furniture and décor were whatever the last owner had left behind, pleasant but nothing he would have chosen and definitely more suited to the former resident's Niman tastes. The back garden hardly lived up to the name, bare of flowers and bereft of planning.

"I wouldn't call it that," he mumbled, reluctantly letting go of her. "It's just a house."

"If you do not like it, why live here?"

"Because it's a godsdamned fortress. Durracrete walls, tarasteel windows, you could open fire on it with a pulse cannon and it would stay standing."

"But it *is* yours?"

"Be hard for even me to steal a whole house," he said wryly. "And yeah, it's mine. I won it in a card game, actually. It belonged to a Niman smuggler who didn't know it was time to stop drinking—or playing tongo."

Jehan eased his blaster from its holster and thumbed off the safety, then keyed in the security code. A retinal scan released the locking mechanism.

He paused in the doorway, his glance darting about, taking stock of the interior.

She touched his arm lightly, her expression questioning, but she didn't speak.

Smart.

He spared her an approving glance then turned his attention to the interior again. Everything looked as he'd left it but—

"I don't think anyone's dropped by for a visit while I was gone," he murmured. "But I'm going to check all the same. Just wait here. I'll be back in a minute, all right?"

She didn't answer and he glanced her way again. Her lovely face was half in shadow.

"Just stay here, okay?"

She nodded and he stepped inside. It smelled stale and he took a spare moment to key in the code to up the air exchange. The living area with its windows looking over the sad excuse for a garden appeared the same as it had when he'd shut the house up to do Helock's run.

The kitchen and dining room, also on this floor, were untouched and he realized that he wouldn't have anything to offer her for dinner except vac rations again.

Guess I'll be taking her to one of those "good Tellaran food" restaurants after all.

He headed up to the second level, suddenly wondering if there were any Az-kye restaurants in Tir-Halea. He hadn't even thought of food from the homeworld in years.

But that's what she'll be used to. It's worth checking into anyway.

He did a quick inspection of the bedrooms and baths on the second level. The place was far too large for just one person and if it hadn't come free and clear—with the taxes kindly forgiven by Chol's office in consideration for his contributions to the governor's fortune—he would have sold it already.

Jehan paused at the bedroom window, looking down into the twilight of the walled yard.

Not exactly the gardens of an Az-kye clanhouse . . .

But the house was light-years better than that miserable shack he'd lived in when they'd first arrived on Halea.

He could still remember his mother's face when she first beheld the two-room shelter that was to be their new living quarters. She was round-bellied with child; none of them even yet spoke Tellaran. Paying the captain who smuggled them out of Imperial space had left them with little but the clothes on their backs.

Jehan had seen the fear on her face, how his father grew even grimmer, the flash of guilt in his sire's eyes that he had allowed them both to follow him into disgrace.

And things had only gotten worse; he swallowed, remembering how angry he had been with them. His mother's saddened eyes, her arms and legs growing thinner every day even as her belly grow, the sharp words he'd spoken to her filled with a venom borne of hunger and fear. Remembered going out into the night to escape the closeness of their miserable shelter.

When he'd returned the next morning he found his father, ashen-faced and shaken.

His mother had gone into labor early. Back on Az-kye skilled healers would have attended her and the babe but this was Tir-Halea. You got nothing you didn't pay for and they were destitute. Desperate, his father had offered his sword, a warrior's most precious possession, as payment. Even it hadn't been enough to entice a healer save mother or child and no warrior long outlived his mate—

Jehan pushed away from the window. It was getting dark. Maybe the place wasn't elegant, but it was safe at least.

"All clear, Liri," he called, heading back down the stairs. "Come on in."

From earliest childhood his father had trained him in a warrior's ways: to observe, to note tiny details, taught him to analyze an opponent's smallest muscle movement to determine the direction and style of attack.

He felt it—the *wrongness*—even before he even reached the bottom of the stairs.

"Liri!"

Jehan was at a run through the living area, past the front door and out into the gathering darkness of the road, his darting glance confirming what his gut already told him.

She had vanished.

13

ᴀ.ᴄᴄ✗ᴄ

Snare

Deftly, Saria avoided another drunken pawing as she made her way through the crowd near the spaceport. Night had fallen but there was more than enough light blazing from the taverns, chem shops, brothels, sweet shops and clothing sellers to illuminate the streets.

Dressed in traditional black, with the height and build of their caste, Az-kye warriors were hardly inconspicuous here. They should be easy to locate again—even in this throng.

Of course any warrior here was by rights a criminal, acting in defiance of Imperial decree against trade with the Realm. But to return the Heiress would win these men not only pardon for their wrongs, but rewards of a kind that only a grateful empress could bestow. Her safe return to Az-kye would raise those warriors—and their clan—to dizzying heights of power and prestige within the empire.

If she could but *find* them!

Saria paused for a moment, trying to get her bearings in the unfamiliar city. She had found her way back to the neighborhood near the spaceport where she had first seen them, gritting her teeth every time her bottom was pinched. The rough crowds, some eagerly heading for an evening's entertainment, others apparently having started their celebrating at daybreak, were now making progress more difficult.

In truth she was surprised by the interest she was getting. Certainly on the homeworld she would have garnered at best shocked stares and at worst ridicule; no Az-kye woman above the status of a slave would ever appear so unattractively attired. Her hair hung free and lacked even a single jewel to enliven it, her face was clean but unpainted, and her coveralls and black boots were more suited to a male Tellaran sewage worker than a woman.

But in Tir-Halea she might well be the most celebrated Companion in the Imperial City for the number of propositions she received. Annoyed by the graphic suggestions—and disgusted by the bizarre ones—Saria steadfastly ignored all offers, and the snickering that often followed her when she did. But despite the aggravation and the urgency of her mission, she could not help curious glances at the Tellarans. They were as wildly varied as the flowers of the Imperial garden, with an astonishing range of eye and hair colors. It was utterly distracting to meet eyes of blue, green, or hazel—each with varying shades within that color—instead of the usual onyx of the Az-kye. Within the empire, blond was a very rare hair color indeed. Here Tellarans sported all hair shades—red and gold, warm browns and black—along with their striking eyes.

Many of the able-bodied Tellarans were scrawny, with the glazed rheumy look of chem dosers. Some of those filling the streets were young, youths or women with children, bedraggled wretches huddled against the buildings, reaching their thin, dirty hands out to passersby to plea for food or money.

One such, a woman, scarcely older than Saria herself and cradling a thin, pale baby in her arms, caught her eye. Flushing, Saria gave a quick, shamed headshake as the woman reached her hand out. She ducked her head, wishing she had but one of the jeweled combs lost with the *Ty'har* to offer against the child's hunger.

Alongside those destitute and desperate were the dazzlingly wealthy of this world. Both women and men flaunted their riches with bright, daring clothes and garish jewels. But for all their lavish display none seemed at ease, as if they knew themselves but a card's turn from joining the beggars they pretended to ignore.

Heritage was all to the Az-kye and without the social cues she knew so well Saria had no benchmark to judge the status of those she encountered. The little experience she had with their people was limited to the few Tellaran Fleet officers that visited the palace for the ill-fated peace accords—her sister's mate among them—and the crew of the *Selini's Song*.

Saria hesitated, glancing back the way she had come.

He would have long since discovered her absence.

I have a duty to the Az-kye to return as swiftly as possible, to reclaim my place. To extract revenge for those dead by Alari's scheming, for the loyal men and women on the Ty'har. *For Naret.*

She wet her lips, fighting the strong pull to return to Jehan. She did not know all his history but one thing was plain: he could never return to the empire. Nor, with only a slave's smock awaiting him there, would he have any wish to. He would never understand "Liri" wishing to return to a life of endless servitude and degradation. He seemed to bear a brooding hatred for those of his kind, for all things Az-kye.

And he would not be well pleased to learn he had given shelter and protection to an Imperial Daughter. . .

Saria squared her shoulders and continued on. She did not know how often warriors visited Halea; she might not see another for weeks if she could not locate these. She craned her neck to see over the crowds, straining to see even a hint of—

"Liri?"

Startled by the feminine voice, Saria turned, instantly recognizing the *Selini's Song's* First Officer.

"I *thought* it was you." Jul's expression was friendly and she glanced behind Saria, puzzled. "Where's the Cap?"

"He is—" Saria offered vague wave behind her that encompassed any number of establishments in this busy section. "Back at the tavern."

"He let you come out here on your own?" Jul frowned. "This isn't a city you want to be wandering around alone in, Liri—especially at night. Jehan should know better."

"You are alone," Saria pointed out.

"I'm used to it. And I'm armed." Jul indicated the snub blaster she wore in a low-slung belt over her sparse clothing. "And a real bitch."

Saria was startled into a laugh. "You would do well at the pal—on Az-kye."

"Oh, yeah? I'll try to make it out that way sometime." Jul smiled. "Maybe after the peace accords are signed, I'll go see what demand is like for a Tellaran Ornament."

"Those of that profession are called 'Companions' in the empire. In fact—" Saria said quickly, "while we were in the tavern I saw three Az-kye warriors pass by. I believe them acquainted with a woman who was once a dear friend." Saria forced a smile. "Indeed, we were close as sisters. I would very much like news of her. Have you seen them?"

"Why would you want—I mean, wouldn't your uh, *status* make talking to another Az-kye a bit . . . awkward?"

Saria spread her hands. "Surely, if he is here in Tir-Halea, he is no traditionalist. And we are in Tellaran space, after all. He may see no impediment to speaking to me here. At worst he will ignore my presence when I address him. In any case I will have lost nothing in the attempt."

"Well . . ." Jul shrugged. "I don't know if they're the same ones you're looking for, but there were a couple warriors going into Vista as I was coming out. I only saw two, though, not three. They might not even be there now."

"Where is Vista?"

Jul pointed. "It's a two-story tavern, the last building other side of the street, green sign. If you see a pleasure house called The Gossamer, you've gone too far."

Saria gave her a quick smile. "Thank you."

"Clear skies," Jul said brightly with a parting wave, the Tellaran woman soon lost in the crowd.

Loud music thrummed through the open doors of Vista, the tavern smelt of food, drink, and pungent smoke. Saria hovered just outside, hoping she would spot the men without having to enter at all, but the interior was dim, the inhabitants moving about in semi-darkness.

Steeling herself against another round of groping, Saria followed at the heels of a tall man, hoping her close proximity to him might make it appear that she had not entered unaccompanied.

The Tellarans inside were not much different from those on the street—though clearly the beggars were not welcome here. Tables crowded the space and a blonde woman, clearly employed more for her ability to hold up the creative costuming rather than her vocal talent, sang a jaunty, suggestive tune from the safety of a forcefield-protected stage.

Despite darkness and the woman's ghastly caterwauling—*This is what Tellarans consider music?*—Saria searched the tavern, from ground level to second-floor gallery, checking every table for the men she sought.

But the warriors were nowhere to be seen.

Returning to the first floor, she paused at the bottom of the wide curved staircase. She bit the inside of her cheek, weighing her chances of pushing through the crowd at the bar to question the servant pouring drinks there. With no better plan, she was turning that way when by chance a sword's pommel caught the light.

At Vista's exit one of the warriors paused for an instant, his face illuminated by the streetlight, then he was gone.

Saria hurried after, grateful for once for her ugly footwear as it gave her needed traction to speed across the dance floor.

She made it back to the street in time to spot the three warriors ahead.

Tellarans hurriedly shuffled aside to make room for the three large warriors but Saria, in her plain coveralls and boots, garnered no such deference. She gritted her teeth, keeping the trio in sight as she wove her way through the crowd, vowing never again to take for granted the parting and deep bows of the Imperial court.

"Honored warriors!" she cried out in Az-kye when she finally managed to get within a half-dozen paces of them. "Hold where you are!"

They stopped and turned back, their dark eyes sweeping over her plain clothing with a mix of puzzlement and suspicion.

A sweeping court dress and a half-dozen well-born maids would have made for a much more imposing approach, but Saria held her head high as she stood before them. She paused, awaiting their bows, but the men simply stared down at her.

"Why do you call to us?" one demanded.

"I am in need of your service," she said.

"Indeed?" he smirked, his glance dipping to her breasts. "And what service can I render you?"

She lifted her chin. "I demand the service of your sword in the name of the empire, *Honored* Warrior."

His mouth thinned, his amusement gone. "Who are you to demand anything?"

This busy thoroughfare was no place to announce her identity, even in their own language. The taverns did not seem a wise choice either. At the moment there was but one option with any hope of privacy.

Saria indicated the alley between the two buildings. "Walk with me."

The men exchanged looks as Saria swept past them into the narrow, deserted space. It smelled of trash and urine. In the dimness something small, with filthy matted fur, scurried away.

Hardly a fitting place for an imperial audience.

The men were on guard, their hands hovering near blasters worn at their hips, and they kept their distance too, requiring her to raise her voice more than she would have liked.

"Your ship and crew are called to my service," Saria pronounced. "You will ready your ship for earliest departure to Az-kye."

The men stared at her and Saria's stomach fluttered a bit.

"You," she said quickly, addressing the first warrior again. "Of what house are you?"

The man glanced at his fellows. "We are of the Ni'raran clan. I am Rudir, our clan leader's sister's son."

"I have not heard your honored name before, Warrior," she said. "But upon my return home I will be pleased to welcome you—and your clan leader—to court."

His eyebrows rose. "To court?"

"I am the Imperial Heiress, Princess Saria." She folded her hands before her and looked at each man in turn. "In the empress's name you are ordered to escort me to the homeworld immediately."

There was silence for a moment, then one smothered a laugh.

Her back stiffened. "My ship was caught in an eddy at the edge of the Badlands. It was destroyed, killing all aboard, save myself. I *am* the Imperial Heiress Saria and you will escort me to Az-kye immediately."

"She is mad." The warrior sent a sweeping look around them, no longer amused. "Or part of a trap to rob us. We should—"

She took a quick step forward. "You *will* escort me to your ship and ready your vessel for immediate departure for Az-kye!"

"I know now what your game is. Nor do I care." Rudir glanced at his fellows. "We are going."

"I do not give you leave to withdraw!" Saria's voice rang out imperiously. He froze for an instant, then turned back, his expression furious.

Her eyes widening, Saria backed deeper into the alley as Rudir advanced on her. She cried out as he seized her upper arm in a painful grip.

"We have tired of your game, girl," he snarled. "Or is he right—is this a ruse to keep us here? A trap set by our enemies?" Saria whimpered as he shook her. "Who sent you, woman?"

"Beat it out of her," one ordered sharply. "If we are to be set upon, we must know by who."

"No!" she cried as **Rudir** raised his hand to strike. "I am—!"

He hit her so hard across the face she staggered, her face going numb at the blow.

"Who sent you?" he demanded.

Tears blurred her vision and she shook her head. "Please! Please—only let me go!"

He hit her twice more. On the second strike she tasted blood in her mouth and only his grip on her arm held her upright.

"Tell me who!" he snarled, shaking her.

"No one!" she whimpered as he raised his hand again. "I am Princess—"

The flash of a blaster bolt scorched the wall just above **Rudir**'s head.

"Let her go."

Snarling at the Tellarans words, the warrior turned, yanking Saria, sobbing, around with him to face the shooter.

"What is this?" **Rudir** roared, indicating his fellow warriors, also held now at blaster-point. "Our own allies now betray us?"

The man pushed back the hood of his black coat to reveal the intricate tattoos across his scalp and face.

"If you wish to remain our allies—and alive—you will let her go." Van smiled, showing teeth sharpened to points. "This woman now belongs to the Brethren."

14

ᚷᛆᛖᚼᛣᛁᚽᛖᚽᛆ

Potentate

Trapped in the groundcar between Van and another unknown Brethren, Saria made herself as small as she possibly could. She was trembling, her face throbbing, her split lip and left eye rapidly swelling.

"Where"—she began, willing herself to control her quaking voice—"where do you take me?"

Van kept his face turned toward the window as the vehicle sped along. "To a meeting."

"A meeting? Who of your ilk could wish to meet with me? I am no one of importance."

The woman operating the groundcar, her scalp showing fewer and less intricate tattoos, glanced back.

"Eyes ahead." Van's tone was mild but the woman visibly tensed, her attention now only on her task.

They were leaving the last outskirts of the city now, the landscape dark and sparsely populated.

Saria wet her lips, flinching as her tongue touched the spot that Rudir had split. Had they overheard her demands to be returned to Az-kye? Witnessed her proclaim her true identity?

"It seems you have suddenly become very important indeed to Helock," Van said.

Saria's hands clenched in her lap at mention of the Brethren leader's name. "Why?"

"I'm sure he'll tell you himself."

Any grace or beauty of the sprawling mansion was ruined by the unsightly thick walls encircling it, the visible force fields and the patrolling guards, each one clad in a black coat and proudly showing his facial rank tattoos.

The force field shimmered as it powered down to admit them. The driver brought the groundcar to a stop at the steps to the main entrance. The Brethren to her left exited the car and Van urged her along outside with him.

Saria shivered in the chill night air. The gate stood open, the force field deactivated. There was a half-kilometer between her and the road beyond, a dozen guards at least.

Upon her first step in that direction, Van grabbed her arm. She gasped as his fingers closed around the spot where Rudir had left bruises.

"We are going inside now," he said evenly. The gate slid shut and the field snapped into place. "I'd prefer not to injure you further but I will, if you do not cooperate." The black tattoos seemed to snake across his scalp and face as he tilted his head. "Do you understand?"

"Y-yes," she managed.

"Good," he said, striding toward the front door, pulling her along with him. "Because Helock hates to be kept waiting."

The interior of the house was no less sumptuous than its exterior. Saria had little experience with any Tellaran home but she recognized the opulence of the furnishings, the craftsmanship of the inlaid crystal floors.

There were other Brethren within as well, and a number of servants. Plainly dressed and busy about their tasks, the servants avoided eye contact with the black-coated men and women, their heads bent over their work in silent terror.

Like the clanless.

Neither servant nor Brethren interfered as Van brought her along the corridor. He signaled to another black-cloaked man, who opened the door to admit them.

The room they entered was as lovely a space as she imagined any Tellaran nobleman might take his leisure in. Gentle music filled the air, seeming to come from everywhere and nowhere.

Seated there, perfectly at ease among the fine artwork and elegant furnishings, holding a crystal goblet of amber liquid, was a broad-shouldered man with a full head of salt-and-pepper hair.

Helock.

A young woman sat curled up on a nearby chaise, her golden hair neatly upswept, her white gown sparkling with jewels, her face haggard under her expertly applied cosmetics. She showed no interest at the newcomers' arrival, and the utter defeat in her form sent a shiver down Saria's spine.

"Did we do that to her?" Helock indicated Saria's face.

"No, Potentate." Van shook his head. "Couple of Az-kye had hold of her."

"Well!" Helock put his glass down on the carved table beside him and stood. "Jehan doesn't take very good care of his toys, does he?"

His height was imposing and his high-collared black coat showed restrained good taste, the fabric fitting his broad shoulders perfectly. He had a presence that effortlessly filled the room and, unlike his underlings, his hair was full, his skin completely unmarked; he could easily be called handsome, even dashing.

Saria raised her chin as Helock studied her. She was well accustomed to the appraisal of a powerful and able ruler. Compared to an Az-kye empress, this paltry Tellaran criminal was nothing.

Then he smiled faintly, just a lifting of his lips, his ice blue gaze crinkling a little at the corners, and Saria felt herself blanch.

Her mother, Empress Azara-behn, could command trillions of warriors with a wave her fan but there was light in her eyes; in this man's there was none. He seemed a creature animated by pure darkness, one poised to strike out with utter savagery. He was terrifying and he knew himself so.

No, it is more even than that. He enjoys it . . .

"Well," Helock began, his deep voice pleasant as he indicated the well-stocked and attractively lit bar that took up most of one wall. "May I offer you a drink?"

"I am not thirsty," she said, both surprised and proud her voice did not quake when she spoke.

"I have a bottle of sparkle wine from the court of King Turan I've been saving for a truly special guest. Ah, but of course, you're Az-kye." He tilted his head. "Do you know who King Turan was?"

Does he know? Or does he toy with all his prisoners?

He waited, a polite smile lifting his lips.

"King Turan was the last monarch to sit upon the Realm's throne," she answered finally.

"That's correct." He inclined his head, like a teacher pleased by a particularly bright student. "Killed when the New Order came to power. We've had a couple would-be kings and queens make grabs at the throne over the centuries," he continued, crossing to the bar and keying in a code to open one compartment. "One nearly succeeded actually. Acknowledged as heir to the throne, the whole

Realm at his feet, but suddenly he just—" Helock spread his hands. "Vanished into the Badlands."

Saria might have kept her expression unchanged but her heart hammered so hard she felt sick.

The racing heart of an animal caught in a trap . . .

"Ah," he said brightly, drawing a bottle out to cradle it in his hands. "*This* was in the king's own collection." He glanced at Van. "You aren't needed any longer."

Van instantly released her arm and took a step back.

Saria resisted the urge to rub her sore arm, instinct telling her that to show any weakness would only amuse Helock.

"Do you have any instructions for me, Potentate?" Van asked.

"I've been thinking you should get away. As reward for your work on the last run," Helock said, busying himself with opening the bottle. The ancient seal gave way and a smile lifted his mouth. "No one will ever forget what you've done for the Brethren over the last few days. I promise you that."

A smile lit his face and Van inclined his head to his leader.

As the door closed behind the man, Helock poured the golden liquid into elegant crystal flutes.

"What about you, Onara?" Helock asked, with a glance at the blonde woman. "Would you care for a taste of royal history?"

She did not answer, nor did she move from her perch, but only watched with silent, hunted eyes.

Helock offered Saria a cheerful shrug. "I'm afraid Onara prefers her refreshments in crystalized form these days."

Onara had the same forlorn look she had seen in some of the city's beggars' faces, that same deadness in her look.

Helock came out from around the bar. Despite their glacial blue shade, his eyes gave Saria the feeling of falling into an endless black pit . . .

He held the goblet out to her and with numb fingers Saria took it from him.

He touched his glass lightly to hers, the crystal clinking pleasantly, then raised it in a toast.

"To the lost crown."

Saria froze, feeling the room pressing in on her as he took a sip.

"Excellent," he proclaimed. "Truly. But you must sample for yourself."

Saria looked at him over the rim of her glass, trying to discern what this man did or did not know, aware that anything she said now might only serve to get herself killed. She glanced at Onara's hopeless face.

Or worse.

"It's not poisoned, if that's what you're worried about." A corner of his mouth quirked upward and he took a step closer. "I'm sure you don't want to be rude . . ."

Trembling, she tipped the glass to sip, wincing as the crystal touched her split lip. The liquor was lovely, smooth as shimmersilk upon her tongue, but she could scarcely taste anything.

"Remarkable, don't you agree?" Helock asked.

"Yes," Saria whispered.

Quick bursts of blaster fire made Saria jump, some of the contents of her glass spilling onto Helock's sleeve. The heavy sound of a body falling made Onara bolt upright on her couch, her painted nails digging into the upholstery.

"Why must they all be so stupid?" Helock grumbled. "Energy weapons in a hall filled with antiques!" He brushed at his sleeve, looking disgusted at the dampness on his sleeve where Saria's drink had spilled. "Could they not even think ahead enough to take him *outside*?"

There was movement in the hall, the bump of something being dragged, the mutter of curses—

Helock plucked the glass from Saria's shaking hand. "I'll get you more."

She and Onara exchanged glances. Even knowing it foolish to hope for help from the broken Tellaran woman, there was comfort to be had seeing another nearby capable of compassion, of humanity.

"So," he asked, "how are you enjoying Tir-Halea?" Helock returned and again held out the glass to Saria. "Don't worry about the jacket," he assured when she made no move to take it. "I've got others. What shall we toast this—"

The sound of another blaster bolt made him blink. The door was kicked open hard enough to hit the wall.

"Evening, Helock." Jehan's dark eyes—and his blaster—fixed on the Brethren leader. "I believe you have something of mine."

15

ᴣᴀᵡᴧᴧᴧᵡᴧᴧᵀᴧ
Unbreakable

Helock frowned. "They were supposed to disarm you."

"They did." Jehan glanced at Saria, taking in the injuries to her face, then turned back to the Brethren leader. "I had a snub blaster in my boot. And with everyone else in the hall occupied with poor Van . . ."

"Sloppy." Helock's mouth tightened. "I despise sloppiness."

"Can't blame them. Not when they're fighting above their class." Jehan closed the door behind him and his glance flicked to Saria again. "The Brethren do that to you?"

Her eyes stung at the sight of him, scarcely holding herself from running to him, from flinging her arms about his neck—

"Actually, Jehan," Helock said, "you owe the Brethren a debt of gratitude."

"And why is that?" he asked.

"My people stepped in, saved her from Az-kye ruffians. She would have been very badly hurt—killed perhaps—if not for us." Helock's smile was back, despite the blaster pointed at his heart. "We were just enjoying a rare vintage." He held up the glasses he held. "Care to try some?"

"I would, but we have dinner plans." Jehan kept his focus on Helock, the blaster in his hand never dipping.

"Come on, Liri. We don't want to miss the hors d'oeuvre special."

"Oh, you won't get out," Helock offered mildly with a careless nod at the door. "I advise you not to try."

"I got in."

"True, but then again," Helock chided, indicating Saria, "it's the second time today that I've invited you, Jehan."

A muscle in Jehan's jaw twitched and abruptly he holstered his weapon. "What are we drinking, Liri? It looks expensive."

What in Ren'thar's name is he doing?

"It is a"—Saria wet her lips—"a liquor once belonging to the Tellaran King Turan."

Jehan gave a low whistle.

"*Very* expensive." He took the glass of sparkle wine and sampled some, nodding in approval even as he placed himself between her and Helock. "And well worth whatever you paid. Where did you get it?"

"Oh, anything can be had for the right price." Helock indicated the blond woman. "You remember Onara, don't you?"

"Of course." Jehan gave the woman a faint smile. "How are you, Onara?"

"It's good to see you, Jehan," Onara said hoarsely, a shimmer showing now in her blue-green eyes.

"But now, Jehan, you must tell me all about your new friend"—Helock indicated Saria—"*Liri* . . . Such a lovely name. Van wasn't able to share much about her—before he left us."

"Not much to tell," Jehan said. "She's the sole survivor of the warship I boarded."

"The only one?" He tsked. "Well, ransom can be a profitable venture, if done right. How much would her family pay for her safe return, do you think?"

"She was a slave. No name, no family. And you already knew that, because Van was there when I brought her onboard."

If Helock was embarrassed at being caught out he did not show it. "She was the only take from that ship?"

"Don't remind me," Jehan grumbled. "It was a once in a lifetime salvage."

Helock turned toward Saria and only Imperial pride kept her from shrinking away from his examination.

"Well, she's a beauty. Or will be, once her face heals." He took a sip of the golden wine. "I do hate to see beautiful things ruined."

Jehan held his glass out. "Any chance of a refill?"

"Of course." He took the glass from Jehan, turning his back to cross to the bar.

Saria gripped Jehan's arm. "Kill him," she breathed. "Quickly."

Jehan covered her hand with his own, pressing it for an instant. Then he took a casual step forward, breaking their contact before Helock turned back.

"On second thought," Jehan said, waving off the drink. "I should get Liri home."

"I was thinking that Liri should stay here for a while." Helock glanced at the blonde woman. "And keep Onara company. She gets very lonely."

"Some other time," Jehan said.

"That warship—" Helock tilted his head. "Was it really all you say it was?"

"More. But Kel made the decision not to board with me."

"Van and Etaran were sworn to me, to the Brethren," Helock pointed out. "Not Kel. They should have gone with you, no matter what his decision."

"Kel gave them an order." Jehan shrugged. "They followed it. You wouldn't want the Brethren to start bucking the chain of command, would you?"

"Kel had risen high in our organization. That amounts to considerable time, training, and resources expended on my part." Helock's lids were hooded. "And you killed him. Why?"

"Partly because he was going to come back here and lay the blame on *me* for his fuck-up," Jehan said bluntly. "And partly because he was about to put a blaster bolt through my brain."

"Then he was, in the end, simply another fool." Helock sighed. "So many of the Brethren climb the ranks only to fail me."

"Maybe moving up through your ranks isn't the same as having leadership skills."

"I could not agree more." Helock said. "The Brethren are in need of new strength."

"Not mine. I'm too pretty to have my face tattooed." Jehan sent a pointed look at Helock's thick mane. "Or my hair burned off."

Helock waved the objections away as he sat in one of the plush armchairs. Behind the Brethren's leader, in the center of the vast dark windows, the distant lights of Tir-Halea were muted and dim. "Won't apply to you. Not as my second-in-command."

Jehan went still. "Second-in-command?"

"I am prepared to make you my lieutenant, Jehan." Helock took a sip of the liquor and on the settee Onara's posture stiffened. "It's a very generous offer."

Jehan sat in the opposite chair, inscrutable now as any Az-kye warrior. "Wouldn't the other Brethren have a problem with me jumping ahead of them?"

"As my lieutenant you'll have the power to deal with any objectors. I think you'll find you'll have a great deal of power. More than you ever imagined."

Jehan's mouth curved into a humorless smile. "Liri is mine."

"Absolutely," Helock assured. "Onara too, if you like."

Jehan glanced at the Tellaran woman. "I think she's fine where she is."

"Well, you *have* caught him, haven't you, lovely Liri?" Helock lifted his glass to Saria. "And the Brethren will safeguard your Liri as they'd protect me."

"The *Selini's Song* and her crew are mine too."

"Yes, of course. After all, it was never your grubby little ship I wanted. It's your resourcefulness, your talent for leadership, Jehan, that I'm buying. That Az-kye ruthlessness of yours, that savagery that lurks just beneath the surface, how you can hide your true nature when the situation requires it." Helock's mouth curved a little. "You and I are alike in that way."

"Except you don't have a drop of Az-kye blood in your veins," Jehan said, indicating Helock's icy blue eyes.

"No," the crime lord admitted easily. "But I have always admired the Az-kye, how they never flinch from a task that leaves a Tellaran whimpering and weeping. And, of course, how their empress holds power."

"Certainly explains the palatial setting." Jehan threw a dry glance at their surroundings. "And the image you've cultivated, the glamor of the potentate. Even people who have no idea what you look like are afraid when they say the name 'Helock.'"

The Brethren leader laughed. "You can thank the Az-kye for that. I used their empire as my blueprint when I molded the Brethren into the force it has become. To rival the power Empress Azara commands in her domain within my own, I set out to create a cult of brutality, with its own rituals and symbolism." Helock raised his glass. "And so I have."

Saria stiffened in insult. As if sensing her imminent outburst, Jehan caught her by the wrist and pulled her into his lap as Helock toasted himself with a fallen king's wine.

Hot words bubbled up but his arm was round her in a hold that shouted warning. His muscles, for all his casual posture, were tense.

"And now you must consider carefully the image that, as my lieutenant, you wish to project."

"We both know the answer to that," Jehan said. "So my living accommodations could probably use an upgrade."

"They will be equal to your new position, as will your share of the Brethren's profits." Helock raised his eyebrows. "Anything else?"

"That's all I need to get started," Jehan said. "Everything else I can take care of on my own. As long as you're serious about not marking me."

"Not so much as a single stripe, my boy. You are now—like myself—Brethren royalty. We must be able to mix freely with the most respectable business leaders, Fleet officers, entertainers . . . we can hardly do that if we look like common thugs. Of course," he added casually, "to assure me that your loyalty is genuine, I will require a blood oath."

Jehan's expression did not change. "You have a knife?"

At that the potentate did smile.

Helock waved to Onara. "Get one."

With slow reluctance the blonde woman rose. She went to the display of ancient weapons above the bar and took down a small sharp jeweled dagger. Jehan put his glass down.

"Thanks," he said, taking his arm from around Saria to clasp the hilt Onara offered him.

"Jehan—" Saria murmured but he swiftly drew the blade across his palm.

"Let the gods bear witness that I, Jehan, do by my life's blood, pledge myself, my loyalty, and my life to you, and no other." Saria cringed inwardly to hear him speak a sacred Az-kye vow of fealty to one so unworthy.

"Nicely said." Helock applauded, his face fairly glowing. "I believe I shall reword the current Brethren oath to match it."

"Might want to get me a cloth or something." Jehan cupped his palm, the blood beginning to pool there. "I'd hate to ruin your carpet."

Helock yanked the shimmersilk scarf from Onara's shoulders and offered it. Jehan quickly wrapped his hand with it, using his teeth to hold the fabric as he tied it off.

"Well, then." Helock's mouth curved and he raised his goblet. "To the Brethren."

Jehan smiled and raised his glass in return. "To the Brethren."

16

Nexus

"Arrena's tits, would you just—!" Jehan grumbled when Saria turned away again from the healing light.

Other than the spare conversation necessary to get to the groundcar outside the gate of Helock's estate, Jehan had kept tense vigil the whole way back to Tir-Halea, his curt manner discouraging any talk. Once safely inside his house, with both door lock and security field in place, he immediately went for a medkit. He took a spare moment to discard Onara's ruined scarf and slap a healing patch over his palm before sitting Saria down on the sofa to treat her injuries.

Holos of peaceful mountains and beaches rippled along the living area walls of his house. Neither they nor the comfortable but serenely colored furniture seemed to reflect Jehan's personality or his Az-kye heritage at all.

And they certainly did not suit his present mood.

"Look, the sooner you let me start, the sooner I'll be done," he said irritably. "And if you aren't going to let me give you something for the pain, it would really help if you would *hold still*."

She scowled at him. "I do not need you to treat me."

"Oh, for gods' sake! Yes, you—Do have to do this *again*? It's been what, twenty-seven hours since the last time I needed to use a medscanner on your face?"

"You pledged yourself to that—that *monster*!" she burst out, her fingers clenching. "I could not believe it! I *cannot* believe it! That you would choose to become one of those honorless Breth—"

"Choose?" he flared. "I didn't *have* a choice about joining the Brethren—thanks to you!"

"Thanks to me?" she cried. "You think to blame *me*? Why did you not kill him when I bid you? You had a weapon, there were none there but us and a weak, terrified Tellaran woman. He was not a dozen paces away— unarmed—with his back turned!"

He snorted. "And to hells with honor, huh, Liri?"

"It was no Challenge!" she spat. "No contest within the Circle between honored warriors! Helock is Tellaran vermin, one that needs exterminated in the most expedient way possible. If that be with a blaster bolt in his back, so be it. You killed Kel without remorse, why then not Helock?"

"You think I didn't want to blow a hole through the bastard?"

"Then why waver? Did you fear you would miss?"

"No," Jehan gritted out. "But if I *had* killed him we wouldn't have made it back to the city—hells, even gotten out of that house—alive. Every last Brethren would be gunning for us. Every one out to prove himself and become the next potentate." He shook his head. "Don't you understand? Killing Helock tonight would create a power vacuum big enough to implode the whole sector. No one except him can control the Brethren; he dies and they'll be like xekodiles tearing into each other. They'd split into factions, rip the planet apart, every section and street belonging to this 'true' potentate or that 'true' potentate. The bloodshed would spread to the Tellaran worlds, into the empire—"

"Why should you care what happens in the empire?"

"I don't," he said shortly. "And I care even *less* now. If you didn't need me here I'd be out hunting down those fucking—"

He broke off, his hand gripping the scanner so tightly his knuckles showed white. Then as if forcing himself to it, the tightness in his shoulders eased.

"I'm tired," he said, his voice level now. "So you've got to be exhausted. Let's get you taken care of, okay?"

Perhaps he was right. Perhaps leaving that beast alive was their only hope of safe passage out of his stronghold. This time when Jehan lifted the medscanner, she submitted to his ministrations without complaint. He worked silently, carefully treating the injuries the warriors had inflicted. Finally, he lowered the instrument, tilting her face this way and that to examine her.

"Sure you don't want something for the pain?"

Saria shook her head. She had refused earlier and now with the discomfort fading she saw no need.

He put the scanner down with a sigh but left the case open. "Are you hungry?"

"Vac rations again?'

"It's late but I'm sure the Brethren would crack open any restaurant—and haul the chef out of bed by his neck— to make us dinner. Personally, though, I'd rather have the vac rations."

"Was there no other choice but to join him? He is a monster, a madman . . ."

"Cracked as a burnt casing," Jehan agreed.

He looked drawn now as if the great weight of his bargain with Helock was settling on his shoulders.

"Thank you," she said hoarsely. "Thank you for coming after me. You saved me, Jehan."

"Oh, fuck, don't thank me." Jehan passed his hand over his face. "The whole mess is my fault."

"Your fault?"

"I was stupid, Liri." He closed his eyes briefly. "And my stupidity nearly got you killed tonight."

"What do you mean?" She frowned. "It was I who ran off when you had offered the protection of your house. The fault is mine."

He shook his head. "Helock's been wanting to recruit me. He's stepped it up a lot over the past couple months trying to sweeten the deal but it didn't work. So he found something that would." He looked down at his hands—old scars, tiny white lines across the palms beside the healing patch where he had cut himself to make the oath. "I brought you onboard the *Selini's Song* but I wouldn't hand you over to Kel. Van and Etaran would have reported that you stayed in my cabin on the journey here. As soon as Helock said he'd invited me . . . I knew. The Brethren had us under surveillance from the moment we made planetfall. They were waiting to see if I'd take you to Bandy or one of the other pleasure houses to sell. They were watching us. Listening too, probably. The Brethren followed you and they—" His mouth tightened. "They stood by—they *watched*—while that filth beat you just so they could step in at the right time."

"I suppose I should be glad they did," she muttered. "I do not know how long he would have continued to strike me."

"Not long. I would have been there in a few moments. And none of those warriors would have lived to walk out of that alley." Jehan raised his eyebrows at her. "That surprises you?"

"I felt quite lost in the crowd," she admitted. "I can hardly believe you would find me at all."

"Inborn warrior instincts. Oh, and Jul wants me to tell you you're a lousy liar."

"And she a good one! I thought I had quite convinced her."

"It wouldn't have mattered even if she'd believed you. She would have told me where you'd gone anyway. But I should have moved faster. I got there just in time to see the Brethren take you away. Of course," he said heavily, "that's exactly what they wanted me to see. He wanted a meeting, remember?"

"That woman, Onara, was she . . ." Saria suddenly found it hard to look at him, "special to you?"

"Still is," he said hoarsely. "But if you're asking if we were lovers the answer's no. Onara's brother, Erit, was my best friend, and after my father died—well, the three of us stuck together, sharing whatever food we scrounged up. Erit and I managed honest scut work sometimes but Tir-Halea's sure no place for a young girl on her own. He took care of her when he could and I watched her when he worked. When I look at her even now, all I see is that little girl, just as much my kid sister as Erit's, skinny as stick but bright and happy as could be, following us around like a snuffer pup.

"I taught them both to read actually." He smiled fondly. "Me, teaching Tellarans to read their own language. When Onara was old enough to be left on her own, Erit and I took berths on a couple of the ships, started to move up on every run. We were doing okay, not great, but one day Erit came back to our quarters proud as all hells to tell us he got himself a ship. He'd borrowed some of the money but he was sure we could pay it back. We did well, too. I was his

First Officer but . . . I didn't know how deep in he was in; how much he'd borrowed from Helock. The interest was insane and he kept falling farther behind on what he owed. He got in so deep, got so desperate, he—he promised Onara to Helock if he defaulted." His face was etched and tight. "When Erit died, Helock called in the loan."

Saria's brow creased. "Died?"

"Shot, almost three years ago now. An argument in a tavern. A dozen witnesses swear they saw him drunk, belligerent, claimed he started the whole thing." Jehan shook his head, his face tight. "But I'd seen Erit drunk— happiest, sleepiest drunk you ever saw. I asked around, spoke to some of the witnesses, and their stories matched up perfectly. *Perfectly.* They all said the same thing, almost word for word."

"Did you—" She felt a fool for asking. "Did you report your suspicions to the Tellaran's Security force?"

"That Helock had Erit killed? That he paid—or threatened—those so-called 'witnesses'?" he asked bitterly. "'Course I did, but there's no justice here you don't buy and Helock had already wiped me out."

"He took the ship?"

"Took everything. The ship, cargo, whatever creds Erit and I had left." He swallowed. "And Onara too."

Saria shook her head, remembering the dead look in the young woman's glance. "Why did you not flee?"

"I wanted to. I had the ship prepped, ready to blast out of here but—Onara wouldn't go. Said we'd be running from Helock for the rest of our lives if we left. Said she had a debt to honor." His lip curled. "*Honor.* Look at her now, only twenty-three and dosing chems. Can't even call her an Ornament, she's Helock's whore. And from the looks of it she won't be alive much longer either."

"I am sorry," Saria said quietly, putting her hand on his. "No one deserves such suffering."

"Not even the clanless?"

"No," she said softly, a lump tightening her throat. "Not even the clanless."

He intertwined his fingers with hers. "Why did you run off?" His face worked for a moment. "Is it—Is it me?"

"You?" she managed. "Of course not."

A rush of relief lightened his features for an instant then he frowned again. "Then why? And why go after those warriors? You lied to Jul; you didn't know any of them."

Saria hesitated.

He gave a heavy nod. "You don't trust me."

"Jehan—" she murmured, her vision blurring. "Those I thought I could trust with my life, thought I could trust until the end of time, betrayed me. I am beginning to wonder if I can ever give my trust to anyone again."

"Let me earn it then," he said huskily.

"Earn it?" she whispered.

"Just give me a chance and I will." He cupped her face, his eyes raw. "When I saw you hurt, saw them take you away…" She saw him swallow. "It was like someone blew a hole through my chest . . ."

He leaned forward, then hesitated, his mouth hovering a spare inch from hers.

"You aren't my slave, Liri," he said, his breath warm against her lips. "No matter what I told the Brethren when I brought you aboard the *Selini's Song*. No matter what I told Helock. You don't owe me anything and I promise—I *promise*—you don't have anything to fear from me." His fingers traced the sides of her neck, to her shoulders. "I want you, so very much. But I need to know you want this as much as I do."

"Perhaps," she said huskily, so possessed of a hunger for his body that her center tingled. "I want it more."

His laugh was breathless. "I don't think that's possible."

"Then let me show you."

Saria lifted her mouth to his and Jehan froze, his breath drawing in sharply at the touch. His lips were soft at first, letting her explore, then suddenly he pulled her closer. His hold was sure, so unlike any she had known before—the confident touch of an *equal*—as he deepened the kiss.

He broke away, his breath quickened, his glance passing over her face. "Not here—"

Before she could ask what he meant, he swept her up into his arms with a warrior's strength, powerful enough to carry her up the stairs. His mouth was against hers the moment he set her on her feet, his hands going to her waist to urge her onto the bed's edge. In an instant he had her low boots pulled off, his palms sliding down the outside of her thigh to pull her against him. Instinctively Saria wrapped her legs around his hips.

He leaned harder against her, one palm on the bed beside her, the other holding the back of her thigh and through her coveralls she could feel his taut shaft, the heat between them burning even through their clothes. She lifted her hips against him and he made a soft moan as she moved, he too catching the rhythm.

Then Jehan straightened, his dark eyes molten, holding her hips to his. Saria lay back as he slid his hand between them, stroking her center through the fabric of her coveralls.

Tingles ran through her hips and buttocks as his fingers pleasured her, his face flushed, his gaze locked to hers. As if aware of how close she was to finding release his fingers slid upward, over her belly to to rest for a moment against the hollow of her throat. Then he was undoing the fastenings of her coveralls with swift sure fingers, arching over her to pull her halter beneath down, the moist heat of his mouth closing over her nipple.

Her fingers threaded through his hair as they pressed him closer, the gentle pressure of his mouth sending shocks of pleasure through her center. She offered herself up to him, hungry for more, and then he was pulling the coveralls off, freeing her of her halter and underwear.

"Gods," he said huskily, his fingers tracing her skin. Saria felt a thrill to be utterly bare and open to his sight, when he was dressed. Not caught now beneath the shadow of the crown and wanted for her position, for the advantages she might bring him and his clan, this was a nakedness not only of skin but of status, even of *name*. This was her own power, her body and scent—her essence—that made Jehan's eyes hot, his breath quickened with desire.

She held his gaze even as she sat up, her legs dangling over the edge of the bed, him standing between her wide-spread thighs. Her fingers traced the curve of his lower lip, the edge of his beard, trailing along his strong jaw. She saw him swallow as her fingers skimmed lower, over the warmth of his skin, the smooth fabric of his shirt and, lower, to the rigid heat of his shaft.

He drew a ragged breath as her fingers ran down his length, straining hard against the fabric of his trousers. Suddenly she wanted him bare too. She slid the jacket from his shoulders, her hand sliding over the trembling muscles of his taut stomach as she pushed his shirt up. He bent his head to help her free him, pulling off his boots alone.

He stood before her again, his face flushed with eagerness. She tilted her head a bit to look at him, her lips curving in a little smile as she slowly ran her fingers along the waistband of his trousers.

"You're doing it on purpose," he said huskily.

"What?" she asked innocently.

His smile was touched with self-mockery, as if he knew that wherever she led, he would follow. "Making me crazy."

With quick, nimble movements she undid the fastenings and, without constraint, his shaft sprung free. He gasped, shutting his eyes at the sensation as she closed her fingers around his thickness, sliding her hand along his length.

She sent an appreciative glance down at the smooth tautness, rubbed her thumb over the drop of moisture at the head. "The gods formed you beautifully, Jehan."

His mouth pursed in what would surely have another quick-witted example of his Tellaran humor if she had not shifted her hips, guiding him to her center. His tip at her moist heat made his mouth part and seemed to scatter his thoughts completely. Saria reached up and put her hand on the warm skin of his shoulder, pulling him forward so he had to catch himself against the mattress. She lay back, and he groaned as his hardness easily slid into her.

The muscles of his shoulders tightened as he buried himself deeply inside her. A heartbeat later Jehan started to move, the angle of their joining allowing him to hit her most sensitive spot with every withdrawal and stroke.

A hot smile flickered over his face as he observed her reaction. He bent his head and his mouth brushed hers. Balanced now on his forearm to free one hand, he ran his fingers down her body to cup her breast, the pad of his thumb teasing at her nipple. The onslaught of sensations tightened her slick center and Saria rose to meet him, her mouth parting, her soft sounds driving his thrusts faster.

She hovered, tingling, just at the edge, the smooth muscles of his hips tightening as he grew tauter inside her. The next stroke had her crying out with pleasure. Her climax robbed him of the last of his control; two more trembling strokes and Jehan stiffened, shuddering, his shaft throbbing as his seed filled her.

He collapsed over her, gasping, their bodies slick with sweat. Jehan raised his head, searching her gaze for a moment, his own raw.

Then he bent his head, his mouth achingly tender when it touched hers . . .

17

ⱮⱯ)ႶᲢᎪ ᎪᏎ 7Ɐ𝘍 ᏞⱯᏎႶᘔ𝘍

Child of the Empire

"He was your lover, wasn't he?" Jehan asked later as they lay in his bed, his voice quiet, almost as if he did not want to pose the question at all. "Your master?"

Content and drowsy only a moment ago, Saria now tensed in his arms.

"Yes," she said hoarsely. "We were lovers."

He brushed the hair away from her cheek with gentle fingers. "Did you love him?"

"I—" Saria tried to swallow past the lump in her throat. "I would have taken Naret as mate had . . . had things had been different."

Jehan closed his eyes briefly. "But he loved you, didn't he?"

"Yes, he did, very much." She shifted against Jehan. "I . . . grieve for him. I am grateful to him, for so much."

"He was your first?" Jehan let a lock of her hair slide through his fingers. "Was . . . was he was gentle with you? Kind?"

"Always."

But how could he be otherwise to an Imperial Daughter?

The memory of her sister and the Tellaran officer, Kyndan Maere, who, even in the depths of her disgrace, took Alari as his mate flashed in her mind. And just as swiftly she knew that if it were she who had stood scorned by the Imperial court, Naret would not have stepped forward to join her in ignominy.

She had been Second Daughter when he had first come to her bed. Soon after, she was elevated to First, to one who would someday be crowned empress. Naret was a true son of the empire, an honorable warrior; without question he loved his princess.

But would he have loved *her*—Saria—for herself, if all she had were cast-off Tellaran clothes given to her out of pity?

Would any of them—her maids, the noblewomen clamoring for her friendship, the men who competed for her favor, her own family—look past a slave's smock and see *her*?

Once I would have said yes, there was one among them all who would love me still.

But I was wrong. And she is now my greatest enemy. . .

Jehan was silent, pensive, and Saria searched those dark eyes. "I cannot tell how how you feel about this."

"How do I feel? I'm glad he was good to you. I'm jealous as all hells." He learned up on one elbow. "I can see it your face—you feel guilty. Because you and I joined?"

"I have no regrets for what we have shared, Jehan. My guilt for Naret is not—He was a brave and honorable warrior. He deserved"—her eyes stung—"so much better."

"He didn't have a problem taking a woman who didn't have the option of refusing him."

"He died for me," she said hoarsely. "He died protecting me."

Jehan was silent a moment. "Then he was honorable after all." He shifted closer, gathering her against him, cradling her in arms. "And I owe him a great debt. I hope his shade knows me for the jealous fool I am. I hope he forgives me for mocking him."

"Tellarans believe in shades as Az-kye do? They call upon them?"

"Doesn't matter if you call one or not, a shade'll show up whenever it wants to," he said, intertwining his fingers with hers. "The Tellarans call them 'ghosts' though. Ever seen one?"

"Sometimes I think the Imperial Palace is home to more shades than living," she said lightly then flinched inwardly at her unthinking words.

"How long were you there, at the palace?"

"I am not sure." She shifted a bit. "More than a year."

The truth within a lie and hopefully an implied time long enough that she should come to know the place and its stories. Long enough, as well, to disguise any future slip.

I must be more careful.

"How long have you been here, in the Badlands?" she asked.

He was silent so long she began to wonder if he would not answer.

"We left Az-kye when I was thirteen," he said quietly. "Almost sixteen years now, I guess. I haven't—I haven't talked to anyone about this since Erit. It's hard even to think about."

"You do not have to tell me, if you do not wish to."

"But I do," he said roughly. "I want you to know who I am—who I *was* . . ." After a moment he gave an embarrassed laugh. "Gods, I don't know how. I don't even know where to start."

Saria rested her hand over his heart. "Tell me your name."

"I needed a Tellaran name to get work, that's how I wound up with 'Dekra.' It was Erit and Onara's idea, actually. It was their mother's family name but I was born"—he swallowed—"Jehan of the B'tai. My mother was clan leader, Esara of the B'tai, her mate, my father, was Delar. Do you—" He covered her hand with his own, his palm damp. "Do you know of them?"

"I do not," she admitted.

"No, I guess if you grew up on Az-kanzar, you wouldn't. I mean, you would have been what, seven, when we fled the empire?"

"I am twenty," she corrected. "Not twenty-three."

"*Twenty*?" Jehan passed his hand over his face. "Gods, you're younger than Onara! And I wondered if I should be taking you to bed when I thought you were three years older."

She raised her head to look at him. "Did you really?"

"Apparently I've got enough honor left to wonder," he said with dry bitterness. "But not enough to stop myself."

"My life has made me older than my years." *Although I would not wish to look it!* "Why did your family flee the empire, Jehan?"

His face tightened. "I'm sure you've guessed that I can't go back. My father—One day, right before the festival of Ren'thar, an Imperial messenger arrived at our clanhouse to summon my parents before the empress. I was their only child and my father would not allow me to go with them, but they went, even with my mother pregnant—Gods, of course they went, it's not like they could fucking *refuse*."

His jaw worked for a moment. "They left early, at first light. I waited for them the whole day. I didn't even go to practice. Usually my swordmaster would have me scrubbing the shrine's stairs for that but he never even came to look for me. The whole clanhouse stank of fear. We ate the evening meal in silence and no one, not the servants, not my cousins, not even my aunt, would meet my eye. I waited just in the courtyard for them and the moons had risen before my parents came back. Their escort was silent, my mother's attendants scattered the moment they set foot inside the gate. They left the litter there, with my mother inside. My father had to help her out himself. I stood in front of them, blocking their way and asking what had happened. My father . . ." Under her palm she could feel his heart speed up. "My father had been accused of treason."

"What had he done?"

"Nothing!" Jehan fairly snarled. "He was accused of plotting to have the Imperial Warlord assassinated."

Saria's eyes widened. She had never heard of any attempt on her father's life but she had been very young then.

And so very much has been kept hidden from me . . .

"It's ridiculous!" he burst out. "My father was loyal to the throne, loyal to the empire! He had no reason to kill the empress's consort—what could he possibly gain from it?"

"But they did not believe him."

"No," he gritted out. "There were whispers, confessions, people he'd been seen talking to. A bunch of flimsy crap that didn't add up to a godsdamned thing but that didn't matter. The empress declared him guilty and that was it."

"Did your mother cast him out of the clan?"

"No," he said roughly. "She wouldn't cast him out. She loved him." His hand tightened on hers. "And he loved her. He was willing to don the white but she was set on going down with him into, becoming clanless too. He'd never allow that and she wouldn't leave him. It was my mother who decided they should run. I was an only child, and until my sister was born, my aunt was Heiress. They decided to run for Tellaran space, leave the clan to her leadership."

"And they took you with them."

"They didn't want to. I insisted."

"Why? Their crime was not yours."

"*Why?* Because my father was everything a warrior should be. He was brave, honorable, lived every virtue the God of War set down in the texts! And what was his reward for honoring Ren'thar? How did the empire repay him for the training and the scars? They destroyed him. They destroyed them both."

Saria's mouth went dry. "You hate her, the empress."

"Of course I hate her!" His lip curled. "I hate every last one of them—fucking Az-kye! With their stupid traditions and their brutality. I wish the Realm would bust through the borders and wipe them out."

"Jehan," she whispered. "I am Az-kye."

"No," he said instantly, his voice softening. "You're aren't, Liri. Not anymore. And like me, you can't ever go back." He drew her closer, cradling her. "But it's okay. You can have a happy life here, even happier than any you could have had in the empire."

Saria tried to take comfort from his strength but even as she lay in his embrace the truth echoed in her mind.

But like all Imperial Daughters I was not born for happiness, only duty, and I must return home.

18

Tuning Up

When Saria awoke it was morning, the place beside her empty. Jehan stood by the window, looking down into the garden with a warrior's alert stillness, his face pensive in the early light.

"Jehan?"

At the sound of his name he seemed to brush off his dark thoughts and threw a smile back at her. "Sleep okay?"

"Very well, thank you." She pushed herself up to sitting and glanced at the window. "What were you doing?"

He shrugged. "Plotting."

"Plotting?"

"As Helock's lieutenant I'm going to be plotting non-stop. I thought I'd get an early jump on it."

"I had forgotten about him," she sighed.

His smile widened and he sat on the bed beside her. "I'll take that as a compliment."

"I am sorry what saving me has cost you."

"Don't be," he said huskily, covering her hand with his own. "You're worth it. That and more."

"How can you think so of a slave? Of one with no hope of position or fortune?"

"Position, fortune, status . . ." He shook his head. "Living in the Badlands taught me you can't measure yourself, or anyone else, by those. They can vanish in an instant and return with one stroke of good fortune. Who you are, the heart of you, is all that matters."

"And my name?" Her eyes stung. "My family?"

"They don't determine who you are. *You* do. Your actions do."

"You are like no one I have ever met, Jehan of the B'tai," she said, her throat tight. "Like no one I could have ever imagined."

He laughed. "I'm going to try to take that as compliment as well."

"It is one," she promised, intertwining her fingers with his. "A very great one."

"What is it about you?' He brushed the hair away from her cheek with gentle fingers. "It's like I *know* you."

She gave a quick, nervous smile. "Perhaps, it is because, like you, I too am Az-kye and forced into Tellaran territory."

"No," he murmured. "I've run into other Az-kye since I've been in the Badlands. Warriors padding their clan's fortunes with smuggling. A handful of escaped slaves. Even a couple of hard-hearted old-timers, left from the days when the empress's mother was trying to colonize every habitable world within reach. But you," he cupped her cheek. "You just seem so. . . *familiar*."

"I lived in the Imperial city." Saria offered what she hoped was a careless shrug. "I am the daughter of a clan leader. Surely that must make me familiar to you."

Saria plucked at the bedcovers, her heart hammering as he studied her. In official holo portraits of the Imperial family she was always arrayed in elaborate court gowns of traditional black, her hair dressed and bejeweled, her face made up—

He shook his head, smiling again. "Doesn't matter. It's a good feeling anyway."

"I was wondering," she began, anxious to turn the subject. "How is it that so many fall to the Brethren, like Erit, but you did not?"

"You mean until last night? Ah, well." Jehan nodded toward the window, toward the population of Tir-Halea, who at this hour were yet sleeping off the previous evening's carousing. "Life's pretty fucking short here. Most of them sign on for a run, then drink and gamble and whore their money away as fast as they can."

"But you did not."

"No." He flushed a little. "Well, not *much* of it, anyway. I saved most of what I earned. I lived in places that would make vole's nests look luxurious, ate well during a run, lived off vac meals when I was planetside."

"And saved enough to purchase the *Selini's Song*."

"Not quite. But a smuggling run is danger punctuated by long stretches of boredom. I was lucky enough to do a couple runs with Chaeya when I was nineteen."

"I do not know of him."

"*Her*. Best tongo player you ever saw. And before you ask why she took such a shine to me—she said I reminded her of her son. She was kind to me, anyway."

"Kind enough to teach you to play this game, tongo?"

"Anyone can *play*." He flashed a grin. "Chaeya taught me how to *win*."

"So you owe your victory to tongo."

He raised an eyebrow at her. "Don't we owe all our victories to Ren'thar?"

"Think you the Az-kye god of war decides the victor of a Tellaran card game?"

"Well, if he does, he winked in my direction long enough to turn my savings into a ship."

"And a house."

"And a house," he agreed. "But that was later. I suppose I'll sell it now. My image as lieutenant demands a showy lifestyle."

Her smile faded. "What are you going to do about Helock? About the Brethren?"

"For the short term?" He shrugged. "Try to stay alive."

"He would kill you? When he has gone to such great lengths to recruit you?"

"Van served pretty faithfully. Look what that got him."

Her fingers tightened around his. "What will you do?"

"Helock is a psychopath, a cold-blooded vicious killer, but even he has his weaknesses. All that matters to him is winning and he has no empathy to get in the way of doing whatever it takes."

"You think that 'weakness'?" she cried. "You have made him sound utterly invincible."

"Love, even self-love, makes us vulnerable, Liri," Jehan said softly. "And great love makes us even more so. Helock craves recognition for his bloodcurdling achievements. He's desperate to have someone he can boast to, gloat to, and he's susceptible to flattery."

Saria's eyebrows rose in disbelief. "*That* is your plan? You are going to charm him?"

"It worked with you."

"I am not Helock!"

"Thank Arrena," he murmured, pulling her against him. "But it *has* worked on you?"

It was very hard to think with him so close like this. "Has what worked?"

His mouth brushed hers, moist and hot against her own. "My charm."

Lightly he flicked the tip of his tongue to the seam between her lips, a promise of other pleasures to come.

Her soft sound of pleasure was the only response she could manage as his mouth trailed lower. She yielded easily as he spread her wide, keeping that promise very well indeed.

19

Counterpoint

"I suppose we'll have a chef and servants," Jehan mused later as he looked over their breakfast of vac rations, spearing some hoss with his fork. "That's a plus for my new position."

"It is not always pleasant to be served," Saria cautioned him from across the dining room table. "It can sometimes be a burden."

"A burden?" His eyebrows rose. "Having meals expertly prepared by your whim? Doesn't sound like much of burden to me."

"Like all artists, the most talented of chefs can be temperamental—and terribly insecure." Saria poured herself another cup of Apovian white tea, the Tellaran drink a favorite now. "When not afforded suitable praise they are prone to tantrums and sulking."

"You had chefs like that at your clanhouse on Az-kanzar?" he asked, lifting his own cup of caf. The dark bitter Tellaran drink was a favorite of his and Saria declared to his great amusement at her first—and *last*—sip, plainly an acquired taste. "I'd think that's a bit too rural for the really ambitious ones."

"I lived at the palace," she reminded. "I sampled dishes created by the very best of the empire's culinary artists. There was often gossip of tempers flaring in the kitchens. One sous chef even went after another with a carving knife and had to be restrained by Her Majesty's guards." She lifted her teacup to warm her hands. "Once the head chef, Haral, spent weeks perfecting a syllabub using a syrup scented with tashi blossoms from the palace's own gardens. He had it carried in by two of his assistants, and placed it on the table before the Imperial family himself with such pride you would think he alone had created the idea of 'dessert.' But when A—the Princess Alari took a taste she . . ." Saria bit her lip. "She—"

"Hated it?"

"Sneezed! And not once or twice—in truth she could not *stop!* I and every Lady present—including Her Imperial Majesty—had to hold our fans over our faces, we were laughing so hard."

"Poor Haral," he said, smiling. "Gods, he must have been crushed."

"He took to his bed for a week and would not rise until—" she caught herself again. "The Second Imperial Daughter sent one of her attendants with her plea to recreate the sweet for her enjoyment."

"Least one of 'em liked it. That must have soothed his pride a bit."

In truth Saria had hated it. But the moment she and Alari were alone in the First's apartments her sister burst into tears at having humiliated the man. Her heart wringing at her sister's distress, Saria forced herself to eat Haral's ghastly concoction every other week for months.

What a fool I was. . .

"Enough to pull him from the edge of despair at least," she agreed, taking a quick sip of her tea.

"I don't think we'll get ones who are quite so mercurial—or talented for that matter—on Halea. But it'll be better than vac rations anyway and the accommodations will be nicer." He gave their surroundings a regretful look. "The Brethren will be footing the bill, as well as providing security detail for us both, but now that I'm going I'll miss this place. At least it's mine."

"Do you not fear giving them such control over you? To have access to you at all times, to have them always at your elbow, in your home—"

"They're my sworn brothers now, remember? Why would I be afraid of them?"

"Because you are not a fool," she said bluntly.

He smiled faintly. "And neither are you, sweetheart. You lived at the palace. The empress and the princesses, they're surrounded by servants, maids, and guards every moment of their lives. While the warlord lived, he had his own household too, with a retinue of armed warriors at his side. The Imperial family has no real privacy. Their safety, their lives, depend on those around them not rising up—like your namesake, Empress Liri, did. Question is—" He leaned back in his chair. "How? How does Azara keep her ass on that throne instead of sailing over the falls to the rocks below?"

Saria's mouth parted at hearing her mother being referred to by name, without due title or honorific, and described in such a manner.

"Come on," Jehan urged. "Helock has gone to all the trouble of re-creating the Az-kye court for himself on this miserable backwater and you and I are about to dance in it with him. So, how does the empress keep control?"

"Tradition. Change is difficult to bring about and dangerous; most people wish only for a life of peace."

"But not everyone."

"No," she admitted reluctantly. "For—some—the lure of ambition, of glory, is far greater than the wish for a life lived as the gods have decreed."

"'As the gods have decreed . . .'" Jehan tilted his head back for a moment. "The Az-kye religion does its part to help everyone dance to the right tune. Each of the Az-kye— *the Children of Heaven*—has his or her place within the universe, our fates woven in the stars by the gods themselves. That's what the temples proclaim, don't they, at every festival and ritual? The empress is blessed by Lashima herself, set to rule as her living embodiment of love and compassion, her consort bestowed by Ren'thar's own sword-arm to act as warlord at her side. The warrior caste's task is to uphold the ancient ways, the merchants to procure, the clanless to suffer in eternal servitude. From the moment we first behold Lashima's stars to the instant we go to the City of the Gods we are told to shut up and accept the fate the gods have given us like good little Az-kye should."

Saria shifted in her seat. "I suppose that is one way to look at it."

"Pardon my cynicism," he said dryly. "It's for a good cause, I promise." He leaned forward, resting on his folded arms. "If you, Liri, had to break it all down to the most basic of motivations, the one thing that keeps the empress and her daughters sleeping safely in their beds, what would it be?"

She bit back the impulse to argue the justness of it, the divine decree that her family—that *she*—rule over the lives of trillions. Instead, with the coolness of mind her tutors had so often extolled her to cultivate, from her knowledge of history, she examined the question.

"Self-interest," she said finally, a heaviness settling over her heart. "A thousand pitfalls stand before those who would act in open rebellion. To unite *one* caste—let alone all of them—against the crown would prove a nearly impossible, likely fatal, task."

"Exactly." His dark eyes fairly glowed with appreciation. "Each piece, each component, is isolated *just enough* so that to rise against the Imperial family would be to invite their own destruction. All that unites the Az-kye—tradition, religion, custom—also keeps each piece, each caste, even each family *within* that caste in competition against the others to survive. And not," he said, his voice low, intent, "going after the throne."

She frowned. "You think the empress has done this purposefully?"

He shook his head. "I don't think anyone can create something as vast as *that* on purpose. I don't think anyone could plan it. It's just evolved that way so that—for now at least—it works."

"Because Her Imperial Majesty maintains it?"

"All Az-kye maintain it, out of habit or ignorance or piety. It's in everyone's best interest to keep all the singers on the right song, right?"

She, least of all, could argue that. "Was it your parents that taught you such, Jehan? To see our society thus?"

"Gods no! My parents would have been mortified to hear me talk like this." He took a swallow of caf. "But again, that's why our people cling to tradition, isn't it? Why none of us ever point out the truth. It makes everything so fucking awkward."

"*Our* people?"

"Slip-up." His smile was chagrined. "You're a bad influence on me, Liri."

She smiled back. "Whenever my sister and I would get into mischief, I admit the idea was always mine."

"You have a sister?"

"I—yes," she mumbled, busying herself by pouring more tea.

"I guess you don't want to talk about it."

"The sister I loved is lost to me forever," she said, her voice low and rough. "I will not look on her again. And dwelling upon what has been lost will only serve to weigh my heart further." She squared her shoulders. "What truths do you mean?"

"You mean besides the clanless? A so-called merciful tradition that spares the empress and clan leaders the annoyance and expense of sharing power with a judicial system?"

"What . . .what else?"

"Uh, how about eschewing the use of blasters when they're so much more efficient than godsdamned swords?"

"Our people have not the means to arm our warriors so! Such armaments would need be purchased from our enemies and the Tellarans would not sell them to us on such a scale."

"The Az-kye could produce them for themselves any time they wanted to," he scoffed. "They arm their warships with similar weaponry."

"Only to defend us against the Tellarans!"

"So why not carry handheld blasters then, to better defend against the wicked war-mongering Tellarans? They'd work hells of a lot better than a sword."

"Because it would dishonor any *true* warrior to carry a coward's weapon!"

Jehan raised his eyebrows slightly and her face warmed to recall that he now wore a blaster at his hip.

And he is no coward.

"Okay," he allowed. "And I'll give you that particular tradition forces an Az-kye warrior to develop a great deal of physical power and courage. Great. But a warrior could keep his sword, his traditional ways, *and* add expertise with a blaster. Why doesn't he? Why have past—and present—empresses done all they can to keep the use of blasters on lockdown?"

"Because . . ." she breathed. "Because it would change the balance of power with the empire. It would recast the very essence of our society." She shook her head in wonder. "Truly, Jehan, you have a gift for strategy that is unequalled."

"Don't be too impressed. Someone else already figured it."

"Some—?" Saria felt herself blanch. "The one who armed Uthar and his warriors on the *Ty'har*."

"Was there anything important on that ship, Liri?"

Her mouth went dry. "Important?"

"It's just *strange*, you know?" His brow furrowed. "Whoever okayed that plan tipped their hand, but why? Unless there was something on that ship they needed or wanted . . ."

"I know not," she said tightly. "To be certain, I was not one privy to the commander's true mission."

He winced. "Sorry. Of course you weren't."

"Jehan"—she wet her lips—"Helock named you his lieutenant. Why has he done such, when you have great reason to hate him?"

"Partly because it suits his purpose to have the Brethren believe the succession is already decided. And choosing a second-in-command from outside their ranks means I come in with no pre-existing alliances among his men. Both strengthen his position. 'Course choosing an heir doesn't mean you trust them or that they should trust you. The two most dangerous places to be are sitting on the throne and standing next to it."

Saria's stomach tightened, remembering Alari, raised to rule, standing alone and disgraced before the whole court. "Like the empress has, with her Heiress."

"To keep power you need to show stability."

"What of those who have risen against the throne?" she asked, perhaps a little too sharply. "Who have sought the crown for themselves and succeeded?"

"I'm sure it will all make for an entertaining show for Helock, to see which of the Brethren will try to kill me. To see if I'll try to kill him. To find a way to kill me. Helock wasn't kidding when he said he'd studied the Az-kye culture." Jehan sighed. "He could teach a doctorate level course in it at a university on Apovia."

"And in copying the Az-kye"—she searched his gaze—"he has inadvertently copied our weaknesses?"

"Gods, I sure as fuck *hope* so. And that's the other reason why Helock chose me, you know. Why he's been after me to join the Brethren all this time. He might have studied them to the point of obsession but he isn't Az-kye. He wants to prove himself by pitting himself against one."

"And he will fall," Saria said huskily, her hand covering his. "Because now he faces two."

"If I could get you away from here . . ." Jehan's fingers intertwined with hers. "Get you safely out of his reach, I'd do it a heartbeat."

"Do not fear for me, Jehan. I think you will find I am well suited to this battle."

His eyes closed briefly. "Liri, I—" The door chime cut him off and Jehan's jaw tightened. "At least the war's thoughtful enough to knock."

"It is the Brethren, then?" she asked, standing with him.

His smile was brief and bitter. "And the dance begins."

20

Inheritance

The moment Jehan opened the door the four Brethren waiting outside bowed their covered heads to him.

In the street beyond passerbys stared. One woman, holding the hand of a boy about five or so, ducked her head when Saria looked her way, hurrying her child along to the other side of the street.

From the tightness on Jehan's face she knew he too, had witnessed the woman's retreat.

They will fear him as they do Helock.

As my mother is feared . . .

"Morning, Brothers!" Jehan enthused with false, brittle brightness, stepping back to allow them entrance. "Won't you come in?"

They filed in, two carrying large bags, their black coats filling the living space with darkness.

"So—" Jehan folded his arms. "I don't know every one among us, but I do know you," he said to the one who stood a bit forward of his fellows. "Welcome, Etaran."

The man pushed back his hood and Saria recognized him as the third Brethren onboard the *Selini's Song*.

"Thank you, my—uh . . ." Etaran faltered, clearly at a loss.

"First," Saria put in quickly. "He is to be addressed as 'First.'"

The men, Jehan included, looked round at her.

She raised her eyebrows, as if it were obvious. "Because he is First among the potentate's Brethren."

"Yes," Jehan agreed instantly. "That's correct. Of course," he cautioned the men, "a Second and Third have not yet been chosen."

The possibility of such swift advancement dangling in front of them widened the men's eyes.

"We made the pickup you requested, First," one of the pair behind Etaran said quickly.

Jehan waved the two men forward. "Let's take a look."

Annoyance crossed Etaran's face as the pair pushed forward. They bent down, each man throwing open the bag he placed on the floor.

Saria was startled. "Dresses?"

"Some other things too. I thought you might like something other than coveralls to wear," Jehan said with a quick smile. He addressed the two men. "Take the bags upstairs. Liri'll show you the way."

Annoyed at being shooed away like a girl to her governess, Saria was about to protest when Jehan caught her eye.

The Brethren will never respect him if his own woman does not and this is a dangerous enough path.

"Of course," she managed sweetly.

The men trailed dutifully upstairs after her and she watched as with quick and careful attention they unpacked, laying out dresses, pants, long tunics—even shoes, a cloak, and a small box of jewels.

"How thoughtful," Saria murmured as they opened a small, folding cosmetics case to show her.

"Is there anything else you wish of us?" one asked, his tone as respectful as if he addressed the High Priestess of Lashima herself.

For an instant the image of this bald, tattooed, black-coated man arranging her hair crossed her mind. Saria bit the inside of her cheek to keep from giggling.

"No," she said evenly. "That will be all."

"I'm sure the First will be selecting Brethren for his staff shortly," he said. "If we've done well, perhaps you could tell him so? I would be happy to serve."

"As would I," the other said quickly. "If it meets with the First's approval."

She inclined her head and the men left. Saria shut the door behind them, eager to examine the choices available.

Fortunately, Tellaran clothing appeared to be designed to be put on and taken off without the assistance of servants. She knew little of their fashion but had seen enough women on the streets here to know the more respectable types wore plainer dresses or long tunics and trousers beneath during the day.

She rid herself of the dreary coveralls in a heartbeat and seized up one green gown with a rounded décolleté and elbow-length sleeves. By tradition an Imperial Daugher wore only black; this was the first time Saria had ever in her life worn color. Despite the Brethren lurking below, Helock's enmity, and her sister's betrayal, Saria could not help but hurry to the bath's mirror to see.

And such a color!

Delighted, she smoothed the skirt of rich emerald shimmersilk, smiling widely. She raced back to the bed, throwing this gown off to trade it for a dress of ocean blue, then back again for another of violet.

When I am Empress, I will wear any color—every color!—and tradition be damned!

She settled on the violet, choosing gold bracelets from the jewel case. Using care, she applied a light shimmery golden powder across her lids. The cheek color proved more challenging. Her maids had perfected its application, but her first attempt left her looking like a second-rate opera singer, her next distressingly feverish. Wiping it off again Saria used a far lighter touch to apply the rouge, using a little at a time until it was right. She shied away from the darker lip colors, choosing a lighter pink tone instead, and her hair she left free as many of the Tellaran women wore theirs.

Saria was choosing slippers when she accidently knocked the jewel box to the floor. She stood there, waiting a moment, then sighed.

As if a dozen attendants stood nearby to retrieve what I have dropped!

Her cheeks warm, Saria knelt to collect the jewelry pieces. She took care to match the earrings but one of the last pair was missing. She felt along the floor for it then leaned down to look beneath the bed.

The earring was there, its bloodstone jewel dulled by the bed's shadow. But just beyond the gem was something wrapped in dark fabric.

Frowning, wondering if the Brethren had managed to secrete such a thing there with her watching, she reached for it. Her fingers brushed the fabric but she could not grasp it.

Lying flat, her head twisted to the side, she stretched and just managed to grab a bit of the cloth. Pulling the fabric, she found the thing very heavy indeed. She moved it bit by bit until she had it out from under the bed.

Saria pushed the rainbow of clothes aside to make room. She lifted the thing to lay it on the bed and quickly unwrapped the cloth to see what it contained.

Her mouth parted, her fingers running along the cool metal.

She started, turning her head when the door opened. Seeing what lay there, Jehan stopped in the doorway.

"You kept it," she whispered. "I did not think you would."

"My father put his sword in my hand just before he died," he said roughly, his gaze resting on the blade lying there, "and told me to become a warrior."

"And you kept it." Her fingers traced the dull metal. "Through starvation and deprivation."

"I don't know why," he muttered. "It's nothing to me."

"Then why is it here? Though you have kept it poorly indeed."

"It's *useless*, Liri," he said sharply. "There's no magic infusion of Ren'thar's power in the blade, no ancient sacred honor woven into the metal! It wasn't even valuable enough to bring a healer to save my mother's life."

"You must polish it," she advised, her throat tight. "Or have another do so. If you do not, the metal will be ruined."

"Yeah, maybe," he said, reaching out to quickly cover the sword with the cloth again. "Funny that I'd see that thing again today."

"What do you mean? Why especially today?"

"Etaran brought news. There's been some changes in the empire that could impact the smuggling runs, luxuries going to Imperial space."

"Changes?" Saria frowned. "What kind of changes?"

"A shift of power. Imperial Daughter Alari has been named regent."

"*Regent?*" Saria sank down onto the bed, heedless now of her new clothes. "How is that possible? There has been no Regency in the empire for more than a thousand years."

"Well, there's one there now," Jehan said grimly.

Saria's throat tightened. "But if Al—First Daughter Alari is regent, what of the empress?"

"The word is she's ill, but she's not making any public appearances, so it's hard to say. The regent could be putting it out that the empress is sick to keep peace." His brow creased. "But if she really is sick she must be pretty far gone for Princess Alari to become regent without a bloodbath between the clan leaders. And there's more. The younger one, Imperial Daughter Saria, is dead."

"Have they—" She wet her lips. "Have they said how she died?"

"Some kind of accident. They're keeping the details fuzzy but the timing is awfully convenient for the new regent. I mean, hells, not a lot of Imperial Daughters have died *accidentally*. It's not hard to figure out who'd want the Heiress gone." His frown deepened. "Did you know that? That Princess Saria had been named Heiress in her older sister's place?"

"Yes." Saria glanced toward the window. "I did know."

"Right." He passed his hand over his face. "Of course you would. They'd have been talking about Princess Alari taking a Tellaran husband on every colony and warship."

"And what of her Tellaran mate? Does he now rule at Alari's side?"

"Now that's a question, isn't it? I can't imagine Az-kye warriors bowing to a Tellaran warlord."

"Do you think the empress really ill?"

"That's what the Brethren have heard."

Saria clasped her hands together to hide their shaking. "Do—do you think she will die?"

"I don't know." He searched her face. "I didn't realize you'd be so upset."

"They are not holo-images on an official portrait to me, Jehan," she said hoarsely. "Not names on an Imperial proclamation or a prayer gate. I *know* them and they too are human. They know joy and laughter, heartbreaks and fear and—and grief." She searched his eyes. "What of you? Are you pleased to hear that she who condemned your father now lies weak and ill? Or even imprisoned by her own daughter?"

"I'm sorry, Liri." He sighed. "It would take a better man than me to say no."

She swallowed. "I see."

"But who knows? Maybe her daughter will be an improvement."

"I think she will prove a poor successor to her mother." Saria stood. "And the regent will find her reign a short one indeed."

21

ᏉᎦ ᎤᏍᏃᏞᎶ Ꮎ ᏴᎠᎶᎠ

At Cliffs' Edge

"The defenses are top of the line." Etaran nodded to the wall of windows that dominated the mansion's living area. The view looked over the city, the setting suns transforming even Tir-Halea into a thing of beauty. "And its position makes it easier to defend."

Saria's gaze ran over the enormous living area with its white and cream furnishings, its white marble floors shined to a high polish. They had already toured the gardens at either side of the house and inspected the six bedrooms, the seven baths, the cavernous kitchen, and the formal dining room with a table for sixteen, each as blanched of color as this room.

"What about the security fields?" Jehan asked.

Etaran glanced at the schematics in his hand. "They're adequate, could be improved. Of course the same could be said for the last two properties."

Jehan raised his eyebrows at Saria. "That just leaves the question of which house the lady likes." When she hesitated, he waved Etaran toward the door. "Evaluate the front security netting. I want to know how long an upgrade would take."

"Of course, First," Etaran said, inclining his head.

The man's footfalls echoed in the space. Two other Brethren, visible when he opened the exterior door, stood guard outside.

"'First'?" Jehan said wryly as soon as the door shut behind him. "You have a very peculiar sense of humor, Liri."

"Helock will be delighted," she promised. "You will see."

"Probably will," Jehan said with a laugh. "At least I got to choose Etaran as my assistant. As Brethren go, I think I hate him the least."

"He does seem the most decent of them," she agreed, recalling how the young man had tried to intervene when Jehan had first brought her onboard the *Selini's Song*.

"Well?" Jehan asked, indicating their surroundings. "What do you think?"

"I am Az-kye," she reminded, thinking of the bright colors and intricate carvings and lush fabrics of the homeworld.

"So this looks like a house in mourning."

"Or a surgical suite."

His laugh filled the bland, soaring living space. "Were the others any better?"

"No," she admitted, scarcely able to recall each of the dozen houses they had visited over the past three days. "None of them had the call of a home."

"This is not a home, Liri," he warned, suddenly serious. "And it's godsdamned dangerous for you to think it that way. Don't get attached to it and don't get comfortable. It's a place of business, a fortress meant to impress, to intimidate, to awe. And one that, with luck, is secure enough to keep us from being assassinated."

Her mouth curved into a humorless smile. "Like the Imperial Palace."

"Exactly," he agreed. "And our criminal's 'palace' has to serve many of the same functions—luxurious enough to impress guests, lavish enough to remind my underlings I'm very powerful, and inherently defensible against attack."

"I suppose," she sighed, with a resigned looked at the furnishings, "the Tellarans who visit will find it to their taste."

"And any Az-kye visitors will be reminded that this is *not* Imperial space," he said a little sharply. "The warrior caste does not rule unchecked here."

Saria caught herself before she could put her hand to her now-healed face. "Have your dealings with other Az-kye been . . . been—"

"Awkward?" he supplied. "Not anymore. I'm 'Captain Dekra' these days and I look Tellaran enough now—" He ran his hand over his beard. "That they just assume I'm Utavian. They're almost as dark-eyed as the Az-kye and plenty of Tellarans have black hair. Besides, most Az-kye in Tellaran space are only here to do business anyway. Even if they do figure it out, they don't care."

"Most?"

He indicated the distant mountains, visible from where they stood. "There's a couple old-timers around, like Anzu. Respectable Az-kye that gods-know-why are obeying Empress Teshir's directive to settle here, even though she's been dead nearly thirty years. They figured out quick my parents and I had fled the empire in disgrace. To them I'm clanless, an unseemly slave who offends the gods by not accepting my place. They're . . . less than friendly."

Saria glanced away. "Do you like the house, Jehan?"

"No," he said with a faint smile. "But it fits the parameters of the base of operations I need. Having a house at the edge of a cliff like this is an added bonus. Attack from that direction is far less likely and we'd have the high ground. There's a good spot on the south side to keep a shuttle for quick escape, and we can use the drop-off as our flight path to avoid flying over an enemy force."

"A war indeed," she said, wrapping her arms around herself.

Jehan nodded past the crowded, crooked layout of Tir-Halea, toward the countryside where the Brethren potentate's stronghold lay. "With the city between us as a battleground."

"That is why you wished to have a house here. Because it would be opposite of Helock's palace?"

"But we'll have a better location. We're closer to the spaceport than he is. Near enough to vanish into the city if it comes to it. He has kilometers of open country between him and Tir-Halea with nowhere to hide."

"Does he never leave his house then?" she asked, frowning.

"Rarely."

"How does he maintain control?"

"The empress doesn't leave the homeworld, barely leaves the palace grounds," Jehan reminded. "She yanks one thread or another across Imperial space from the comfort of her throne—like a fat spider in the middle of her web."

"You have never set foot in Her Imperial Majesty's presence," Saria snapped. "And you may accept my word that Empress Azara is not 'fat'!"

"I didn't say she was fat," Jehan said, frowning. "I compared her to a 'fat spider.'"

"You will not speak so of Her Imperial Majesty!"

"If you two are such good friends, how come you aren't at the palace right now?"

"That was no doing of *hers*! She never harmed me!"

"Well, she sure did her share of harm to *me*!"

Saria felt her face flush and she softened her voice. "Forgive me. I did not think of the suffering your family endured by her command."

"She's lucky to have such a champion in you," he said after a moment, his tone conciliatory too. "And as far as fat spiders go, I was actually talking about Helock."

Saria glanced toward the front door. "Should we be speaking so here?"

"We're okay for now," he said. "And Mig'll do regular sweeps to keep the house and shuttles clear of 'ears.'"

"You intend to induct Mig into the Brethren?" she asked, surprised.

"Oh, hells no." He flashed a quick smile. "But you'll see a familiar-looking housemaid coming in every day. Well," he said with a sigh, "I guess we've picked our base of operations. We'll be moving in today so let's send Etaran to settle up while we go pack."

"Now that I *have* things to pack." Her fingers brushed the shimmersilk of her skirt. "I did not have the opportunity to thank you for the clothes."

"I'm just glad you found something you like." He looked her over appreciatively. "It sure fits you well."

"Any one of them would." Saria indicated the dress. "They were all my size."

Jehan shook his head, his grin flashing. "Jul's showing off. I wouldn't know a woman's size if you put a blaster to my head."

"Jul? You mean your First Officer?"

"She's part owner of a boutique in Tir-Halea, The Curled Ribbon. She works a bit there whenever she's planetside but Mig says she only does it so she gets first pick what comes in."

"First Officer, Ornament, shopkeeper. She is a busy woman."

"She is that," he agreed. "The Ribbon stocks some of the best stuff from both the Realm and the empire. Apparently even the governor's wife shops there. When I've got enough guards to make it safe I'll take you there and you can choose some gowns for yourself."

"Safe." Suddenly the temperature of the room seemed to drop. "We are far from safe."

Jehan looked toward the door, where the Brethren awaited them outside, his expression grim now. "Helock'll be coming at me any way he can. I don't know when or how. But I do know I don't have a lot of time."

"To win the Brethren over with your charm?" she asked, trying to lighten his mood.

"Well, I can try to get them to love me. But if you could ask the empress what a ruler given the choice between love and fear should pick, she'd tell you you're better off with fear." His smile was bitter. "'Cause fear lasts longer."

22

Ghosts

Saria jolted awake, her heart hammering as she stared into the unfamiliar darkness. Instinctively she reached across the bed for Jehan and found the place beside her empty and cold.

Even now, weeks later, neither rested easy in this cavernous mansion. The burden of his new role grew daily, and it showed in the shadows under his eyes, in the heavy set of his shoulders. He was in frequent contact with Helock via holo and comm but the potentate, as Jehan had predicted, never left his stronghold.

The *Selini's Song* might be Jehan's but her last run was completed under the captaincy of another, junior, Brethren. Jehan's days were filled with the remote coordination of smuggling runs, the collection of revenues from illegal trade with the Az-kye to add to Helock's fortune—and his own. His lofty rank entitled Jehan to twenty percent of the syndicate's revenues, a staggering amount but modest compared to Helock's seventy.

Although Jehan seemed to delight in lavishing luxuries on Saria, and frequently brought her little gifts purchased at Jul's shop, his growing wealth and influence appeared to give him no other pleasure. And while she held no status within the Brethren save that of Jehan's mistress, he had her with him whenever possible, bearing silent witness to the many dealings of the organization. He seemed to draw strength from her nearness.

His gregarious and even-handed leadership was gaining him popularity among the Brethren but he trusted none of them—save perhaps Etaran. The young Brethren had shown himself loyal and capable, and offered her a warm smile whenever Saria joined them. By Jehan's order, at sunset the house emptied of all Brethren and household staff, even Etaran. The evening meal was left laid out for them, kept on warming trays so that he and Saria might serve themselves. The last servant to leave to the house was always the shy housemaid. She kept her head down, her red hair tucked under a gray cap, any listening devices Helock or his spies sought to leave in the house deactivated and secreted into her frayed bag.

From sunset to sunrise no one was permitted entrance to the house. Brethren acted as guards, patrolling the grounds outside, but the security force fields protecting the house itself were under Jehan's sole control.

Only when he had activated the house defenses, nightly changing the codes and tying them to his retina scan, would some of the tension ease from Jehan's shoulders. They spent the evenings together discussing the day's events and he sought her insight and opinion on all that she had heard and observed. He had a talent for bringing some joy to their luxurious confinement with conversation, holo plays, and concerts. But even after the sweet release of loving, when Jehan would wrap his arms around her, their bodies slick with sweat and lull her to sleep in the warm strength of his embrace, he himself found little rest.

Saria activated the light on quarter power and wrapped a shimmersilk robe around herself. The Novician marble was icy beneath her bare feet, the moons giving off just enough light through the hall windows for her to see her way. Shadowy figures moved about on the grounds below—black-coated Brethren on patrol.

He was right; this is not, and never could be, a home.

"Jehan?"

The flickering of changing light drew her to the living room—

Alari's onyx gaze met hers.

Her sister's white garments floated around her. Her face, mouth, neck, and hands pale as Tellaran marble. A single slash of red split her lower lip, her dark eyes sunken, the skin beneath reddened and raw, her black hair hidden beneath the Regent's high crown.

Saria darted back as a tall shadow walked right through her sister's ethereal form.

"Liri?" Jehan, clad in only silken sleeping trousers, caught her gently by the shoulders. "Are you okay?"

"It—" Saria's glance went to the spectral image of Alari. "It is a holo."

"Pretty creepy, isn't she, in all that Imperial mourning crap?"

"Has—" Saria managed. "Has the empress—"

"No, she's alive. Well, as far as I know anyway. This recording was made weeks ago."

"If not the empress—why has Alari donned mourning dress?"

He ran his hand through his short hair, ruffling it further. "This is a recording of the funeral rites for Imperial Daughter Saria."

"Her—" For a moment the room seemed to tilt. "Funeral rites?"

"Didn't I tell you the younger princess died? I'm sorry, I thought I did."

"Yes." Saria stepped forward, drawn to the life-sized holo of Alari. "You did."

Just as in real life, her sister stood shorter than she and the image was so clear, so sharp, Saria felt she could reach out and touch Alari's cheek, feel her sister's smooth, soft skin.

"She . . ." Saria whispered. "She looks grieved."

"She's supposed to," Jehan pointed out. "That's the whole idea."

"I do not mean the garments, the cosmetics to make her appear as if she cannot rest, cannot cease her weeping. She is suffering, burdened."

"I would be too if I'd murdered my sister."

"Her eyes show pain—*true* pain." She reached her hand toward her sister. "This is not pretense. Truly, she grieves."

Jehan gave Alari's image a doubtful look. "If you say so."

"Reset it," Saria urged quickly. "Let me see it all."

Clearly puzzled, Jehan crossed to the controls. For an instant the room was plunged into darkness and then the holo came to life again as the funeral rites within the temple of Meithea began.

Saria watched her sister enter behind the High Priestess of Meithea, queen of the underworld. Alari's mate, Kyndan, accompanied her into the temple wearing the Tellaran Fleet dress uniform of blue and white. Arrayed too all in mourning white, as she had not appeared since the death of her consort, was the empress.

Saria sank down to the room's circular couch as her mother was carried into the temple.

How ill she is—how thin and frail—

Alari presided over the funeral rites at the High Priestess's side, the temple behind her filled with priests and priestesses, councilors, and prominent clan leaders, their warrior mates. More than once during the rites Alari's mate discreetly moved to steady her. Every line of her sister's body reflected agonized fatigue, as if she walked within her own nightmare.

The recording stopped just as the High Priestess was lifting the cup containing the Goddess's perpetual flame. The room went dark.

Then Jehan brought the lights up to half illumination.

Saria wiped at her face, brushing impatiently at the wetness there.

"Funeral rites are private, sacred," she said hoarsely. "How do you have such?"

"This recording was smuggled out of the empire for the Brethren. And with half the Imperial city in attendance, you could hardly call it private." His brow creased. "I didn't realize it would upset you so much. To see people you used to know like that."

Among those present had been members of Naret's clan too, their faces etched with grief.

"Why?" she asked suddenly. "Why were you watching it?"

His frown deepened. "I wasn't really. The Brethren keeps tabs on all major events, Tellaran and Imperial. Etaran regularly submits a collection for me to review. I was skipping through this when I saw you come in."

Saria clasped her shaking hands together as Jehan sat beside her.

"This is more than just seeing people you knew when you worked at the palace, Liri. What's going on?"

"I *cannot* now believe Alari tried—Had her sister killed."

"You *can't*? When you look for a murderer you start with opportunity and motive—at whoever would benefit most from the killing. I can't think of anyone in the empire who had more to gain from Princess Saria's death than the regent."

"But there is no victory in her manner, no satisfaction in her face! She does not have the manner of one who vanquished an enemy but one who . . .One who has lost someone she loved greatly."

"Doesn't make her innocent. She might have loved her sister, might even be feeling guilty because she had her sister killed."

"The empress is desperately ill," Saria said hoarsely. "But now I do not think that is recent. There were times—when I was at the palace—her Imperial Majesty seemed fatigued, short-tempered . . ."

Was it illness that made her mother so enraged when Alari declared for her Tellaran mate rather than the warrior who had been chosen for her? Was that why she had imposed such a cruel—such an uncharacteristically impulsive—punishment on her eldest daughter?

A chill ran up Saria's spine.

But . . . if is not Alari who sought my death . . .

"The empress disinherited Princess Alari—humiliated her—when she chose a Tellaran mate," she said slowly. "And she elevated the Second Imperial Daughter to Heiress."

"Yeah," he said, puzzled. "And?"

Saria wet her lips. "If she . . . *regretted* what she had done, felt her younger daughter not well suited to rule the empire, to reverse her decision, to restore Alari as Heiress, would be a near impossible task unless—unless—"

He stared. "You think the empress had her younger daughter killed?"

"I do not like to think so," she whispered hoarsely. "But there are few with both the power to arrange the death of an Imperial Daughter and have it be named an accident. The empress is among them."

Jehan shook his head. "Why the hells would the empress want to put the daughter who married a Tellaran on the throne?"

"She might not wish to, but she would—*if* she though it best for the Az-kye," Saria said, suddenly feeling bone-weary. "If she thought by doing so she could stave off war with the Tellarans. A Tellaran consort can protect the empire as no Az-kye warrior *could*. If he is loyal to Alari, he will use his knowledge to defend her from Tellaran attack."

"A treaty would do the same damn thing."

He is right. No one stood to gain more than Alari by my death. It is only seeing her again, even as a holo, remembering how I loved her, that has made me doubt . . .

"Jehan, I—"

His warm hand rested on her back. "Sweetheart?"

I must tell him who I am, not yet. To do so would burden him further. I cannot do it now, when he needs all his focus to defeat Helock . . .

"Come on, Liri." Jehan urged her to her feet. "Let's go back to bed."

"I do not think I will be able to sleep," she murmured.

"Well," Jehan slid his arms around her to draw her close, and pressed a soft kiss to her temple. "Then let me see if I can make staying awake more fun . . ."

23

ᏉᏁᏗᏠᏗᎶ ᏔᏮᎶ ᏗᏮᎮᏗᏴᎶ

Beside the Throne

Jehan threw her a chagrined smile as they walked along the center street of Tir-Halea a week later. "Good to get out of the house for a while?"

The Brethren guards kept their hoods up, surrounding her and Jehan like a flock of black birds. Ahead a group of rough-looking spacers avoided eye contact, quickly scurrying out of the way of the Brethren's lieutenant.

"Not when we are greeted everywhere as the goddess Meithea Herself, come to fetch their souls to the underworld." Saria said dryly.

"They're just showing respect."

"You mean fear."

His nod to a shopkeeper made the poor man freeze, his face deathly pale. "All this flows from Helock's rule, just like an Imperial Servant can walk down the worst alley on Az-kye and not be set upon."

"Because Her Imperial Majesty's subjects revere her," Saria chided.

"They do," he agreed. "The empress is the blessed daughter of the gods. She's carefully cultivated an image of benevolent power. But the Az-kye love the First too, for being their hope of good things to come."

"Ah," she said, smiling a little. "So truly we are not come simply to 'walk around, enjoy the sunshine, grab some lunch' as you said."

"You didn't really believe that?"

"Certainly I did," she protested innocently. "As I believe you will purchase for me the new gowns you promised."

He laughed, his whole face lighting with it as he took her hand. "Well, of course I meant *that*."

She lowered her voice, leaning closer to him. "So you hope to sway the populace to your side."

"Helock is a bloodthirsty scary lunatic," he murmured then flashed a smile. "And I'm an approachable, likable fellow."

"And a very handsome one as well."

"Well," he shrugged. "If *you* say so. Actually, you gave me the idea. I was thinking about how the empress made her daughter regent. How she's showing everyone her chosen successor, giving her responsibilities and power. Empress Azara is trying to give Regent Alari some of that Imperial glamor before she dies."

Saria looked away. It was a moment before she could speak. "And?"

"Helock won't do that for me, of course." He nodded to another shopkeeper, this one a scantily-dressed woman readying her tavern for opening. She sent a cautious smile back. "So I'm going do it for myself."

"You show them a pirate crown prince, the dashing hope of the future." She smiled at him sidelong. "Perhaps you should not have brought me, then, to distract them from your glory."

"But you are Lashima to my Ren'thar." His smile was tender now, his dark eyes aglow. "You are my softness, my compassion. You are what makes me vulnerable. You, sweetheart, are what makes me approachable."

Saria laughed. "In truth, you are too charming for your own good."

He took her hand in his warm broad one. "I mean it, Liri."

The false name was like a blade to her heart and she dropped her gaze.

He stopped. "Liri?"

She indicated the black-coated men around them. "This is not the place to speak so."

Jehan sighed and started walking again, her hand still in his. "Okay," he said, bright again. "Lunch first, then you can pick where—"

He broke off, murmuring a rough curse under his breath. Saria followed his gaze to see another group of Brethren approaching, that group twice the number they had and there, at their center, was the potentate himself.

But he never leaves his—

Jehan recovered swiftly, raising his hand in welcome, his smile already in place. "Helock!"

"Jehan, my boy!" Helock offered a friendly smile in return as Jehan hurried Saria along to meet the potentate's entourage. "Come now," he scolded his guards. "Let your lieutenant through!"

The two men embraced briefly as though were brothers in truth. Ignored for an instant, Saria glanced around to weigh the reaction of the Brethren to this warm display. They looked pleased indeed.

"I suppose it's been a while since you saw Liri," Jehan said.

"As if one could ever forget such a beauty," Helock chided, taking her hand and pressing it gently between his own. "How are you, my dear girl?"

Saria smiled, resisting the instinct to yank her hand away. "Very well, Potentate. And you?"

"Oh, no, this will not do," the Brethren leader said lightly, taking her hand to press a kiss to it. "You must call me 'Helock.'"

"Thank you—Helock." She turned her body to continue their stroll, the demure action also serving to withdraw her hand from his grasp. "Is Onara not with you today?"

"Suffering another of her headaches."

"How unfortunate," Saria said. "Jehan has promised me new gowns from The Curled Ribbon—"

"I think I said '*a* gown,'" Jehan mock-grumbled.

"He said 'gowns,'" Saria said to Helock.

"I am sure she would have enjoyed accompanying you," Helock said. "The Ribbon is a favorite of hers. I have purchased a number of clothes for her and—others—there over the years."

"It would be pleasant to have another woman to shop with." Her heart wrung at the suffering Onara endured. But possibly, as Jehan's power grew, they might find a way to somehow free her . . . "Perhaps may I come someday soon and collect her for an excursion?"

"Of course! But you mustn't put off your shopping today." He raised an eyebrow at Jehan. "And surely your protector can afford more than *one* gown, my dear."

"Now you've done it." Jehan threw a grin at their Brethren walking with them, including these men in the joke. "She'll bankrupt me."

A few of the men gave echoing smiles.

Clever, clever man . . .

"Not until *after* lunch," she promised sweetly.

"Well then, you must join me for the midday meal—as my guests, of course," Helock put in quickly as if he had suddenly become aware how much the Brethren had warmed to Jehan and his companion. "I'm just on my way to The Bountiful Harvest. The chef Cobin is renowned for his culinary creations."

Jehan shrugged. "Sounds good to me."

"Excellent!" Helock caught the eye of one of the Brethren. "Tell them to ready a table for three."

The man inclined his head in acknowledgment and hurried off ahead.

"I hope we won't bore you too much with talk of business," Helock said to her.

Saria offered a little pout. "I too hope so!"

The men chuckled at that but as ever, Helock's smile did not brighten his eyes.

Abruptly he turned to Jehan. "I received news just a few minutes ago that may have a great deal of impact on our runs into Imperial space."

Jehan quickly closed the space, walking now between Helock and Saria. "What's going on?"

"The new regent's consort has been named warlord."

Jehan's eyebrows rose. "A Tellaran is Imperial Warlord? I didn't think they'd accept him."

"I don't think Regent Alari gave them much choice," Helock said. "And now a former Tellaran Fleet commander heads the Az-kye war machine. With knowledge of not only the Realm's forces but known smuggling avenues and close contacts—*very* close contacts—within the Tellaran Fleet, he could impact our operations drastically."

Saria had forgotten her sister's mate was also the son of a Tellaran admiral. "Will he work with the Tellaran Fleet, do you think?" she asked. "The new warlord?"

"Jehan and I should prepare for the eventuality," Helock said. "In fact, my boy, I think we should move our outpost on—"

A shout from one of the Brethren ahead was cut short. Saria cried out, instinctively protecting her face as blaster bolts sizzled all around them, slamming into the durracrete and filling the air with the sting of ozone.

Jehan knocked her to the pavement, his body covering hers. Trapped there, she could hear the crackle of weapon-fire, the screams of city dwellers, the shouts of the Brethren, the dull thud of falling bodies—

There was a break in the onslaught as the Brethren rallied to fire back.

"Come on!" Jehan shouted, hauling her up.

He half-carried, half-dragged her to the shadowy cover of a nearby alley. Shoving her behind the scant protection of tarasteel refuse containers, he took up position in front of her, blaster in hand.

"Who are they?" Saria pressed closer to the corner of the smooth pre-fab wall of the building and the chill of the metal container, trying to make herself smaller to allow Jehan more cover.

"Someone who wants Helock dead," Jehan said shortly. "So that narrows the suspects to about ninety-seven percent of the population."

"What do we do?"

"Get the fuck out of here." A glance around the container made his expression even grimmer. "They've cut down half our men already, the others have taken cover."

"Helock?"

"I can see him—"

A new volley of blaster fire cut off his answer and he twisted to shield her as a number of the stray shots scorched the alley walls and pavement.

When it let up a bit, he took a quick look.

"Godsdamn it! He's pinned down." Jehan lifted his blaster. "Stay here."

"What are you doing?" she cried, catching his arm as renewed blaster fire lit the alley. "When he is dead you will be free! Leave him!"

"I'd fucking love to," Jehan gritted out. "But if they *don't* kill him—if Helock survives this—and I *didn't* help him—" He shook his head. "But hopefully I won't make it in time to save the bastard."

"Jehan!" She scrambled to hold him fast.

His dark eyes claimed hers. "I love you, Liri."

Her breath caught. "Jehan—"

"I know." A smile encompassing joy, embarrassment, regret, self-mockery lit his face. "I have lousy luck and worse timing. Should've told you before—" His wry glance went to the tarasteel containers, the alley. "Or at least someplace decent." Then all the self-deprecating humor fled from his face, leaving his gaze raw. He caught her cheek in his palm and pressed a quick, desperate kiss to her mouth.

"Just stay here," he murmured hoarsely. "Just stay safe, sweetheart."

Then he was gone.

24

ᴶᵡᴧᴧᴧ

Traps

"Jehan!"

Horrified, her palms pressed to the cold metal of the container, Saria watched as he plunged into the street, Blaster bolts scorched around him, burning the ground in his wake. He fired upward in the direction of the attack as he ran but they were random, desperate cover shots. He had no hope of sighting them, let alone hitting anything.

Her fingers clenched as he stumbled blindly forward.

Do not die! You cannot die!

Only by Ren'thar's own hand would Jehan make it to where the potentate huddled behind a blaster-gouged groundcar, two Brethren already dead at his side—

But he did.

Though if Jehan hoped to save Helock by rushing to his side, his presence there only gave their attackers the two prime targets in one place—the potentate himself and his lieutenant. Blaster fire hammered the groundcar, giving the men no opportunity to escape or return fire.

No one can survive such an onslaught . . .

She glanced around the corner, upwards, to where the blaster emanated.

One assassin!

It was impossible to tell from here if the gunman was male or female but she could clearly see a lone assailant. Dressed entirely in black, masked, wearing vision-enhancing goggles and armed with a blaster rifle, the attacker could continue the onslaught until the ground car was obliterated. Jehan, pinned down with the Brethren leader and armed with only his handblaster, had no chance against such a weapon.

One of the Brethren lay face down nearby. His upper body was partway in the alley's shadow, a blaster still in his hand.

Her heart hammering, Saria hugged her way around the container. Keeping her body pressed to the building wall, she crept to the building's edge. The bodies both of Brethren and unfortunate bystanders littered the sunny street but all others had fled. If the governor's security force had been alerted, it was plain they were content to let this battle to play out without them.

The tarasteel of the groundcar's side was starting to glow, heated near to melting by the energy weapon's strikes. Jehan could not remain sheltered there much longer.

The blood of a thousand empresses runs in my veins. I will not shame them with cowardice!

Saria darted forward, throwing herself over the body of the fallen Brethren. Trembling, she yanked the weapon from his grip, the blaster surprisingly heavy in her hand. She scrambled back, her shoulder hitting the wall painfully, and drew her legs up against her body.

She stayed there a moment, expecting blasterfire to shatter the durracrete wall.

But the assassin kept his sights on the groundcar and the targets huddled there.

Her back pressed against the wall, Saria got her feet under her, and stood on wobbly legs, the unwieldy blaster now gripped in both hands. The fallen Brethren would have already disengaged the safety.

Saria had never used a blaster before and she would have a heartbeat at most before the assassin fired back.

Wetting her lips, she quickly pulled one of her slippers off. Keeping her gaze on the groundcar, she flung the shoe to the other side of the alley.

Jehan, sheltered behind the vehicle, caught the movement.

Clearly seeing her intention, he started to shake his head sharply but Saria took a quick breath and pivoted, her body only half covered by the wall. Using two hands to heft the bulky weapon, she took aim at the attacker and fired.

Any prayer she had to hit him went unanswered. Her shots went wild but she kept her finger on the trigger, recklessly draining the charge with continuous fire.

If the marksman was startled by her sudden attack, it did not impede his response. As if in slow motion the assassin smoothly swung her way, the rifle now pointed directly at her—

Three quick bursts blew through his chest.

Knocked backward by the force of the kill shot, the assassin's shot hit high, and Saria flinched as pulverized durracrete sprayed dust over her.

Her breath roared in her ears in the sudden silence, the heavy blaster gripped painfully tight in her hands. Smoke rose from the assassin's wounds; he would not rise again. She let her leaden arms fall but could not seem to unclench her fingers to drop the weapon.

Across the battle-scarred street Jehan looked her way. His blaster at the ready, his glance scanning for any sign of further assault, he pushed off from the groundcar and sprinted toward her.

He grabbed her arm, yanking her deeper into the alley, pulling her again back behind the protection of the containers.

"What the fuck did you think you were doing, putting yourself in his sights like that?" His chest heaved, perspiration dampening his hair, dirt and dust dulling his fine clothes. "I told you to stay *here*!"

"You were in danger!"

"Yeah, it's called a 'firefight'!" he snapped. "Exactly what you were supposed to stay *out* of or didn't I make that clear?"

Saria gaped up at him. "I saved your life!"

"I didn't need your help!"

"The hells you did not!"

"I was fine." Jehan's dark eyes were stormy and he wiped impatiently at his forehead. "I had a plan."

"A plan?" she challenged. "Another moment and the groundcar would have melted! You would have been driven into the open and picked off like a kytala bird snapping up a shimmerworm!"

"I would've thought of something!"

"And I *did* think of something!"

"You could have been killed!" His shook his head, his voice raw. "I could have lost you. Don't you understand that?"

"Yes," she said hoarsely. "I do, Jehan. For if I had waited, or hesitated, I would have certainly lost *you*."

His face worked for a moment, then he pulled her against him. His shirt was sweat-soaked, his breath ragged, and she felt him trembling as she wrapped her arms around him.

"I'll get you—get *us*—out of this," he murmured roughly against her hair. "I promise."

"What you said—"

"I meant it." He drew back to look at her. "I love you."

"Jehan." Her vision blurred. "There are things I have not told you. Things about myself—"

He cupped her cheek. "You think I don't know that?"

"And it does not"—she searched his eyes—"trouble you?"

"If you're asking do I want to know all your secrets— hells, yeah, I do. But they aren't going to change how I feel because they won't change who you *are*."

"You do not know that," she said hoarsely.

He dark gaze was soft. "It won't change the way I feel, Liri."

"Jehan, I am—"

"Are you two all right?"

Reluctantly Jehan let her go and turned to face Helock. A dozen Brethren reinforcements had arrived, taking up position outside the alley and in the street.

"Yeah," Jehan said. "What about you?"

"Alive," the potentate said grimly. "Thanks to you."

"Any idea who it was?" Jehan asked.

"Not yet," Helock said. "But we have the body. We'll get his identity, track down his employer, if he had one."

"I want to get Liri back home," Jehan said, taking her hand and drawing her along. "You should get out of Tir-Halea too." He threw a meaningful glance at the rooftops and windows. "I don't think either of us should be out in the open like this right now."

"Get me a groundcar," Helock snapped, and pushed one of the black-coated men in the direction of the street. "And you," he directed another. "Go to The Bountiful Harvest and tell Corin he'll cook for me at my house instead. And signal all our brothers and sisters. The Brethren *will* retaliate."

Still feeling as if she had scarcely escaped drowning, Saria, bathed and dressed in clean clothes, found Jehan in his office.

The Brethren were everywhere, around and in the house. Jehan had already doubled the patrols for the coming evening.

"Is there any word?" she asked as she closed the door behind her.

"Not really." Jehan sat back in the chair and passed his hand over his face. "But I sure wouldn't want to be in the city right now. Helock's shut everything down, including the spaceport. The Brethren are hauling people out of their homes, questioning everyone. The governor's security officers have retreated."

"They have abandoned them to a monster."

"We outnumber them," he reminded. "And we outgun them. Retreating is their only option."

"So Helock rules this world now."

"Maybe he has for a long time," Jehan murmured, looking toward the window, toward the city. "He just never made it so . . . *obvious* before."

"Perhaps even he did not realize how powerful he has become." Saria came to stand beside him. "I do not think that—even once he has found those responsible for the attack—he will release his grip."

"No," he murmured. "He won't."

A chime at the office door had Jehan glancing at the security readout. "It's Etaran." He released the lock from the control on his desk to allow the young Brethren entrance. "You have news?" he asked after the door shut.

Etaran's throat worked. "Not of the attack, First."

Jehan raised his eyebrows. "Something else, then?"

Etaran took a step back. "I think this was a mistake—"

"Hold on," Jehan said sharply, standing. "What did you come to tell me?"

The Brethren hesitated, half turned away.

"Well?" Jehan prompted. "I have the house constantly checked for Helock's ears, if that's what you're worried about. And anything you can say to me, you can say in front of Liri."

"I wouldn't have come to you but my sister—" Etaran squared his shoulders and faced them. "Taya lives in Tir-Halea. Her husband was killed a while back so it's just her and the kids. I help as much as I can of course, but she's really been struggling to keep things together and she's— Taya's had to work at the pleasure houses just to keep the kids fed."

"I'm sorry to hear that," Jehan said, his voice a bit cool. "Does your sister need money?"

"What she *needs* is—" Etaran closed his eyes for an instant. "I know what happened today shouldn't have happened." His fists clenched at his sides. "But innocent people are getting hurt out there. My sister and her kids are there in the middle of Tir-Halea and we're—*Helock*—is tearing the city apart! Look, I know this might just get me a blaster bolt through the head but I also know . . . You aren't like him. You have feelings, friends. You've had your share of fights, we all have, but you'd . . . you'd never butcher people." He swallowed again. "Like Helock does."

"You're taking quite a risk," Jehan pointed out. "Talking like this to me."

"Yeah," the young man said heavily. "I know. But I have to do something. *We* have to do something."

"We can't," Jehan said shortly. "These are the potentate's orders."

"I think—" The young Brethren wet his lips then took a quick step forward and lowered his voice to a whisper. "You remember Kel?"

"I, for one, am not likely to forget him," Saria said of the Brethren Jehan shot on the bridge of the *Selini's Song*, the man who'd demanded he hand her over as part of Helock's cut.

"Everybody knew Kel was about to be named Helock's lieutenant," Etaran continued. "But he wanted to make sure his position was solid so he . . . got some of the other Brethren on his side."

"What do you mean "on his side?" Jehan asked.

"Being second-in-command of the Brethren isn't exactly the safest job to have, and Kel sure wasn't planning on *staying* there." The young man lowered his voice even further, almost feverish. "Somehow Kel got access to Helock's command codes and duplicated *everything*. I'll give them to you." "With Helock's codes and yours—*you* can become Potentate."

Jehan went still.

Saria shook her head. "Jehan become—?"

"You have Helock's command codes?" Jehan broke in. "How the hells did *you* get them?"

"From Van," Etaran stammered. "He was pegged to be Kel's second-in-command. Van only brought me in after you shot Kel; he was going to use the codes for his own takeover—he just didn't live long enough to do it."

"Why do you not use these codes then?" Saria challenged. "Become potentate yourself?"

The young man blanched. "Because even if I thought the Brethren would follow me, I don't want the job."

"So what do you get out of this, if you help me become potentate?" Jehan asked sharply. "To be the new lieutenant?"

The young man shook his head. "What I've wanted for a long time—*out*."

"Out?" Jehan echoed.

"Yeah," Etaran said roughly. "I want out of the Brethren, new IDs for me, my sister, and her kids and enough money to make myself look *normal* again. Enough so I can get out of this shithole and never come back. You becoming potentate, you letting me go, is my only chance to leave the Brethren—alive anyway. You *know* that. But becoming potentate is your only chance too."

"Really?" Jehan asked. "How do you figure that?"

"You probably think I'm just some dumb street kid and maybe I am," Etaran said, his face tight. "But even I can see that once Helock has hold of this planet, of this *sector*, and the last thing he'll tolerate is a second-in-command who's more popular than he is. If he's somehow taken down by the Fleet or the governor's forces you'll get executed right along him, *First*. And if he wins, he's going to get rid of you. If you want to stay alive, if you want both of you" —he glanced meaningfully at Saria— "to survive, you have to take Helock out. I'm willing to stand with you because I know you can do it. You can take control of the Brethren— if you do it *now*."

Jehan looked toward the city, toward the chaos in the distance, the fires . . .

When his eyes met hers again the bleakness in his gaze tightened her stomach. "Jehan?"

"I'm sorry, sweetheart," he said hoarsely. "I thought I'd found a way out for us. I was going to tell you today— But that doesn't matter anymore. We're out of time. I have to take Helock out now, tonight, whatever the cost." Jehan's expression changed, suddenly as inscrutable as any warrior's. "How many of our brothers will support my becoming potentate?"

"A third had already committed to Kel," Etaran offered. "Van said he figured most of the rest would fall into line once he'd taken control. Most will follow you."

"But not all."

"No," Etaran admitted. "Van figured—and I agree— that about ten percent are die-hard loyal to Helock. We'll have to eliminate them."

"How do you know the codes Van gave you are active?" Saria demanded. "Helock could have changed them."

"Old codes will work." Etaran gave Jehan a steady look. "*If* we have a retinal scan to go with them."

"I really don't think Helock is going to be eager to help me overthrow him," Jehan said grimly. "The only way to pull this off is to capture him and replicate a retinal scan. With a retinal replication we can fool the system. Then all Brethren everywhere will follow whatever orders I give them. I'll use that to maneuver myself into full authority."

"Will you have enough men to take the stronghold?" Saria asked, frowning. "Enough time before Helock summons reinforcements?"

"What if—what if we didn't use force to get in?" Etaran asked suddenly. "What if you told Helock that Liri didn't feel safe here? That you both wanted to shelter at the stronghold till the city was secure?"

"No," Jehan snapped. "I don't want her anywhere near Helock."

"But it is a good plan and a story that Helock will believe." Saria offered Jehan a small smile. "Two of us, remember?"

His dark eyes were raw. "I remember."

Etaran shifted uncomfortably, breaking the moment between them.

Saria straightened. "Well, if my girlish fretting is to be our excuse to gain entrance to Helock's stronghold then we must move forward without delay. Once whoever tried to kill you both is in Brethren hands the whole thing will sound like nonsense."

"So, the assassination attempt today—" Etaran began, frowning. "You didn't set that up?"

"With Liri there?" Jehan demanded. "Hells no! Besides, I was getting shot at too, remember? Trust me, Helock doesn't need *me* to kill him; he has a sector full of enemies."

"But . . . you *will* kill him?" Etaran asked.

"No."

"But you can't leave him alive!" Etaran exclaimed, his voice cracking.

"I can't kill him." Jehan's mouth thinned. "I need him as a bargaining chip."

Saria's brow creased. "What do you mean, 'a bargaining chip'?"

"If I'm going to hold power as potentate I'll need support from outside the Brethren too."

"Support from who?" Etaran asked. "Who else would go up against Helock?"

"The only other person who needs Helock removed as much as I do." Jehan glanced toward the city again. "Governor Chol."

"The governor?" Saria's frown deepened. "Think you he will rally to your side, Jehan?"

"I don't think I'll ever be his best buddy. But if we hand Helock over, Chol will look like a hero and Helock is neutralized. Good deal all around."

"There's still the Brethren loyal to Helock," Etaran reminded.

"You know who they are, right?" The young man nodded. "Then we take care of them later. Liri and I will keep Helock busy while you and the Brethren loyal to me take the stronghold from the inside. Once you let me know we have control, I'll deal with Helock." He let his breath out. "I'll have the Brethren under my control in a few hours."

"There are Brethren both here and at the stronghold I know we can trust," Etaran promised. "All you have to do is talk your way in."

"Do not fear on that account," Saria assured. "The gods themselves could not resist his charm."

"Well, fuck, we saved the man's life today," Jehan muttered. "That should at least get us invited over for dinner. Go choose an escort from the Brethren you're absolutely confident will follow me when the time comes, Etaran. I'll contact Governor Chol and cut us a deal, then I'll start sweet-talking Helock."

25

⅀⟋⍀⟋⟋ ⋀⊀⌐⋀⋀

Masquerade

"Liri, how lovely you look," Helock said two hours later as he greeted them in the foyer of his mansion. He took her hands in his, his skin hot and dry. "I want you to know that you are both welcome to stay as long as you like. You are very safe here, my dear."

Saria suppressed a shudder, forcing herself to endure his paternal kiss to her forehead.

"Jehan, my boy." Helock embraced him briefly, his expression one of deep affection as he held Jehan by the shoulders. "Until today I never knew what true loyalty was. Until today I never before had one who I could love as a son."

"I only did what I had to do," Jehan said.

"Too modest!" Helock shook his head. "What you did was no less than heroic. I owe you my life! But come—" He ushered them inside. "If we are to shelter together for safely, I insist we enjoy ourselves. It's early for dinner, I know, but Corin has prepared a meal for us that is beyond compare!"

A look passed between Jehan and Etaran as Helock took Saria's arm to lead her.

"Is this not magnificent?" Helock asked, indicating the table.

"It is," Saria agreed. The table fairly groaned under crystal and fine settings. Twenty dishes awaited them, held to perfect temperature and moisture by their serving dishes. As Helock settled her in a chair to his left she imagined this would be but the first of many courses.

As fine a selection as the empress would enjoy.

Helock indicated that Jehan should occupy the chair to his right but before he could sit the door opened again.

Onara, beautifully dressed in a rose-gold gown of elaborate beading, her golden hair again upswept, entered.

"Ah," Helock said. "I am so glad you decided to make an appearance today, Onara. The new gown I chose suits you well, although," he continued, lifting his glass and sending a secretive smile at Jehan, "I have the feeling it is more our guests that draw you from your—rest—than *my* company."

Onara, eyes downcast, silently took her place at the foot of the table.

Nor was her or anyone else's participation required. Helock kept up the conversation all on his own, flattering Saria's beauty and praising Jehan, telling grand stories—all prominently featuring himself—making jokes as they dined on the chef's magnificent creations.

The food was excellent and the wines were of rare vintage, but Onara neither ate nor drank; she seemed lost in her own world. Jehan, like Saria herself, seemed to have little appetite for the exquisite meal either. It was bloodcurdling, watching Helock gorge himself while, in Tir-Halea, his men tore innocent lives apart.

"Well," Helock said brightly as he stood at the end of the meal, "dessert, caf, and brandy are set up in my study." He sent a smile toward Saria. "If I may be allowed the indulgence of escorting your lady in?"

"I'm sure Liri would be honored." Jehan stood and offered his arm to Onara but the Tellaran woman simply sat there, unmoving.

"Onara!" Helock's snarled and the girl jumped at the break in his courtly façade.

She pushed away from the table and stood, her movements jerky as she took up position at Jehan's side, her gaze on the floor.

For an instant Jehan pressed her hand and her eyes rose to meet his, a sheen glossing them before she dropped her gaze again.

As promised, delectable treats awaited, arrayed on tiered dishes, the dessert display itself a visual feast. But Saria, who had always loved sweetmeats, had even less appetite now. The study had not changed since she had been here last, bloody and shaken from her beating by the Az-kye warriors.

"We have a great deal to celebrate tonight, Jehan," Helock said, releasing Saria. "And I have something special for the occasion."

"Another rare wine from a Tellaran king's stores?" Jehan guessed, smiling.

Helock dismissed the idea with a wave. "No, no, something far more spectacular. A bottle of kanak lifted from the Imperial Palace itself, one that dates back to the time of Empress Xar."

Jehan's eyebrows shot up. "How did you manage to get *that*?"

"I have my ways," he said, pouring the dark red libation and Saria's heart sank as she recognized it. Kanak turned her stomach on the best day.

Apparently her dismay showed on her face because Jehan gave her an amused look.

"I think Liri would be happier with her usual white tea." Jehan indicated the dessert display which held caf as well. "There's some there, you see?"

Helock brought around two glasses, offering neither to Onara. Apparently the Tellaran woman's choice of intoxicants still did not include liquor.

Jehan eyed the glass. "Mind if I have this over ice? Straight up kanak has always been a little much for me."

"If you like," Helock said amiably, handing Onara the glass and waving the Tellaran woman that way. Onara, her gaze downcast, shuffled to the bar. "Though personally, I prefer the traditional way."

"Well," Jehan shrugged, "I'm hardly the traditional type."

When Onara returned and held the glass out to Jehan, her hand was shaking. He took it from her with a quick nod of thanks and she returned to the bar, apparently to await Helock's next command.

Knowing that beyond that door Etaran was arranging a coup to bring the brethren down, it was a relief to have something to do. Saria poured the tea, taking comfort in the soothing scent of it, the warmth of the cup in her hand.

"In grateful thanks for your brave acts today—" Helock lifted his glass. "To you, Jehan, and your future."

Jehan raised his glass in return and drank with Helock while Saria sipped her tea.

"Well?" Helock asked. "What do you think?"

"Excellent." Jehan admitted, swirling the dark red liquid in his snifter, the ice clinking against the crystal. "But you have good taste."

"I do indeed," Helock agreed, chortling, then drank again.

"We really should be drinking to Liri, though," Jehan said. "She distracted the assassin long enough for me to take him out."

"Quite right! To Liri—I cannot thank you enough." Saria managed a smile as the men drank to her.

Helock drained his cup and snapped his fingers at Onara. Silently the blonde woman fetched the ancient bottle and refilled Helock's cup.

Jehan held the snifter between his hands. "Any news on our would-be assassin?"

There was a chime at the door.

"Something now, I hope," Helock said.

He took a deep draft of the liquor and placed his glass on the bar, then activated the control to release the door.

Seeing who it was, Saria tried, as casually as she could, to place her cup on the table.

"Yes?" Helock raised his eyebrows as Etaran entered and shut the door behind him. "You have news?"

"Everything's been taken care of as per your orders," the young Brethren inclined his head to Helock, "Potentate."

26

The Web

We are betrayed!

Saria felt the blood drain from her face. Her eyes met Jehan's to see that same awful knowledge reflected there.

"What's going on?" Jehan asked tightly.

"Well," Helock said with a frown, "that should mean that the men who accompanied you here, the ones loyal to you—who would have betrayed me for you—are dead." He looked to Etaran. "That's correct, isn't it? None remain within my compound who are loyal to Jehan?"

Etaran inclined his head. "To my knowledge, every Brethren loyal to Jehan, everywhere, is dead."

A muscle in Jehan's jaw twitched. "You bastard," he said to Etaran. "You set me up."

"Etaran doesn't deserve any credit; he was simply following my orders. In the end it was quite easy, actually." Helock lifted his snifter to Saria. "All I had to do was put *her* in danger and you jumped at the chance to betray me. Caring for her," Helock curled his lip, "was your mistake."

Jehan's dark eyes were murderous. "My only mistake was saving your life."

"Oh, but you didn't, my boy," Helock said cheerfully.

"But I—" Jehan's face blanched. "You staged it."

"I confess," Helock took a deep draft. "It was great fun, trying to guess if you would wait to see if the assassin killed me or try to shoot me yourself. Not that you would have succeeded, of course. I had you under surveillance the entire time. If you had aimed for me, you would never have gotten off a shot."

"You killed your own men," Saria said numbly, "for amusement?"

"The Brethren exist to serve me. They live—and die—by my will. I only wish I could have let the game go on longer." Helock sighed. "Brilliance—and boredom—are my curse, as much as you, Liri, are Jehan's."

The potentate offered Jehan another salute. "But while I do appreciate your efforts against *me*, you had no more chance of winning this game than a rodent in a lab maze has of earning a doctorate."

"A lot of trouble to go through," Jehan pointed out, "when you could have just killed me."

"And deny myself the enjoyment of seeing you crumble and join me after years of resisting? To watch you twist and struggle to free yourself?" Helock tsked. "Do you see now, how stupid you are? How I have shown you what you really are?"

"And what is that?" Jehan demanded.

"A simple-minded Az-kye," Helock said. "A warrior I bested with barely an effort."

Jehan's teeth bared. "I'm no warrior!"

"Don't bother." Helock made a dismissive wave. "You're like the rest of them—dumb, blindly stumbling in a galaxy that left his kind behind ages ago. You cannot escape what you are Jehan—and at heart you will always be Az-kye."

"Just as you are a vicious beast!" Saria spat. "A monster that needs be destroyed!"

"I've *won*, Liri." His smile turned cruel. "And in the years to come you will learn—as Onara has—that I always do."

Etaran shifted his weight as Helock finished his drink and headed to the bar for more. "Is there anything else you will require of me, Potentate? I should return to co-ordinate the patrols."

"Of course," Helock said. "And I'm sure with your skills and patience you will rise very high indeed within the Brethren."

Etaran inclined his head. "Thank you, Potentate."

"Oh, Etaran—" Helock called, placing his snifter on the bar just as the Brethren reached for the door control. "You forgot something."

Etaran paused, puzzled. "Potentate?"

Helock turned back, lifting his blaster. "I'd never allow that."

Before he could cry out, Helock drilled two blaster bolts through his chest.

Saria scrambled back as he fell and glanced at the door, but no guards appeared to attend their Potentate. Either the room was soundproofed against even blaster fire or the men outside had been ordered not to interfere.

Helock turned his weapon on Jehan. "Would you be so kind as to hand your blaster over? The hold out one you're carrying too. No, better yet, Onara—" His lips twitched. "You go disarm him."

Trembling, her face pale, Onara scurried forward.

"I'm sorry," she whispered as she took the snub blaster hidden in his boot.

"It's okay." He met her gaze as she took the sidearm from the holster at his hip. "It's not your fault."

"Well, what shall we drink to now?" Helock asked, taking Jehan's blasters from Onara and tossing them aside before holstering his own. "I know!" The Potentate lifted his glass again. "To your efforts, Jehan, to garner support among the disaffected of my Brethren," Helock said, taking a sip of his liquor. "You have helped me cull the herd."

"Didn't Kel ferret them out for you?" Jehan asked.

Helock shrugged. "He gathered a list of those who 'might' follow him. Not the same as committing themselves to *your* cause." He tilted his head. "You were far better liked than Kel. Even some I thought would never follow him were eager to join *you*."

Jehan sank down, the snifter in his hand. "So they're dead then? All who were with me? That's nearly a third of the Brethren."

"A little more, actually," Helock waved. "But yes, dead. Every last one."

Jehan closed his eyes for a moment.

"You've lost it all. And now I have everything. Including"—his icy glance flicked to Saria—"the woman you love." His mouth curled into a cold smile. "I promise I will make good use of her."

Saria stiffened in revulsion, but Jehan regarded the potentate with the inscrutable look of an Az-kye warrior.

"Didn't you hear me?" Helock asked sharply. "I've beaten you! No one is coming to help you, the house is surrounded by my *loyal* Brethren and you will die here, very slowly, watching as I rape your woman!"

Jehan's expression did not change. He simply sat, his dark gaze never leaving Helock.

"I *won*!" Spittle appeared at the corners of Helock's mouth, his cheeks showing two bright spots of color. "Are you just going to sit there, dullard? Do *something*!"

"I am doing something," Jehan said. "I'm waiting."

"Waiting?" Helock scoffed. "Waiting for *what*?"

Jehan lifted his goblet and the glass caught the fading light of the afternoon suns, turning the liquor within blood red. "For the poison to kill you."

"*Poison?*" Helock burst out, a touch of fear reverberating through his disbelief. "There's no way you could have—"

"You should know to be more careful," Onara snarled, "who you trust with your liquor, Helock."

The potentate's eyes widened. As if the thing were filled with venomous snakes he dropped the glass, the contents spilling across the white carpet as he threw himself in the direction of the bar, frantically inputting a code on the control panel.

Nothing happened.

"I've had a very talented engineer doing runs with me for years on the *Selini's Song,* but"—Jehan set his own glass down on a nearby table and stood—"I'm sure you know that. Mig mouths off like anything, throws a mean punch too, but she knows how to remotely isolate a security system better than anyone."

"It's not possible!" Helock hissed, inputting the code again. "I had her followed! She was never near this house!"

In an instant Onara darted forward to relieve the potentate of his blaster. Helock turned to catch her and stopped short, clutching his belly with a groan as Onara leveled the weapon at him.

"No," Jehan agreed. "But one of the owners of the shop where you buy so much of Onara's wardrobe is a friend of Mig's, and of mine actually. She's a good first officer and—I'm told—a fine Ornament. She's one hard-working girl, our Jul, knows a lot about clothes—and, of course, smuggling contraband."

"Thanks for the new gowns." Onara indicated the beading at the shoulder of her dress. "Turns out they had of all kinds of goodies."

Clutching his middle, Helock took a step toward the door, toward the loyal Brethren guarding the hall.

"I'd be surprised if you made it half way there," Jehan mused. "But if it makes you feel better to try, by all means, Potentate . . ."

Helock took another stumbling step, then doubled over, panting.

"And you know I hate to break my word to anyone so," Jehan continued. "I will be keeping that deal I made with Governor Chol after all. I'll order the Brethren out of the house using your codes. Along with the rest of your glorious, *loyal* brothers; they'll be picked up in that massive sweep I arranged with Chol's security force. I'm sure some of the Brethren will shoot it out with Security but the survivors will spend the rest of their lives on penal colonies, scattered throughout Tellaran space."

"They will . . . hunt you . . . *down*!" Helock spat.

"No one's going to be looking for me," Jehan assured. "I'm sure Etaran already relayed to your loyal Brethren that I wasn't going to be leaving here alive. My name—along with Onara's and Liri's—will be on the governor's 'killed before apprehended' list. But *you*, Potentate, along with all your wealth, will vanish. Governor Chol will see to it the story leaks out that you cut a deal in return for freedom, your money and a new identity. Word of your betrayal will spread, even to the surviving Brethren on the penal colonies."

"No—no one will—"

"Believe it?" Jehan supplied. "After you once marooned half your crew on a drifting wreck and left them to die? After you just personally ordered the deaths of hundreds of Brethren? You've built an empire on other people's blood, Potentate. No one will doubt you betrayed the Brethren to save your own hide. Although anyone who comes looking for you to get revenge"—he spread his hands—"will be chasing a ghost."

"Your word—!' Helock panted, his face red and soaked with sweat. "In this room you—made a blood oath of—loyalty—"

"Yes, I did," Jehan said solemnly and his eyes met hers. "I just didn't make it to you."

Saria's throat tightened. "Jehan . . ."

"The codes I gave Etaran are—fakes," Helock choked out. "Your own codes have been wiped out. Only *my* command sequences control the Brethren now." His mouth stretched into a pained, gleeful smile. "And you don't have them."

"You're right, I don't," Jehan agreed. "But Onara does."

"O—Onara?"

Jehan tilted his head. "Why do you think I left here when you offered her to me that first night? She's my friend, my best friend's sister, why the hells would I leave her behind—leave her with *you*? It wasn't because I was worried Liri would be jealous, though I'm sure that's what you thought," he said as the blonde woman came to stand next to him. "I needed someone at your stronghold, someone you didn't consider a threat."

"You thought you broke me long ago." Her clear blue-green eyes narrowed as she looked down on her tormentor. "That I'd become a pathetic glit biter, a terrified whore.

That I'd be far too timid to steal your codes, to help orchestrate your downfall," Onara bared her teeth. "To fill your drink with poison."

Helock's fists clenched, his face purple with rage. "You fu—"

But just as he reached for her his face contorted in pain and he collapsed.

Onara knelt beside him. "I came here to settle our debt, remember?" she asked when Helock's pain had eased enough for him to look up at her. "It's taken years for me to collect, to make you pay for murdering my brother. You destroyed everything he worked for and you took him from me so now I'm taking everything of yours, Potentate—your wealth, your so-called 'dominion', those filthy thugs you call the Brethren. Oh," she added as Helock gasped, his back arching in pain, "and, of course, your miserable, worthless life."

When the spasm passed, Onara turned his face toward her.

"There's one last thing I want you to know before you go, Helock. We"—she leaned forward to speak in his ear—"*win!*"

The Potentate made a final choking sound then went still, his ice-blue eyes staring sightlessly.

"Onara?" Jehan asked quietly.

Onara pushed her fingers against Helock's fleshy throat then let out a shaky breath. "Dead."

Jehan offered her his hand to help her up, and the Tellaran woman trembled as she stood. "Are you okay?"

She nodded. "I will be. Now."

"How did you do it?" Saria shook her head at Onara. "We were all watching. How did you manage to get the poison into his cup without any of us seeing? Without Helock seeing?"

"She couldn't," Jehan gave a rueful smile, his face pale. "I told her to put it in the bottle before we got here."

27

Race

"But how can that be? You—" Saria eyes widened in horror. "Oh, gods!"

Jehan held up his hand. "I'll be all right. I drank a whole lot less than he did. And I cut it with ice, remember? I have plenty of time to get treatment."

"He's lying," Onara said bluntly. "He doesn't know that."

"We must get you to a medcenter now!" Saria cried, seizing his hand.

He resisted her pull. "Nobody wants to get there faster than I do, believe me. But all this will be for nothing if we don't destroy the Brethren."

"Jehan, you cannot—!"

"Liri," he broke in, perspiration dotting his brow. "I have enough time to bring down the Brethren and get to the medcenter but I absolutely *don't* have time to argue about it." He cupped her cheek, his dark gaze intent. "You and I will never be free—or safe—unless we smash the Brethren completely. I have to do this."

"If you will not go before that—" Saria nodded reluctantly. "Then let it be done quickly. What is needed?"

"We've got to get to a working control panel. Onara, is there another one in this room?"

"No, but there's one in the dining room."

"We can't let anyone see me and we sure can't let anyone see *them*," Jehan said with a glance at Helock and Etaran.

"Wait here," Onara said, already turning that way. "I'll go."

"Hold on!" Jehan caught her by the arm. "There's at least a dozen Brethren inside the house and even more on the grounds!"

"Brethren who are *used* to seeing me running around doing Helock's bidding!" Onara shook him off impatiently, every bit of the frightened, drug-addled prisoner gone. "I'll make sure the dining room is clear then I'll lock the doors and obscure the windows."

His jaw hardened. "You aren't going alone. Give me my blaster back and—"

"And what?" Onara demanded. "How far do you think we'll get in a running firefight if they see you? We wouldn't even reach the security shield! Besides, I'm not done taking from Helock yet. Leaving the Brethren intact is *not* an option. And you've got your own work to do here, remember?"

Jehan's mouth settled into a grim line but he let her go. Onara hurried to the door to the dining room, and in an instant she slumped her shoulders and lowered her head—once again transforming into the beaten concubine.

"Never piss off a Zartani woman, Liri," Jehan grumbled as soon as the door shut behind her. "Not even Ren'thar can be as vengeful as they are."

"I shall remember it so," Saria assured him, searching his pale face. "What did she mean, your own work? What needs done?"

He pulled a small metal card from his pocket. "It's not going to be fun."

She gaze went to the dead potentate. "You need to copy his retinal scan."

"And quick," he agreed, heading to where Helock lay. "Before the tissue degrades."

"Tell me what to do," she said instantly.

"I'll need about a quarter glass of water," he said, readying the device.

When she returned with the cup he was kneeling beside the Brethren leader. She took up position on the man's other side.

Jehan readied the recording device. "I need you to moisten the eye a bit so I can get a good scan. The replicator will do the rest." His gaze met hers. "Can you do this?"

"I think you will find"—she hardened her jaw—"I can do whatever is required of me."

He gave a faint smile. "You're a lot tougher than you look."

"Most women are," she said, bending to her work. "How long will this replicated scan last?"

"If we're lucky? An hour. But that's all we'll need if we get a good imprint."

Jehan frowned as he manipulated the device. After a long moment the replicator flashed green.

"Okay," Jehan said, shifting position. "Let's get the left."

"Do you need both?" Saria asked. All the other locks she observed the Tellarans use required only one eye scan.

"Most people use their right eye for a scan." He readied the replicator again. "You might be able to rig a lock to pilfer one eye scan without your subject catching on but not two. If I were Helock I sure as hells wouldn't trust the power to control my personal army to a single scan.

There," he said, standing, as the device flashed green. "We're done."

Even crossing the room to retrieve his blaster had Jehan's face blanching.

"Perhaps you should rest," she urged.

He holstered his weapon, sweat beading on his forehead. "No time and it wouldn't help anyway."

Saria caught his hand. It felt clammy in hers. "Jehan, we should leave, *now*, go to the medcenter and leave the Brethren for—"

"No. I have to order the Brethren out of the house first, away from the compound, and get them where the governor's forces can capture them easily. That's the only way we'll be free, Liri." His fingers intertwined with hers. "The only way you'll be safe. Ren'thar to your Lashima, remember?" He offered a wry smile. "You're bringing out all my nasty honorable instincts."

"We're clear," Onara said sharply from the doorway.

"Come on." Jehan urged Saria into the dining room but she froze as a couple of black-coated Brethren walked by the window.

"It's all right." Onara's gaze narrowed at the passing men. "We can see out but they can't see in. Jehan," she urged, hurrying across the room, "the panel's here."

"Well, let's see how good these copies are."

Saria stood at his shoulder, watching as he activated the panel. As soon as the ID input flashed, he held the replication up to the red scan light. For a moment there was no response. Saria held her breath. Suddenly another scan input lit up.

"Told you," Jehan said, holding up the copy of Helock's left retina.

A heartbeat later the system came online. Jehan moved aside as Onara entered Helock's command codes.

"We're in," The Tellaran woman said shortly and stepped back.

"Time to spread the net." Jehan's fingers flew over the controls, sending orders to the Brethren throughout the system.

"That's it," he said quietly.

Saria turned toward the windows, her stomach sinking as the men continued their patrols.

"Come on," Jehan muttered, the hair around his temples damp now. "Come *on*."

Saria hardened her jaw, ready to insist that they fight their way out—

"Look!" Onara cried.

Outside, the Brethren were swiftly gathering, pulling the bewildered and frightened household staff along with them as they ran from all parts of the compound toward the shuttles—which even now were powering up. From all throughout the stronghold Brethren were heading for the shuttles, loading the servants in and scrambling onboard themselves, the first lifting off now.

"They have obeyed your commands." Saria caught Jehan's hand, his fingers like ice now. "It is time to go."

"Not safe yet, not till the house is clear," he said hoarsely. "Not until the last of them are gone."

"Jehan—"

He rallied for a moment, cutting her off. "Liri, in a few minutes the whole compound will be empty, the security field shut down, and we can just walk out of here." Jehan caught himself against the wall. "Scratch that; we'll borrow one of Helock's groundcars and *drive* out."

It seemed an age until the last of the black-coated men was onboard, till the doors closed on the last shuttle before it lifted off, racing away like the others toward the eastern mountains.

"Enough," Saria said firmly. "We are going *now*."

"You're the boss," he said, his voice scratchy. "Just let me get the security fields down and lock the system."

He swayed a little and Saria caught him, pulling his arm around her shoulder and wrapping her own around his waist. "Onara!"

Instantly the Tellaran woman took over, putting in the codes herself and unlocking the dining room door.

"I'll get a groundcar!" Onara called over her shoulder, heading into the empty hall at a run. "Meet me outside!"

It was twilight now. Gooseflesh rose on Saria's skin at the echo of their footsteps in the marble hall. The mansion seemed nothing now but a cold sprawling, mausoleum, empty but for them, its dead master, and the recreant who had betrayed them.

Apparently Jehan felt it too. "Think he'll haunt the place?"

"I think—" Saria huffed. Jehan, tall and broad as any warrior—and as heavy—was leaning hard on her. "Helock will be too occupied suffering the greatest torments of the nine hells to dally here."

If the potentate's spirit did indeed stalk behind them he could not pass the threshold of the front door because Saria felt instantly warmed despite the gathering darkness as they stepped down into the courtyard.

At the controls of the lavish vehicle Onara came fast around the corner—so fast the groundcar's back end swung out as she slammed to a stop.

The door opened upward and Jehan, groaning, practically fell in.

"Go!" Saria cried, scrambling in beside him.

Onara had clearly overridden the safety protocols because she engaged the forward drive before the door even shut: Saria had to grab at the seat padding to keep from being thrown out. She ducked her head, holding her hand to her face protectively as pebbles and dust spat at her through the opening. The door finally sealed shut just as they blew past the gate of Helock's compound.

"Hold on, Jehan!" Onara increased the groundcar's speed. "I've already signaled ahead to the nearest med center. We need to keep him conscious so keep him talking, Liri!"

Saria shifted to pull Jehan against her.

"Sweetheart," he rasped. "If I don't make it, I've already told Mig to—"

"You gave me your vow to live!" Saria cradled him closer, his head against her shoulder. "I do not take promises as lightly as Tellarans do, Jehan!"

"Okay, subject change." He was shivering, his face and hair soaked with sweat. "You been following the bolo ball playoffs? I'm rooting for the Apovians, myself."

"How could you do such?" she demanded, ignoring his attempt at humor. "Stand before me and drink *poison*?"

"Believe it or not this wasn't my original plan. This one just got thrown together at the end. You know—" He shifted, his brow knitting in pain. "I really liked my other plan better."

"Why did you not tell me what you intended to do?" she asked tightly.

"I just had this crazy idea that if I told you, you might be against it. Besides, from childhood, warriors teach their sons to show no fear, hide their feelings behind a mask. They don't do that with the girls, and good thing too—" He gave her a smile, his brow damp now with perspiration. "After all, how the hells would us men know when we've said something really stupid?"

"You feared I would give you away?" she asked, hurt. "Did you not trust me?"

"It was more like I didn't think you'd be behind the whole 'drink poison with the potentate' idea and you'd wind up scowling at me. And see? I was right."

"You would not let me drink it," she realized. "You nudged me toward the tea so I would not."

"I didn't have to push that hard, Liri. You looked like a kid at Lashima's sweetmeats celebration about to be handed a plate of vegetables instead."

"How did you know what he would drink? What to poison? He might have chosen any liquor."

"To crow over the defeat of an Az-kye?" Jehan snorted. "No, as soon as I got Onara's message this afternoon that Helock acquired an ancient bottle of kanak I knew that's what he'd be drinking. I suppose he thought it was funny."

"No wonder you were so confident you could gain entrance to the house. Helock *wanted* us there." Saria wiped his brow with the skirt of her gown. "Did you know Etaran would betray us?"

"A Brethren with a soft heart, one fretting over a sister and her kids in danger, who just *happens* to show up with Helock's stolen codes and ready to throw his support with me just when I need him?" Jehan's laugh turned into a cough. It was a long moment before he could speak again. "I might be charming, Liri, but I'm sure as fuck not that lucky."

"You knew it all along? He fooled me completely."

"No. I didn't trust him, of course, but I was starting to think he was a decent man—for a Brethren anyway. But I had Mig run a check on everybody Helock assigned to me, so when Etaran came offering to make me potentate tonight I knew he never *had* a sister. But fuck, he had skill, I'll say that for him. Made a point to say he was a Tir street kid—like Erit and me and Onara were—implied that this was the only hope to protect you, led me along just enough so I'd think the decision was mine." He clasped her hand tightly. "I hated taking you there, sweetheart, to Helock's, knowing it was a trap. But I also knew it was a golden chance—our best chance. Helock was going to dispose of whoever had sided against him anyway and—" He wet his lips. "It's not honorable by any stretch but he killed nearly a third of the Brethren for us today. All I had to do was let him."

"And you feel guilty?" she asked gently. "For their deaths?"

"These people got shot in the back by their 'brothers.'"

"But not by you," she said, stroking his hair. "Nor could you have saved them, any more than you could the Brethren who died for Helock's staged attack this morning."

"Gods, that man was a lunatic." He shook his head, his brow damp with perspiration. "It never occurred to me he was behind that. Speaking of fooling people, Onara—if I'd known why you went years ago . . . I would have been there for you and I'm really—"

"Don't worry about that now," the Tellaran woman said shortly. "We've avenged Erit. Our job now is to outlive the bastard who killed him by decades. Got it?"

"And so you," Saria said to Onara, "passed messages to Jul and Jul to Mig and then Mig," she looked at Jehan, "to you."

"Only way," Jehan rasped. "With Helock monitoring our every move, every comm call and everyone around us being subjected to scans. No fancy codes, no comm trace, just tiny handwritten notes hidden in a woman's hair."

Saria frowned. "But Jul's hair is cut short."

"Well—" He coughed again. "She might have hidden them somewhere else; I didn't ask."

"I was right." She shook her head. "You truly are incorrigible."

He grinned, his dark eyes in stark contrast to his pallor. This time the coughing wracked through his chest. "I"—his lips pressed together and it was a moment before he could continue—"love . . .you."

"And," her vision blurred as she stroked his hair, "I love you, Jehan."

His pained eyes opened wide. "You—?"

She smiled down at him through tears. "Did you think even I could resist your charm, beloved?"

His face softened. "Liri, I—"

He gasped, arching back against the seat, the tendons of his neck standing out, his mouth open in silent agony.

"Jehan!"

Suddenly he went limp against her, his mouth slack, his face deathly pale.

Saria shook him, his head lolling to the side. "He is not breathing!"

In response the Tellaran woman accelerated, the groundcar hurling through the city streets, hapless pedestrians racing to get out of their way. Frantically Saria felt at Jehan's neck but there was no sign of a pulse. She pressed her hand to his chest, desperate to feel a heartbeat.

There was nothing but stillness.

"Onara, we must—!"

The groundcar came to such a sudden stop that Saria was pitched off the seat, hitting her shoulder against the padded back of the driver's seat.

Jehan landed atop her, hard enough to knock the breath from her lungs, pinning her on the groundcar's floor under his weight.

Then the door opened, letting in cool evening air and the bright light of the medcenter.

"Here!" Onara cried. "He's here!"

"Move!" One of the medtechs pushed Onara aside, seizing Jehan under his arms and yanking him out. Two other medtechs were quickly maneuvering a stretcher into place.

"Ready?" the medtech snapped to one of his fellows. The other man caught Jehan's legs and together they lifted him onto the stretcher. Instantly monitors on the stretcher sprang to life and sounded alarms. Then the men were speeding with Jehan, moving at a run through the center doors.

The remaining medtech gripped Saria's arm to help her out, already running an instrument over her to check her for injury.

"Release me this instant!" Saria snapped, yanking her arm out of his grip.

"Just a—"

She pushed against the groundcar to launch herself forward, beating Onara through the doors and into the center.

For a moment the bright interior, the quiet civility of the medcenter, disoriented her. Then down a long hallway she spied them maneuvering Jehan's stretcher into one of the rooms. She broke into a full run, Onara at her heels. At the threshold to Jehan's door Saria skidded to a stop.

Tellaran healers were crowded around him, their displays showing green.

One of the healers, a white-haired man, sent her an annoyed look then gestured to one of his assistants. "Get them out of here!"

"How is he?" Saria cried. "I command you answer me! How is he?"

The healer shook his head and gestured to one of the medtechs. "Shut it down."

"Damn it," Onara choked out. "Damn it."

"No!" Saria's frantic glance went from display to display as the staff, a moment ago so focused, stepped back dejected. "He breathes! His heart beats!"

"He's on total support," the healer said shortly. "But he's gone. I'm sorry."

"*No!*" A medtech caught her arm and Saria struggled against the man's pull. "Let me go! *Jehan!*"

28

ᏇᏃ ᏆᏃᏏᏂ ᏉᏐᏃᏂ

At the Gate

Jehan's eyes flew open.

A brilliant blue sky above came into focus. Gasping, he pushed himself up, instinctively taking a fighter's crouch. His frown deepened as he took in the open field, the soft, cool grass under his fingers, the sweet scent of meadow flowers on the air.

He quickly scanned the grassland but he was alone here. There was no sound.

No birds, no rustle of leaves, no insects.

None.

"What the fuck?" he muttered as he stood, the black leather of his clothing supple and smooth.

Startled, he looked down to see himself in full warrior clothing. Instinctively he reached over his shoulder, only to find the scabbard at his back empty.

"Have you lost it?"

He spun around at the Az-kye words, his heart thundering, forgetting for once that there would be no one there—

"Father?" he breathed.

Delar of the B'tai raised his eyebrows. "Have you forgotten me, my son? You stare at me so."

"You're just . . ." Jehan shook his head. "So young. And . . . *short.*"

His father laughed, a deep booming laugh. He'd forgotten that, the sound of his father's laughter.

That his father had *ever* laughed.

"You have grown taller than I indeed, my son." His father looked at him in warm approval and his smile turned wistful. "But your eyes are still your mother's."

Jehan shook his head. "What are you doing here? You can't be here. You're—Wait . . ." He turned, his glance darting about the verdant landscape. "Where the hells are we?"

"I do not care for this coarse language, Jehan."

"You want me to stop cursing?" Jehan rounded on him. "Then tell me where the fuck we are."

His father's heavy brows came down in a scowl. "You are the son of a clan leader and—"

"And you need to tell me where we are, Father!" Jehan broke in.

His father indicated the sunny meadow. "The fields."

"The fields?" Jehan echoed. "*What* fields?"

"The fields . . . Between."

His father looked back, and Jehan followed his glance. In the distance where before there had been nothing now stood a city, a vast, ancient, brilliant city full of color—

"Az-kye," Jehan whispered, shivering despite the sunny day. "We're on Az-kye. That's the gate of the Imperial City."

His father shook his head. "That is the Gate to the City of the Gods."

"Wait, you mean—" His shivering got worse, like ice was running through his veins. "I'm dead?"

"You are *Between*."

His shoulders fell in relief. "So not dead?"

"Between," his father assured.

"Why is it so cold here?"

"*I* am not cold."

"And even if you were," Jehan grumbled, shivering, "you wouldn't complain, would you?"

His father smiled faintly. "No, I would not." He studied Jehan. "Why are you here?"

"You mean instead of inside the city where it's probably nice and toasty?" He rubbed his hands together, trying to get the feeling back into them. "I guess the gods don't want me there. Because I'm Tellaran now. Because I didn't live like a warrior."

"You are my son," his father reminded. "You are clothed as a warrior. Surely the gods have not erred to garb you so."

"I don't have a sword," Jehan pointed out. "And you do. Which makes no fucking sense since I know for certain that sword is hidden."

"Perhaps that is why you do not have your sword," his father said. "Because it is hidden."

Jehan blew his breath out. "It's the same sword, Father. You *gave* your sword to me, remember?"

"Then you have not lost it after all." He tilted his head. "But that does not explain how you came to be here."

Jehan wasn't sure whether he really was outside the City of the Gods or the poison was just making him delusional, but it suddenly seemed really, really important to explain this to his father in a way a warrior could understand.

"There was an enemy—a Tellaran—someone I had to defeat. I tricked him, I defeated him, but to do it I had to drink poison with him. I guess I'm—*Between*—because I didn't get here the way I should have."

His father's eyebrows rose. "And what way is that?"

"Combat, fighting a Challenge, the warrior way—*your* way."

"You chose to drink poison?"

"You think I wanted to drink it?" Jehan demanded.

"Then why do so?"

"Because he was evil. Because guile was the only way I was ever going win against a complete fucking sociopath!"

"No, Jehan—why?"

"I just *told* you." Jehan passed his hand over his face. Dead or not, getting his father to understand anything not strictly traditional—not Az-kye—was a huge pain in the ass. "It was the only way to win, Father!"

"You could have run. You had money to disappear. A fortune at your command." Delar held out his hand. Resting in his palm were the astuk crystals Jehan had taken from the *Ty'har,* the rainbow-hued jewels breathtakingly radiant in this otherworldly land. "Enough to vanish into the Tellaran worlds, did you not?"

"And what kind of life would that be, Father?" Jehan threw his hands out in frustration. "To spend our whole lives looking over our shoulders—never knowing if she's safe from that monster!"

His father tilted his head. "She?"

"Liri," he said hoarsely. "It was the only way to protect Liri. She's—I love her."

"To sacrifice yourself," his father said gravely. "To keep your mate, your children, safe requires far more than a sword." Suddenly the crystals in Delar's palm crumbled into bright, glittering dust that rose, swirling, to be carried away by the breeze. "Perhaps you are more of a warrior than you know, Jehan."

"I'm sorry," Jehan blurted, "about that night. The things I said—"

His father's hand came to rest on Jehan's shoulder, the only warmth in this frigid place. "You were little more than a boy then. A frightened child in a strange place. We should have left you on the homeworld, safe in the clanhouse with your aunt, your cousins, not wandering Tellaran space, outcast with us."

"I wanted to come with you. I wouldn't let you leave without me," Jehan said thickly. "But—can you tell Mother? How sorry I am?"

His father's face turned toward the distant, bright gate.

"Is she—" Jehan followed his father's glance. "Is that where Mother is?"

"Oh, yes," his father replied easily. "My Esara sups in Lashima's hall, strolls with her ancestors through the heavens in the evenings."

"You said I'm not dead," Jehan frowned. "But you *are.* Why are you here?"

"Once through the Gate of the City of the Gods, it is forbidden to return." Delar met his gaze. "Before she died your mother bade me safeguard you, Jehan. So here I stay. *Between.*"

He knew he hadn't been imagining those annoying nudges at the edge of his consciousness, the whispered reproaches about how a warrior should comport himself, but . . .

A lump formed in Jehan's throat. "You made yourself a spirit—for me?"

"For you." His father sent a longing look toward the city. "And for her."

"You don't have to stay here alone anymore, Father," Jehan said thickly. "Go inside. Go to Mother."

His father smiled. "We will go in together and be home in time for the evening meal."

"Home?"

The warmth of his father's hand on his shoulder spread through Jehan's body and suddenly he wasn't cold at all anymore.

"Yes." Jehan smiled back. "Yes, let's go home, Father."

The city wasn't as far away as he'd thought; it was close enough now that it wouldn't be a long walk at all. From here it seemed very like the Imperial city he remembered from childhood, with gardens and music and the smell of the sticky quen'dila the street vendors sold—

No!

"Liri?" Jehan stopped short, hesitating just outside the brilliant gate.

"Come along, Jehan," his father urged. "Your mother is waiting for us. Do you not see? She is just there ahead."

"I can't." Here it was sunny, warm and brighter than ever, but there, in the distance, where *Liri* was, a storm raged. "She's alone . . . She's in pain. Father, I have to go back!"

The moment he turned his father's hand slipped from Jehan's shoulder and a cold blast slammed into him, the icy wind blurring his vision.

Let me go!

"Liri!"

He leaned hard into the gale, fighting for every step, seeking her in that dark chaos.

Jehan!

The storm ripped through the fields, blotting out the sun, sending such a wave of icy pain through his body it forced him to his hands and knees. His fingers digging into the ground, he crawled toward her, gasping against the agony tearing through his belly.

His teeth chattering, he looked up to find his father had followed him back into the fields.

"Father, go!" he choked, forcing the words through the pain, trying to be heard above the howling wind. "Go to the City!"

"I will abide here a while longer, my son," his father said smiling, himself untouched by either cold or storm. "Between."

Jehan drew breath to argue, but the air was foul and he choked on it, coughing. The tempest closed around him, smothering him. For a moment he flailed in it, and then somehow, in the darkness and pain and chaos, he caught hold of her hand—

29

Paths

His eyes fluttered. "Liri . . ."

"I am here." Saria's heart warmed, and she sent up a prayer of thanks at the strength in his grip now. "How do you feel?"

She had fought bitterly with the Tellaran healers, cursing them as they cut support, the machines going dark. They let her go to him then but all she could do was stand at his side shivering, silent tears running down her face. Sobbing, she took her hand in his, murmuring his name. . .

Then suddenly his fingers closed around hers and he gasped, drawing breath again on his own.

Now, hours later, his face was pinched, his lips pale as he took in the medcenter room around him.

"Water . . ." he rasped.

She poured a cup and helped him, holding the cup steady, supporting his shoulders as he drank.

Jehan nodded to show he'd had enough and fell back onto the pillows, a touch more color in his face now. "It's evening. Same day?"

"Yes."

"Doesn't seem like it." He shivered. "Why do they keep these places so fucking cold anyway? I feel like someone just filtered all my blood through ice."

She went to the room's small closet and spread another blanket over him. "They did filter it," she said, brushing his hair back. "But I do not think they used ice. It was the only way to completely clear your system of the poison."

"That's a little better." He gave her a smile. "Don't suppose I could get you to climb in here with me?"

"I do not think your doctors would approve."

He raised his eyebrows. "Well, you're awfully dour."

"*Dour?* You were *dead*, Jehan."

"I know," he said quietly, all humor gone from his face, his fingers entwining with hers. "I remember."

"You remember?" she asked, startled. "What do you remember, Jehan?"

"My father—" He shook his head. "Never mind. Where's Onara?"

"Overseeing the transfer of funds with the governor's representative."

"Making sure the good governor takes only the third we promised him of Helock's fortune, I'm sure." The skin around his eyes tightened. "The Brethren?"

"I am told nearly half of those left were killed. The others have been captured by the Tellaran Security forces."

Jehan glanced at the door. "And the governor's kept his word?"

"Two of his guards stand outside but I have been assured that all record of your being here has been deleted." She tilted her head. "Somehow I think the governor is surprised you were able to succeed."

"My father raised me to either win or die with honor," Jehan said. "Since I can't do the latter, I'm stuck with the former, I guess."

"And now that you have won," Saria ventured, "what will you do?"

"Accept my third of Helock's wealth and my sparkling new ID from the governor," he said, sitting up. "And finally do what I've wanted since my feet hit Halea's dirt: get the hells out of here. Have a home again. I don't even care which Tellaran world really—Okay, not Zartan. Zartan might as well *be* in the Empire with all their traditions and noble bloodline crap. Maybe Sertar. The only difference between the Sertarians and the Brethren is a very thin veneer of civilization. I'd likely do very well there."

Saria looked away. "You might as well stay here then."

"I don't care which world, you pick. Apovia, Nima, even Zartan if you like, and I'll be happy. If you're with me." He looked younger somehow and his fingers lightly intertwined with hers. "If you'll marry me."

"Marry?" she breathed.

"It would have to be in Arrena's temple," he said, his words coming out in a rush. "There are no temples to Lashima in the Realm but maybe the Tellaran's goddess of love could stand in for the Queen of Heaven just this one time, don't you think?"

She wet her lips. "You do not sound sure."

"Oh, I'm sure," he said. "And thank the gods I'm not a warrior 'cause I'm just going to say that my heart's going like a tantalope right now." He cupped her face. "But I love you, Liri. I love you and I want to marry you."

"Jehan," she whispered, "the things I have kept from you—"

"They won't make any difference."

Her vision blurred. "I fear they will change everything. I cannot marry you," she warned hoarsely, "until I have told you all."

A grin spread across his face.

"Why do you smile so?" she demanded. "I am serious, Jehan!"

"You said 'until.' You just agreed to marry me."

"I did not! I said—"

"You *said* 'until,'" he insisted, grinning. "That means 'yes.' Yes, you'll marry me. Just say it."

Saria wet her lips. "I—"

Alari now sat upon the Az-kye throne with her Tellaran mate by her side and by all accounts over the past several weeks, she ruled well. And Alari's mating to a Tellaran man, despised as it had been, placed her in a far better position to stave off war with the Realm. A Tellaran Consort would do a great deal to smooth the way to peace.

The Princess Saria was thought dead but the succession had been decided. For her to return now, to demand she be restored as Heiress, would throw the empire into a civil war that would tear it apart. Even to simply go home, to take up the place of Second, would split the clan leaders. Many would rise up in favor of her rule, but just as many would seek her death—

To go home meant her only hope to survive would be to destroy Alari and her supporters. In the end she, like Empress Liri, might indeed be victorious and claim the throne, but the cost would be staggering. The empire itself would be soaked with innocent blood to place that crown upon her head.

She was an Imperial Daughter, taught from birth that the needs of the Az-kye must come first, no matter what sacrifice it demanded of her personally.

Alari was First, always. It is her birthright to rule. I despised being in her shadow, despised that my life would be lived on the edges, always the lesser sister.

Perhaps we have both come to be, my sister and I, where the gods always intended we should. Alari on the throne and I—

She looked into Jehan's joyous eyes, her heart so full for a moment she could not even speak.

"I love you, Jehan," she said softly. "And if, when you know my secrets, you want me, then I will marry you."

30

ᎳᏣᎵᎦᎧ Ꮣ᙭ᎱᎦᎧ

Clear Skies

Jehan's face fairly glowed as he pulled her toward him. "Liri . . ."

His utterance sent a slashing pain through her chest. "Jehan, first you must know—"

The opening door cut off her confession and the man, his gray uniform marking him as a member of the governor's staff, his eyebrows rising at the intimate scene, stopped in the doorway.

"Apologies, I didn't mean to interrupt."

"But since you have," Jehan said, annoyed, "what do you want?"

"I—of course." The door closed behind him, his boots clicking across the medcenter's white floor as he walked. "I am Nel Praom, Governor Chol's personal secretary. I will escort you to the governor's palace as soon as the doctors release you from their care."

Saria and Jehan exchanged a look.

"So soon?" she asked. "Surely he needs more rest."

"I have just spoken to the chief physician. His preference is that you remain another night. However"—Nel straightened—"he does deem you well enough to be released under the circumstances."

"In other words, the governor wants me off-world as fast as possible," Jehan said.

"It was you, Captain Dekra, who insisted upon the need for both speed and secrecy," the man pointed out. "As well as the establishment of new IDs and a considerable monetary reward."

"Actually we're giving *him* a share of Helock's wealth," Jehan corrected. "Not the other way around."

"Nonetheless." He clasped his hands behind his back. "I am sure you are as eager to conclude this business as His Excellency is." He glanced at Saria. "And to return to your own affairs."

"What you lack in diplomacy, Nel Praom," Saria said coolly, "you more than make up for in tactlessness."

Nel's mouth parted but Jehan laughed, cutting the man off before he could speak.

"All right, Praom, go get me released and we'll get this over with."

"I have arranged transport for you both to the governor's palace but I must also orchestrate an inconspicuous departure from the medcenter," he said shortly. "We should be underway in twenty minutes."

With a final narrow look at Saria, he left, shutting the door behind him.

She turned toward the room's small wardrobe. "Your clothes are—"

"Not so fast," he said, catching her hand in his. "You have a few things to tell me, don't you?"

"I—" Saria's mouth went dry.

"I know you're afraid." He intertwined his fingers with hers. "There's no reason to be. If I can down a snifter of poisoned brandy, I think I can handle a few secrets."

"I hope you speak true," she blurted. "I pray you love me still."

"Are you already married?"

Her brow knitted. "No."

"Killed anyone?"

"No." Her frown deepened. "Should we reckon Helock's death? I was culpable in that, I think."

"You didn't kill him. Onara and I did. Ugly as it was, it *was* justice—well, as close to justice as you get in the Badlands—for Erit, for a thousand other lives Helock destroyed. I know it lacked the glory of fighting in the Circle, with Ren'thar's blessing choosing the winner," he said dryly. "But in this case I think even *He* would just want that scum dead."

"I wish I could argue," she said. "If only for form's sake, but I cannot."

"Well, I know you disapprove of stealing, smuggling, and piracy, so I can't imagine you're guilty of any of those. You sure didn't seem interested in working at a pleasure house so that's not it—not that that would bother me."

Her eyebrows shot up. "In truth? You would marry me freely, even if I had worked as a Companion?"

"Sure. You'd have to retire, of course. I wouldn't be on board to have you *keep* working as one. Hmm," he considered. "Deeply in debt?"

"No! And I do very much doubt, Jehan," she said exasperated, "you will *guess* the truth."

"Tell me this—" His expression turned serious. "That first night on my ship, you toasted Ren'thar, asking him for vengeance. Vengeance against who?"

"My . . . my sister."

"What did she do to make you hate her?"

"I was my mother's Heiress. My sister—" She wet her lips. "*Someone* betrayed me, tried to kill me. I believed it was she. Now . . . I am not sure."

"That's how you wound up a slave on the *Ty'har*?" he asked, his frown deepening. "Because someone tried to kill you?"

"I will tell you all if you wish; I vow it. But when I do, it will be your secret to keep as well. One that must never even be whispered." She searched his gaze. "Are you sure you want to bear such a burden, Jehan?"

"A burden shared is a burden halved," he said with a quick kiss to her palm. "We'll bear this one together."

"There is so much, you will have many questions, and I would answer them all—"

"And we're going to need more than the twenty minutes we have to get through it all," he finished for her. "Get Praom back in here. I'll tell him we'll see the governor tomorrow."

"I do not think it wise to delay this meeting," she warned. "If we are to have the life we wish, you must—*we* must—have the new identities he promised."

"It's not like he won't give them to us if we don't go tonight."

"Are you sure of that? Do you trust Governor Chol?"

"Damn it." He passed his hand over his face. "No, I fucking well *don't*. Right now we have set everything set up so he has to keep his word if he wants his share." He sighed. "Okay, sweetheart, but once our new IDs are set and the money's transferred we're getting off this rock. The minute we're spaceside, I want to know everything. And then"—he pressed a kiss to her mouth—"we get married."

31

Another Palace

"Tellarans must compensate their public servants quite well," Saria commented as their groundcar turned onto the elegantly-curving driveway and the splendid entrance came into view.

It was full night now but even that could not dim the grandeur of of the governor's palace. Thanks to the many lights illuminating it, the building's beautifully cut, brilliant white stone sparkled even at this hour, but seen in daytime, from their cliffside mansion, it had dazzled the eye indeed. The sprawling mansion was placed in such a way that it rested high on the city's eastern side, better to catch the rays of the setting suns—when most of the population of Halea would be up and about.

"Not usually *this* well," Jehan said. "But His Excellency best serves those who remember to line his pockets."

Nel Praom, the governor's secretary, regarded them with thin lips but did not disagree.

Jehan sent Praom an annoyed look as the driver went around the building and brought the groundcar to a stop at a darkened side door.

"Servants' entrance? You'd think our considerable contribution to His Excellency's fortune would buy us the *front* door."

"It hardly serves secrecy to have you enter by way of the lit façade," Nel said shortly, out the groundcar's door as soon as it opened.

"Well," Jehan muttered, offering his hand to Saria to help her out of the vehicle, "at least we'll start our new lives in style."

"We will not be here long," Saria reminded.

"Good. Onara's waiting for our signal to make the final transfer and I'm more than ready to say goodbye to this world," he murmured, gently urging her along. "Let's get this meeting over with."

"This way," Nel prompted, when they joined him inside.

This part of the governor's palace was clearly never meant for guests to see. Bare of decoration, with floors and walls of a dull, oppressive gray, it was utilitarian at best. Saria could hardly imagine having to spend most of her waking hours in such places and she suddenly wondered if the Imperial Palace had also been outfitted with such low-ceilinged hallways and cramped stairs for its servants, the ugliness kept hidden away.

They followed Nel along another corridor and up a set of dark, narrow steps. Just as Saria's chest was beginning to feel tight from the claustrophobic passage, Nel opened a door that led from behind a sweeping staircase and into a large open hallway. From the inlaid jeweled border of the marble floors and the soaring space it was clear they now stood in the receiving hall, facing the main entrance of the governor's palace.

The mansion was surprisingly quiet, no servants or guards about. Saria guessed that the staff had likely been sent to other parts of the palace in anticipation of their arrival.

"Just through here." Nel indicated two tall carved double doors. They, like the *objets d'art* of the hall, were antiques, clearly brought to this frontier colony at great expense.

A governor at ease with corruption indeed . . .

Nel turned the heavy handle and pushed the door open. It was a warm night but the palace was cooled by air exchangers, likely for the sole purpose of allowing a fire to burn brightly here.

"At last!" Chol was an older man, gray-haired and very thin with a mustache that only served to emphasize his cadaverous cheeks. His expression peeved, he rose from his chair by the ornate fireplace. "We have been waiting here an age for you!"

The woman with him, dark-haired, prettily plump and far, far younger than the governor, remained in her chair. She too looked so visibly relieved at their arrival.

"My apologies, Your Excellency, my Lady," Nel said. "May I present Captain Dekra and his . . ." he glanced at Saria, "companion, Liri."

Whether Nel knew that among the Az-kye the term was reserved for those compensated for their sexual attentions or not was unclear but Jehan threw Saria a half-amused, half-apologetic look.

"Considering the events of the evening, I would like to do another check with our security forces in the city," the secretary continued. "With your permission, Excellency?"

Chol waved his assent. As the door closed behind Nel, Jehan stepped forward.

"Your Excellency." Jehan turned his attention to the dark woman who smiled and rose, smiling, to offer her hand to him. Her many jewels—nearly as many as Saria herself had often worn—caught the light when she moved. "Lady Chol."

"We needn't be so formal," the governor's pretty wife purred. "I absolutely insist you call me Rinna."

Saria's mouth thinned at the charming smile he gave the governor's lady.

"Rinna," he repeated. "Although," he said with a curious glance toward the governor, "I confess we weren't expecting to meet you as well this evening, Rinna."

"Well," she said, not letting go of his hand, "when Trum told me what you'd done I could hardly pass up the opportunity to meet the man who saved us all from those dreadful Brethren."

"I can't take all the credit," Jehan demurred. "It was a group effort."

"I'm sure you're being too modest," Rinna simpered. "May I offer you a drink?"

"No!" Jehan said instantly then softened his tone. "I mean, I think I'll pass tonight, thanks."

"I as well," Saria volunteered, though clearly Rinna was not eager to offer *her* anything.

"In fact," Jehan put in, "we wouldn't want to take up any more of your time than necessary, Your Excellency. On the matter of our—

"Oh, surely there's no rush." Rinna linked her arm with his, her mouth forming a pout. "You must stay to supper. I'm afraid Trum's position"—she made a dismissive wave in her husband's direction—"often keeps me from meeting anyone *really* interesting."

"Unfortunately," the governor said with a tight smile, "I *do* have other matters to attend to tonight, my dear, so I think we'd better let Captain Dekra—"

"And *I* think we could at least offer the man a meal."

"That's kind," Jehan said. "But we actually have a friend already waiting for us and believe me, she's really not someone to annoy."

"But Captain—" Rinna leaned in a bit, her breast just touching Jehan's arm. "Surely there's something I can offer to whet your appetite?"

"They're in a hurry to be on their way, my pet." The governor's mouth thinned. "And as it happens, there are one or two matters I must discuss with Captain Dekra—in private. If you'll excuse us, Rinna?"

"Oh, I couldn't run off when we have guests," Rinna protested, "it would be too rude."

"You are quite right." Chol glanced at Saria. "Why don't you take our *other* guest on a short stroll through the gardens while we conclude things? Gardening is quite a passion of Rinna's. She sometimes spends half the day out there."

Over the governor's wife's head, Jehan threw Saria a frustrated glance.

"But right now," the lady gritted out, "I am quite content to stay he—"

"I would *very much* enjoy seeing the gardens." Saria took a step forward and gave her best court smile. "If you will be kind enough to show me, Lady Chol."

"Yes," Jehan put in, quickly disengaging his arm from Rinna's. "We'd both be grateful for your hospitality while we finish up in here."

Rinna threw Saria a petulant glare, accepting defeat with poor grace indeed.

"This way," she fairly snapped, sweeping past Saria.

Jehan caught Saria's arm with a grateful look. "I won't be long."

"Do not be," Saria muttered before following Rinna, who had not even bothered waiting for her, into the hall.

"You have done all this on your own?" Saria asked, impressed, as she walked beside Rinna along the garden path.

Lit to allow for the enjoyment of the greenery without detracting from the beauty of the starry evening, little enclaves dotted along the garden's serpentine paths, each honoring one of the Tellaran gods or goddesses.

Saria indicated a lush flowering tree, its purple blooms giving off a heavenly scent. "What is this one called?"

"How would I know?" Rinna asked, annoyed. "We have *gardeners* for all that."

"Oh, but—" Saria broke off as they passed a lovely, tucked away little spot dedicated to Arrena, the Tellaran's equivalent of the Az-kye's Lashima.

A fine spot for a rendezvous indeed.

"How long have you lived here?" Saria asked.

"Five years." Rinna turned her face toward the warm breeze. "I'm Trum's third wife, actually. The first one died, the second—well, she was a Zartani noblewoman. Living here didn't suit her at all."

"I did notice an age difference," Saria said diplomatically.

"Age, energy, interests." Rinna kicked at the path, sending some of the pebbles scattering. "There's a galaxy of difference between us."

"Was it an arranged match then?"

"No, just an advantageous one—for both of us. I got this," Rinna said with a gesture that took in the gardens, the governor's palace. "And he,"—she indicated her face, her figure—"got *this* standing next to him at official functions."

Saria frowned at her bitterness. "Can you not leave him?"

"Oh, he'd never let me leave. And what would I do if he did? I have no money of my own, like his second wife did. Besides," she said heavily, "he supports my mother, my brothers and sisters too. Because of this, they'll all have educations, futures."

Saria's frown deepened. This young woman—likely her own age really—was, despite her jewels, her youth, her beauty, and her position, utterly miserable.

But how happy was I, as an Imperial Daughter?

As Second, she had been no more free than this woman was. With so many depending upon her behaving properly, on graciously accepting the mate the empress would have chosen for her to solidify a political match, there was little chance for her to fashion her own life. Once mated she would have spent her time serving in the temples or acting as a patron of the arts or some other acceptable but dull pastime expected to absorb the time and attention of the younger sister of an empress. She might have indulged her love of history, perhaps even penned texts worthy enough to add to the Imperial library, but even that pleasure would have dimmed in time.

She had been even less free as Heiress. Barring Alari, who ultimately betrayed her, she had no true friends. She had cursed her fate but if Alari had not acted against her, she never would have come here, never would have known Jehan . . .

A shiver ran down her back at how close she had come to a splendid life lived with an empty heart.

"Don't feel sorry for me," Rinna said stiffly. "I've done very well for myself and all I have to do is pretty up the palace, and show up when he needs someone to stand next to him."

"I do not feel pity," Saria said honestly. "Those who sacrifice their happiness for the good of others have great courage and strength." She indicated the gardens, the shrines within it. "And I cannot but think that your gods will someday reward you for it."

Rinna searched Saria's gaze as if wondering whether she were sincere or not.

"Thank you," she said slowly. "That was . . . kind." She glanced away. "You should get back to the house. They're probably done by now."

"Are you not coming?"

Rinna shook her head. "Once you two leave, Trum'll just head into his office for the rest of the night. We're both very busy, you know. Sometimes we go days without seeing each other."

"Then it was a pleasure to meet you, Lady Chol."

Rinna smiled. For a moment she was quite lovely indeed. "You too, Liri."

Saria glanced toward the house, uncertain. "How do I—?"

"Oh, easy." She pointed. "Just follow along this path, take a left when you come to the statue of Jandar, then, at the end of the path, take a right. You'll see the stairs back up to the balcony."

Saria inclined her head to Rinna and left the pretty woman there, wondering as she walked along the path if there were a guard—or a gardener—that Rinna habitually met out here.

Some small happiness for her, I hope. . .

But to be certain, her husband must know it was not *gardening* that drew his comely wife to spend her time out here.

Together at the hospital, she and Jehan had chosen Nima as the first of the Tellaran worlds they would visit. They would explore the powder-soft beaches and crystal-clear water, and as Arrena was that world's patron goddess, marry at Her great temple there. Having seen nothing but the homeworld and Halea, combined with anticipating her new life with Jehan, had Saria's fingers tingling with excitement.

She quickened her pace and soon came upon a shrine featuring the imposing statue of a mighty Tellaran god, his muscled form composed of shimmering blue. His bearded face, both intelligent and stern glaring down at her as she passed by.

Certainly forbidding enough to be Jandar . . .

But when she reached then end of the path and turned right, the carved arch she and Lady Chol had entered under was not there. Saria frowned at the high hedge blocking her way and turned right, walking alongside it, looking for a pass-through or gate, but there was none.

She could *see* the curving stairs up to the balcony that ran the whole back side of the house; she simply could not *get* there.

Despite Rinna's instructions, Saria hurried along the other way a bit, but there was no arch through here either, only more paths leading back into the thick of the gardens.

She breathed out in annoyance. Onara awaited them already and Jehan should have concluded whatever the governor required of him. Either Lady Chol deliberately misled her or that muscular blue statue had not been of the

Tellaran war god after all and she simply had taken a wrong turn.

Dismayed to think she was delaying the beginning of their new life with her own foolishness, Saria narrowed her gaze up at the balcony into the house, visible from where she stood. She could retrace her steps and hope for Rinna, or someone else, would lead her out or—

Saria walked along until she found a spot where the hedge was sparsest and, Imperial Daughter though she was, got down on her knees to crawl through.

Sparse or not, the branches caught at her clothes, face, and hair. Setting her jaw, she managed to push her way through.

She stood, brushing dirt from her palms and clothes, passing her hands over her hair to free it of leaves. Proud to have taken the most expedient way and *very* much hoping that she had not been observed from the house—she could easily imagine Jehan's laughter at seeing her battle the hedge—Saria hurried up the stairs.

Crossing the balcony, she turned the handle of the first glass door, only to find it locked.

The next four were locked as well. Muttering one of Jehan's favorite curses she went on to the fifth, vowing that if this one did not open she would pound on it until someone came. Luckily, the antiquated handle turned.

Saria found herself in a small, unoccupied sitting room. She went through the open door on the opposite side of the room only to find herself in what appeared to be the library. Saria scanned the rows of ancient texts longingly but did not pause to explore. She had to pass through two more rooms before she at last found herself back in the main hall.

"There you are!"

Saria jumped at the governor's exclamation. He was bearing down on her from the opposite side of the hall, scowling. Her cheeks went hot, feeling very like a naughty child caught sneaking about.

"I apologize," she said quickly. "I believe I took an incorrect path from the garden."

His mouth thinned. "And where is Rinna?"

"She found the night air refreshing and wished to remain outside." She glanced behind him. "Where is Jehan?"

"Looking for you, as was I," the governor said shortly. "You have no retinal scan on file, it seems. I will need one to finalize the ID." He indicated the doors on the opposite side of the hall. "Come into my office."

Just then Nel came around the corner, a little out of breath. "You found her!"

"At last." He waved his secretary toward the back of the house. "Go find Captain Dekra, will you? He insisted on going out to the gardens to look for her."

"Yes, Your Excellency," Nel said, turning that way.

"Well, come along," the governor snapped. "I do have other matters to attend to this evening, you know."

"Of course," Saria mumbled, following him to the other side of the hall.

Chol held the door open for her to precede him. Saria hurried into the room and stopped short, her mouth parting.

Dimly she heard the governor shut the door behind her, the sound of the lock being engaged, but her wide gaze stayed fixed on the man seated at the desk.

He stood; she had forgotten how tall he was. Nearly as tall as an Az-kye warrior.

Though with his striking blue eyes, this man would never be mistaken for one.

"Princess Saria," Kyndan said formally. Her sister's mate, now the Imperial Warlord, smiled. "I had nine hells of a time finding you."

32

Rescue

"And you are absolutely certain, Commander Maere?" Governor Chol circled round to look at her as one might examine a particularly strange curiosity in a shop. "This woman is an Az-kye princess?"

Kyndan raised his eyebrows at her.

She lifted her chin, clasping her hands together to hide their trembling. "I am Imperial Daughter Saria."

Jehan! Sweet Lashima, where is Jehan?

"Extraordinary," the governor murmured, shaking his head. "Well, now that I have delivered Her Highness to you"—Chol turned to face Kyndan—"I believe this takes care of my . . . difficulties?"

"If by 'difficulties' you mean a life sentence in a correctional facility on Utavia for corruption," Kyndan said dryly, "yes."

"Excellent! Then if you—"

"Provided," Kyndan interrupted, "Princess Saria's recovery is kept strictly confidential."

"I'm a man who can keep many secrets," Governor Chol reminded. "But," he glanced at her, "she is known here—but as Liri, of course."

"'Liri'?" Kyndan asked. "Like Empress Liri of the third dynasty? The one who flayed half the court when she took the throne?"

"You have been studying our history, Commander," Saria remarked.

"It's good bedtime reading," he returned. "And even for an Az-kye empress, Liri was a homicidal maniac."

"She is my ancestor," Saria reminded sharply, "as well as Alari's."

Kyndan's smile was cold. "Those particular genes might have skipped a descendant or two. But in any case, *this* 'Liri' is about to vanish into thin air."

Chol hesitated. "There are those who will ask about her—"

"Discourage them," Kyndan snapped. "By whatever means necessary. Or I'll bring the Fifth Fleet here, impose martial law, and remove you from your"—his gesture took in the palace around them—"civic duties. And then, just for good measure, I'll order mass arrests and make sure every smuggler and two-cred glit biter in the sector thinks you, personally, sold them out."

The governor's thin lips went white. "The populace of Tir-Halea has long since learned the wisdom of not digging too deeply. I'm sure the disappearance of one woman— whom the official record now lists as deceased—won't be a problem."

"If it is," Kyndan said coldly, "it'll be *yours*." The Imperial warlord waved a dismissal to Chol. "Make sure no one sees us on the way out."

"Of course," the governor mumbled.

"We'll be heading up to the the *Dauntless* as soon as the governor's people have been cleared from the area," Kyndan continued as soon as the door shut behind Chol. "My First-in-Command, Lieutenant de'Cator—you remember Nisara, don't you?—will be coordinating your transfer to the ship, Your Highness."

If he is in the garden seeking me out, as Chol said, he might yet be safe . . .

Unbidden, the agonizing idea wormed into her mind: that Jehan had simply collected his ID, his share of Helock's wealth, and walked away without so much as a backward glance.

"You look like you've gotten by okay," Kyndan said, glancing her over. "In fact, if I didn't know better, I would have mistaken you for a Tellaran."

Saria looked at him coolly. "I could hardly walk about on Tir-Halea in full Imperial court dress."

"True." He folded his arms. "But it's a damn good disguise."

"Then how did you find me?"

"I had an idea, a hunch really, and we were lucky enough to intercept a Az-kye ship trying to make a run for Imperial space. The crew saw the wisdom of cooperating in the warlord's investigation." Kyndan shrugged. "Once they were aboard my cruiser with a dozen Fleet blasters pointed in their faces, that is."

Her head came up. "They recognized me, those warriors?"

"Hardly. Or I'm sure these warriors—if you can call them that—would have happily ransomed you back to the empire. The dead Heiress returned to life? You would have funded the building of some very grand clanhouses. But no," Kyndan continued. "I just asked them politely—well, more or less anyway—if they knew of any young Az-kye woman who had showed up in this sector in the past few weeks. They told me of a woman fitting your description having been being taken prisoner by a syndicate calling themselves 'the Brethren.' Gods, where did they *get* such a stupid name?" He leaned on the edge of the desk. "Of course you can imagine my joy at arriving here at the Governor's Palace to demand Chol's official help in the search, only to discover that the Brethren have just been disbanded and you, here, under the governor's own protection. Though, Your Highness, I gotta say, I'm wondering why you didn't try to return to the empire."

"I did," Saria said bitterly. "The warriors that I called upon for assistance did not believe me to be an Imperial Daughter. It was they who handed me over to the Brethren. But now that you have found me," her gaze narrowed, "I imagine you intend to kill me."

"*Kill* you? Oh, hells no! I need you alive and well, Princess." Kyndan's blue eyes fairly glowed. "You see, you're going to help me conquer the Az-kye Empire."

Jehan pressed back deeper into the darkness as the Fleet troops passed by. For the hundredth time in the past half-hour, he cursed himself for giving in when Praom had ordered their driver to halt outside the security field and made it clear they weren't going anywhere near the governor until Jehan handed his blaster over.

He might not trust the governor so much as an inch but there was no fucking way Chol would have called in the Fleet to give him up to them. Chol was knee-deep in a thousand dirty deals throughout the sector. The governor's fortunes depended on the Fleet staying the hells *out* of his territory.

Which meant that the Fleet was here for their own reasons—very possibly to arrest the good governor himself.

And if that were true, he sure picked the wrong time to visit the governor's palace for a bunch of forged documents.

But as he'd said to Liri, charming he might be, lucky he was *not*.

Liri . . .

His stomach clenched. She'd come out here twenty minutes ago with the governor's wife and that gnawing feeling in the pit of his stomach—that *otherworldly* urging—had pushed him to interrupt Chol's long-winded discourse, to insist on heading out here to find her.

He'd covered half this insane labyrinth searching for her, and only by chance did he see the Fleet troops before they saw him. Using the maze's dark enclaves and corners he'd managed to keep out of their sight—so far.

The governor's own security force was distinctly, disturbingly absent. Either they had already surrendered or—wisely if Chol was now in disgraced free-fall—had abandoned their posts to seek out a berth on the first ship that would get them off-world.

Jehan could feel him again—his father—standing at his shoulder now as if that warrior was at high alert, his sword drawn and at the ready.

He could also feel the small hold-out blaster secreted in in his right boot.

But one small weapon wasn't much against a whole Fleet squadron—

A timid footfall, the soft rustle of leaves had him quickly bending down, easing the blaster from his boot. A shadowy figure moved, a slender form but one far too short to be Liri. Jehan yanked the woman back against him, his hand smothering her startled scream.

"It's Jehan Dekra," he hissed. "I'm not going to hurt you!"

Rinna relaxed a bit against him. He eased off, letting her go as quietly as possible and she turned, her face, even in this dim light, very pale.

"The Fleet's here!" She was young but she was smart enough to keep her voice to a whisper.

'Course, being Governor Chol's wife would have smartened her up fast.

"I noticed," he murmured, glancing back the way she'd come. "Where's Liri?"

"I don't know. She went back to the house and I stayed out here to meet—" Rinna shook her head. "I don't know if she made it or not."

"Wonderful," he muttered, peering into the darkness for any sign of red Fleet uniforms.

She plucked at his sleeve. "What are they doing here? Are they arresting Trum?"

"Now why would they be arresting your husband?" he asked dryly. "I don't suppose your, uh, *friend* would have any way of finding out what's going on."

"He could—if he were here," she murmured bitterly. "He took off as soon as we spotted Fleet troops."

"Any chance you know a nice, quiet way past the security field? Oh, and I won't believe you if you say you *don't*."

"There's a doorway hidden beside the outside stairway. It leads under the house and to one of the outer buildings. From there you can get to the city and, if you're lucky, the spaceport, unseen."

He glanced toward the house. "Is the door marked?"

"It's smooth so it blends into the wall. It's about three paces past the last step on the right. Come on!"

He shook off her hand. "You go ahead."

"You're armed and I know my way around. We're better off together." When he didn't answer she continued peevishly, "They've probably already taken her into custody, you know. You're being an idiot."

"Isn't the first time," he muttered. "Sure won't be the last."

Even in the faint light he could feel the weight of her glare. "Fine," she snapped. "But I'm going."

"If you see Liri—"

"I'll wave goodbye," she hissed and crept forward, clearly knowing her way around this place well enough to make a minimum of noise as she left.

It was possible that Liri had also seen the Fleet troops before she was spotted and was hiding out here. It was equally possible she made it to the house only to be caught in whatever mess Chol had made for himself.

The Fleet officers wouldn't buy that he and Liri were just guests here and let them go. Onara would have seen to it his share of Helock's money was already safely transferred to untraceable accounts and his new ID would be as solid as they came.

Or it *would* have been if Chol had actually finished creating it before Jehan headed out here.

Liri hadn't been around for her final scan either, which meant if she got picked up she wouldn't have any identification—one thing sure to send alarm bells ringing for the Fleet types. 'Course those alarms would really blare if they got hold of him; he had at least a dozen warrants outstanding and as a known smuggler—

The Brethren thing probably won't help much either . .
.

Jehan hardened his jaw. *The house it is.*

His father and swordmaster had trained him from a young age how to move in silence and stealth. But moving quietly in an unfamiliar place meant moving fucking *slowly* when all he wanted to do was sprint that way, find her, and get the hells out of here—

Jehan was almost to the house when two of the balcony doors were thrown open. He ducked back into shadows, watching as red-clad Fleet troops poured from the house and down the stairs like blood from a wound.

Liri was right in their center.

She walked beside a familiar-looking Fleet commander but right then Jehan couldn't be bothered to place the guy.

His eyes had gone hot at the sight of Liri surrounded by the troopers. Her shoulders were tight as if trying make herself smaller in their midst. Jehan breathed hard as he followed, every instinct demanding he howl out a challenge, his hand just *itching* for a sword—

But this was the Badlands and these were Tellaran troops. Running out there like an enraged Az-kye warrior to get himself killed—or captured—wouldn't do her any good.

She was in their custody, likely under arrest, and they were taking her to their shuttle. Once on a Fleet cruiser or at a Fleet facility she would be damn near unreachable.

The commander waved his troops aboard but remained at the bottom of the ramp to speak to Liri, a blonde female officer with them. Jehan was close enough now that he could hear their voices, although he could not make out the words. Liri was arguing with the commander and Jehan's jaw tightened as the man took a quick, angry step toward her.

Those two Fleet officers were armed but their blasters were holstered. The shuttle powered up, the noise providing the perfect cover.

There was no time—in a moment they would take her aboard, take her gods knew where.

Jehan eased to the edge of the shadows. With smooth, practiced movements he leveled his blaster and fired—

"Chol is scum," Nisara said to Kyndan as they left the mansion and headed out onto the balcony. "I can't believe you're actually leaving him in charge here."

"Oh, he's not staying," Kyndan said briskly. "You can bet the governor is already on his way to shove every last credit into an untraceable account and vanish."

The blond woman made a sound of disgust. "And you're just going to let him go free?"

"I'll contact TelSec as soon as we get back to the shuttle," Kyndan said. "Chol won't even make it out of the spaceport."

Saria glanced about as she walked beside her sister's mate, seeking Jehan in the darkness. But if he was here, the bright lights of the Tellaran military shuttle hid him from her sight.

"'Course Chol does have one card to flash in his favor," Kyndan continued. "He rescued Her Highness from the Brethren. He might turn that in for a little leniency. Though I'm a little curious, Princess, how you managed to get off the *Ty'har* and all the way to Tir-Halea."

If Chol claimed to have rescued her from the Brethren, eager to claim glory for himself . . .

Saria glanced away. "A passing freighter received our distress call. By the time they arrived to offer assistance I was the only one on board left alive."

"Wasn't someone with you?" Kyndan asked. "Alari said there was someone . . . special."

"Naret," Saria said hoarsely. "Naret of the Az'larna. He was a good man, an honorable warrior." She sent a narrow glance at the Tellaran beside her, a man who dared claim the title her father had once borne. "A *true* son of the empire."

Kyndan snorted. "Highness, after what I've been through the last couple days, throwing a barb like that isn't going to get you much blood out of me."

"Has my sister lost control of the empire so soon? In truth, she did not wear the regent's crown long at all." Saria remarked acidly. "What a disappointment she has turned out to be."

Kyndan's face flushed and he stopped short at the shuttle's ramp.

"Onboard, all of you!" he barked at the troops around them. "Fire her up and let the *Dauntless* know we're lifting off momentarily."

As the others hurried aboard, Saria turned toward him. "I am an Imperial Daughter. Think you truly I would ever help you, Commander?"

"That's 'Imperial Warlord.' And what I *demand*, Saria, is that you to behave like a Daughter of the Shina' clan, a princess of the Az-kye, and act in your people's best interest."

"Conquest by barbarians is in the Az-kye's best interest?" she sneered. "Using Tellaran tricks to prop up the rule of my incompetent sister is—"

He took a quick step toward her. "You know, I may need you back on Az-kye, *Your Highness*, but I am perfectly capable of gagging you till we get there."

"Think you to cow me, Tellaran?" She lifted her chin. "You do not frighten me."

"Maybe not, but what's happening in the empire *should* scare the hells out of you. If I don't get you back to the homeworld—and fast—the empire will crack apart. And if that happens, I can guarantee you when everything is done, it won't be Alari *or* you who's wearing the crown." His blue gaze narrowed. "Your mother the empress, is ill, did you you know that? Well," he continued at her scant nod. "Her illness is no accident. The storm that your ship was caught in wasn't an accident either. Someone was trying to kill you, Princess."

"Truly?" she snapped. "The warriors my sister sent to slaughter those loyal to me with Tellaran blasters *did* make me suspect so, Commander."

"*What?*"

"Do not pretend ignorance to me!" she flared. "Plainly it *was* Alari who won the commander of my ship to her side. It was she that bade him lead his forces against me." Her lip curled. "And who better than *you* to arm them with Tellaran weapons?"

"Oh, hells no! Whatever happened on that ship, I had nothing to do with it and Alari—" He shook his head sharply. "Never! Alari loves you. She would never hurt you."

"Then tell me, *Warlord*, why have you come on a Tellaran ship with Tellaran troops to "rescue me"?" Saria demanded. "Why has my sister, the Imperial regent—who loves me so—not sent an armada of Az-kye warriors to bring me home? Why has my mother not? Or will you pretend now that Alari does not keep it secret in the empire that I still live? My sister would 'never hurt me'?" She gave a short bitter laugh. "Think you I believe *that*?"

"You'd believe it if you'd seen Alari when she heard you were dead! When she had to perform the rites at your funeral, if you'd seen her"—his voice tightened—"at night when everyone had finally left us and she could weep for you." He straightened. "And I'm here, Princess, because I'm the one who figured out that you might have survived the *Ty'har's* destruction. But no one in the empire, especially Alari, trusts me right now. The only way to convince her of the truth is to get you home. Alari—the *Az-kye*—need you on the homeworld, Your Highness. When the empress—when *Alari*—sees you're alive all that woman's plotting to take the throne is going to fall apart. And I promise you this—" His teeth bared for an instant. "I am going to make that bitch *pay* for taking my mate away from me."

Saria searched his face, something of the sincerity in his suffering giving her pause. "But if Alari—if my mother—did not seek to have me killed, who—"

A blaster bolt caught Kyndan in the upper chest, knocking him backward into Nisara.

"Liri!" Jehan shouted, stepping out into the light, his blaster still leveled.

Kyndan lay on the ground, the wound in his chest smoking. Nisara was shouting orders to her troops.

Saria took a step toward Jehan.

If neither sought my destruction, if my sister and mother—if the Az-kye—are in truly in danger—

"Liri, come on! *Run!*" Jehan fired again, high enough to hit the edge of the shuttle, forcing the troops there to dart back. "Come on!"

I am an Imperial Daughter!

Her vision blurred. "Jehan . . ."

Nisara had her own blaster out, the weapon trained on Jehan. Saria threw herself into the Tellaran woman, knocking the blaster aside. Nisara twisted her hand free and caught Saria with a fist to the face.

"Liri!"

The Tellarans poured from the shuttle as Jehan ran toward her, firing off shots.

He grunted as a bolt hit him straight on, dropping him instantly.

Saria's breath froze and she pushed Nisara away, running to him, the grass slick beneath her slippers.

She fell to her knees at Jehan's side, already turning him when Nisara and two other Tellarans caught up. Saria rolled him onto his back, her hands frantically going over his chest, but she could find no wound.

"Stunned." Nisara glanced at one of the men beside her. "Good shot."

The man had his rifle at the ready. "Thank you, ma'am."

"Corporal!" Nisara snapped as a third man joined them. "Commander Maere's status?"

"The medtech's with him now," the man reported. "He'll make it but we need to get him to the *Dauntless*'s medunit."

"Right," Nisara said, keeping her blaster at the ready. "You—and you." She indicated Jehan. "Get his sorry ass onboard."

"Leave him be! He was but defending me!" Saria cried as the men pulled her from her. "He is—a friend."

"I don't give a damn *who* he is," Nisara gritted out. "He just tried to kill our commander. He's coming with us to face charges for attempted murder."

Jehan groaned as he came to.

He recognized this feeling—it wasn't something you forgot. The awful headache and insects-crawling-on-the-skin sensation that accompanied waking from a stun shot had all the charm of a beastly hangover with none of the preceding fun.

What he didn't recognize was where he was.

There was the familiar feel of a mattress beneath him and a thin pillow beneath his head. The light made his burn and the white walls were too clean, too new to be the *Selini's Song*, too utilitarian to be their mansion . . .

Liri!

He bolted upright on the cot, the movement drawing another pained groan. Jehan held his pounding head between his hands in an effort to keep it from exploding.

But at least he knew where he was now. The red uniform of the Fleet guard standing on the other side of the security field made that pretty plain.

The man gave him a narrow look and activated the comm at his ear. "He's awake."

"Fleet holding cell, huh?" Jehan croaked. A stun shot also left you dehydrated as hell. "It's my first, believe it or not."

He pushed himself off the cot, swaying for a moment before he found his balance, his glance going around the pristine, sparsely-furnished space. There was the bunk he'd just stood up from, equipped with a thin pillow and blanket. A wash station and open 'fresher—*Oh, that'll be fun*—a recessed shelf in the wall where his meals would be sent through and, of course, a shock field active across the cell archway to keep him contained.

"It's nicer than I thought it would be." His legs felt leaden as he made his way over to the sink. A wave of his hand activated the water and, gritting his teeth against the renewed pounding as he bent over, he used his cupped hand to drink. The water was cool, and though it hurt his throat to swallow at first, he kept cupping and drinking till he'd quenched his thirst.

He straightened. The guard hadn't moved and now eyed him warily.

Jehan glanced around the cell again. "Mind telling me where this holding cell is?"

"You're onboard the *Dauntless*, Captain Dekra," answered the blond female officer as she came to stand beside the guard. "I am Lieutenant Nisara de'Cator, the *Dauntless*'s second-in-command."

"Nice to meet you." He tried to keep his pace even as he crossed to her but after the stun his balance was less than impressive. Behind the guard was a plain wall. If there were other cells on this deck he couldn't see them from in here. But they would have designed the brig to make sure prisoners couldn't interact.

"I have come to inform you that you will be held here until we can transfer you over to a TelSec facility," Nisara continued. "There you will stand trial for your assault on, and attempted murder of, Commander Kyndan Maere— along with any other outstanding charges. Considering your colorful career, Captain, that should make for a very long list. I would advise you to engage an excellent legal advocate, although, of course, as your sizable accounts have now all been frozen, that might prove challenging for you." Her blue eyes narrowed. "Starting to regret shooting a Fleet officer, pirate?"

"Not really." He glanced behind her. "You took a young woman into custody along with me. Where is—"

"You don't get to ask questions," the lieutenant snapped.

Jehan's teeth bared, his hands clenching into fists. *"Where is she?"*

There was a commotion outside the cell, infuriatingly beyond his line of sight. The lieutenant turned that way, her brows rushing together. "You aren't permitted in this—"

The breath exploded from his chest as Liri came into sight.

"I am here, Jehan!" she cried. "I am here."

"Liri!" his heart thudding, he got as close to the field as he could without getting shocked. "Are you all right?"

Another one of the Fleet guards followed after her, looking frustrated. "I'm sorry, Lieutenant. She insisted—"

"You can't be here," Nisara snapped at Liri. "Return to your—"

Liri rounded on her. "Do not presume to order *me*, Lieutenant!"

"This is a Fleet ship," Nisara reminded. "You have no authority here."

"Think you it is wise to offend me?" Saria's voice was icy.

The blonde woman bristled. "Princess, this really isn't your—"

"Princess? What—" Jehan shook his head, his voice rising. "What the hells is she talking about, Liri?"

"I am not Liri," she said hoarsely. "I am Imperial Daughter Saria, Heiress to the Az-kye throne."

34

ᎣᎦ᎚ᏥᎥᎢ

Chasm

Jehan shook his head again. "You *can't* be—"

She stepped closer so that only the spare centimeters of the shock field separated them. "I am Princess Saria."

"That's not fucking possible! When I found you, you were a—" His fists clenched. "The empire spent *weeks* in official mourning. They performed her funeral rites! Imperial Daughter Saria is *dead*!"

"I would be," Saria agreed, "but for you."

He searched her sweet gaze, wanting to deny it—wanting *her* to deny it—his heart cracking open at the truth he saw there—

"It's because you were on that warship." He swayed, shutting his eyes briefly. "That's why so many of the warriors had blasters. Some were assassins—"

"And some my protectors."

"And who wouldn't be willing to kill or die," he said numbly. "With an Imperial Daughter at stake . . .?"

Saria glanced at Nisara. "Drop the security field."

"The fuck I will! This man shot our commanding officer!" Nisara's blue gaze narrowed at Jehan. "I'll drop this field when I hand him over for trial."

"Commander Maere is wounded," Saria snapped. "He will survive. And you will free Captain Dekra."

"He's a criminal! A dangerous—"

"Jehan rescued me from the *Ty'har*. He is the only reason I survived the warship's destruction. It is thanks to him I survived in the Badlands. You will release him. Now."

"I most certainly will not!"

"All charges against him will be dismissed," Saria continued sharply, and Jehan's heart hammered at how her posture, her very face, changed to one of cold—*regal*—authority. "His ID will be clear of any taint and his fortune restored. Before we leave orbit he will be escorted by shuttle safely to the spaceport on Halea where he will depart this world or one of his own choosing."

"I am a Fleet officer—"

"If you wish my cooperation on Az-kye," Saria said, her tone no less threatening for its chill, "you will bargain for it now."

"I don't have the authority to make this call," Nisara bit out.

"Then contact one who does."

The blonde woman bristled. "I'll have to speak to Commander Maere."

Saria inclined her head then glanced at the guards. "Drop the field and leave us. I am perfectly safe with him while you make arrangements for his release."

"You heard Her Highness," Nisara grumbled.

Reluctantly the guard keyed in the code, the field flashing for a moment before it came down. Both guards followed the lieutenant, leaving Saria and Jehan alone.

For a moment there was silence between them as they looked across the threshold at each other.

"'Her Highness,'" Jehan echoed hoarsely. "Jul was wrong about you, *Princess*. You are a damn good liar."

Saria stepped forward, into his cell. "I longed to tell you the truth. I tried—"

"You didn't try very hard."

"I told them—" She wet her lips. "Those warriors, the men who beat me, I told them who I was."

His eyes widened. "*That's* why you ran off, why you went after them? You thought they would take you back to Az-kye? But—" Jehan shook his head. "You're an Imperial Daughter, for fuck's sake! Those warriors should have jumped at the chance to serve you! Why the hells would they—"

"They did not believe me." Her shoulders trembled. "They called me a madwoman, a liar, and they—they—"

"You knew I loved you," he said roughly. "Did you really think I could ever hurt you?"

"You loved Liri." She dropped her gaze. "And I am daughter of the woman who destroyed your family."

"And you thought—what? That I'd hold *you* responsible for something your mother did? That I'd take vengeance against you for something that happened when you were—maybe *four*? You're not your mother, Li— Saria—and I'm not my father. We have our own lives to lead."

"And I . . ." She reached out, resting her hand lightly on his arm. "Even I think it foolish, Jehan, but I began to wonder if, so far from the homeworld, with the storms between us, the gods had lost sight of me. That somehow, if I told you when we were still so close to Imperial space, that if I dared whisper the truth, the gods would hear me, remember me, and—" She swallowed. "Our time together would end."

His breath stopped. "Like it has now, you mean."

"I am Heiress, Jehan," she said softly. "One day I will be empress."

"You were right," he rasped. "When you said it would change everything."

"Not all of it." She stepped closer. "Not the way I feel for you."

He took her hands in his, in wonder as always at the softness of her skin. "Then come with me! Let your sister have the empire. We can be married, have a life together in Tellaran space—"

"That is not possible now." She wet her lips. "There is a battle being waged for the throne. The lives of my people, of *our* people, hang upon the outcome. I cannot put my own wishes above the Az-kye. My heart would never know peace if I abandoned them." She looked at their hands, clasped together. "I could bring you no happiness if I came to you with such a darkness in my heart."

"I can't come with you." His grip on her tightened reflexively. "I can't cross Ren'thar's Sword. I'd be enslaved the second I entered Imperial space!"

"I am no more free to stay here." Her eyes were bright with unshed tears. "History has taught me well how very few of the Imperial line ever know happiness. As much as I wish it otherwise, beloved, I am an Imperial Daughter." She let go then, and the few inches between them became an abyss. "I am Az-kye."

His throat closed. "Something I can't ever be again."

The sound of sharp footfalls approaching reached them and Nisara, her face flushed in annoyance, stopped at the entrance to the cell.

"Looks like you could ask for Arrena's diadem and get it, Your Highness." The blonde officer clasped her hands behind her. "It's your lucky day, pirate. Commander Maere has given the princess his word that your record will be wiped clean. You're free to go." She jerked her head toward the open door. "So *go*."

Saria rose up and pressed a final soft kiss to his mouth.

"Wait—" he croaked, reaching for her. "Please—"

"Go, beloved." Her tears overflowed as the Tellaran officers marched into the cell, clasping his arms to escort him out. "Go—find your home."

35

Heiress

"Sister?"

Once, the newly discovered scroll from the Xe dynasty unrolled across her desk would have absorbed and delighted Saria. Now, seated in the quarters of the First and again garbed in full court dress of Imperial black, Seria realized she had been staring at the ancient text for some time without seeing it at all.

Alari smiled. "But I should say 'Heiress' again, should I not?"

The nearby rustling of silks made Saria sigh inwardly. Chosen from the best families and eager to serve the next empress, her new maids hovered around her, crowding her so that at times she felt she could scarcely breathe. Since the moment she had returned home weeks ago, someone was constantly at her elbow—a maid, an advisor, a clan leader needling for a favor—but never the one she wanted. Only long after the moons had risen, when she had sent her maids away, when she was finally alone, could she give in to her heartache without fear of her tears being noticed, gossiped about . . .

Saria stood. "Leave us."

The maids went reluctantly, disappointed at missing an opportunity to witness talk between the Imperial Daughters, to carry whatever snippets of information they could glean to their clans.

Spies all . . .

Alari tilted her head. "You look fatigued, Saria."

"I do not rest easy these days." Saria shook her head. "And when one so close to us, a trusted kinswoman, has betrayed us—"

"She made a fool of me," Alari said, her sweet face pained.

"She fooled us all. Nearly *killed* us all."

"But it was I," Alari continued, her voice tight, "whom she tricked into casting off her mate."

"Kyndan forgives you. He loves you."

"And I him." Her sister's voice took on such tenderness when she spoke of her mate Saria had to swallow her envy.

She looked out over the gardens, past the walls of the palace, the Gate of the Blessed, to the Imperial city itself.

Why should she have her love, and not me mine?

"I heard the announcement," Alari ventured.

Saria sank with a groan onto a plush silken chaise. "Why must it be done so soon? I have scarcely set foot on the homeworld!"

"You are Heiress now," her sister reminded, sitting beside her. "You must have a mate, a child."

"You sound like Mother."

Alari winced. "Never that."

"That is my duty now. To bear Imperial Daughters," Saria said bitterly. "Girls to be walled up within the confines of the palace, hemmed in by their appointed roles. The eldest ever envied, the younger ones left to rise up and destroy her sisters or else live out as Second or Third in the bitter shadow of the eldest."

Alari looked stricken. "Was it like that for us? Did you hate me always?"

"No!" She shook her head sharply. "I love you but I—coveted your place. I wanted to be First."

"Well," Alari huffed, not without amusement, "I knew *that*."

Saria sighed. "Apparently only *I* thought it kept well hidden."

"And now you are First," her sister said, her expression a little sad. "But there is a price that comes with glory that the Second never knows."

"Why must I be mated this year?" she burst out. "Why not next year or the year after? Why does everyone push me so? Surely I might be given time—given time to—"

Alari took her hand. "No one living understands your burdens as I do."

"And you shook them off with the flash of blue eyes!" Saria pulled her hand from her sister's and stood. Her heart hammered as she crossed the balcony to rest her hands there, looking at the walls beyond. "You chose your own mate! And a Tellaran! And soon you are going away with him."

"I was raised to be First. I have ruled as regent." Alari's voice took on a thread of tarasteel, her skirts rustling as she stood too. "I know far more of responsibility, of wielding power, than you, little sister. And far more of its press upon the heart."

"Wait!" Her cry stopped Alari at the door and Saria ran to embrace her sister. "Forgive me! Forgive me my bad temper and my pettiness! I wish you all happiness, sister. It is—it is only I—"

"I will miss you too," Alari said, hugging her tight.

Saria sat beside her mother, facing the court. The Imperial family did not dine publicly as often they had when her father lived, but since her recovery and Saria's own return to the palace, the empress commanded these dinners take place every other day.

Alari—now an Imperial Daughter but happily relieved of her place in the line of the succession—and her Tellaran mate were excused from this duty.

Saria envied them greatly.

"Thank you," she murmured as the servant refilled her wine glass.

The servant froze, mortified, and Saria's face went hot at her mother's glare.

With a sharp flick of her hand the empress dismissed the serving maid. The servant made a brief bow and scurried away, eager to be free of the awkward scene. At her mother's dark glance the other attendants retreated as well.

"Forgive me," Saria mumbled. "A custom learnt in Tellaran space."

"An unseemly one for an Imperial Daughter and one you will not repeat," her mother snapped. "Our rule has been shaken to its core by upheaval and betrayal. Your sister will soon quit our palace with her mate for Tellaran space. We must reclaim the influence of the throne and I will tolerate no other taint to our rule."

And to recall one marked as clanless to the empire, to find some way to free him, restore his honored name, would be to send the empire spinning—

Even to make such an attempt was not in her power. Her mother, while still weakened, grew in strength every day. It would be many years before Saria would take the throne as empress.

He will have long since taken a Tellaran wife by then, had children with her, a home . . .

"Yes, Imperial Majesty," Saria murmured.

"I am glad we are agreed." The empress took a sip of her wine. "We will begin preparations for your mate's choosing tomorrow."

"Did you not think to ask me first?" Saria heart hammered but this time not even her mother's sharp glare could silence her. "That perhaps I do not wish to take a mate now?"

"I was saddened to hear of Naret's death," the empress said, not unkindly. "Were he alive I would permit you to take him as mate but that is not possible now. You and I, Saria, are all that hold our dynasty now."

"My sister—"

"Will never again sit upon the Az-kye throne," the empress said evenly. "*You* are Heiress now. You must secure your succession. Now, more than ever, the Az-kye need the assurance and stability that only your daughters will bring. You must take a mate—a proven warrior worthy to rule beside you as warlord."

"Did you love my father?" she asked tightly.

Softness and pain flashed in the empress's face. "Yes," she murmured. "Very much." Then her shoulders squared and she reached for a hiti fruit, her hand painfully thin from the attempt on her life. "But it was my duty to take a worthy mate. I would not have chosen him if he were not a suitable match, an honorable warrior of excellent family. So it must be with you."

Beyond the high, arched windows darkness had fallen, the lights of the Imperial City blotting out any sight of those far-off stars.

And I will live out my life here, within the palace walls. But no matter how many years another sits beside me as consort, it will be you, beloved, who has my heart . . .

"Yes, Imperial Majesty," she murmured.

36

⟡⟁✗⟁⟁⟁⟁⟁

Bargain

It was a shit walk to the house.

Too full of bramble brush to land a shuttle, too overgrown for a groundcar, the only way to cover the last twenty kilometers was on foot.

It was dry as the sixth hell too, the dust burning Jehan's nose, scratching his throat as he slogged on. The pack on his back was heavy with supplies, and he wore blasters on both hips in case he stumbled on a nest of crimson vipers. Only an idiot would live out here at the edge of the Zeg-Halea wasteland.

Or a stubborn old bastard like Anzu.

Jehan was panting when he finally reached the house, his shirt soaked with sweat. The structure had started out pre-fab maybe forty years ago. At one time the place might have been decent enough but over time Anzu had done patches here and there, unsightly testaments to his ineptness at the chore. Now the whole thing looked like it had been clapped together by a lunatic with a laser torch.

Which, of course, it *had*.

The door was locked but it didn't take much knowhow to bypass the ancient security lockouts. He could have managed it even before he and Erit had signed on for their first run.

The inside of the house was nearly as dusty as the outside, the smell of food—apparently Anzu was no more a cook than he was a craftsman—lingering.

There was a stirring of air, a flash of metal. Jehan ducked and twisted to knock the weapon aside. In a heartbeat he had the old man disarmed, slamming Anzu against the house wall in a puff of plaster, pinning him by the throat.

Despite Jehan's tight grip, the elder man showed no fear.

Tough old thing . . .

"Hey, you aren't dead after all!" Jehan said cheerfully. "Good news for both of us."

"What"—Anzu rasped, struggling to speak against Jehan's choking hold—"do you here?"

"I was in the neighborhood. Thought I'd stop by." He let go and stepped back as Anzu gasped for breath. "You recognize me, don't you? I know you've seen me over the years—looked *through* me, more like. My name's Jehan."

"I care none for what you call yourself. If you are come to rob me," Anzu snapped, "you are a fool."

"Well, I am that," Jehan agreed, wandering through the tiny living space. "But I haven't come to rob you. Don't—" he advised amiably when Anzu's glance went to his sword, now lying on the floor. "I'll have to stun you, then wait for you to wake up again before we can talk. It took me a week longer to get back to Halea than I thought it would so I'm a bit pressed for time now."

"I am no mercenary, no smuggler, far past my prime as a fighter. We *have* no business."

"I have five million creds that says we do."

"Five mil—?" Anzu's lip curled. "You have come far from that filthy urchin grubbing for a meal."

"You mean the scared orphan kid you wouldn't even speak to?" Jehan bit out. "Sorry, he's long gone, Anzu. You have to deal with *me* now."

"What do you here?" the old man demanded. "I have nothing of value. The land here is worthless, the house worthless. I have nothing you could want."

"Oh," Jehan said, his voice low and tight, "now that's where you're wrong. You *do* have something I want—very, very much."

Anzu's dark eyes sharpened with suspicion. "And what is that?"

Jehan's mouth curved. "A name."

Anzu's brow furrowed, his silver hair catching the light. "A *name*?"

"Your name. I want you claim me as your son."

"My *son*?" Anzu's wizened face could not conceal his shock. "To what purpose?"

"Because within the empire's borders *you* have a name, a clan. And I don't."

"I do not know much of you but clearly you are a wealthy man now. You have freedom here. You have no reason to risk return to Imperial space, nor would it be seemly for such as you to do so."

"I don't want your opinion or your advice," Jehan snapped. "The deal is simple. My money for your name. You interested or not?"

"Think you you can *buy* honor?" Anzu sneered. "You know nothing!"

"I know you've stuck in this miserable dust bowl for years." Jehan gave the shack a pointed look. "The cost of passage back to the empire could buy a clanhouse and you're poor as the wasteland's soil. None of your *honorable* clan is going to bother crossing the Sword to bring you home." Anzu flinched and Jehan spread his hands, his tone softening. "But I can get you home, Anzu, on an Az-kye ship registered in your own name, no less. You'll return to the homeworld a very wealthy man. A credit to your clan, welcomed home with open arms."

Anzu's face went bright for an instant then his expression closed. "You toy with me."

"I need your name, your claim." Jehan's jaw hardened. "Without it, the moment I cross into Imperial territory I'm clanless, a slave. Without your name I can't enter the Circle and fight."

"The—? *You* would enter the Circle?"

In a smooth movement Jehan drew the sword from the scabbard he wore on his back, the blade catching the sunlight that streamed in through the window.

Holding it flat in the palms of his hands, he offered it to Anzu.

After a moment, the warrior shuffled forward and took the weapon, turning it over in his raw-boned hands, testing its balance and heft.

"A fine weapon," the old man allowed, running a practiced, critical eye over the blade. "Even if the price was high indeed, the merchant did not cheat you."

"I didn't buy it." He'd cleaned it before he'd come here, the very act bringing back the scent of tashi flowers blooming. His own hands had been small and childishly chubby when he'd first learned those skills at B'tai clanhouse barracks. "It was my father's sword. Now it's mine."

Anzu snorted. "Then it is the weapon of a criminal."

"My father was no criminal! He lived and died a true son of the empire!"

"Indeed," Anzu said coolly. "And what crime did they condemn this 'true son' for?"

"An attempt on the life of Warlord Kohren."

"A crime against the house of the empress herself! And still think you he was not guilty?"

"Do you think I—and my mother—would have followed him to this hellhole if he were?" Jehan demanded. "She *died* here, you know. Along with the child—our clan heiress—that she carried. Because we both knew him, and we knew that, whatever they said, not only did he *not* try to kill the warlord, he *couldn't* have. I was with him when the attempt was made."

"Why then did you not bear witness to his innocence?"

"I was a kid; who would listen to me? Besides, the empress had already made her decision and that was the end of it."

Why was he even trying to convince this old Az-kye of his good name? Tradition taught that for those consigned to wear the white, like his father, like himself, there could be no redemption.

"I am sorry," Anzu said stiffly. "For the loss of your mother and sister." His mouth worked for a moment. "And for that of your father."

Jehan went still at the unexpected kindness. "Thank you."

Anzu raised the blade a little. "Have you ever even wielded a sword?"

"I lived in the clanhouse barracks from the time I was eight till I was twelve. When we fled the empire my father trained me—till he died. You can teach me the rest."

Anzu shook his head. "You are too old."

"Look who's talking," Jehan threw back. "My father was a warrior. I'm as strong he was, as fast as he was. And, godsdamn it, I'm *taller*."

"You are not a warrior."

"And you're nothing but an old drunk. But you were an Az-kye warrior once. And now *I* need to be one."

"To what purpose?" Anzu asked, exasperated. "You will be cut to pieces, do you fight."

"That's not your problem, is it? You'll get the money—*and* to go home—whether you have a live son or a dead one."

"Why do such?" His glance went over Jehan, his mouth thinning a bit at his Tellaran clothing. "It is not for honor you fight."

"You're fucking right about that. It's the prize I'm after."

"*Prize?*" He gave a wheezing laugh. "What Az-kye prize would a Tellaran pirate risk dying for?"

Jehan's jaw twitched. "The Princess Saria."

"You do not mean . . ." Anzu stared. "You are mad! Every clan will put forth their most powerful warriors to fight in the Tournament for the Imperial Daughter!"

"Well, lucky you." Jehan jerked his chin at Anzu. "'Cause you got me."

"Like as not you will die in the first round!"

"Let me make the decision a little easier for you. Take me to the homeworld as your son, train me to be a warrior, and I'll make you my heir here. You can't lose, Anzu. If I die there you inherit everything I've got left here too, in addition to the five million. But just"—Jehan smiled—"think of what it will mean to you if I *win*."

Anzu's dark eyes met his.

Jehan might not give a damn about status and bloodlines but through that warrior stoicism he could see it sure held sway over Anzu's Az-kye heart.

"You'd be sire to the mate of an Imperial Daughter," Jehan continued. "Your clan will rise higher than it ever has. And someday you, Anzu of the He'lar, will be grandsire to an *empress*."

With a swift, practiced movement Anzu offered him the sword. "Do our clan proud and may Ren'thar grant you victory, my son."

It felt funny, *disloyal,* to call another man by it—

"Yes, Father," Jehan said, sliding the sword back in its scabbard.

"We will begin your training immediately. Once, of course, you are dressed properly and"—Anzu's silver eyebrows rose—"your Tellaran will has been registered."

37

Homecoming

Saria broke stride when she saw him, the bright sunlight of the palace corridor dimming around her.

In deference to the Heiress's approach courtiers, servants, officials, and clan leaders drew aside to make way and bow as she passed—and he was among them.

It had been nearly a season but the curve of his face, the breadth of his shoulders, was burned forever into her memory. The sight of him clad in warrior black *here* in the Imperial Palace made her heart speed up, her palms damp.

Looking at him sidelong as she passed, she quickened her steps to an undignified pace. Forcing herself not to break into a run, Saria was faintly aware of the stir she left in her wake, of her maids hurrying to keep up.

Her heart was thudding in her chest when she finally reached the unoccupied receiving room where she was to receive petitioners. As soon as she was inside, the guards closed the doors behind her, thankfully blocking her from the curious gaze of the court.

Perspiration dampened the skin beneath her breasts and she pressed her hands against her ribs, shivering despite her wide shimmersilk scarlet court gown and the warmth of the day.

Tilanna, lately of her sister's service, regarded her with a puckered brow. "Your Highness?"

"I cannot breathe." The vast room seemed to be closing in around her; the huge carved doors of the receiving room appeared flimsy and utterly inadequate. "I must have light. I must have air!"

She stumbled across the room, skirts billowing out around her, and threw open the window open herself. Saria leaned there against the windowsill, shaking, leaning forward to gulp the fresh, sweetly fragranced air of the Imperial gardens below.

"Your Highness?" Tilanna cried. "Shall I fetch a healer?"

Her maids gathered around her, their faces etched with concern.

"Give me some air!" Saria snapped open her fan as they scurried back, waving the delicate jaha feathers quickly in front of her face, willing more breath into her lungs.

"Please, allow me to send for a—"

"I am not ill!" Saria's hand clenched into a fist. "And I do not care for your badgering!"

"As you wish," Tilanna murmured. "My apologies, Princess."

"What?" Saria whispered. "What did you say?"

The maid spread her graceful hands, her lips parting in fear.

Saria took a step toward her. "What did you say?"

"I—" Tilanna stammered. "I offer my apologies." She bowed, trembling. "For offending you, Princess."

Saria's gaze went from Tilanna to her other maids, taking in their finery, the richness and elegance of this room. She turned, looking past the Gate of the Blessed to the wild colorful sprawl of the Imperial city itself.

Suddenly her lungs filled and her shoulders fell.

"Who has requested an audience this morning?" she asked, her voice steady, calm now.

Her women exchanged apprehensive glances and then Celin, the maid burdened with the task of tracking her appointments and appearances and obligations, which sometimes changed by the hour, consulted her notes.

"Lady of the Sah, then the master of the mining consortium," Celin said. "The Arbiter of the Tournament is here again as well, he wishes to discuss the commencement of—"

"Cancel them all," Saria snapped, striding past the women.

"But—Your Highness!" Celin blurted, hurrying after. "You have declined to receive the Arbiter for nearly—"

"I said, cancel them all!" she ordered, her raised voice echoing through the high-ceilinged room.

Celin bowed then scurried across the polished floor. She ducked into the hallway where the Tournament Arbiter, an honored and elderly warrior, waited, shifting foot to foot with unseemly agitation to be admitted to her presence.

Standing in front of the elaborate throne where she usually sat to receive petitioners, Saria squared her shoulders.

"Tilanna, there is a warrior in the hall who bears the crest of the Ni'raran clan. His clan leader is with him." She looked at the maid. "Go now and bring him here. Him and the clan leader both."

Tilanna inclined her head, hurrying to her task.

Saria closed her eyes. Birdsong floated in through the open window, along with the distant thunder of the falls, where the Empress Liri had nearly met her end all those centuries ago . . .

Behind her, the carved door swung, squeaking on its hinges like a snouse caught in a firehawk's talons.

"As you commanded, Your Highness," Tilanna said from her place at the door. "The warrior and his clan leader await admittance outside at your pleasure."

Saria turned. "Admit them."

Her maid opened the door, urging the pair inside.

"Clan leader of the Ni'raran and her escort," Tilanna announced as soon as the guard outside shut the door behind them.

Both the warrior and his clan leader bowed deeply.

"You may approach," Saria said, standing before the Heiress's throne.

Without raising their eyes, the two came forward. When they were within five paces of the Heiress, both sank down to their knees, their heads bowed.

"Lady of the Ni'raran," Saria said, addressing the clan leader, "I know your crest but I think we have not met before."

The woman, dressed entirely in the black of the court lifted her gaze. She was a round-faced woman, perhaps the empress's own age, and clearly not one to deny herself the pleasures of the table.

"To my great regret we have not," she said. "I have been several times at court but I have not, before now, had the honor of speaking to Your Highness."

Saria glanced at the warrior. "And who is this warrior who accompanies you to the palace today?"

The clan leader smiled. "One of my nephews."

"And he serves in your house well?" Saria asked.

"Oh," the lady said, a little smile tucking her pudgy cheek, "he has accomplished much on our behalf."

"Far more than any at the palace could imagine, I am sure. I hope," she continued, addressing the warrior, "you do not exhaust yourself in your labors?"

The warrior raised his head.

And their gazes met.

"Do you recognize me now, Rudir?" Saria swept forward in her court gown of Imperial black, spreading her fan as she turned slowly for his inspection. "Or shall I have the room darkened and trash strewn about? Would that better call to mind for you, I wonder, the alley"—she stopped, fixing him with a cold look—"where you handed me over to the *Brethren's* tender care?"

The Ni'raran clan leader looked perplexed but the warrior had gone pale.

Very pale indeed . . .

"Your—Your Highness—" Rudir croaked.

"Ah!" Saria clapped her hands, smiling down at him. "So you *do* know me for your princess. At last."

His eyes were wide. "Heiress, I cannot begin to beg your forgiveness for—"

She quickly held up her fan to silence him.

"Oh, but you can," Saria purred. "I have cleared my morning so that you may beg my forgiveness for breaking Imperial law to fill your clan's greedy coffers." The Lady of the Ni'raran blanched, her mouth parting. "For acting as no warrior can and keep his honor," Saria continued. "For taking the sacred strength Ren'thar granted you to protect and instead using it to beat a woman pleading for your help.

"You *will* beg my forgiveness, if you hope to save your clan from destruction. Although"—Saria sat, her maids gathering around her throne as she narrowed her gaze at him—"I doubt it will do any good."

"Stop scratching!"

"I can't help it!" Jehan growled. "It . . . fucking . . . itches!"

"You must look like a warrior now," Anzu hissed, his glance darting about the crowded street of the Imperial city. "You must act as a warrior!"

"I *know* that." The follicle stim that guaranteed he'd have the long hair of a warrior by the time they got to Az-kye itched like crazy.

Five thousand creds and I feel like I've got blear bugs crawling all over my scalp.

Anzu slapped his hand away. "I said, stop!"

"I'm trying!"

Jehan gritted his teeth, clenching his fists to keep from digging his nails into his scalp again. But Anzu was right: giving in to any un-Az-kye behavior here in the middle of the temple district of the Imperial city was not just stupid, it was *dangerous*.

"You must *speak* always as a warrior!" Anzu continued. "As a proud son of the He'lar. You speak our language now like a Tellaran whore!"

Jehan bared his teeth. "*Your* lang—"

He stopped short.

Being on this world, hearing the buzzed language of his boyhood all around, raised the hair on the back of his neck. The smell of the city, the dust kicked up by dozens of litters—no groundcars *here* in the most sacred home of the empress—stung his nose. Even the distant mountains, the way the suns lit the sky made his chest ache like a metal band around his ribs, but—

There, its polished stone a riot of color and decoration, the powerful spray from falls half a kilometer high splitting the sunlight around it into an aura of shifting rainbows, sprawled the Imperial Palace.

And somewhere, beneath the splendor of those golden spires, was Saria.

"I will be mindful of such," he said in perfectly accented warrior-caste Az-kye, "Father."

Anzu regarded him for a moment, his wizened face stern. Jehan sighed inwardly, resigning himself to what was surely going to be a new tirade on the subject of his many shortcomings.

As soon as Jehan showed the Az-kye clothing he'd brought along, Anzu wouldn't permit him to wear anything else, even for training, even in the middle of the day in the dustbowl that was the Zeg wastes.

He'd had to shave too, of course. Warriors didn't wear beards and Anzu wouldn't stand for it—called it "slovenly." He'd already had the follicle stim treatment before he sought Anzu out. His hair was falling into his eyes before they even headed to the spaceport in Zeg-Halea. Now it hung halfway down his back, tied with a thin leather strip like any Az-kye warrior.

That morning the man looking back at him in the mirror was the very image of an Az-kye warrior: a big, hulking, black leather–clad dolt ready to fight to the death for any slight against clan honor. A throwback armed only with a sword, who could be knocked on his ass by a fourteen-year-old apprentice fan dancer with a blaster.

He hardly recognized himself.

Surprisingly Anzu offered a short nod. "Acceptable."

Better than my sword work anyway.

If he'd thought that all those years in the dustbowl of the Badlands had softened Anzu up, one day under the old man's tutelage had cured him of that. Anzu gave his word to make Jehan a warrior—or kill him trying apparently—

pushing him so hard that Jehan was trembling with fatigue at the end of the day.

The week-long trip from Halea to the homeworld hadn't been a respite either. Even within the confines of the Az-kye cruiser Jehan had purchased for their voyage Anzu designed drills for him to do.

But his swordsmanship was crap and they both knew it.

And with only days left until the start of the Tournament, Anzu might just find himself heir to Helock's fortune before the end of the week . . .

"Here," Anzu said shortly.

Jehan followed the old man's gaze to the other side of the broad avenue. "That is it?"

He eyed the sprawling estate, its colorful tiling, the blooming tashi trees bright with purple flowers. In many ways it was typical of a clanhouse. The walled garden, the sloping roof, the outbuildings beyond that would house the obligated lesser families—the *g'sil*—of this clan, and even farther afield were the barracks where unmated warriors were housed.

But only *this* clanhouse had the power to bring a sheen to the eyes of the old warrior at his side.

"How long has it been?" Jehan asked quietly. "Since you were home?"

"Thirty-eight years," Anzu said, "Since Y'an and I obeyed the empress's call to settle upon her new colony beyond Ren'thar's Sword.

"You had a mate?"

"Yes," Anzu said hoarsely. "And no woman was ever fashioned more beautiful than my Y'an."

"I'm sorry," Jehan blurted, stunned into forgetting all about his accent. "What happened? I mean—"

"She died." His chin trembled a bit before he controlled it and straightened his back. "On Halea."

"And you . . . survived that?" Jehan asked stupidly. "I mean, bound mates usually don't, uh . . ."

"I never expected to live past her loss—nor wished to. I can think only that the gods had forgotten me, so far was I from Az-kye soil."

"It wasn't about the money at all, was it?" he breathed. "You just wanted to get back to the homeworld to—"

"I would you remember to say you are of the He'lar with great pride," Anzu interrupted sharply. "When your name is added to the Tournament lists, which you may yet achieve—*if* you can prove yourself not such a bumbling fool when you lift your sword."

"Right," Jehan muttered.

"Come then, son. Let me show you your home."

Anzu had been gone so long the new clan leader, a woman only a few years older than Jehan, not only didn't remember him, she didn't even recognize his name.

And for such a long-awaited homecoming, this one sucks.

They were left outside in the dusty street to wait while the clan leader sent for servants who looked like they had been old when *Anzu* was young for gods' sake, before she even allowed them admittance to the house.

Once the old man's clan affiliation had been confirmed and he was at last allowed to pass over the threshold of the house where he'd been born they were brought to before the clan leader.

The new Lady of the He'lar, Y'lanni, sat sipping on iced fruit as she looked them over. She hadn't even bothering to stand up to greet them

"I am certain Mother said nothing of you to me, nor my grandmother either, Anzu," the lady said petulantly. "And this is your son, Jenar?"

He caught himself about to roll his eyes. "Jehan, my Lady."

Her brow puckered. "But you are so young. Were you and your mate not of an age, Anzu?"

"He was a late and . . ." The old warrior shifted his weight, "*unexpected* blessing."

"In any case," Y'lanni said, shrugging it off, "the estate is at capacity already. Certainly there is no room in the house for you. Everyone is come for the Tournament, you know."

"My son will be competing," Anzu said.

Her expression went cold. "I fear you have come far for nothing. Our clan could not possibly afford to provide the entrance fee or to pay to clothe him properly. And—did he win—the cost to pay formal courtship to an Imperial Daughter would be exorbitant. In fact, the harvests from our outer estates have been so paltry that—"

"*I* will provide all he needs," Anzu interrupted. "My own monies are more than adequate to woo even an Imperial Daughter."

"I see." Y'lanni shifted in her seat a bit. "I did not expect that you would have done so . . . *well* in the territory beyond the god's Sword, cousin."

"Father has bested even pirates," Jehan said solemnly. "Indeed, he made the bulk of his fortune outwitting the greatest of them."

"The house *is* full but—" The Lady tapped her feather fan. "I am sure some room may be found in the barracks for you both." Then she graced Jehan with her first smile of the interview. "And may you do honor to our clan in the contests."

"He will," Anzu promised. "Despite his injury."

Injury? Jehan barely managed to keep his expression to the proper stoicism. *What the fuck is he talking about?*

"Injury?" She tsked. Jehan imagined that was her "sympathetic" face. "How unfortunate."

"A muscle tear in his back, suffered shortly before we quit Tellaran territory," Anzu continued. "It has impacted his sword work so that you would hardly know him a trained warrior." He spread his hands. "I fear it has left him as clumsy with a blade as a pregnant sular."

Her over-plucked eyebrows rose. "Had you better compete in the Tournament, cousin, if you are injured? To be certain there are many young women—even some within your own clan—who would be appreciative of a warrior such as you. I have a younger sister who is yet unmated. Certainly to engage in such a grueling contest when you are at a disadvantage is not wise, Jenar."

"Jehan," he corrected *again*. "I thank you but there is but one Grand Tournament, one opportunity to become the princess's consort. I will be ready."

"And to that end you must train hard," Anzu agreed. "If you will excuse us, my Lady?"

"Of course," she said, fanning herself. "I look forward to seeing you compete."

"At least she did not forget your name this time," Anzu murmured as they left the Lady to her sun and sweets.

"Only because she did not use it," Jehan grumbled. "How is she related to you again?"

"The lady is your second grandmother's great-niece."

"I thought I saw a resemblance. Was her grandmother anything like that?"

"Why think you my mate and I agreed to settle the colony?"

"Wait." Jehan blinked. "Were you just . . . *funny*?"

"No." The old man's pace quickened. "Ah, good. We have not missed the afternoon drills. Come, Jehan; now you will see how *true* warriors train!"

Jehan's step slowed, his brow knitting as black-clad warriors of the He'lar clan poured out of the barracks, already jumping into what would be the third round of workouts for the day.

He'd forgotten about the reality of life for unmated warriors. Grass-stuffed mattresses, community quarters, drills at dawn—

"Oh, this," Jehan muttered under his breath, trudging after Anzu, "is *really* going to suck . . ."

38

Trancendence

At least I will rule an empire at peace.

It was unusual weather for this late in the year, cool but with a feeling of springtime. The streamers hung for the peace accord celebrations bright in the sunshine. With servants about everywhere to attend her if she had need of them, and craving some semblance of quiet in the midst of the festivities, Saria released her maids and sent them to enjoy the party. She walked among the many guests here in the eastern park of the palace, her smile firmly in place but her heart heavy.

Today the homeworld celebrated the peace agreement. Tomorrow the Tournament would begin . . .

She spied her sister ahead and quickened her pace to join her. No longer regent, or Heiress, Alari's face shone with joy as she took in the Az-kye and Tellarans mixing here in the Imperial gardens. The empress had granted her sister's dearest wish—her freedom—and soon she would leave to live with her mate in Tellaran space.

"It is going very well." Saria shook her head, smiling, at her sister's gown. "I did not think to ever see you in colors."

"Nor I you." Alari indicated Saria's own dress. "You may be the only First Daughter who has dressed so since the Xar dynasty."

"Yes, well, I have your mate to thank for that," Saria said, "but we *all* have much to thank your mate for."

Despite Jehan's nearly killing him, Kyndan had fought his way back to Az-kye in time to unmask the traitor in their midst, saving the lives of both the empress and the mate he loved so passionately.

Alari's gaze went to where the empress stood talking with the Tellaran ambassador. "Do you think she was disappointed?"

"When Kyndan named his reward? I think our mother would have your heart happy." Saria laughed. In return for his service to the empire he asked two things—for Alari to study art as she had always wished, and from that day all Imperial Daughters would honor Azis, the goddess of the rainbow, by their bright attire. "But I do think the court as equally scandalized by the new wearing of colors as they were to hear their former regent would now be a Tellaran artist."

"I will still be Az-kye," Alari said, a little defensively. She had since childhood kept her wish to be a painter secret from all, save Saria. "And the Dethara Academy is one of the finest schools of art in Tellaran space."

She took her sister's hand as she had when they were girls, her throat tight. "I will miss you."

"I will come home to visit as often as I can," Alari promised. "And I will be the artist I longed to be."

"You are still Second," Saria reminded.

Alari laughed and put her hand over her heart. "And I do beg you, sister—choose a mate soon so I may be just an Imperial Daughter!"

Saria forced a smile. Many of the warriors who had entered the Tournament had come to the celebration and Saria made it a point to avoid them. She did not wish to like a man who would see his end tomorrow, nor take a dislike to one who well might triumph. It would be unfair of her to offer encouragement to any of them.

Most wisely kept their distance but in that moment one warrior's dark eyes met hers, hot and far too bold to be proper when meeting the gaze of an Imperial Daughter.

Gods, it cannot be . . .

"Do you know that warrior?" Alari asked, her brow creased as the man turned away to speak to the elderly warrior at his side.

"No." Saria quickly let go of her sister's hand before Alari could feel how her palm had dampened. "I do not."

She should stay, speak to Alari, or have a word with the departing Tellaran ambassador, but she could not stop herself from following after him any more than she could stop the moons from rising in the evening.

It is not him. It cannot be him!

Clearly not recognizing the Az-kye Heiress without her entourage, a group of Tellaran admirals strolled past, blocking her way and her view of the man.

Saria craned her neck, silently infuriated to find herself with no decorous way of getting past the Tellaran dignitaries. She could not order them away and certainly an Imperial Daughter pushing past diplomatic guests would instantly attract attention.

By the time the Tellarans had passed the man and his companion had vanished. Saria's glance darted about but the pair were nowhere in sight.

It is because of Rudir! Recognizing one face from Tellaran territory now has me imagining the most foolish of things.

Saria turned back toward the veranda in time to witness Kyndan catch her sister in his arms and press a kiss to her temple, both their faces aglow.

And I am so envious I am sick with it. Alari has her love and I will never have mine—

"Looking for someone?"

Saria spun.

"Jehan . . ." she breathed.

Impossibly his hair was long now, tied back as any warrior would wear it. He was clad too in a warrior's black clothing, the leather supple and the shoulder beading of the finest quality. His beard was gone, his square-jawed face smooth and shaven.

He was astonishing, beautiful. The very image of an Az-kye warrior. . .

"Yes, your Highness." He inclined his head respectfully, his warrior-caste accent flawless. "Jehan of the He'lar."

She shook her head a little. "What?"

"I am Jehan, of the clan He'lar." He indicated the festivities. "Are you enjoying the celebration, Princess Saria?"

"You cannot be here," she whispered, shaking her head again. "You cannot be here!"

His eyebrows rose a touch. "I *was* invited. I am pleased to attend the commemoration of the new peace accords. Truly a remarkable day in our history. You are a great student of the past, I understand."

"This is not—" She broke off, throwing a quick, frightened glance about. Already their encounter was being observed.

"The suns are too bright today. I will retire to the quiet of one of the summer houses now," she said, a bit loudly. "Walk with me."

He inclined his head. "I am honored, Princess."

Thankfully even the Tellarans had been informed which structures were to be reserved for the use of the Imperial family and their personal guests. Saria strove to keep her pace unhurried as she led him to a belvedere set far back from the main party.

Fortunately, this pavilion was equipped with dark linen curtains to allow some measure of privacy and Saria hurriedly yanked them shut herself.

"What are you doing here?" she hissed.

"You told me to follow you . . ."

"No jokes, Jehan," she warned. "You, here, on the homeworld, at—*Gods!*—the palace? Are you insane?"

"Yeah." He considered for a moment then nodded. "Yeah, definitely."

"We must get you out of the city, off Az-kye before anyone discovers you here. My maids—no, I dare not trust them." She pressed her palm to her forehead. *Think, I must think!* "The Tellarans. Alari's mate can arrange for you to—"

"Fuck, he recovered quick, didn't he? I need to work on my aim."

Saria stared up at him. "Are you truly blind to your peril, Jehan? My mother would see you chained by your ankles and hanged from the Gate of the Blessed for your defiance of the punishment the gods have visited upon you, for claiming a name not your own." She indicated the beading at his shoulder. "If the He'lar discover you masquerading as one of their clan—"

"I am one of their clan. In fact, I'll be representing them in the Tournament tomorrow."

Saria felt the blood drain from her face. "You cannot."

"My name is already on the lists." He frowned. "Arrena's tits, sweetheart, you could at least read the names of the men ready to kill each other for you."

"You are no warrior!" she cried. "You will be cut to pieces, do you fight!"

"Why does everyone say that?" he muttered. "But yeah, I'm in the Tournament and I'm fighting tomorrow. It's tomorrow, right? Maybe I should leave the party early. I don't want to be too hung-over."

"No!" She shook her head sharply. "No. I will not permit this, Jehan! I will—"

"Tell the empress?" he supplied. "Tell the Imperial guard to throw my ass out of the palace?"

"I will—" She raised her chin. "I will have your name struck from the lists. I will deem you unsuitable to be my mate."

"Huh." He folded his arms. "For what reason? And—unless you're trying to shine Lashima's own light on me personally—you'll have to cut at least a couple of other warriors too so as not to raise suspicion. And I don't know about their clans," he shrugged, "but *mine* will certainly have something to say about you throwing me out of the contest for no good reason."

"No lady would be so ill-bred as to defy the Heiress's express wish."

"You haven't met the He'lar's clan leader."

She recognized that fire in him. It was the same look as when he had decided to take on Helock . . .

"What of—What of Onara? And your ship? Surely you wish to return to—"

"Onara's at Bathena's great temples, up in the mountains of Lema. And if the goddess of peace should grant *anyone* healing and inner calm, it's Onara. I sold the *Selini's Song* to Jul. I tried to cut her a deal but she wasn't having it. She paid full price and hired Mig on as First Officer." He gave faint smile. "But Jul was always a keen judge of character—except she can't spot a liar near as well as she thinks, can she, *Princess*?"

"What choice did I have?" she whispered. "I revealed myself to my own subjects and earned a beating for it! I had to hide myself in such a place, surrounded by—by—"

"Criminals?"

"I do not think you a criminal, Jehan."

"Just not good enough for you."

"What would you have me say?"

"Well, I'd *like* you to say you'll keep your promise and be my wife."

Her eyes stung. "Such is impossible now."

"You'll have to marry me when I win the Tournament."

"Do not do this." Saria clutched his arm desperately. "Do not fight!"

"Hardly great advice for a future warlord, sweetheart."

"They will kill you!"

His face tightened. "I survived seventeen years in the Badlands. You think I can't win against a bunch of idiotic Az-kye?"

"*I* am Az-kye." She dropped her hand. "Jehan of the He'lar."

"It's a name," he shot back. "That's what you care about, right"—he stepped closer, lowering his voice—

"Liri?"

Her gaze—the proud gaze of an Imperial Daughter—lowered. "I did not set out to deceive you."

He snorted. "Right. 'Liri, the poor slave girl!' Just the kind of woman I would rush to rescue."

"Nor did I intend to entrap you by my disguise," she said, her voice strained. "I did not know your past then."

"My past?" he echoed. "Because my honor is only as good as my father's? As my mother's, as my clan's? *I* don't count for anything?"

"Only Tellarans think that way," she scoffed. "That they are the leaf alone and not merely an offshoot of the tree."

"Easy to say when *your* leaf is one of those basking in the sunshine."

"I have my own duties, my own responsibilities, my own hardships."

He raised an eyebrow. "You have gemstones set into the tops of your shoes."

"My life is not all wealth and privilege," she said hotly. "There are limits—constraints—even for a princess."

He nodded past the billowing curtains, to where the glittering dignitaries mingled to celebrate the peace accords. "Your sister seems to have bounded right past them."

"I know now that Alari never wished for the throne."

"But you do."

"What would you have me say, Jehan?" she cried, throwing her hands out.

"Would you have married me if the Imperial consort hadn't come for you?"

Her chest squeezed. "I—"

In the next moment his mouth was hot against hers, his broad warm palm cradling the back of her head.

Instinctively Saria softened against him as he deepened the kiss, her arms going round his neck to pull him closer.

Perhaps it was that his taste was the same but his skin smooth and shaven, or that his warm scent mixed with the sweet flowers of the Imperial garden, but the sensations left her feeling as if she were in two places, two worlds, at once, and Jehan alone occupied this numinous place with her.

He broke off, his chuckle a little breathless. "Any more and we'll need more than curtains to hide what we're doing up here."

"Jehan—"

"Don't worry, sweetheart." He gave her a hot smile. "Soon I'll do a whole lot more than just kiss you. But tomorrow, I got a busy day."

Then he pushed the curtain aside, leaving her alone and shivering in the chill shadows of the pavilion.

39

⅂Ⅎᒋ ⅃Δ ӾᒋᒷℲᒋᐱ⅄⅂

The Tournament

Okay, I am officially out of my fucking mind . . .

The pageantry to commence a contest for an Imperial Daughter exceeded even that of the Festival of Ren'thar, the competition to be held on the grounds of the Imperial Palace itself. Over a hundred clans had put forth their finest warriors to compete for the opportunity to share Saria's throne, to sire the next Empress of the Shina' clan dynasty.

And Jehan was *way* outclassed.

Lined up beside the best the clans had to offer, he blended right in. His clothes were of the finest sular calfskin. His shoulder bore the crest of the He'lar clan woven with precious stones. His hair, having finally stopped growing—and itching—was now held back with a traditional leather tie. His fluency in his native tongue, tarnished by his years in the Badlands, had returned. In the past few days he'd hardly ever caught himself thinking a word in Tellaran and scrambling to remember it in Az-kye.

He looked every bit an Az-kye warrior—till he swung a sword anyway.

The men standing beside him had trained for hours daily in the years he'd spent running the streets of Tir-Halea. Their swords were more than just weapons now; those blades had become an extension of themselves, a way to channel the very essence of what it was to be a warrior, to be *Az-kye*.

And it sure as hells wasn't something you could pick up in a few short weeks.

Anzu trained him morning till night, pushing him hard, but as the Tournament grew nearer, even behind the practiced inscrutable expression of a warrior, Jehan could see doubt in the old man's eyes.

The previous day he and Anzu arrived at the palace barracks where contestants would be housed for the duration of the Tournament. At the final afternoon practice, Jehan got his first look at what he was up against.

He had to struggle not to be sick.

He thought the He'lar warriors were impressive but these men were tarasteel leviathans.

Suddenly the enormity, the *insanity*, of what he was doing hit him. He knew with gut-wrenching certainty that Anzu and Saria were right—he wasn't going to survive.

He wasn't the only contender who realized he was in over his head. Thirty of those who had arrived yesterday found quick, albeit honorable, reasons to withdraw from the Tournament and were gone before morning.

He was tired too. Nerves kept him tossing and turning on the uncomfortable pallet and he desperately wanted a cup of caf.

The lists were called, announcing which warrior would face which in the first matches. Those who survived to triumph would be pitted against the day's other winners and so it would go on day after day until only one warrior remained to be declared victor. The stands were packed with courtiers and powerful clans eager to witness the blood sport, but the seat reserved for the Imperial Daughter herself, the woman so many would die for over the next few days, remained empty.

Nor would she attend, until the last day when the final challenge would take place.

"Are you unwell?" Anzu asked, the old man searching his gaze when Jehan met him in the preparation room below the stands where the contestants would ready themselves for the coming Challenge.

"No." Numbly Jehan handed his sword and scabbard over, already pulling his jacket off. By tradition all Challenges were fought barefooted, the men clad only in black loincloths, the sword their only weapon and their only protection.

When Jehan had stripped down, Anzu handed the sword back to him, silently following him back to the arena. Across the circle of stones Jehan locked gazes with the man who would very likely kill him in the next few minutes.

"Well," Jehan said faintly, "at least he seems like a nice fellow. With luck he'll get this over quick so he can rest up for the next round."

"You are not as bad a fighter as you think you are, Jehan."

"Wow," Jehan muttered. "That's as close to a compliment as you've ever given me."

"Mind your speech," Anzu scolded.

Jehan closed his eyes briefly. *What the nine hells does it matter now?*

"You have trained hard." Unexpectedly, Anzu placed his hand on Jehan's shoulder. "You will do well, my son."

"Right," he mumbled, the sword hilt gripped in his now damp palm.

An astonished stir ran through the crowd as, accompanied by her guards and maids, dressed from head to toe in glittering, dazzling Imperial black, Princess Saria entered the gallery.

In the stunned wake of the Imperial Daughter's arrival those in the stands scrambled to their feet. Like the crowd, like the warriors in the arena itself, Jehan too bowed to her.

Unlike all the others, when Jehan raised his head it was *him* she was looking at.

And the moment their eyes met across that gulf all his fear, his nervousness, his doubt vanished like mist in the sunlight.

The princess sat, her attendants taking their own seats as the crowd settled into their places again, their conversation buzzing with excitement and speculation.

The Arbiter raised his hand, calling forth the first competitors. Jehan stepped forward, pausing at the Circle's edge for the judge's signal to begin.

I really am out of my mind.

Jehan planted his feet and shifted his hold on the sword as he locked gazes with his first opponent. A small, grim unwarrior-like smile lifted the corners of his mouth.

And I'm going to fucking win . . .

40

Final Challenge

Jehan hissed, baring his teeth, "Tell me again why we have to do this without painkillers."

"A warrior endures without complaint," Anzu reminded, his head bent over his work, closing the wound on Jehan's leg, the result of a lucky sword swipe on the fourth day of competition.

But not lucky enough.

"As I recall, you said I'm no warrior."

"You would do better," Anzu admonished as he finished, "to end the challenges more decisively."

"I'm winning, aren't I?" Jehan demanded. "That's the point, isn't it?"

"It is not seemly for a warlord to show such . . . restraint. You must show, even now, that you have the strength to act with quickness and surety."

He was no swordmaster but the ugly street fighting of the Badlands served him in the contests far better than any skill with the blade could have. He had all the finesse of a Sertarian casino bouncer, but the same skill that lent these warriors such grace handicapped them against such an unpredictable fighter. Since childhood these men had been taught "this" riposte to "that" attack but no matter how practiced they were with the prime parry, a sucker punch in the face ended the Challenge *fast*.

He'd knocked the last guy out cold with the butt of his sword. For form's sake he looked to the Arbiter to make a ruling, already knowing the official would never insist he slaughter an unconscious man.

In the Grand Tournament killing was allowable but it wasn't *necessary*, and he'd managed to get this far without taking a single life.

Jehan gripped the side of the table. "I don't know what you're complaining about," he said through clenched teeth. "The current warlord is a full-blooded Tellaran and—hold on—" He stared, astonished past the point of pain. "You sound like you actually think I'm going to win."

"Think you, you will not?"

"I *have* to. I'm just surprised that *you* think I'll win."

"Of course you will win." Anzu gave a short nod. "You are of the He'lar clan. Even now our clan leader plans your victory celebration."

"Poised to cash in, is she?" Jehan asked dryly. "She might want to wait to order the pricy wine until I make it to the final round."

These contests were grueling, terrifying, a constant and exhausting high and crash of adrenaline. It didn't help that after them he was back in here, covered in dirt and sweat from fights that left him shivering in the cool room, the stink of fear and blood clinging to him and nothing but Anzu's gruff bedside manner to look forward to.

He passed his hand over his face. "How long till the next one?"

"There is a—"

A sharp knock cut the old man off. Anzu instantly drew his blade.

Jehan stared. "What are you *doing*?"

"None of our clan would disturb you now." The warrior tightened his grip on his sword. "And at this crucial time in the Tournament any visitor is an unwelcome one."

"Wait—you don't think someone's here to kill me off?" He glanced at the door. "*Outside* the Circle? Why not wait and have the fun of killing me in front of a cheering crowd?"

"Because it is not one of the Tournament entrants who has come. You are but three challenges from becoming warlord, Jehan," Anzu reminded. "In a few hours you will be poised to become the most powerful man in the empire. You have more enemies now than you have ever had."

"Wow," Jehan muttered, reaching for his own weapon as the knock came again, "that *is* saying something."

They took up places on either side of the door.

"Wait—" Jehan whispered as Anzu reached for the door handle. "What if it's the Arbiter? I don't want to skewer the judge. It might count against me when he has to make a call."

"It is *not* the Arbiter," Anzu hissed, his sword at the ready. "These passages are now the abode of dangerous men."

The flash of blades that greeted them proved him right.

An upheld hand stopped them all short.

"I hope"—Saria began, pointedly looking past the drawn weapons of her guards to Jehan's and Anzu's raised swords—"I have not come at a bad time?"

"Li—uh, Your Highness," Jehan said and like Anzu, hurriedly lowered his weapon.

The guards, however, were not so sanguine.

"We, uh," Jehan continued, glancing at the grim-faced men, "thought you were someone else."

"I am glad to hear it," Saria said wryly. "May I enter? Or shall I conduct this audience from the hallway?"

"No! Sorry, come—uh, please enter, Your Highness," Jehan said, stepping back and finally remembering he was supposed to bow. "You honor us."

"Indeed," she muttered, sweeping past her guards. She raised her eyebrows at Anzu. "And this is . . .?"

Jehan shifted his weight. "My father, Your Highness. Anzu of the He'lar."

"How proud you must be"—she threw a sidelong glance at Jehan—"of your son, Honored Warrior."

Anzu bent his head. "Jehan would be the pride of any clan, Your Highness."

She gave a tight smile. "How lucky, then, that yours claims him. And now, I would speak to your son in private. Leave us." She glanced at her guards. "All of you."

Her warriors looked none too happy but they obeyed. Anzu bowed out, closing the door behind him.

"You should be careful," he chided. "People might think you like me or something."

"Your *father*?" she asked, indicating the closed door. "Who is he?"

"One of the colonists your grandmother sent to settle the Badlands."

"The He'lar's wealth is neither impressive, nor their influence great," Saria said, "but he is of a respectable clan."

"Hey, I wouldn't have just *anyone* as my pretend father."

"Why?" She shook her head. "Why would an honorable warrior lie so—claim a son he does not have?"

"I bribed him."

"You *what*?"

"Bribed. Him." Jehan spread his hands at her stare. "Hey, my share of Helock's money was quite a pile.

Enough to buy even *me* a respectable name and a place in the Tournament."

"Jehan, you have done well in the Circle—"

"By that you mean I'm not dead."

"You have fought well and I am . . . honored."

"Oh, well, then it's all worth it." He turned, limping back to the treatment table. "Mind if I sit, Highness?"

She hurried after him, frowning. "You are in pain."

He stifled a groan, using his palms to push himself onto the padded surface. "Hells yeah, I'm in pain! Dozens of us are injured, dozens of men are dead in this lunacy."

"This contest was not my wish," she said tightly. "Not by my choice but by the empress's order."

"Why isn't *she* here then? Watching us butcher each other?"

"Why do you speak this way to me?" she demanded. "What have I done to so offend you?"

"It's not what you've done, it's what you came here to do," he gritted out. "And you can forget it."

"Jehan, many of the contestants have honorably withdrawn—"

"No. Hey, mind if I rest a sec?" he asked, lying down. "Trying not to get hacked to pieces isn't as much fun as it looks."

"I insist you withdraw from the lists."

"Nope."

"I did not wish to take such action but if you will not go peacefully—" She squared her shoulders. "I will expose you. I will unmask you for the fraud you are and denounce the clan who has falsely claimed you."

"The hells you will." He looked up at her. "What, are you afraid I'll win and you'll have to keep your promise?"

"Promise?"

"That if, after I knew your secrets and wanted you, you'd marry me. You owe me some vows."

"Those words were spoken a lifetime ago, half a galaxy away. I will not be bound by them."

"Hey, don't let the gods hear you say that. They hate it when Az-kye break their word."

"I waste my breath to try to speak sense to you!"

He sat up, catching her arm gently before she could turn away. "You really *should* be more careful. These passageways are tight quarters for your warriors to fight off an attack. They're just as likely to get in each other's way as they are to defend you. It wasn't that long ago that someone tried to end your whole dynasty, remember"—his mouth curved—"Liri?"

"You need not be concerned for me," Saria said shortly, pulling her arm away. "If you will not acquiesce to my wishes, I see no reason to come down to you again."

"You won't have to," he called before she could reach the door. "'Cause I'll be coming up to you, Princess."

"He sure is one ugly bastard," Jehan muttered, eyeing the warrior who paced back and forth at the Circle's edge.

"Kih of the Li'ru is a merciless fighter," Anzu warned. "He has killed every opponent while you spare yours." The old man fixed him with a look. "Do not seek to spare this one."

Jehan's muscles were trembling from nerves and fatigue. "Probably a good plan."

The Arbiter raised his hand and both men passed the stones that marked the boundary of the arena.

Kih let out a bellow and ran at Jehan, his sword lifted. Probably his best attack, meant to end the Challenge with Jehan's head flying from his body. But Jehan knocked Kih's sword aside and spun, jamming his elbow into the back of the other warrior's neck.

And nearly lost his head to Kih's backswing.

A ripple went through the crowd as Jehan jumped back, the sword so close it nicked his throat. The path the blade took across his skin stung like a bitch but Jehan knew better than to drop his guard to reach for the wound.

"I look forward to killing you," Kih snarled, slashing at him again.

"It's good to have goals," Jehan panted, scarcely blocking in time, watching out for that wicked backswing. Jehan kept his feet moving, circling Kih, keeping eye contact at all times just as his father had taught him.

"Know you," Kih spat, "you fight like the son of a whore?"

"What does that even *mean*?"

"I have watched you—your tricks and games." Kih's lip curled as he stalked forward. "You do not fool *me*. You are hiding a lack of skill. You are no swordsman."

"Takes more than sword work to win a fight." Jehan dodged out of the way. "And in case you hadn't noticed I've made it to the last round."

Kih's heavy brows rushed together and Jehan realized he'd spoken with a Tellaran cadence, in the Realm's way of running words together.

"You are not even of our caste!" Kih sneered. "You are not *fit* to be our princess's consort!"

Whether it was the strain or exhaustion, he didn't know, but Kih's words suddenly rang so true Jehan glanced at Saria.

It was a deadly mistake.

The sword slicing across his chest made him cry out. In two quick moves that Jehan barely blocked, Kih had him off his feet and in the dirt of the Circle.

Jehan rolled out of the way just as Kih's sword came down, the dust stinging his wounds, and scrambled to his feet.

Kih's lip curled. "You do not even fight like a warrior."

"No," Jehan growled. "I fight like a winner."

This time when Kih swung, Jehan didn't dodge but stepped *forward*, blocking Kih's arm. He hooked his foot behind Kih's and slammed the butt of his sword *hard* right into the side of the other warrior's neck.

Kih staggered and fell hard. His chest heaving, Jehan stood over Kih's unconscious form, the sound of the crowd's cheers pounding against his eardrums.

Trembling with fatigue, he faced the galley where Saria now stood and lifted his sword high to her in victory.

But the official judge did not raise his hands in acknowledgment of Jehan's triumph. He held his hand out, palm down. After a few confused moments the crowd quieted.

All but Anzu.

"What is this, Arbiter?" he demanded, every line of the old man's body stiff with offense. "Declare him! Jehan of the He'lar is the victor!"

"Arbiter!" Saria rose. "Declare the victor!"

"I cannot, Your Highness," the Arbiter said, throwing her an apologetic glance. "There is . . . one more contender."

"One more—!" *What the fuck?* "All the lists have been called! I have beaten every combatant!"

The Arbiter glanced toward the east side of the Circle as a warrior entered through the arched doorway. As he drew closer, Jehan's frown deepened, wondering why this man looked so familiar.

Saria's wide gaze was fixed on him. "Naret . . ."

41

Benediction

Jehan felt his face blanch as Saria's lover came to stand beside him. The handsome Az-kye's face was tilted up to meet her gaze, his expression adoring.

"How—?" Saria shook her head. "How can you be here? You died aboard the *Ty'har*."

"I often wish I had." Naret closed his eyes briefly. "So greatly did I fail in my duty to protect you, my Princess."

"I cannot . . ." She shook her head again. "I cannot believe it."

"When I awoke you were gone, the ship like ice. I called for you, searching the ship, hoping you had gone to the shuttle bay. Lashima answered my prayers but it was not I who acted as your protector that day. I saw you running. I saw you stumble and another take you up and carry you aboard a Tellaran vessel. Ren'thar granted me the strength to reach one of our shuttles, but before I could rescue you from the barbarians—" Naret lowered his gaze. "I lost consciousness. A ship patrolling the Az-litha colony found me. I lay within their medical bay for ten days without waking. When I awoke they told me you were—" He shook his head. "But that does not matter now."

"Why did you not reveal yourself before now?" Saria asked.

Naret's face was pained. "I failed you. When I thought you dead I had no reason to rise from my bed and when I learned you lived—It is only now that I am strong enough."

"You did not fail me," she said gently. "You are the reason I survived."

Jehan's jaw was clenched so tightly it hurt.

"You are too generous, my Princess." Naret bowed his head. "But no kind words can wash away my shame. I was once your protector; I would fight now to reclaim that right."

Saria hesitated, her glance going to Jehan but she'd know history better than any of them. "The Tournament has been decided—"

"I beg your pardon, Your Highness," the Arbiter said. "Naret of the Az'larna was appointed your protector by the empress herself. There *is* precedent for him to challenge the victor."

"Did he wish to fight, why did he not add his name to the lists?" Anzu erupted, glaring at Naret. "Why wait till now to put himself forward, when the Tournament has already been decided?"

"As Her Highness's appointed Protector, it would be unseemly for him to fight one other than the victor," the Arbiter reminded sourly.

And fuck, why wear yourself out if you don't have to?

"Saria," Naret said, plainly desperate enough to forget her title. "I failed you once but I never will again. If I win, I will devote myself always to your protection and your happiness. If I lose"—he swallowed—"I will be free of my guilt and welcomed in Ren'thar's Hall."

"Naret," she began, shaking her head. "You cannot—"

"No!" A shock ran through the crowd at his interrupting an Imperial Daughter, but Jehan stepped forward, his glance taking in Anzu, Saria, and the Arbiter before he turned to hold Naret's gaze. "I will fight him."

"I cannot believe the Arbiter allows this travesty!" Anzu fumed. "For you to face, *now*, an opponent who is fresh and unfatigued when you have fought for days! When you have already won the Tournament—and done so with both honor *and* mercy!"

"Yeah," Jehan muttered, bending to sharpen his sword. "That'll teach me."

"You shall not be forced to this! We will call upon the empress! Our clan will insist the Council of Elders examine Naret's claim to combat—"

"Man, you'd do anything to get a clan member in the palace."

"Perhaps, Jehan," Anzu said brittlely, "I simply do not want you to die."

His head came up and he met the elder warrior's gaze. "I'm grateful for all you've done, you know. I might not be your son, Anzu, but I can tell you any one you'd had would have been proud to call you 'Father.'"

"I—" Anzu's chin trembled. "I saw you many times about on Halea as a young man, Jehan—a child really when your parents died. To my shame I could not see past tradition, past status, then. But know I deeply regret I that did not take you into my home." A sheen came to the old man's eyes, his voice thick. "I should have done, for any man would be blessed to have you as a son."

Jehan's throat tightened. "Thank you for that."

Anzu gave a short nod. "If he was chosen by our empress to be the princess's protector, Naret of the Az'larna is a superior swordsman," he said grimly. "He has not been exhausted by the contest as you have, but fight as you have fought, Jehan, and you will triumph."

"No. Winning with Tellaran street fighting against Naret, wouldn't make me feel like I'd really won. And Saria . . . deserves a warrior at her side."

Anzu put his hand on Jehan's shoulder. "You are a warrior, Jehan. You *are* Az-kye."

"Well," Jehan said, standing, "then I guess I better go act like one."

He walked to the edge of the stones, trying to the hide the limp he'd picked up when he twisted his knee fighting Kih. The crowd cheered when he came into view but if he were fooling them, he wasn't fooling himself.

He ached all over, his sword arm so fatigued he could hardly hold the weapon up.

The temples taught that Ren'thar selected the warrior who won. That even now the god raised his hand to bless with victory the warrior best suited to the task of warlord. But Naret was fresh and rested, he was younger, well-trained, chosen by the empress herself to be her daughter's protector.

And he *loves Saria too . . .*

The Arbiter lowered his hand and he and Naret stepped into the Circle.

Jehan lifted his sword, circling, waiting for Naret's attack.

If you're really watching, Ren'thar, remember I'm a warrior's son too. Remember my father—my mother—and the wrongs done us.

Give me victory.

When the attack came, Naret moved like lightning. Not for him the brutality of Kih, nor the quick but weak attack of Jehan's first opponent. This young man had skill with a sword that showed him not just proficient but a master.

Naret's first coulé forced Jehan off balance. He parried Jehan's attack and responded with a quick compound-riposte. Jehan's breath caught, a ripple running through the crowd when Naret's blade neatly sliced his cheek.

Jehan fell back, breathing hard, squinting against the sweat in his eyes. His throat tightened at Naret's slow approach. Onlookers might have thought the younger man was simply being cautious but Jehan realized that as much as he himself wanted to win the *right* way, so did Naret.

The man was giving him every advantage, every opportunity to recover before the next onslaught.

Gods, he's going easy on me!

His chest burned at finding himself the object of Naret's pity. Despite Naret's masterful swordsmanship, Jehan could have won a half-dozen times if he'd been willing to resort to Tellaran street fighting.

But he wouldn't do it, not this time; Saria deserved a warrior.

Even if it wasn't him.

Then suddenly, as if the goddess Lashima Herself drew back the curtain of time, Jehan could see Naret standing at Saria's side as consort. He saw the kind of warlord this man would make but one who, when the crucial moment came, would fail her—

Saria!

The vision left him gasping. The horror of her path if he failed here today twisted his stomach.

I can't let him win! I can't!

Just as Naret swung the death blow Jehan raised his blade, his lips drawn back in a roar.

Ren'thar! Let your sword sing through me!

A rush of energy shot through his body, the smell of tashi flowers that bloomed beside the B'tai clanhouse barracks in the air. Suddenly every lesson his father drilled into him, every movement his father could demonstrate with flawless skill, was *his*.

The power coursing through him was a beast of its own will and thought. It possessed him utterly, pouring into and through him so that Jehan no longer felt the aches or pains of the past grueling days, nor was he restrained by the limits of his own human strength.

He had a brief flash of Naret's eyes going wide, the man's sword swinging upward as he tried desperately to stem the onslaught of Jehan's blade—

The energy suddenly vanished, leaving Jehan trembling, painfully mortal and blinking down Naret's body.

The roaring mana that had filled him, and pulsed through the very air around him, was gone, leaving only the sound of blood rushing in his ears, his gulps for breath, and the wild cheering of the crowd.

Gasping, weary in mind and body, he found he couldn't even heft the sword aloft in victory as he should. He kept his fingers around the grip but just barely as his arm gave out, the blade's point throwing up a tiny puff of dust as it fell to the dirt of the arena.

Swaying with exhaustion, surprised to see that Naret had landed a few blows he hadn't even felt, Jehan raised his head to meet Saria's wide gaze. She'd left the Imperial box, leaning forward and gripping the rail as no Imperial Daughter should do.

"Saria—"

There was no way she could hear him. He couldn't even hear himself over the crowd shouting his name.

"Sweetheart," he rasped as blackness took him, "I won."

42

ᵍᴧ ᵡᴧᴧᵑᴧᴇ

Courtship

"Why?" Saria cried, on her feet as soon as the reception room doors shut behind the courtiers.

The moment his injuries had been treated and he was dressed again in warrior black, his "clan" brought him to be formally presented to her. Without even permitting their clan leader to finish her insufferable flattery and get to that task, Saria had thrown everyone out of the room.

"Why did you not refuse to fight?" Saria continued, blood pounding through her temples. "You stood victor already!"

"Naret wanted that fight, not me, remember?" Jehan snapped. "He entered the Circle of his own free will. He knew going in only one of us was going to walk out!"

"You could have spared him if—"

"You think *he* would have spared *me*?"

Her mouth tightened. "You spared the others!"

"Did you love him?" he demanded. "Is that what this is about?"

"He was a good man! An honored warrior—"

"This is what you wanted!" Jehan's nostrils flared. "You wanted to be Az-kye—for us *both* to be Az-kye! The Tournament needed a definitive winner and the empire needs a strong warlord. I only behaved the way any honorable warrior would act in the Circle. This is our way!"

"*Our way* condemns you a as slave to the end of your days!" she said hotly. "Strange how you pick and choose what you will of our traditions, Jehan." Her hands curled into fists. "And you are hardly one to speak of honor!"

"Because disowning my own father would be honorable? That's all I had to do—all my *mother* had to do—for *honor*! Cast him out and we would have been welcomed anywhere in the empire!"

"Your father was a criminal!"

His dark eyes went molten. "And the very stones of your palace reek of innocent blood."

"Leave me, Jehan of the He'lar," she said through clenched teeth. "I will not look on you again."

"Oh, hells no. I won and I'm not about to give up my prize. Our formal courtship begins tomorrow." Jehan turned his back. "I'll see you then."

"I have not given you leave to withdraw!"

"You're not going to stop me from going, Saria," he said without pausing in his stride. "And you're sure as fuck not going to get me to give up!"

The door slammed shut behind him and Saria's mouth tightened.

We will see . . .

"Tell him I am ill," Saria said firmly the next morning. She turned over in bed. "I cannot see him today."

"Shall I send for a healer?" her maid, Tilanna, asked. "If you are too ill to see your intended—"

"I do not require a healer," Saria snapped. "All I require is that you send him away! In fact"—Saria pulled the jaha-down quilt up to her neck—"inform him I will not be able to see him tomorrow either."

The maid hesitated and Saria threw a glare at her. "Do as you are told!"

Tilanna scurried away to do her bidding and Saria yanked the covers over her head.

Tomorrow I will announce to the court we are ill-suited. That a mating between us would be—

The door to her quarters closed sharply. Startled by the sound of so many approaching, she sat up quickly. Jehan strode into her bedroom and Saria frantically tried to smooth her sleep-rumpled hair. Just behind him came a half-dozen priestesses of Behur.

"What is this?" she demanded. "How dare you invade my quarters so!"

If these women who served the god of healing looked cowed by their Heiress's scowl, Jehan decidedly did *not*.

"I dreamed that my intended might be ill," Jehan said. "So trusting in the gods' guidance, I summoned healers from the temple of Behur to attend you. Clearly my vision was a true sending, evidence that the gods smile upon our coming marriage. Of course, I have already sent word to Her Imperial Majesty that you are unwell. The empress bids you be given a *thorough* examination to determine the cause of your illness and its treatment, no matter how unpleasant the cure might be." He took a step aside to allow the women to pass. "But do not fear; I will not leave Your Highness for a moment."

Glaring and outmaneuvered, Saria had no choice but to submit to the healers' examination. Each, of course, was intent on finding a cause for her "illness" and they badgered her with questions. Finally, the elder priestess determined that she was overwrought from the strain of the Tournament and prescribed both rest and a suspension of her duties for the time being.

"At least," Jehan said, leaning casually against the wall after the women had been ushered out, "that gives us lots of time together."

Sitting at her dressing table now and wrapped in a silk robe, Saria gave him a sour look. "You had no dream."

"And *you* didn't even have a sniffle."

"I awoke with a headache."

"Well, I'm just glad I could help you to such a speedy recovery."

"You should not speak like that," Saria grumbled.

He raised his eyebrows. "Like what? I'm happy you aren't really sick."

"You do not sound Az-kye," she said irritably. "You must mind your diction. Do not let your words run together as Tellarans do."

"Well," he said, his accent again in keeping with the warrior caste, "I would not wish to embarrass you."

"I am more concerned that they will discover you are an imposter and throw you from the falls."

"Like Liri was?"

"*Empress* Liri," she reminded sharply. "No honored warrior would call her simply 'Liri.' And in the name of Lashima, Jehan—stand tall! Not slumped like a Tellaran street caller."

"You sound like my old swordmaster," He straightened. "Next you will deny me dessert for the tarnish on my sword."

Her head came up. "You have not polished your sword?"

"I haven't been with you in weeks." He put his hand over his heart. "You have my word, sweetheart, my sword is well-polished."

It was only when he grinned at her furrowed brow that she caught his joke. Her cheeks went hot. "Still with a Tellaran's sense of humor."

"Still *have* one, yeah," he agreed. "Sorry—*yes*."

"I wish the healers were here still," she muttered. The gaze of all those venerable women at least served to keep her in check. "I would have them concoct something for my headache."

He stroked her hair and instinctively she leaned against him. "Do you really have one? I can call them back."

"It is nothing. I could not sleep last night."

"I was going to talk to you about that. I think I should sleep here from now on."

"No!" she cried, pushing to her feet.

"Someone tried to kill you," he reminded seriously. "And your sister. And your mother. She may have had help."

"The empress's new spymaster will uncover her confederates if any remain."

"The last one missed a plot to take over the throne," he pointed out. "What is the matter? Do you not trust me?"

"Sooner or later you will slip, forget yourself, and my maids will hear you," she hissed. "They will expose you."

"I would not want your maids exposing me," he said solemnly.

"This is not a joke or a game!" Her hands clenched at her sides. "You must leave, Jehan! Now, before you are discovered!"

He took a step closer and just his nearness sent her heat rising.

"What . . ." she managed as he bent his head toward her. "What are you doing?"

She had a flash of dark, fiery eyes then she was against him, his mouth hot on hers. His face was jarring in its smoothness, shaved as a warrior's should be, but his scent, so warm and male, was the same. After many nights of longing for him, weeks when not even the demands upon the Heiress could distract her, then the torment of days spent watching him fight, her breath stopping at every miss, her nails cutting into her clenched fist at every swing, left her with no will to fight that need now.

His hands left her for an instant as he freed himself of the sword at his back.

"Saria," he murmured hoarsely. It occurred to her that this was the first time he would love her, knowing who she truly was.

For a moment she held her breath, fearful that his touch would have changed, no longer one of equals, no longer of one who saw her as a woman, not a princess.

But this was her Jehan, with courage unmatched even in legend, and though they stood in the Imperial Palace itself, he was neither cowed nor hesitant. He undid her fine linen robe, the gown beneath falling as he pushed the thin straps from her shoulders, catching the back of her head, his fingers threading through her hair to slide his lips against hers.

Saria wrapped her arms around his neck, meeting his heat with her own, helping him cast off the black clothes of a warrior, reveling in the feel of his warm skin, the broad muscles of his shoulders as he lifted her onto the bed.

She was ready, open for him, the tip of his hardness at her center.

He pulled back and slid his body down, the warmth of his muscled belly between her legs now, and he gave a breathless laugh.

"I wasn't kidding about the sword polishing." He flashed her a quick smile, his long hair soft against the top of her thigh. "But we have to slow this down. I don't have it in me to last long, sweetheart."

"I thought of you," she said, her voice husky. "Here in my bed, I thought of you as I brought myself to pleasure."

His face flushed with hunger, his eyes molten now. "Well, I sure didn't come all this way to disappoint you . . ."

His gaze held hers, as he bent his head to flick his tongue against the apex of her breast. The heat of his mouth was followed by cold as the air touched the moisture left by his kiss. Saria shivered with wanting.

Jehan's lips slid lower, over her belly, as his fingers traced her center, lightly touching, and Saria arched at the tightening pleasure of it. Gently his fingers parted her folds to press a kiss, as soft as the flutter of a gossamerfly's wings, there. Saria gasped as the kiss changed to gentle suction, drawing her in, his tongue flicking against her.

He sank a finger into her folds, pressing that sensitive place inside, sending her release crashing over her. Still trembling from her climax, she wrapped her arms weakly around his neck as he positioned himself over her. Balancing on his elbows, he held her gaze as his cock slid inside her slippery folds and he trembled a bit as he filled her completely. He started to move then, his face and body taut, the muscles of his stomach trembling as he thrust. Saria moved against him, her hands on his hips to press him deeper, and he made a strangled sound as she cried out again, contracting hard around him.

Jehan thrust once more, deeply, and stiffened, his shaft throbbing as he came.

He gasped, his head bent, his mouth open and moist against the skin of her neck.

Her hand went to the back of his head, to his long thick hair held with a warrior's tie. "Jehan . . ."

"Don't worry, sweetheart. After all these weeks without you" —he gave a soft chuckle, rolling off to cradle her against him— "I promise, whatever I do next here, it sure won't be sleep."

The last of the afternoon suns' light warmed the room as Saria shifted against him.

"You cannot stay here," she murmured, her cheek resting on his bare chest. "Your very presence in Az-kye space invites disaster."

"We beat Helock together," he reminded, covering her hand with his. "We can handle a couple of courtiers."

"Helock was a madman who led a band of thugs." Saria pushed herself up on her elbow to look him. "My mother rules an empire of trillions with an ocean of warriors at her command. You must leave!"

"Leave?" His eyebrows shot up. "Why the hells would I do that? I won the Tournament. From what I hear even the empress likes me."

"Her Majesty likes Jehan of the He'lar." She remembered all too well the conversation the previous night when her mother urged her to take him as bound mate without delay. "A warrior who does not even exist!"

"He does now," Jehan countered. "Just ask the He'lar clan leader."

"Does she know?" Saria frowned. "Is she too part of this fraud?"

"Anzu told her I'm his son. She had no reason to doubt him and he sure would not want to know the truth now."

"Think you your deception will go undiscovered?" she cried. "When every eye in the empire is upon you now?"

"What is this about, really? Is—" She saw him swallow. "Is this about my father then?"

"No," she whispered. "I can find no reason why your father would still keep to our ways, why he would wish his son to become a warrior if he himself were capable of acting with such dishonor, so I cannot but think him so."

"Then . . . what is it?" His face was grave. "Do you not want me, Saria?"

Her mouth parted but she could not answer.

"I know you think Naret was the better man," he said quietly. "Maybe you think he should have won."

She dropped her gaze. "That was for Ren'thar to decide."

He was silent for a moment. "You wanted to know why I did not refuse to fight him," Jehan said finally. "And the answer is because I knew—" He shook his head. "It sounds crazy when I say it out loud but I *knew* right there in the Circle that if he became consort . . . Do not ask me how I know, but a great trial is coming, one that will test our people, test you. Something about Naret's character, about *his* way of looking at things, would tip the balance the wrong way. Something he would do, just because he was who he was, would not let our people survive another generation." She saw him swallow. "Would not let *you* survive."

She frowned, searching his haunted gaze.

"There was another reason too," he continued softly. "A very selfish one. I knew if I did not face him there and then, if I did not fight him as a true warrior would, there would have been doubt in your eyes whenever you looked at me. Looked *on* me," he corrected with a faint smile. "There, you cannot say I do not sound Az-kye now."

"I would not have doubted you," she said hoarsely.

"Yes, you would have. And I would rather have died in the Circle than lived with that." His voice quieted. "I wanted to win but I didn't want to kill him. I think—I think maybe it's what *Naret* wanted though—to go to Ren'thar's Hall. And for what it's worth, I think the god welcomed him there."

"Jehan, I could not bear it if—You *must* go." Her vision blurred. "Even if you take my heart with you when you do."

"I love you—whether you're Liri or an Imperial Daughter or an—" A smile touched his mouth again. "An *ex*-Companion. Sweetheart, the gods—Az-kye, Tellaran, who cares which ones—have given us a chance to be together, *here*, on the homeworld, with you someday as empress, and me as warlord. We can have our whole lives together." His warm broad hand cupped her cheek. "It's worth the risk, it's worth everything—if you love me."

"I do love you, Jehan," she said hoarsely.

His gaze softened. "Then marry me."

"Jehan . . ."

"Wait! Don't answer yet!" He flung himself away, to the side of the bed, to grab his warrior's jacket, patting at the pockets and drawing out a case. "I have a courting gift for you."

"A courting gift?" Saria took the elaborately carved ancient box into her hands. She lifted the lid to peer inside and her mouth parted at the sight, each jewel sparkling with inner rainbow colors. "The crystals . . ."

He lifted the necklace, all five of the gems beautifully set into gold. Gently he brushed aside her hair and fastened it around her neck.

"But—" Saria frowned at him, her hand resting on the gems around her throat. "Why did you not sell them? You risked your life to take this treasure from the *Ty'har*."

"Because deep down I knew, even then"—his mouth curved, his dark eyes soft as he lightly traced the curve of her cheek—"there was only one treasure I was taking from that ship."

Her vision blurred. "Yes."

"Wait—what?" He blinked. "You mean, 'yes'? As in, yes, you'll marry me?"

"I am only being sensible. If you will not go then it is the only way to assure your safety. No one would dare offend the Imperial family with the outrageous lie that our warlord was once a Tellaran pirate, or could possibly be one of the clanless."

"You mean it?" he asked hoarsely. "You aren't teasing?"

"I mean it." She smiled at him through tears. "I will take you as my bound mate, Jehan."

43

Introductions

Jehan was early for his audience with the empress. To better woo the princess and, no doubt, to get the court used to him as a force within the empire, he had been given quarters in the palace itself.

Anzu and the Lady of the He'lar—puffed up with the stratospheric rise in her clan's influence—had not yet arrived, and though he had spent the night in the Imperial Daughter's bed, he had to wait outside till he could be properly presented to the empress.

Her Imperial Majesty's majordomo Jelara gave him a fretful look. He hadn't realized how showing up early like this would put the woman in an awkward position. She couldn't announce him before the empress bade him enter but she was clearly anxious not to offend the next warlord by leaving him to wait out here either.

He tried not to shift his feet. If his ordeal in the Circle had been both terrifying and exhausting, navigating the court, even in the short time since he'd been declared victor, was proving no less treacherous.

Word had flown through the palace that he'd spent the afternoon and night with Saria in her bedchamber, that he was to be presented to the empress, and afterwards the marriage date was to be announced. Clearly things were going well.

He smiled inwardly, remembering the previous afternoon and night . . . and this morning.

Very well indeed.

And the members of the palace, high and low, were eager to make an ally of the man firmly on the path to becoming consort and Imperial warlord. The smiles that greeted him lacked warmth, everyone seeking to draw him into their tangle of alliances and plotting and ambition.

It reminded him a lot—and very unpleasantly—of dealing with the Brethren. Saria hadn't been kidding when, challenged with facing Helock and his men, she'd said it was a task she was well suited to.

Yeah, but am I?

"There you are!"

Startled, Jehan turned and found himself looking into the bright blue eyes of the man he'd tried to kill.

Kyndan Maere.

He wore a Tellaran commander's dress uniform of blue and white, his boots polished to a high shine, his brown hair regulation Fleet cut. Jehan glanced at the blaster Princess Alari's mate wore at his hip.

"I hear you're up for *my* job."

"Job?" Jehan croaked.

"Sorry, Tellaran term. I meant it looks like you're going to be the next warlord."

"Yes," Jehan said, his heart hammering. "If the Heiress honors me by consenting to be my mate."

"You know—" Kyndan's brow furrowed. "You seem . . . familiar."

"I am an Az-kye warrior." Jehan did his best imitation of his father's stoic expression. "I think we are not much different—one from the other—to a Tellaran."

"True enough," the former Imperial Consort agreed. "Black leather, big swords. Small brains."

Jehan didn't even twitch.

The Tellaran's blue eyes narrowed. "Usually that kind of thing gets me dragged into the Circle."

Jehan offered a warrior's slight shrug. "Truly I have spent enough time in the Circle for the time being, I think. And I have never had complaints about the size of brains or my"—Jehan gave a meaningful glance at the weapon strapped to his back—"sword."

Kyndan gave a surprised laugh. "An Az-kye warrior with a sense of humor! I didn't think they came that way!"

"There are those who would say no Tellaran possesses honor."

The Tellaran's gaze narrowed a bit. "But you wouldn't?"

"I have known such." Jehan inclined his head. "It pleases me that our people will be at peace"—Kyndan was Imperial Daughter Alari's mate and a former consort and warlord but Jehan had a hunch he would prefer to be called—"Commander."

"I am too." Kyndan sent a glance at the courtiers and lowered his voice. "I hope they treat an Az-kye poised to be warlord better than they did a Tellaran."

"If they treated you worse," Jehan muttered, "your time here must have been a journey through the Underworld."

"I know it's overwhelming," Kyndan said quietly. "That right now you don't know who to trust. You just need to remember one thing and you'll be fine."

"What is that, Commander?" Jehan asked, frowning.

"*Her.*" Kyndan nodded toward the throne room, where both his own mate and Saria waited. "She's in the middle of this storm. Your real job is to be her rock, her protector. Be the one that she can always trust and turn to, no matter what. Do what's best for *her*, and the hells with the rest of them."

Jehan's shoulders fell. "That I can do."

Kyndan gave him a nod and an encouraging smile. "Then you'll be fine."

Maere's a good leader. A good man.

He was starting to feel pretty bad for shooting the guy now.

'Course can't hardly say that aloud, now can I?

"Jehan—cousin!" The Lady of the He'lar, her rounded figure laced into a too-tight court gown of Imperial black, hurried his way, her heels clacking against the polished floor, the tall jaha feathers in her hair bouncing with every step. "Are we late? Tell me we have not offended her Imperial Majesty with our delay!" Y'lanni threw a narrow look back the way they had come, at the courtiers, servants, and officials that crowded the hall. "You simply must—I do not know!—make a proclamation or some such that they are to *clear the way* when we approach!"

Anzu gave him such a long-suffering look that Jehan had to bite his cheek to keep from smiling.

"That honor is reserved for the Imperial family," Jehan said, trying to force some regret into his voice.

"But we *are*!" Y'lanni objected, her plump cheeks flushing.

"We are not of the Imperial family, my Lady," Anzu said, as if this were the hundredth time he was repeating it.

"Well—" She indicated Jehan with a wave of her elaborately jeweled feather fan. "Nearly so, in any case!" Huffing at finding no ally in Anzu, she sent a pleading look at Jehan. "I entreat you, dearest cousin, speak to Her

Highness! Surely the Heiress would not hear of her mate's clan leader so despicably treated!"

"I am not her mate yet." Jehan's voice had a touch of tarasteel to it. "And does she choose me as consort I will leave our clan to join hers. I think it wise—*cousin*—that none of us forget that."

Y'lanni's mouth settled into a pout and Jehan caught Kyndan's understanding, and sympathetic, look.

The majordomo was waving at them frantically.

"That's us," Kyndan said to Jehan. "You're stepping onto the high wire and I'm stepping off." He gave a friendly smile. "And good luck to both of us."

"I understand his visit to you yesterday went well," the empress murmured. "He did not leave until long after the suns rose this morning. It is the talk of the court."

As First, Saria sat now at her mother's side on the Heiress's throne while Alari, once regent, now an Imperial Daughter only but beamingly happily so, stood at her mother's side.

Saria stiffened. "Is *everything* I do a matter of common gossip?"

"As First?" Alari said dryly. "Yes."

"Of course, I have no need of gossip," the empress reminded, "when I have a spymaster."

A spymaster who in his eagerness not to fail where his predecessor had might yet sniff out the truth of Jehan's identity . . .

"I have considered Your Majesty's counsel," Saria said quickly. "And I agree. There is no reason to delay. I shall take Jehan of the He'lar as my bound mate as soon as it can be arranged."

"Excellent," her mother said. "I will consult with the priestesses of Lashima for the earliest auspicious day."

"Are you certain, sister?" Alari asked worriedly. "You have known him only a short time."

"You did not know Kyndan at all when you chose him to be your mate and you are happy, sister. And—" Saria shifted a bit. "And—the god has favored him with victory. I see no reason for delay."

Just then the doors of the throne room opened and the majordomo led Jehan, his "father," and the Lady of the He'lar in.

With them came Kyndan Maere.

Saria's mouth went dry. She had done her best in the last days before Alari's departure to keep her sister's mate and Jehan as far apart as possible. Now the men stood side by side!

Her frightened glance met Jehan's and, clearly aware of exactly what she feared, he gave her a reassuring look.

Both men, along with Jehan's companions, bowed deeply to the empress. When they straightened, the majordomo extolled the noble lineage of Jehan's "clan," recounted his victory in the Circle, and—to Saria's ears anyway—seemed to gloss over the fact that even this invented history had Jehan growing up in Tellaran space.

But even if Jelara, the majordomo, tried to downplay that fact, it had not escaped the empress—or perhaps her new spymaster.

"We are grateful for the loyalty you showed our mother, the Empress Teshir, in obeying her command to colonize beyond the Sword," the empress said to Anzu. "It cannot have been an easy existence."

"It was not," the elderly man agreed, the etchings of sorrow clear on his face.

"We too are pleased to have welcomed him home," the Lady of the He'lar hurriedly put in, a bit too loudly, her mouth stretched wide in a smile, "Your Most Gracious Imperial Majesty."

The old man looked pained and Saria tensed, praying for Jehan to control any urge to smirk.

"He is a credit to your clan," the empress said kindly. "And Ren'thar has chosen well. He has proven himself in combat and graciousness—an example to all. He will make a fine consort to our Heiress. You are most welcome to our palace, Jehan of the He'lar," the empress said to him. "As you will be to our clan."

Saria held her breath, her heart thudding in her chest as Jehan raised his gaze to meet the eyes of the woman who had sent his father into disgrace, had forced his family to abandon their home and flee to Tellaran territory, whose orders resulted in their deaths.

"I am grateful for your kindness, Majesty," he said in perfectly accented Az-kye. "I will endeavor to always be worthy of the Princess Saria."

The empress favored him with a smile then turned her gaze on Kyndan. "And you, warlord and mate of my daughter, have come to beg leave to depart our court?"

"I have." He gave an utterly Tellaran smile. "But with your blessing, I hope, Your Majesty."

The empress sent a glance at Alari, who beamed at her then stepped down from the dais to stand beside her mate.

"I bid you protect the Princess Alari. She is"—the empress's eyes shone for an instant with unshed tears—"very dear to us all."

Kyndan took Alari's hand and inclined his head to the empress, solemn now. "As she is to me, Majesty."

"Do you know, Kyndan Maere"—the empress regarded him for a moment—"I believe I will miss you as well."

"I thank you for that," Kyndan said, pleased and surprised. "While Alari and I will make our home on Nima, I know we will both look forward to visiting Az-kye. And—" He glanced at the majordomo, who waited by the doors. "The new Tellaran ambassador is here." He shared a smile with Alari. "And may this one be less trouble to your court than the last have."

"I should certainly hope so," the Empress returned dryly as the doors were once again opened.

Also wearing the Tellaran's dress uniform, the Tellarans' new representative entered. Saria felt herself blanch.

Protocol demanded the blonde woman keep her attention forward but for just an instant she glanced Kyndan's way—

"Sir!" Nisara cried, her weapon instantly in her hand. A shock ran through the courtiers at the action, dozens of swords unsheathed as the imperial guards ran forward. Saria shot to her feet. "Behind you!"

"Hold where you are!" Kyndan, as yet Imperial warlord, snapped at the guards then took quick steps to confront his former First Officer, wrenching the blaster from Nisara's hand himself. "What the hells the matter with you?"

"Don't you recognize him?" Nisara cried. "That's Jehan Dekra! That's the pirate who tried to kill you, Kyn!"

"What is this?" the empress demanded.

"This Tellaran is mistaken, Your Majesty!" Saria insisted. "He is—"

Jehan stepped forward. "No, she's not."

Saria shook her head. "Jehan—"

"If nothing else, Princess," he said hoarsely, "I *will* be a warrior worthy of you." He addressed the empress. "I was known as Jehan Dekra when I lived in Tellaran space, but I was born Jehan of the B'tai."

"How—" the empress began, frowning. "How is your clan name known to me?"

His expression tightened. "Maybe because you condemned my father, Delar of the B'tai, for the attempt on your consort's life."

"Traitor!" she gasped. "Assassin!"

"My father was innocent!" Jehan shouted. "My father—my *family*—was loyal to you!"

"Mother—"

The empress glanced at the Lady of the He'lar. "You are here by deception—to murder us—"

"Don't blame them," Jehan said quickly. "The lady I misled. And Anzu"—he wet his lips—"I threatened his clan. I forced him to bring me here."

"That is—" Anzu began.

"He acted to protect his house," Jehan said, talking over the elder warrior. He faced the empress squarely. "The blame is mine alone."

"No!" Saria cried. "Please—"

"Take him!" The empress's shout echoed through the throne room. "Take this criminal from our sight!"

Nisara fixed him with a look. "Sorry you shot my commander now, pirate?"

"Actually," Jehan grumbled, as the warriors swiftly relieved him of his sword and seized him by the arms, "I'm just sorry I didn't shoot *you*."

"Punish him if that is your will, Mother!" Saria burst out the moment they were alone. "Banish him to Tellaran territory!"

Even now, in the evening and alone in the privacy of her quarters, the empress raised her eyebrows to be spoken to so. "Why would I do so?"

"Because he is favored of Ren'thar. Because I demand it so!"

"Tread carefully, my child," her mother said coldly. "You do not demand of your empress."

"I am First, she who will be empress after you."

"You have a sister," the empress reminded.

"I may have a sister, but you only have one Heiress. Alari does not wish to return to the throne."

"What your sister wishes and what will be demanded of her may be divergent indeed." The empress's fan flicked like the tail of an angry sercat. "I should think you would be more concerned with your own future, daughter."

"Would you remove me as Heiress?" Saria challenged. "Disinherit me as once you did Alari for choosing the 'wrong' man?"

"Do not tempt me," Azara said coldly. "I may yet do so."

"Alari will refuse the throne." Saria narrowed her gaze. "She is less afraid of you than she once was and has a strong Tellaran mate to protect her."

"Alari was regent, a fine and dedicated leader of the Az-kye, while you were off spreading your legs for a slave in Tellaran territory. She will take the burden again if she must."

"I have gone mad then," Saria said tartly. "As I seem to recall you proclaimed the same man all a warrior could be and entreated me to take him as consort without delay."

"I did not know of his deception, that he dared claim to a name not his own. It only compounds his disgrace—if such a thing is possible. I would have this slave laboring in the mines till he died for even daring to look upon you, had I known."

The empress regarded her. "Did you know who he was? The truth of his past?"

"Yes, I did know." Saria lifted her chin. "And I alone will bear the responsibility of my choice."

"Unapologetic, unflinching strength." A faint smile of pride touched Azara's mouth. "The crown demands much of those who would wear it, Saria. But someday, my daughter, you will be a great ruler indeed."

Saria shoulders fell. "You will pardon him then, allow him to return to Tellaran space?"

"His fate can be no other now," the empress said, rising. "Tomorrow he will be thrown from the falls."

44

Falling

Saria bit her lip to keep from crying out when the guards dragged him in.

Jehan was held between the warriors by the upper arms, his hands tied tightly together at the wrists with a leather strip, his long hair free. His eyes were shadowed, his face gray, his feet bare.

He wore the white smock of a slave.

The hallway was filled with courtiers jostling for a glimpse into the grand throne room, another morbid look at the condemned. Perhaps aware how close to losing control her Heiress was, the empress had declared this sentencing as private a one as possible. The majordomo shut the doors herself as soon as the prisoner was inside.

Saria sat beside her mother on the dais while Alari and her mate Kyndan standing nearby. Alari's own pleas to their mother, even Kyndan's suggestion that Jehan be remitted to the Tellaran authorities for trial instead—where he would face imprisonment but his life be spared—had not swayed the empress.

Alari, whom she had once so unfairly maligned, whose downfall she had cold-heartedly plotted, stayed by her side through the long sleepless night. Listening as Saria raged, raising her up when tears brought her to her knees, Alari offered the only comfort she could—her presence and support.

"Kneel," one of the guards snapped when they reached the foot of the dais.

"Oh," Jehan said with false cheer. "Do you think that will help?"

"Kneel!"

The guard pushed him hard, knocking him to the ground so that he had to catch himself with his bound hands.

"Daughter," the empress murmured when Saria tensed to stand.

Jehan pushed himself up, sitting now back on his heels, and flinging his hair back. His gaze locked with Saria's for a heartbeat, then he turned his gaze to the empress.

He raised his eyebrows. "Somebody said you wanted to see me?"

"Your disrespect only confirms you the son of a traitor," the empress said coldly.

"Well," Jehan smirked, "if there's anything Your Majesty excels at—it's being a great judge of character."

At the mention of the recreant, the beloved member of the Imperial family the empress had trusted completely, at how close Azara had come to losing her throne, her life, and the lives of her daughters, the air in the room went glacial.

"You assumed a false identity to enter Imperial territory," the empress continued. "You disguised your dishonor through deceit and you entered the Circle without a name, an offense against the gods themselves."

"And, somehow, Ren'thar chose me as victor." Jehan's brow knitted with a mock frown. "Wait—you don't think *He's* in on it too, do you?"

"You only worsen things with your heresy," the majordomo said sharply.

"I'm about to be thrown from the falls," Jehan snapped. "At this point I'm not really worried about making it *worse*, thanks."

The majordomo's lip curled. "You will be barred at the gate of the City of the Gods, left to wander the darkness of the Underworld, nameless as your sire."

"Oh, I'll get past the Gate," Jehan assured. "I know people there who'll sneak me in."

"You are unrepentant in your disgrace!" the empress's voice rang through the soaring throne room. "The very worst of what an Az-kye can sink to. Take him—take him now and let the falls crush his bones on the rocks below!"

"*No!*" Saria cried, on her feet now.

The empress rose. "Daughter!"

She paid her mother no heed, racing down the stairs to fall on her knees before Jehan. She caught his bound hands in her own.

His face went white. "Saria, don't—"

She threw a glare up at her mother. "Throw him and I will fall to the rocks as well."

The empress took a step forward. "I warn you, Heiress, do not defy me."

Saria yanked the crown from her head, painfully taking hair with the small combs that held it into place, and flung it, sending the ancient diadem skidding across the polished floor.

"I renounce my place as First! I cede forever my status as an Imperial Daughter! Let his fate be mine!"

"Sister," Alari gasped, her face ashen. "Get up!"

Saria threw a sorrowful look at her sister, guilt churning her stomach at forcing Alari to a place she had no wish to occupy.

Then she lifted her chin. "Alari will be empress after Your Majesty, and may her rule be long. But"—she met Jehan's wide gaze—"the gods have given to me my true mate. In life or in death, I will not be parted from him."

"I love you, Saria," Jehan said, his hands cradling hers. His gaze went over her face as if he were seeking to memorize every shadow and curve to take with him into eternity. "And I'm not going to let you do this."

She shook her head. "You cannot stop me. No one can."

"You are the bravest, most courageous woman I have ever met." His gaze was soft. "And you will make a great empress. Our people will need a strong ruler, one who can guide them through what's coming—and that's you. My life is over." His hold on her tightened. "I won't let you throw yours away."

Her vision blurred. "If you die, I die."

"Sweetheart," he began hoarsely, "I think from the minute I stepped aboard your ship I've been standing at the Gate to the City of the Gods. The storm, the Brethren, Helock, the Tournament . . . I've been standing a hairsbreadth from death for months. I had all night to think about it"—his smile turned rueful—"And Ren'thar might not have chosen him but—I think I was *supposed* to die in that storm. That it was Naret who was supposed to be the one who saved you from the *Ty'har,* not me. I think all that's held me among the living is that I love you too much to go."

"Jehan—"

"I made a promise to safeguard you, I made a blood oath to you, but you're home now. Safe now. And gods know, I would give anything to share your life with you—but I can't." Tears shimmered in his dark eyes as he lifted his hands to trace the curve of her cheek. "But I promise, Saria, after your long and glorious reign, when you finally get there, I'll be in the fields outside the Gate, waiting for you."

Tears spilled down her cheeks. "No . . ."

He lifted his head to address the empress. "Forgive her renouncement. She *is* the one to rule after you," he said hoarsely. "And for the love of the gods, don't let her follow me. Keep her safe. Keep her safe for me."

A tiny frown puckered the empress's brow, as if she were seeing Jehan for the first time. "I will."

"Okay." He swallowed then gave a short nod. "Let's get this over with."

45

ᒥ ᑎᒐᑎᐤᐧᐦ

Justice

"No!" Saria held on even as the guards yanked him up. "*No!*"

From outside the throne room came the sounds of raised voices, someone pounding sharply on the door. With the nearly successful coup painfully fresh in their minds, everyone in the room froze. The guards that held Jehan between them, the only ones at hand to protect the Imperial family, tensed and looked toward the dais for guidance.

"I'll find out what's going on," Kyndan said, stepping forward, his sidearm already in his hand.

"Kyndan Maere!" the empress called. "I have not given you leave to do so!"

"Actually, I don't need your permission," he pointed out. "Technically, I'm still Imperial warlord and since this is a matter of your protection, I get to make the call."

"Be careful!" Alari cried.

"Aren't I always?"

Kyndan jogged across the throne room, his blaster at the ready, listening at the double doorway for a moment before he leveled his weapon and cracked open the door to look.

Whatever he saw there made him lift his blaster to the "ready" position. He sent a glance back at those around the dais then opened the door a little further.

"Fuck," Jehan muttered.

Saria rose to her feet as Anzu pushed his way past Kyndan. He strode into the throne room, pulling along with him a cringing young woman. Kyndan quickly slammed the door against the curious eyes of the court.

"What the hells are you doing here?" Jehan snapped at Anzu. "Go home, godsdamn it!"

The old man ignored him, his jaw set as he strode past Jehan and Saria to set himself square before the empress. He bowed to her briefly, by his action pulling the woman with him.

The woman's clothes marked her out as a noblewoman but she was not in court dress, as if Anzu had dragged her from her clanhouse, giving her neither warning nor choice about her journey to the palace.

"We have been merciful to you, Anzu of the He'lar. You are foolish indeed"—the empress's lip curled—"to risk appearing before us again."

"I have come to keep you from the committing the gross injustice of executing Jehan!"

"This man has neither name nor clan," Azara said coldly. "And as to his execution, you are dangerously close to joining him."

"Anzu," Jehan hissed. "Shut up and get—"

"My mate is lost to me," Anzu interrupted. "And I am long tired of living, but I will not go until justice has been done. Your Majesty, I bring before you De'narra, Lady of the B'tai."

Jehan started to hear his clan name and the young woman, trembling, sent a terrified look at the empress.

"I have been clan leader less than a season, Your Majesty!"

"Tell her," Anzu snapped, giving the frightened woman a shake. "Tell them all!"

"I—" Her gaze darted around, her face blanching deeply when she met Jehan's. "I became clan leader upon the death of my mother, Ressi of the B'tai."

"Know you this name?" Anzu asked Jehan sharply.

Jehan frowned. "Of course I do. Ressi was my mother's sister."

"Her *younger* sister, Majesty," Anzu clarified.

"What of it?" Alari asked, stepping forward. "And why do you bring the lady before my mother now?"

"Tell them," Anzu repeated, his grip tightening on her arm.

"I knew nothing of it!" she squeaked. "My mother told me the day she died!"

"Told you what?" Saria asked, frowning.

De'narra glanced at Jehan uneasily again. "How she came to be clan leader." She wet her lips. "Of the bargain made with the traitor—"

"That vile creature has been cut from the Book of Lineage!" the empress interrupted sharply. "By my own decree her name is *never* to be spoken again. Do you seek to join her, De'narra of the B'tai?" The empress indicated the window behind her. "The falls await your answer."

The lady's lips trembled. "I beg your forgiveness, Majesty."

"What bargain?" Jehan demanded.

"That—*she* would arrange to have your father accused, would orchestrate his downfall and make my mother clan leader in her elder sister's stead. In return, when the time came my mother would support—uh—" The Lady of the B'tai's lips trembled. "*Her* when she took the throne."

"We have come to know well," the empress said darkly with a glance to each of her daughters, "the depth of her deceptions."

Jehan shook his head again. "But your mother could only become clan leader if my mother—"

"Accepted disgrace," Anzu finished. "Or fled to Tellaran space with her mate."

"She knew," Jehan said flatly to De'narra. "Ressi knew my mother loved him too much, that my mother would follow him, even to the Badlands. She *died* there, you know. They both did."

"It would not have mattered if your mother stayed on the homeworld," De'narra mumbled. "In time, she too would have been accused, found guilty of some crime or another. And my mother made clan leader in your mother's place."

"A season?" the empress asked sharply. "You knew of this an entire *season* and yet you said nothing?"

"In truth," the lady cried, "I did not know what to do! You were deathly ill and—the traitor—constantly at your side. She would have kept me from you, suspected my intent to betray her plotting before I even crossed the Gate of the Blessed! And I had no proof of her betrayal to offer Your Majesty but my dead mother's word."

"And after?" Saria demanded. "My mother is restored to health, the conspirators revealed"—she sent a grateful look at Kyndan—"you could have come forward then."

"To my death!" the lady wailed, tears spilling down her cheeks. "I have scarce slept for weeks, fearing the spymaster's discovery of my clan's collusion in the plot! I am condemned by my mother's scheming and jealousy, not my own!"

"'Course I knew," Jehan murmured, his eyes a little unfocused. "I always knew, Father."

Saria frowned at him and Jehan gave a teary laugh.

"Sorry." He was smiling as if a huge weight had been lifted from him. "Just saying goodbye to someone, for now."

"Majesty!" The Lady of the B'tai fell onto her knees, sobbing, and spread her hands. "I beg your forgiveness—your mercy!"

"Mother?" Saria asked, her throat tight.

The empress waved her hand. "Release him."

At her word the guards let him go so quickly Jehan stumbled.

Anzu's hand was on the hilt of his sword and he looked at the empress. "With your permission?"

She nodded assent and Anzu swiftly cut the tie that bound Jehan's hands.

The skin of his wrists was raw. Saria reached for his hands only to find herself caught up in his arms, held tightly against him.

"He was innocent," Jehan said into her hair. "He's free now."

"As are you," Saria murmured.

"The matter remains," the empress reminded tersely, "of his entering the Tournament under false pretenses."

"There was no lie!" Anzu objected.

"Oh, do stop blubbering!" the empress snapped at the Lady of the B'tai. "And get up! Your clan will send tribute to the palace as retribution for your transgressions and that will be an end to it." She looked back at Anzu. "He entered the Grand Tournament as your son, which he is *not*."

"I say to you, Majesty— I vow before Ren'thar himself—that Jehan *is* my son." Anzu's voice shook. "The son of my heart, if not my body." He lifted his trembling chin. "And one I am proud to claim."

"Thank you, Anzu," Jehan said, his voice rough. "Thank you for that."

"I think you're running out of objections here, Your Majesty," Kyndan said. "You might just want to give in now."

"Jehan and his family have been much wronged by you, Mother," Alari added.

Azara gave her eldest daughter and her mate an exasperated glance. "Think you I do not know it so?" She rubbed at her temples. "There are moments I think my whole reign will come to nothing but untangling—*her*—web!"

"Mother?" Saria asked tightly.

The empress lowered her hands and met Saria's gaze. "In truth, I cannot promise your rule will bring you joy, my child. But this at least I can give you. Jehan of the B'tai"—she glanced at Anzu—"and the He'lar clan. By the favor of Ren'thar and the grace of Lashima, by the honor of—*both*—your clans, I deem you worthy to be consort to the Princess Saria."

Jehan looked down at Saria wide-eyed.

"We're getting married," he said, the words half-question, half-statement. "For certain."

Saria laughed. "Yes, without a doubt," she promised and pulled his head down for a kiss.

They finally broke away, a little breathless and blushing to find themselves observed by all.

The empress waved to the majordomo. "Issue a proclamation, Jelara," she ordered. "And let it be known throughout the empire."

"But I—"

Saria and Jehan exchanged a look, then Saria raised her eyebrows. "Jelara?"

"Your Highness—" The majordomo's glance went from face to face, then she spread her hands helplessly. "I cannot think how to fit this all into one proclamation . . ."

46

ᐱ ᐧᐃᐧ ᐃᐧ ᐁᐧᐸᐧ ᐊᐧᐸᐧᐳᐧᐱᐧ

Woven In the Stars

"You were right," Saria whispered in Jehan's ear as the empress moved off. "She *does* like you."

Around them, every part of the palace, the grounds, and the Imperial city itself was alight with decoration to celebrate their nuptials.

"She had better," Jehan said, and surely even the staunchest traditionalist among the courtiers would forgive a warrior for smiling on his wedding day. "'Cause I'm not going anywhere." He nodded at the couple strolling toward them. "But here are two who are."

"Sister," Alari said, warmly embracing her. She smiled up at Jehan and gave him a quick hug. "And, by both Az-kye and Tellaran tradition, 'brother.'"

"It pleases me greatly that you remained for the wedding," Saria said to them both.

"Congratulations," Kyndan said, offering his hand to Jehan, "Warlord."

"Thanks again for your support," Jehan said.

Kyndan laughed. "Whatever the support of a Tellaran warlord means around here."

"Don't downplay your role, Kyndan," Jehan said. "In fact, as I recall, *you* were actually the one that let Anzu into the throne room that day."

"Oh, I did that for me," Kyndan said, waving it away. "Or else it would be me and Alari where you're standing now and *no one* wants that."

"Still," Jehan said, "I feel kind of bad, you know, about shooting you."

"I'll get you back someday."

"Kyndan," Alari gasped. "You threaten the life of the Heiress's consort?"

Saria glared. "This can only be answered in the Circle!"

Both men looked round at her wide-eyed. The princesses burst out laughing.

"Funny," Jehan muttered.

Saria grinned. "Yes."

"Well, I think we'll go grab a drink," Kyndan said, eyeing his sister-in-law a little warily. "Before I wind up seeing the falls from the top, and then the bottom. If you'll excuse us, Your Highness? Imperial Warlord?"

"I can't believe you did that," Jehan muttered after they had bowed and retreated into the crowd. "He's my friend, you know."

"I thought you liked jokes, my mate."

His grin widened. "*Almost* your mate."

"I am eager to be bound to you, Jehan," Saria murmured, smiling up at him

A warm flush spread over his cheeks. "When can we duck out?"

Saria glanced at the crowd. "It will be some time."

But she had not looked away quickly enough.

"Saria?" His arm went around her to pull her close. "What is it?"

"I was—I was just thinking of how much of our future will be dictated by tradition, by the demands of our roles." Her smile was rueful. "I know it is not the home you envisioned, the life you wanted."

"Sweetheart, whether it's in a pirate town or an Imperial Palace, the only life I want"—Jehan leaned down to brush his mouth against hers—"is the one I get to spend with you."

Other Works
by
Ariel MacArran

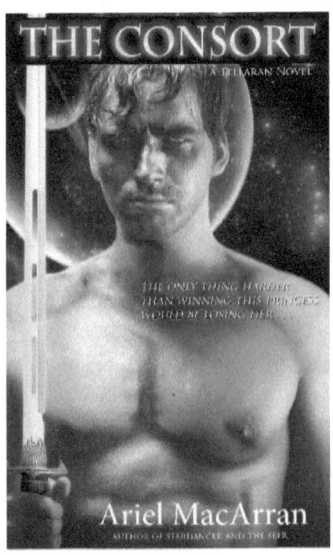

After spending a year enslaved by the Az-kye, Commander Kyndan Maere has good reason to hate them. On the eve of peace between the Tellaran Realm and the Az-kye Empire, Kyndan finds himself drawn into a duel for the hand of Alari, the First Imperial Daughter.

When their passion ignites Kyndan learns the only thing harder than winning this princess would be losing her . . .

Kinara's quest for revenge goes horribly wrong when she crosses into Az-kye space. Defeated and enslaved Kinara offers herself to Aidar, the Az-kye commander, in exchange for her crew's protection.

But this warrior wants much more than just her submission, he wants her to give herself completely . . .

Discovery means death but Arissa risks everything to save Fleet officer Jolar's life. Repaying this telepath means saving her from execution but Jolar will do whatever it takes to clear his debt to her.

The only thing he absolutely cannot let himself do is fall in love with her . . .

ANOTHER
MAN'S
Bride
Ariel MacArran

Historical Romance

Fleeing charges of witchcraft at the English court, Lady Isabella Beaufort agrees to a marriage arranged by her cousin, Queen Joan of Scotland. Deep in the Highlands, Isabella is captured by Colyne MacKimzie, an enemy to the king and a man set on claiming a rich ransom for her return.

Even as she is drawn irresistibly to Colyne, Isabella's visions show her terrifying images of him. Colyne knows giving into his desire for this beautiful, haunted woman invites his swift destruction just as he knows he will risk anything to have . . .

Written as Willow Danes

Jenna McNally is tending to the heartrending task of clearing out her grandfather's cabin when she's knocked off her feet by the impact of a nearby plane crash. She races into the snowy North Carolina woods to help and discovers that this is no plane that's crashed.

Ra'kur's people have been brought to the brink of extinction by war. After years spent searching for a compatible mate to bond with, an enemy attack lands him on a backward, primitive planet and right to the very female he has been seeking. And a Hir warrior's first task in claiming a mate is to capture her . . .

Historical Romance

Fleeing charges of witchcraft at the English court, Lady Isabella Beaufort agrees to a marriage arranged by her cousin, Queen Joan of Scotland. Deep in the Highlands, Isabella is captured by Colyne MacKimzie, an enemy to the king and a man set on claiming a rich ransom for her return.

Even as she is drawn irresistibly to Colyne, Isabella's visions show her terrifying images of him. Colyne knows giving into his desire for this beautiful, haunted woman invites his swift destruction just as he knows he will risk anything to have . . .

Written as Willow Danes

Jenna McNally is tending to the heartrending task of clearing out her grandfather's cabin when she's knocked off her feet by the impact of a nearby plane crash. She races into the snowy North Carolina woods to help and discovers that this is no plane that's crashed.

Ra'kur's people have been brought to the brink of extinction by war. After years spent searching for a compatible mate to bond with, an enemy attack lands him on a backward, primitive planet and right to the very female he has been seeking. And a Hir warrior's first task in claiming a mate is to capture her . . .

Acknowledgments

I owe a great many thanks as always to my editor, Erin McCabe. Working with her is an amazing experience. I learn so much and my writing is so much richer for her insight, ideas and gentle guidance. I am humbled by her generosity and very grateful for her hard work.

Thanks to Christine LePorte for her final polish.

Thank you to Adam McLaughlin, a very talented actor and audiobook producer, for his incredibly valuable feedback on this book.

Thanks again to my cover designer Steven James Catizone for the gorgeous new cover design.

Thank you to my friends who supported and encouraged me and, most of all, to my family.

About
Ariel MacArran

Ariel MacArran has had a lifelong love of books, stories and writing. Nothing makes her happier than the opportunity to give back some of the magic of being swept up into a story that other writers have given her.

Ariel loves hearing from readers! Please visit her websites:

www.arielmacarran.com

www.willowdanes.com